MW00654867

THE
LOVECRAFT CODE

THE
LOVECRAFT
CODE

PETER LEVENDA

IBIS PRESS
Lake Worth, FL

Published in 2016 by Ibis Press
A division of Nicolas-Hays, Inc.
P. O. Box 540206
Lake Worth, FL 33454-0206
www.ibispress.net

Distributed to the trade by
Red Wheel/Weiser, LLC
65 Parker St. • Ste. 7
Newburyport, MA 01950
www.redwheelweiser.com

ISBN: 978-0-89254-217-8
Ebook: 978-0-89254-633-6

Library of Congress Cataloging-in-Publication Data
Available upon request

Book design and production by Studio 31
www.studio31.com

[BP]

Printed in the United States of America

DEDICATION

to

Donald and Yvonne Weiser

From BBC News April 12, 2003:

Looters Ransack Baghdad Museum

Thousands of valuable historical items from Baghdad's main museum have been taken or destroyed by looters. Nabhal Amin, deputy director at the Iraqi National Museum, blamed the destruction on the United States for not taking control of the situation on the streets. On Saturday, Unesco—the UN's cultural agency—has urged the US and Britain to deploy troops at Iraq's key archaeological sites and museums to stop widespread looting and destruction. ... The museum's deputy director said looters had taken or destroyed 170,000 items of antiquity dating back thousands of years.

PROLOGUE

… those who are without are my adversaries, hence they oppose me. Nor do they know that such a course is against their own interests, for might, wealth, and riches are in my hand, and I bestow them upon every worthy descendant of Adam. Thus the government of the worlds, the transition of generations, and the changes of their directors are determined by me from the beginning.

—*Kitab al-Jilwa*, the Yezidi Book of Revelation

… the deathless Chinamen said that there were double meanings in the *Necronomicon* …

—"The Call of Cthulhu," H. P. Lovecraft

Mosul, Northern Iraq
April 15, 2003
Operation Iraqi Freedom

Faruq, the plainclothes security officer of the *Mukhabarat*—the Iraqi Intelligence Service—bent over the victim. The skinny old man was tied to a pipe that ran the length of the basement room where he was being held. He had not eaten in days. He had not bathed in weeks, not since the water had been shut off during the bombing, and he smelled like a corpse. His clothes consisted of a tattered pair of shorts, which was all that was left after the guards ripped off his clothes as they laughed. The security officer had insisted that his groin be covered so he would not have to look at the gaping wound. He had nothing but contempt for the man, who was not even an Iraqi but a Yezidi.

"We should have wiped out all of you when we had the chance. We did our best, anyway. Chemicals, biologicals, bombs. Whatever

came out of Saddam's box of tricks. But it still wasn't enough." Faruq
spat in the face of the man, who had long since ceased to react to
anything but the worst pain. To men like Saddam, the Yezidis—like
the Kurds—were not Muslim. They were not even Arab. He didn't
know what they were, and he didn't care. All he knew was that they
threatened his hegemony over Iraq and for that reason had to be
destroyed.

"I will ask you again, *kafir*. Where is the book?"

The victim was long past whimpering. He knew that another
punch, another kick was inevitable. More electricity, probable.
Another dunking of his head in the overflowing toilet, extremely
likely. He had surrendered what it was to be human. What it was
to be a human being. His soul was now hovering over his body,
straining at the golden cord that connected them together.

The victim had once been a man. But that was before the attack
on Baghdad with its feeble excuse of weapons of mass destruction.
That was before the events of September 11, 2001 ruined everything
for everyone. He had been a man. Before the Mukhabarat found
him cowering in a neighbor's house and dragged him out and onto
the back of a flatbed truck. He had been a man before they kicked
him so hard and so often in his genitals that it no longer mattered
what gender he had once been. Whatever it was, he was no longer.

He had been an employee in the Baghdad Museum. He had
been one of the last to leave when the Americans came earlier that
month. They had tried—all of them, all of the museum staff—to save
what they could before the barbarians and the bombs destroyed Iraq's
ancient inheritance: the artifacts from Babylon, Akkad ... Sumer. He
had done his share, grabbed what he could, and made for the north.
For Mosul, near the ancient city of Nineveh. Mosul was at the edges
of Kurdish territory, and he had friends and family there who would
hide him and his treasure.

Some cylinder seals. A vase from the time of Nebuchadnezzar.
Some steles. And a book.

The book had been wrapped carefully and placed in a waterproof box. He had not dared open it, but one night before the Guard came to arrest him his neighbor's daughter had been too curious. Only eleven years old, she had pried open the box when he was asleep. She could not read the ancient lettering, the handwritten manuscript that covered hundreds of brittle pages. But when he woke up—the victim who had once been a man—he saw what she had done and before he could scold her he recognized the title of the book.

It was not a title page the way modern books are printed. It was only mentioned in the opening paragraph. *Kitab al-Azif.* It is a strange name in Arabic. *Azif* refers to the sounds made by insects. "Buzzing," perhaps. Or "whining," as in the sound made by a mosquito. Or the strange choral chanting of the cicadas. He did not know the English word, but he knew the reputation of the book.

It was not as old as the other antiquities in the Baghdad Museum. By comparison, it was almost modern. Ninth century, perhaps. Under normal circumstances it should never have been in the museum at all, but the fame and notoriety of the *Kitab al-Azif* made it an invaluable part of the museum's collection. Like many of his people, he knew its history and the purpose to which the book had been put, centuries ago.

And he knew the only ones who could be entrusted with it now.

His arrangements had been made only a day before Mukhabarat Division 5—Counterintelligence—found him. The lackeys of the great Saddam did not care about the steles or the cylinder seals, and the vase merited only a passing glance. They only wanted the book.

And the book was the very last thing he would give them. He would give his life first.

There was a rumbling beneath the ground that traveled up the feet and along the spines and shook the very skulls of the guards. Tanks. Armored vehicles of all types. The dreaded helicopters. "Boots on the ground." The Americans were in Mosul. Time was running out.

The security officer was in better shape than his victim, but not by much. He had only eaten some dry bread in the past twelve hours, washed down with weak tea. This operation was off the books as far as Iraqi intelligence was concerned. They could have cared less at this point about the *Kitab al-Azif.* Everyone was scrambling to save themselves and whatever money or valuables they could find before scurrying across the border west into Syria or north into Turkey, their uniforms left behind so as not to identify them. Some, the Shiites, were getting a warmer welcome in Iran but to get there they would have to go through Kurdish territory.

Kurdish territory was a dangerous place to be for a member of the Iraqi security services. The Kurds had a long list of grievances against Iraq and especially against the brutal, murderous regime of Saddam Hussein. He and most of his colleagues were caught in a trap between the Coalition forces to the south, and Kurdish territory to the north and east. He would have to go across into Syria from Mosul, if he could avoid Kurdish and Coalition patrols along the way. No matter; his job before the American invasion had been to infiltrate the Syrian intelligence networks that were constantly sending spies across the border into Iraq. He knew who they were and how they operated, and how to cross over into Syria undetected.

But Faruq was no ordinary policeman. He was a member of a sect that made even the hated Crusaders look like orthodox Muslims. And this was their last chance to get their hands on the one document that would give them the power to unite the secret tribes across all of the Middle East and Central Asia into one victorious army that would take back what had been stolen from them during the time of the Prophet. His brothers were scattered from Kailash to Kashmir, descendants of races that had been converted to Islam with fire and sword but who worshipped the Old Ones in secret, in clandestine shrines deep within the mountains and valleys of an ancient empire that had stretched from the Mediterranean to the Indian Ocean.

And all that was standing between them and the ultimate

revenge was a skinny academic with a broken body and a soul that was struggling to leave it.

An explosion rocked the street above. Mud and plaster rained down on them from the ceiling. The victim did not seem to notice, but his captor was intensely aware that time was running out. He had to make this fool talk, and his options were limited. They all talked eventually, but he did not have the luxury of time. Baghdad had fallen a week ago. Mosul was already in Crusader hands. If he was going to escape Iraq he had to do it now, today. Yet he did not understand why this man was so resistant. Prisoners usually started babbling as soon as they saw the chains, the electrodes, the filthy toilet. This man—he glanced again at the museum identification card in his hand—this Fahim Abd Al-Latif was an archivist, no more than that. They had located his family, but most of them had already fled, including his wife and two sons. The only leverage he had was the neighbor and the neighbor's young daughter.

It was from the girl that they got the confirmation that the book existed, and they did not have to torture her to get it. She seemed eager to please. Her father, on the other hand, proved more recalcitrant. They could hear his screams from the cell next door. Pointless to torture him now, but the guards were angry at the fall of the regime and were taking it out on the fat man who had fathered such a beautiful girl.

The security officer went to the door and called for the girl to be brought in.

Fahim did not look up, nor did he give any indication that he knew what was going on. *It might already be too late*, thought the officer.

The girl was brought in.

She was young and wore no veil, and was dressed simply. Her eyes were an amazing blue in a dirty but otherwise very pale complexion. She was Yezidi, there was no doubt about that. Even her hair was light in color, what might have been a honey brown hue if it had been washed and combed properly.

The officer took the girl by the hand and stood her in front of Fahim, who still had not looked up from the floor. He felt the front of her dress, rummaging across her chest, and understood that she was already on the verge of womanhood.

She whimpered.

He lifted up her coarse cotton gown and felt along her thighs and buttocks while she squirmed against him. In another year or so she would be ripe, probably sold in an arranged marriage to a wealthy sheepherder or carpenter. Ordinarily, Faruq would have raped her by now, just on general principles and because he had not had a woman in several weeks due to the fighting and the constant bombardment. He liked the very young girls. There was no chance of disease, and their skin was so soft. He liked the way their eyes widened in pain and shock when he entered them. Sadly, there was no time for this now.

He withdrew his revolver.

"Fahim, pay attention," he said softly.

The man hung limply from his restraints, but his chest moved slightly, in and out, so he was obviously still alive and breathing.

"Fahim. I have Jamila. She is right here. Can't you smell her? The sweet smell of innocence and purity?"

The victim, the thing that had once been a man, stirred.

"Look up, Fahim. This is the last chance you will have. You cannot save yourself, you are nearly dead already. But you can save Jamila. Beautiful young Jamila."

Slowly, as if opening his eyes was physically painful, he raised his head to look straight ahead of him. What he saw nearly made him pass out.

The security officer was holding Jamila away from him, by her neck. He had his revolver jammed between her thighs.

"You will tell me where to find the *Kitab al-Azif*, and you will do so now. Otherwise, I will take young Jamila's virginity in my own way. Do you understand?"

He drew the hammer back on the revolver, cocking it. The sound was loud, even in this cell beneath the embattled streets of Mosul.

Jamila began to wet herself, and the urine stained the barrel of the revolver, but the officer did not withdraw it.

Fahim looked up, pleading in his eyes, first at the officer then at Jamila. Jamila's eyes were shut tight, as much against the humiliation as the fear.

"I will count to three. If you have not given me what I want to know by three, then Jamila will be raped by the bullets of my revolver and I will leave her body next to yours as you die slowly of thirst and starvation in this godforsaken hole in the earth."

Fahim tried to form a prayer in his mind, but the words would not come. The images were fretful and fleeting. He knew that this time of horror would one day come, the time of facing his own death. He knew that he would be reborn in the garden of the Peacock Angel if he lived his life correctly. But he did not know if protecting the Kitab was more important than protecting Jamila. What was the worth of a book when compared to the life of an innocent young girl?

Normally, the answer was a simple one. A book had no value when compared to the life of a human being, any human being.

But his people had given their lives to save their own Holy Books, hadn't they? They had been persecuted and murdered in large numbers because of their religion. Because of their *texts*.

"One ..."

Jamila kept her eyes shut. She did not want to see the pathetic figure of her father's friend in the state he was in. She was horrified and humiliated, but even more she knew that her secret had to be kept at all costs. Her family had been keeping secrets for generations. A secret was worth more than gold. But she could not control her body and the rush of urine from between her legs made her feel disgusting and unworthy of so sacred a task as this.

"Two ..."

Fahim struggled with his decision. His people would never forgive him for betraying them to the Iraqi police. He knew the value of the book, but also knew that it must be kept out of the hands of those who would use it for the destruction of humanity. If he gave it up now, all would be lost and his name would be cursed for generations ... if indeed there were generations left to curse him.

But then he felt a strange warmth take hold of his heart. Something like fingers—gentle fingers—had touched him inside with a sensation so profound he thought it was a physical touch. But nothing had moved in the airless cell. Maybe it was a heart attack. Maybe he was already dying.

He looked at the young girl, whose eyes were now open and staring directly at him, and into his own.

Jamila had made the decision for him: for Fahim and for the evil man with the gun between her legs, too.

"Three ..."

The explosion rocked the tiny cell, dislodging the iron pipe so that Fahim fell free, his hands still tied but no longer attached to the cell. There was a fog of dust and plaster everywhere. Piles of debris. He felt a small hand take his own in a darkness made absolute with the termination of all electric power in the city. He dragged himself upright, as best he could, his legs shaking and threatening to fail him at every step. He stumbled when his feet struck the body of the security officer, who did not move. *Incredibly*, Fahim thought, *I have outlived the man who was going to kill me. If even for a moment, I have survived.* His brain tried to make sense of what had happened. He knew it was an artillery shell, or a rocket fired from one of the Crusader's gunships, demolishing this house or the house next door. But how to explain that sudden determination in Jamila's eyes, or the warm hand that held his heart in its palm only moments before the blast?

Dazed, he let Jamila lead him out of the cell, out of the basement, and eventually all the way out of Mosul.

Red Hook
April 15, 2014

At the same moment, but exactly nine years later and thousands of miles away, Gregory Angell—scion of a long line of Rhode Island Angells and great-grand-nephew of the celebrated but long-deceased George Angell, professor of Semitic languages at Brown University—woke from a restless sleep in his basement apartment in the Red Hook section of Brooklyn, drenched in perspiration. He turned on the lamp next to his bed and stared up at the water-stained ceiling for a long, anxious moment. Was it the scurrying of rats in the walls that woke him? Or was it the scuttering of old nightmares through festering holes in his porous, paper-thin dreams? A young girl. A starving man. A darkness that seemed to breathe poison. Iraq.

His left hand rubbed the sleep out of his eyes. His right hand held the gun he kept under his pillow.

Through the flimsy plasterboard walls he could hear the radio in the apartment next door. It was the morning *azan*, the Muslim call to prayer. His neighbors were Syrians, from Damascus. They were also the supers of the building he lived in. It was the *azan* that woke him up. The warbling, floating cry of the muezzin roused feelings and memories in him that he preferred to have left buried, back in the frontier between Iraq and Turkey. Kurdish territory. No man's land.

It was the land that gave the world the three great religions of Judaism, Christianity and Islam.

And it was the land where he lost his faith in God entirely.

Instinctively, he checked the automatic's ten round magazine. With one in the chamber he had eleven shots ready for whatever would come through the door or lurked in the shadowy corners of his book-congested apartment. Nothing ever did, of course. Not in the more than seven years since the massacre at Mosul where God died, buried there with the women and children who were dragged

off the bus in front of his eyes and machine-gunned in the street.
Yezidis. *Kafirs.*

Victims.

It was about four a.m. The worst time of the day for him, that
sliver of dubious existence between night and day, between darkness
and light. It was the hour when shadows took on substance and
where function, impossibly, followed form. For a man who no longer
believed in God, he was more than afraid of ghosts.

He felt his pulse, and slowed his breathing, counting off the
seconds. Ten seconds in, hold for ten, exhale for ten, hold for ten.
Ten seconds, ten rounds. A ten count. It was how he lowered his
blood pressure. That, and his Glock 9mm, was how he got through
the night.

Sweating. Trembling like a man suffering from the DTs. Glock
tracing an arc through his small apartment, looking for a target of
opportunity. A flesh-and-blood target to stand in for the invisible,
creeping thing he could not name.

He cradled his head in his hands. There was a longing in the
music now coming from the room upstairs, a longing that he felt as
acutely as if he had lost the same love at the same time as whoever
had written that song, or as whoever was listening to it now in order
to ease the pain of distance or loss. Their distance was his distance,
their loss was his loss. The music—the plaintive sounds of Syrian-
accented Arabic lyrics against the yearning strain of the oud—could
have been wrung from his own heart.

It was a love song, and it was being sung by a man to a woman
who had left him for another country forever. A lost love. To Angell,
it was still a love song: not to any human woman but to a presence
once as strong as the most cherished sweetheart, the most adored
spouse.

It was a love song to a dead God.

Angell knew he was losing his mind. He heard things that
weren't there. He saw things out of the corner of his eye that could
not possibly exist. Shadows. With guns. And when he closed his eyes

against the pressure of too much sight, the image—*that* image—of an afternoon in Mosul was conjured up before him like a monster from the pages of some suppressed grimoire. Instinctively, Angell knew that conjuring a demon from Hell had been forbidden by the Church not least because, once raised, that demon could attack God, kill him, and change the world forever. After all, that is what happened to him.

Terms like *unspeakable horror* and *loathsome putrescence* were used by pulp fiction writers as shorthand for things they had never really seen. But Angell had seen them. Angell knew what *unspeakable horror* was: he saw it committed on a side street in the Hell that was Mosul. He knew what *loathsome putrescence* was, because Iraq was a museum of rotting corpses, clouds of flies, and the stench of death that never left you. Not even on the flight home to the land of deodorant and mouthwash, washing machines and frozen margaritas, cable TV and hot showers.

Most of all, he knew with a deadly certainty that God was dead. He knew that humanity was alone in the vastness of space, on the brink of extinction on a tiny planet in the middle of a nowhere galaxy, where science and technology were exactly as Carl Sagan had characterized them: as candles in the dark. Cold comfort when the apocalypse was upon them. More like "whistling in the dark."

Better to let your eyes get accustomed to the eternal night.

Angell kept his madness from seeping into his daily life, into his classes at the university, by staying alone as much as he could so that others would not notice his sudden loss of attention, his gaze drifting to a point somewhere in the distance, his inappropriate comments, his "lack of affect." To many he was just the stereotypical absent-minded professor, an eccentric who had nonetheless served his country as an advisor in Afghanistan and Iraq, a man fluent in strange tongues and living in a world of ancient faiths. He was allowed those moments when he seemed to disappear into another world. He was indulged in his little insanities.

They didn't know about the Glock.

It was the nine millimeter that kept him sane, for it was his way out. His ticket home. He relaxed into the peace that the presence of that weapon gave him, for it was *right there*, like a promise he knew would be kept. Any time it got to be too much, the solution—the escape route, the *exit strategy*—was there. Not like God, who was *not there*.

It was fully-loaded, but that was just for show. He knew he would need only one bullet.

Pretty strange lifestyle for a professor of religious studies at Columbia University.

BOOK ONE

CHATTER

The sciences, each straining in its own direction, have hitherto harmed us little; but some day the piecing together of dissociated knowledge will open up such terrifying vistas of reality, and of our frightful position therein, that we shall either go mad from the revelation or flee from the deadly light into the peace and safety of a new dark age.

—H. P. Lovecraft, "The Call of Cthulhu"

CHAPTER ONE

REMOTE VIEWING

Damascus
738 C.E. / 120 A.H.

Before the Grand Mosque. Steps away from a shrine containing the head of John the Baptist. In the blinding sunlight of noon, reflecting off the stones of the mosque and the stones of the plaza before it. A man. A madman. In rags, holding a scroll of paper. He is chanting something incomprehensible. It may be poetry. It may be a prayer. It may be divine. It may be blasphemy. A crowd gathers.

It is Ramadan, the month of fasting and of forgiveness. No one has sipped a drop of water since before the sunrise *azan*. Men and beasts are crazed with piety and thirst.

There is dry, nervous laughter. The Umayyid Caliphate is in its last days. Within twenty years, it will be gone. Like the desert sands in a windstorm. The Law of the Prophet—Peace be upon him—has rooted out the demonolatry of the pagan tribes and replaced it with the scented pages of the Holy Book, the Qur'an. But some members of the Quraish—the Prophet's tribe—still hold to the old ways, in secret, worshipping the dead gods and pouring libations onto the broken stones of a dead faith. They have rescued the idols from the Ka'aba—and from the Prophet's wrath—and built hideous altars in the mountain caves north of the city. Altars bathed in the blood of sacrifice.

The madman is not of the Quraish. He is a Sabaean, of Yemen, and they say he is a cousin of the false prophet 'Abd Allah bin Saba, the Shi'a heretic who proclaimed the divinity of Ali, and who will soon be executed after revolting against the Caliphate from his sanctuary in the sacred city of Kufa. Others, that he is an adherent of the Mazdaks, an ancient cult that existed before Islam, obsessed with the manipulation of numbers and the making of magic squares and *jadwal* to which they put obscene and blasphemous use. Or a worshipper of the Old Gods, A'ra and Hubal, Azizos and the daughter of Allah, Manat. Or perhaps a devotee of Qos, he of the shrine of black basalt whose cult was known—and suppressed—at Wadi Hesa. Indeed, the madman's descendant—in another thirteen hundred years—will unleash a tidal wave of apostasy and violence on the earth.

Today, however, the madman is alone and wailing before the Grand Mosque.

His words are gibberish, a kind of poetry, rhythmic syllables of an ancient tongue which was old when Moses—Peace be upon him—was a priest of Aton in Egypt, learning Egyptian magic. In the shrine of the Grand Mosque, in the shadows of the crypt, the head of the Baptist moves.

The crowd grows larger. The Caliph's men are moving slowly towards the madman, uneasy about arresting someone who may have been touched by God. Their scimitars flash in the noonday sun.

A single, strangled word escapes the lips of the muttering madman and sails like a winged curse above the heads of the faithful. Three syllables that strike fear into the souls of the *ulama*. They retreat a step before him, and the Caliph's men do likewise.

In that moment, in the sight of God and man and the Grand Mosque, the madman's left arm is ripped from his shoulder in a shower of blood and gore and terrible, terrible pain.

The hand that ripped it cannot be seen. Not in sunlight, nor in shadow. The blood drips on the stones as the crowd stares, uncomprehending, before it retreats in horror.

The screams can be heard in the deepest recesses of the mosque. The head of the Baptist can be seen to shiver in its reliquary, its jaws struggling against age and death and memory to open, to give voice to the eternal, to the black well of terror at the heart of the human condition, to the Dreadful that has already Happened.

The madman's severed arm is nowhere to be seen. It has vanished, as if into the air itself. Something can be sensed, something ...

Another violent twist of invisible force and his right leg disappears and his body falls to the dust and gore beneath him. His screams have become so loud and penetrating that they are no longer heard with human ears. He is being devoured, slowly, before the eyes of the faithful in the square, before the Grand Mosque. The scroll of papers in his left hand has fallen and its leaves are being blown by an invisible wind to the four corners of the Caliphate. His mouth is stretched wide in a rictus of pain and terror and the faithful begin to scatter, to flee from the jinn who have possessed this madman and caused him to be torn asunder before their unbelieving eyes. His left leg disappears into the craw of some unseen Beast and his torso flops helplessly on the ground as, finally, his remaining arm is chewed to the shoulder and all that is left of the seer, the prophet, the madman is his head and what remains of his shredded abdomen. As his head is swallowed up into the maw of the voracious monster his last word finds its expression in the lips and jaw of the Baptist—Peace be upon him—as the head rattles in its reliquary of gold and silver, screeching in a voice rusted shut with disuse over seven hundred years of death and hollow prayer:

Qhadhulu …

The "Manson Family"
Fort Meade
April, 2014 C.E. / 1434 A.H.

The viewer collapses into his chair. He rips the electrodes from his head and chest and screams for water. He is shaking, perspiration dripping from every pore and soaking into the chair and the floor of the air-conditioned room in the basement of the secure location at Fort Meade.

His handler rushes into the room and shouts for the medic who is always on call.

It is the year 2014 and the location is the headquarters of the Remote Viewing team that had been tasked with locating the author of the September 11, 2001 attacks on the World Trade Center and the Pentagon: Osama bin Laden. They are what is left of the CIA's Bin Laden Issue Station which was officially disbanded in 2006, but whose most fanatic members—those calling themselves the "Manson Family" because of their obsessive and alarmist mentality—have regrouped under other operational names, other black budgets, in order to continue a new search for a new threat: Abu Bakr al-Baghdadi, former leader of Al Qaeda in Iraq and now head of the notorious Islamic Caliphate, or ISIL. This search has made use of every possible means, every conceivable tool, in order to accomplish its mission. No matter how strange. No matter how unorthodox. And that includes the seeming witchcraft of remote viewing.

The rooms where the viewing was taking place were thirty meters below ground. The walls were a meter thick, reinforced concrete. The lighting consisted of racks of long fluorescent bulbs behind wire mesh screens in the ceiling. Doors were made of titanium steel. Soundproofing was everywhere. Desks were bolted to floors. Its inhabitants referred to it as 'Spahn Ranch'—the infamous head-quarters of the real Manson Family—and it tried very hard to live up to its reputation. Guards were posted at every doorway. They were armed. Heavily armed.

Back in the 1970s, this operation was captioned variously as GRILLFLAME, or the fantastically-suggestive STARGATE, or any one of half-a-dozen other cryptonyms. Military personnel with high level security clearances were trained in the art of spying on the enemy using only their minds.

It was not a new art, and hardly a science. It had been used by the Nazis during World War Two to locate enemy submarines, and the Soviets were rumored to be using the same methods during the Cold War. In the 1980s, the operation had been terminated even though the remote viewers had claimed some impressive wins. No matter; to a newly-Christianized American government the whole thing smacked too much of demonolatry, and with the demise of the Soviet Union and the removal of the Berlin Wall, STARGATE went the way of all other forms of HUMINT—Human Intelligence—until the events of September 11, 2001.

With the pressing need to find Osama bin Laden and others members of Al Qaeda the remote viewing program came back on-line. Due to all the cutbacks at CIA and the firing of literally hundreds of field agents that began in the immediate post-Watergate era, agents on the ground in Afghanistan, Pakistan, Iraq, and Iran were few and far between. Domestically, the FBI had virtually no agents who could speak and read Arabic fluently, far less anyone with knowledge of Farsi, Urdu, or any of the other languages of the Middle East. Until Homeland Security could come up with the expertise it needed—and could cultivate the kind of in-country espionage networks that had existed throughout the region during the Cold War—other means had to be found for spying on the enemy.

Basically, remote viewing is the simplest form of intelligence-gathering one can imagine. One needs a human brain capable of thought, and at most a sheet of paper and a pencil. That's all. If the Pentagon needs to know what kind of resistance to expect at a given location anywhere in the world, the remote viewer is tasked with nothing more than coordinates: longitude and latitude. The viewer then relaxes and enters a kind of mild trance state during which time he or she "sees" the location mentally. The paper and pencil are there to facilitate imaging: the viewer may start to draw general outlines of what is seen, or specific characteristics that seem important or especially clear. At the end of the session the drawings are analyzed for their intelligence value. If there are no drawings, the viewer may be speaking aloud into a recorder, describing what is seen and heard in the trance state.

While most missions of this nature were concerned with military and intelligence targets, once in awhile something totally off-the-wall would occur. Sometimes teams of remote viewers were sent on a "mission" and their results compared; in that case, often the viewers were seeing the same location but at different angles, some from high altitudes and others from underground. There was never any satisfactory explanation for the phenomenon.

"What the hell was *that?*"

The viewer has been revived, his veins pumped full of drugs so he can be debriefed before he collapses again and his memory conflated with dreams, fevers, childhood memories, nightmares. He is holding a plastic cup of cold water and his nervous trembling is causing the water to spill, unnoticed, onto his lap. They have caught his voice on digitized tape and run it through their computers, but what he saw—what the viewer actually "saw" in his heightened psychic state—has to be described, orally, for the analysts. The papers on which he was drawing his vision are a scrambled mess of ruined architecture, dead bodies, alien landscapes, and cartoonish monsters. Nothing makes sense. They are looking for Al-Qaeda's infamous new leader and imam, not for gothic horror.

"It was ... it is Damascus," he manages to get out.

"Damascus? That's not possible. Damascus is locked up tight as a drum. Assad hates al-Baghdadi and ISIL and the feeling is mutual. There's no way al-Baghdadi is in Damascus. Not yet, anyway."

The conversation swirls around and over the head of the remote viewer, who is shuddering from some nameless dread. Exotic names, like al-Nusra and Peshmerga, Al Qaeda in Yemen, Al Qaeda in the Maghreb. *Daesh.*

"Yeah, but al-Baghdadi would try to take advantage of the momentum and infiltrate his people into Damascus. They already have Raqqa, and Fallujah in Iraq. There are entire towns that are going over to the rebels ..."

"I don't see him leaving his cave and traveling to Damascus. Too risky. He's always been better with audio and video tapes to Al-Jazeera..."

The agents stopped in mid-sentence as the viewer spoke up, looking into the middle distance as if he was still in the trance.

"It wasn't ... it isn't ... today. It was ... some other ... when ..."

The look of terror on the viewer's face is making the debriefers uncomfortable. His grammatical degeneration adds to this sense of unease, as if his vision had given rise to a kind of aphasia. This isn't particularly scientific. A remote viewer is tasked with a simple mission and he or she simply goes into a light trance and follows the suggestion as far as it will take them. Finding lost ships. Locating hidden missile bases. Weapons caches. Secret agents on the run. Of course, there had been "accidents" in the past; remote viewers seeing alien landscapes, UFOs, ghosts ... but those were anomalies, predictable side effects from the strange process of psychic traveling through space and—it seems—time. One of them, one of the "accidents"—the superstar viewer Jason Miller—had simply gone off the deep end after one such session. Disappeared without a trace. Collateral damage, according to some. MIA, according to others. His case was legendary among the Family. He tested the highest of all the potential RV recruits; aced the Zenner cards, demonstrated some limited PK ability, and did that famous real-time RV feed on Tora Bora when they were close—so close—to finding and killing OBL the first time.

But Jason Miller up and left one sunny afternoon and, with all his spycraft intact, melted effortlessly into the void.

"You were looking at the future?" one of the debriefers, a man in a uniform with no indication of rank or service, suggests.

The viewer shakes his head.

"No ... not the future ... the past. Long ... long ago. Men in turbans. Scimitars. John ... John the Baptist ..."

"Jesus!"

The viewer looks up, sharply.

"No. Not Jesus. John the Baptist. His head. In a cage. In a mosque. Speaking."

The debriefers look at each other, alarmed. Their viewer was clearly losing his mind. He would need to take some time off. Even worse, the session had been fruitless.

"Okay. Go on. John the Baptist was talking to you."

"Not to me! To … to … I don't know. But there was a man and … and he … it was horrible." He swallowed, and took another sip of cold water.

"He was shouting to the people in front of the … the mosque. And then he … his arms … they were gone … they were there, and … they were gone … there was blood … so much blood… he was being … eaten … by something, something I couldn't see … no one could … see … "

"What was he shouting?"

"What did he say?"

"Did you understand it?"

"What language was it?"

"Can you write it down?"

The viewer began shaking his head back and forth, back and forth, and silently weeping. He knew what was happening. He saw it happen to a Spec-4 named Brewer who had begun drawing weird animal shapes, like bats that were flying underwater, relentlessly and without stopping until they pulled him off duty and sent him to a special facility to reacquaint himself with his mind. He saw it happen to that lieutenant in the Air Force who had been selected due to her unnatural ability at Blackjack, who kept clawing at her throat and mumbling words in a language that no one at Fort Meade could identify. He remembered how, in the weeks after that incident, linguistics experts were called in to interpret her ramblings (without knowing their source, of course, or the conditions under which they had been obtained) but to no avail. The language spoken had elements that seemed to be Gaelic or Celtic in origin, but other words were clearly Indo-European. "Perhaps proto-Sanskrit," suggested one scholar, but even he was not convinced of the theory.

These examples stood up and trembled like ghouls in the graveyard of the viewer's memory. He knew what had happened to the Air Force lieutenant. She was in the psych ward of a VA hospital, in a special secure wing reserved for spooks who went crazy in the field. He knew that Brewer was no better off. All in all, of the seven remote viewers who had begun with this mysterious special program the previous year—a mission they referred to as "Cielo Drive," another Manson reference—only one was still left.

Him.

The previous casualty was Captain Danforth, who had blurted out the weird phrase "the Ishtar Gate! Close the gate! Close the gate!" before lapsing into a vegetative stupor about three weeks earlier. He didn't want to go there. He didn't want to become another RV statistic like Brewer and Danforth and Miller and the three others. He had to be careful of what he said, of what he sounded like. His career—hell, even his life—hinged on how he handled the next few moments.

But there, on the desk in front of him, were his drawings. They seemed like diseased things, the product of a deranged mind or a seriously impaired child, the signed and notarized affidavit of madness. There was writing, but in what language? There were buildings, but they were architecturally impossible. And then there was the last thing he wanted to see: a winged creature. Like a bat, but with gills. An underwater bird of some kind. The same thing that Brewer had seen before … well, before they picked him up and brought him tenderly to his next posting in the Dali-esque landscape of his own fractured mind.

"What did he say?" they demanded, crowding him now. Insistent. Nervous, maybe. Shouting orders. They knew better than this. They knew you didn't browbeat a viewer who had just come out of a trance. It was like slapping a sleepwalker.

"Do you remember the sounds? The madman in the square. *What did he say?*"

It was all over for him. He knew that now. There was no escaping his fate. Brewer's fate. Danforth's. He could hear the cell door slamming on his future. With a great heave of his shoulders, an intake of breath, and a shudder of his soul, he nodded and surrendered. *Time to man up*, he said to himself. He tried clearing his throat, but it came out as a death rattle. He tried again.

"It was … it was … it sounded like … *ku … tu … lu …*"

"What?"

"Say again?"

"*Kutulu*. It sounded like '*kutulu*.'"

A man in uniform with no visible insignia or sign of rank rummaged through the drawings the viewer had made during his session. Most were incomprehensible. Some vaguely Asian architecture, perhaps. Weird, anthropomorphic figures. But along the border of one page he noticed a string of squiggles. Meaningful squiggles. A word in Arabic. A word that the viewer could not possibly have known. And yet had written down. In a trance.

The viewer looked from one officer to another, from one agent to another. He was suddenly small. Helpless. Frightened. In a sickly sheet of perspiration that had spread from his forehead to his face and neck and which was now a stain was spreading across his back. A man who had served in Operation Iraqi Freedom. A man who had earned a Bronze Star for bravery under fire in Fallujah.

"What does it *mean*?" he pleaded in a last bid for clemency. "What did I *see*?"

The man in the uniform, the man in the uniform with no insignia of rank or service, left the room and wandered to a secure phone in the inner office of the Remote Viewing Unit. He picked up the phone and was immediately connected to a similar phone a few miles away, in a small office belonging to the Defense Intelligence Agency.

"Chatter confirmed," is all he said.

He hung up, looked at his watch, and knew he had enough time to make the next flight to New York City. Time for the flight, but not much more than that. If the Old Man was right, they had at most weeks—possibly less—before all Hell would break loose.

It was time to bring Gregory Angell on board. By force, if necessary.

Chapter Two:

Chatter

"Chatter confirmed."

On the other end of the line in the small office in Silver Spring, Maryland a quiet man of a certain age hung up the phone and stared into space. Dwight Monroe's hair had gone prematurely white decades ago. And while he kept himself in shape as best he could, he knew he did not have that many years—or even months—left to him. His doctors had been kind, but frank. Yet age and advancing decrepitude did not disqualify him for the role he had to play in the defense of the country. He had buried stronger men than he. He had gone to their funerals, and had handed their numberless widows numberless American flags and "the gratitude of a grateful nation". He knew every name behind every star in the lobby of the headquarters of the CIA at Langley, and he knew of many more stars that should be there and weren't.

He sat motionless in his soft leather chair. The campaign desk in front of him was an antique. It was said that it had once belonged to Ulysses S. Grant, appropriately enough, for there was a bottle of Laphroaig and a single glass on the edge of it, waiting for him to pick it up and dull the blow of what he had just heard.

"Chatter confirmed."

From the days of the Korean War when he was just a brilliant, twenty-something consultant to the fledgling CIA in matters of psychological warfare and behavior modification, to the Phoenix program in Vietnam when he was in his late thirties running ops against the VC and the Russians, and from there to Africa, Latin America and Eastern Europe—there was always this sense that there was another factor in the world, a mysterious force that influenced world events, something just out of sight beyond the horizon. As Monroe grew older, and witnessed the incredible and the improbable,

on the battlefield and off, he became more convinced that they were
all—all of them, all of the spooks and the analysts and the official
historians and the career politicians—missing something. Something
of vital importance.

It all began, for him, that mortal day in Dallas in November,
1963 while working on a deal with Bell Aerospace on behalf of
CIA. When Oswald was arrested for the assassination of President
Kennedy the tumblers began to fall into place on a safe that was
locked away somewhere deep in his unconscious mind. He made
the connections because he knew the players. When it was revealed
that a woman named Ruth Paine had opened her home in Texas
to Lee Oswald and his Russian-born wife, Marina, and their two
children the name rang a bell: Bell Aerospace, to be precise.

Ruth Paine's husband Michael worked as an engineer for Bell
Aerospace, a company that had been founded largely on the strength
of the revolutionary Bell helicopter. The Bell helicopter had been
invented by Arthur Young, a genius engineer and visionary who had
left the world of the military-industrial complex to devote himself
full-time to the study of the paranormal. Arthur Young's wealthy
socialite wife, also named Ruth, was Michael Paine's mother and
Ruth Paine's mother-in-law.

Monroe had met Michael Paine and shook his hand during a
business meeting only an hour before the assassination.

And there it was: Oswald to Ruth Paine, Ruth Paine to Ruth
Young, Ruth Young to Allen Dulles. Dulles, the former head of the
CIA until the disastrous Bay of Pigs operation—and a man who
despised Jack Kennedy—was only four handshakes away from Lee
Harvey Oswald, through his mistress Mary Bancroft who was Ruth
Young's best friend.

That was the improbable.

When Monroe began, quietly and unobtrusively, to investigate
the Dulles-Oswald relationship he gradually became aware of the
incredible: that Ruth Young and her husband Arthur Young were
members of an elite group that had been formed by the inventor

Andrija Puharich back in the 1950s, a group called The Nine. He knew Puharich, who was a captain in the US Army at the time. Had worked with him during the Korean War days at Edgewood Arsenal and had attended one of Puharich's lectures to the Army on the weaponization of psychic powers, real black box stuff. He lost touch with the eccentric genius after Korea so did not realize that Puharich was deeply involved with some bizarre theory concerning extraterrestrials and their influence over political and historical events. Puharich had been one of the first to research the psychic potential of hallucinogens back in the 1950s, an area that was of intense interest to CIA. His colleague at the time was Gordon Wasson, the famous discoverer and popularizer of the magic mushroom. Wasson was himself an associate of a mysterious European man with shadowy intel credentials, George de Mohrenschildt. Wasson's phone number was in de Mohrenschildt's address book when the latter died under unusual circumstances.

It was de Mohrenschildt who introduced Lee Harvey Oswald to Ruth Paine in Texas. It was Ruth Paine who helped Oswald get his job at the Texas School Book Depository. It was Ruth Paine who was the daughter-in-law of Arthur Young. It was Ruth Paine who visited Arthur Young in Pennsylvania only weeks before the assassination in Dallas. What they discussed in that meeting remains a mystery.

Oswald had been surrounded by members of Puharich's mystic circle, and he never had a clue. Furthermore, he never had a chance.

Neither did Jack Kennedy.

It was then that Monroe started to involve himself in research that went beyond-the-pale. Psychic phenomena. Secret societies. Serial killers. Murderous cults. The UFO phenomenon. As he rose in the hierarchy of the intelligence community—now with CIA, then with DIA, and finally with his own berth at DHS (the Department of Homeland Security)—he made a point of collecting what data he could. Other men would have used his position and authority to advance their careers or, like J. Edgar Hoover, blackmail their enemies. But Monroe was not interested in that. He was a career intelligence officer. His forte was knowledge: the accumulation and analysis of data.

And in the process he acquired two degrees—one in astronomy and another in archaeology—earned during a hiatus after the fall of Saigon in 1975. He already had advanced degrees in psychology and anthropology from his Korean War days, but he needed a vacation from Vietnam and all that he had experienced there as part of Operation Phoenix, which many people thought just referred to the assassination of Viet Cong leaders but which also had a strong psy-war component. His colleagues thought it odd that he would waste his time in pursuit of degrees in such arcane subject matter, but they put it down to a desire to broaden his education in areas that were not germane to intelligence-gathering. A kind of hobby to break the monotony, maybe. When one of their own, another Phoenix alumnus who was a colonel in military intelligence, retired to become a Satanist and the founder of something called the Temple of Set (the ancient Egyptian god of Evil), the attention was deflected from Monroe's studies onto the man with the weird eyebrows and his wife, a former fashion model. That was just fine with Monroe. But the fact that another Phoenix operative was now involved in occultism bothered him. It seemed to be a harbinger of what was to come.

What his colleagues did not know was that Dwight Monroe was running his own intelligence network, a spider-web of contacts that spread through most of the agencies now under the DHS umbrella, developed carefully over the past thirty-odd years. Since it was informal, and since there were no official meetings or minutes taken, no one really knew it existed. Not even, in some cases, the participants themselves.

It was run on a "need to know" basis, and so far the only one who needed to know was Dwight Monroe.

He roused himself from his reverie, and reached for the bottle of single malt Scotch.

"Chatter confirmed."

As he opened the bottle he thought of how those two words had just altered the course of history: his own, and everyone else's. The chatter that had been coming in from their overseas listening posts and the ELINT (electronic intelligence) and SIGINT (signals intelligence) satellites and computers had been meaningless to most at NSA. None of the search terms had been flagged. Not officially, at any rate. Most of the conversations between known or suspected members of the various terrorist cells were the usual mundane accounts of family matters and the occasional religious or political reference. When one of the search terms did surface, it was noticed only by members of Monroe's own private network and the data handed over to him personally for analysis. That is the way he had it set up, and so far it was working fine.

But when the chatter intensified and the search terms began jumping out at him in greater intensity, he needed another source for confirmation. The implications were too severe, too outrageous. He couldn't rely on chatter alone. He needed corroborating data.

That's when he turned to the remote viewing operation that did not show up on the government's books but which had been in full flower during the hunt for Bin Laden, a hunt that had taken on new energy with the election of an American president with a Muslim name, Barack Hussein Obama, and his demand that the architect of 9/11 be located and terminated. That was when the remote viewers were put back on-line, the "Manson Family" called out of retirement, and new energy infused into the program after a long hiatus.

He supplied fresh sets of coordinates to the RV team through his contact at the DIA. Ostensibly they were looking for Bin Laden and Al Qaeda cells in Afghanistan. Later, the target had shifted to

ISIL and to al-Baghdadi who took over from the dead Bin Laden. But as always the coordinates had been encrypted so that even the officers in charge of the remote viewing teams were unaware of the target locations. The viewers were not allowed to open the envelopes which contained the numerical data points for latitude and longitude—which were, in any case, written in a code invented four hundred years earlier by a Catholic monk, the occult scholar Abbot Trithemius, the father of modern cryptography. Instead, they were to hold the sealed envelopes and begin viewing.

The results were far better—and much worse—than even Monroe had anticipated. The data he had accumulated over decades of research and analysis into the purported existence of a worldwide cult with ties to terrorist cells, drug operations, and human trafficking was not only confirmed, but expanded with much new information showing the degree to which this cult had penetrated foreign governments as well as diverse ethnic and religious communities in the United States of America.

The fact that the Middle East was a hotbed of weird religious cults—the Alawis, the Nosairis, the Druze, and the Yezidis, not to mention the Nestorians, the Assyrians, the Copts and other assorted Christian and quasi-Christian groups—rarely was rarely reported upon by the mass media. Even the Wahabbis—the Sunni group now in charge of Saudi Arabia—was considered heretical by some doctrinaire Muslims. What was going on now in the Middle East was a cult war of enormous proportions ... and enormous implications for the rest of the world.

And beneath the surface of all of these warring factions was another cult, something far more ancient and far more dangerous than Al Qaeda or Jemaah Islamiyyah, Lashkar-e-Taiba, or even those sadistic poseurs of the Islamic State. Playing one sect against the other, one terrorist group against the other, this nameless cult had managed to build a powerful organization whose power was directly proportional to the degree to which it was unknown. Unlike Al

Qaeda or ISIL, whose influence far outweighed their actual ability to conduct sophisticated military operations, this cult's ability to forever change the balance of power in the Middle East—and by extension the world—was far greater than its reputation.

The remote viewers had confirmed it. The word he had dreaded hearing—the term that had come up so often in the chatter from Tunisia to Turkey and beyond—had surfaced in a secure sub-basement at Fort Meade, uttered by a man who had no inkling of its meaning or its importance. The transcript of the viewing session would arrive on his desk within the hour, but Monroe already a good idea of what it would say. It had been predicted almost a century ago by an introverted, nativist author of ghoulish short fiction who lived and died in the claustrophobic embrace of Providence, Rhode Island.

CHAPTER THREE

MOTHER NIGHT

What is love? There is nothing in the world, neither man
nor Devil nor any thing, that I hold as suspect as love ...
Therefore, unless you have those weapons that subdue it, the
soul plunges through love into an immense abyss.

— Umberto Eco, *The Name of the Rose*

Providence, Rhode Island
598 Angell Street
1915 CE / 1333 A.H.

The newspapers were full of the story of the American occupation
of Haiti, which began on July 28 that year. The date was noted as
possibly significant; its proximity to the pagan cult of Lammas ordinarily celebrated on the eve of August 1 was probably coincidental,
but its relevance would be confirmed nineteen years later in 1934
when the US occupation officially ended on August 1.

But all Howard Phillips Lovecraft could think of at the moment
was of the noble US Marines occupying a tropical island infested
with the horrible cult of voodoo. Who knew what ancient gods
and demons would be disturbed by the presence of so many white,
Christian soldiers? Who could tell what the ramifications would be
as unspeakable beings were roused from their underworld crypts?

And how would their co-religionists react, those gathering in
secret, arcane rituals in the swamps outside New Orleans, in our
very own United States? He had heard of the orgiastic rites taking
place among the devotees of the African gods, accompanied by the
hideous pounding of the huge drums as naked men and women
writhed uncontrollably, their souls in the grip of fiendish creatures
from some other dimension.

Not that he believed in any of that. But he knew that *they* did, and that is what mattered.

As he lay down the newspaper, he could hear her screaming outside the door. His mother. His poor mother. She was seeing them again. The creatures. It was particularly bad this evening. Rats in the walls. Lurkers in the dark. She was surrounded by beings visible only to her. She was either losing her mind, or she was seeing what others could not. Or both.

He knew the feeling.

He tried to cover his ears to block out her rantings. He would be twenty-five years old this year, and had spent all of that time in one house or another on Angell Street with his mother. His father had died, insane, when he was quite young. His beloved maternal grandfather, the noted businessman Whipple Van Buren Phillips, a Freemason, had died in 1904. Young Lovecraft's only succor had been his dreams. Locked away in his room, surrounded by books (many of which he salvaged from his grandfather's library), he would let his mind wander all over space and time, collecting ideas and images and sensations that would ordinarily be out of reach for the ordinary man living in an old house in the eldritch city of Providence, Rhode Island.

But how he loved Rhode Island! The smallest state in the Union, it was a manageable place even though it was populated by ghosts, demons, the spirits of dead Indians, and the lingering gaunts of ancient peoples who had once lived in these forbidding New England forests and raised stone altars to the noxious creatures they thought were gods. Rhode Island was the whole world, as far as he was concerned. Everything he needed was within a short walk of his home. The university. The libraries.

Cemeteries.

"Get away! Get away from me!" his mother screamed in the hall.

Lovecraft sighed, and got up from his desk and opened the door.

"Mother ..."

She stopped where she was as if pole-axed, her arms ceasing their windmilling as she batted away unseen terrors. Instead, she pivoted on her axis and pointed a raised finger at her son.

"They're coming. They're coming for *you*!"

And then she tore off down the hall cackling a manic laughter, a screech designed to fool the demons, to convince them she could defend herself against their vile blandishments. A laughter fueled by terror. Lovecraft stood there, a deep sadness erupting from his heart like cold lava from a trembling volcano. His father, dead. His grandfather, dead. His favorite uncle, Frank Chase Clark, had died only a few months ago, in April. His cousin, the young Phillips Gamwell, has only a year left to live. And now his mother, hopelessly insane. He was not yet twenty-five, and his whole family—aside from some aunts—was disappearing into the void. For a man who valued heredity and ancestors as much as he did—who gloried in bloodlines and breeding, classical literature and the genteel arts of bygone ages—he was being robbed of his own. There would soon be nothing left of the Lovecraft line.

His mother had come from a noble and wealthy family with ancestors who came on the Mayflower, but had married beneath her station: a traveling salesman of jewelry and baubles. A man who went bonkers in a Chicago hotel room during a business trip and who died in a hospital in Providence shortly thereafter. His mother had never come to terms with her egregiously bad fortune. Her father had stepped in to do what he could to lift his daughter and her strangely nervous son up from the fringes of poverty into something more respectable and comfortable, but then he too had passed away. Lovecraft missed him as much or more than his own father, whom he had never really known.

It was twilight in Providence on a summer's day. Shadows lengthened. Stars were almost visible, shining with ancient light from unsettling distances and harboring who-knew-what kind of beings on unseen planets. And as the shadows grew long on Angell

Street, his mother became more agitated. She saw threatening forms in every corner of the house, materializing as if from the very walls themselves. On the street, it was even worse. They would come jumping out at her from the sides of buildings, doorways, overhangs: hideous creatures with long, claw-like fingers and wide unblinking eyes. He had to be sure to watch her and not allow her to wander outside where her illness would become apparent to their neighbors and where she might possibly harm herself or others in the process. It meant she could never be left alone, not even for a moment. Lovecraft was shackled to his mother and to their five-room apartment like a dog on a leash.

It was an exhausting way to live.

At least Lovecraft was not particularly interested in going anywhere. Sometimes, when he knew his mother was asleep, he would go for long walks in the evening. Providence was a different city at night, and he could almost believe that the creatures his mother saw in her derangement actually existed in some dimension perpendicular— and not parallel—to our own. As if there was a road through reality, traversed by all manner of alien traffic only occasionally observable by the sensitive, the artistic ... the insane.

Lovecraft knew that his dreams were the stuff of his vision. His dreams had fueled his perception of what others called reality. But he had also suffered his own nervous breakdown a few years earlier. It marked the beginning of his withdrawal from the world, but it also gave him the space and time to write. From scientific articles and essays on politics to short stories about beasts and alchemists, Lovecraft had embarked on his own peculiar arc of story-telling and cultural observation. But in the background was the constant percussion of mental imbalance and isolation. He had wanted to be an astronomer ... but his fragile emotional state had ruined the chance. He would have to travel to the stars in some other way.

He was a firm believer in scientific principles, and had written learned articles on astronomy at a very young age. But at the same time he had to acknowledge the power of the irrational in his understanding of horror. Science had not protected his family from sickness, madness and other evils. Science was not able to cure his father, grandfather, uncle, or mother. Of course, neither was the church. His belief in science, he knew, was practically a religious one. It was a preference for science over superstition, for facts over suppositions. He wanted science to be perfect, to answer all of humanity's questions, to be the panacea it promised it would be.

But in the meantime ... night gaunts, lurkers in the dark, rats in the walls.

And dear old Mom.

He got to work on another story. In his mind, he could see the lineaments of a world beneath the flat surface of our own. It was a world peopled by strange beings, or at least they appeared strange to the untrained observer. In order to maintain a form visible to us in three dimensions they had to assume weird, asymmetrical shapes that represented their best option for physical manifestation. But the result was often hideous.

The creatures he imagined were vaguely anthropomorphic but they also possessed appendages that were more cetacean, with fusiform bodies and vestigial limbs projecting from malformed crania. Mammalian mysticeti, amphibians with teeth that suckled their young, they were monstrous but their monstrosities enabled them to survive below the sea and in the far reaches of interstellar space ...

Or so he imagined. Or thought he imagined. It was hard to tell the difference between imagination and hallucination, between hallucination and reality. Especially when you lived with madness every day of your life and were forced to treat it as real.

But in his dreams he heard voices. He saw cyclopean architecture. He heard screams. Sometimes those screams were identifiable as coming from his mother's bedroom as she struggled with horrors not dissimilar to his own. But at other times the screams seemed to come from his own throat, modulated by a vocal apparatus not traceable to forms resulting from human evolution.

At the age of five, he had dreamed the name *Abdul Alhazred*. It was an impossible name, at least in terms of Arabic orthography and grammar. But he had heard it nonetheless. A name that haunted him his entire life. It rang out in his dreams as clear as the cry of the muezzin in Damascus at dawn. Perhaps it was not Arabic. Perhaps it was a name from another race, another tongue, filtered through an Arab speaker's sensibility. He did not know.

The other word—*that* word—also came to him in a dream. He heard it like the lugubrious moan of a condemned prisoner. It represented all that was evil, all that was heinous in the human condition as far as that condition was contingent upon the good will of the Great Old Ones ...

What? What did that mean?

Lovecraft looked up. Had he fallen asleep again? He listened for sounds of his mother but she was back in her room, possibly asleep already, exhausted by her flight from her waking nightmares. He looked down at the pages he had been writing. The sentence had stopped in the middle, somewhere. Abandoned its train of antique phrasing. *Great Old Ones*. He had been day-dreaming. Lost contact with the world around him for a moment. That always happened when he focused on the word. *That* word. And there it was, at the bottom of the page, standing alone and defiant as if written by another's hand:

Cthulhu.

CHAPTER FOUR

THE ANATOMY OF MELANCHOLY

As the man said, for every complex problem there's a simple
solution, and it's wrong.

    —Umberto Eco, *Foucault's Pendulum*

Monroe spent a long time staring at the glass of Laphroiag, seduced
by its power to calm the soul and dull the senses. He sighed, and
resisted its pull. Instead, he reached into a locked filing cabinet next
to his desk and within easy reach of his leather chair, and withdrew
a large manila envelope whose contents were held in place by a
thick rubber band. Not exactly high-tech, but it was a file he had
been compiling since those early days of the Johnson administration
when he realized that everything was not what it seemed. He dared
not commit its contents to any electronic medium, for he could not
afford even the slightest chance of the file making its way onto some
server somewhere, hacked and cracked by an adolescent malcontent
or a sophisticated Chinese cyber-warrior. No. This file—most of it
handwritten, some of it typed on a manual typewriter, and all of it
compiled by hand—had to remain off-grid.

There were architectural drawings, astronomical charts, glossaries
of Kurmanji, Sanskrit, Sumerian and Zhangzhung. Chronologies
of the lives of select artists, writers, musicians. Tables of Kabbalistic
correspondences. Weird diagrams cribbed from occult literature.
Organization charts of terror cells, secret societies, and obscure
corporations. Maps of Asian landscapes. Correspondence with
scientists and schizophrenics. Newspaper clippings. Articles from
medical journals. Alchemical drawings.

Obituaries.

Taken individually, they were the pages of a tortured mind and
a broken soul. Pieced together, all that dissociated knowledge, and
read as a whole they told the story of the beginning, and of the end.

48

Of everything.

"Chatter confirmed."

He glanced at his watch. The chatter had confirmed everything he had been tracking since the 1960s. All that work, all those sleepless nights. All those obscure reference works from libraries and archives around the world, wherever his official missions had taken him. The suspicions had turned to possibilities, the possibilities to probabilities, and now his life's clandestine work had transformed suspicion to reality. He thought of all those conspiracy theorists out there, those who believed that the world was controlled by a secret government of malicious and greedy men. He almost laughed out loud. Would that it were so! Would that there existed a government of men who controlled … everything. The reality—now confirmed—was far, far worse. Faced with the alternative, the conspiracy theorists would have embraced an Illuminati or a New World Order and considered themselves blessed.

There was a discrete knock at the door. His agent had arrived with the transcript of the RV session. He put his large manila file—the Lovecraft Codex—back in the locked cabinet, and then opened the door to admit one of the few men in the world who had an idea of what was about to happen.

"It's true, then?"

"Sir. I'm afraid it is."

"Then we haven't much time."

"No, sir."

"Angell. Where is he now?"

"Still in Brooklyn. He has no classes today."

Monroe scanned the transcript, but it was as his agent had said. He looked at the scribbled drawings with a silent shudder. They were crude, but oh so familiar. They represented the heartbeat of some huge and diseased thing that had been pulsing since before life appeared on earth, transmitted down the generations to our own.

Monroe could not go to anyone else with this. It would be months before anyone would take him seriously. He could not go to the President, nor to the Joint Chiefs. His operation was still—as it had always been—off grid. A black op. With a black budget, filched and fudged from other departments, other operations. And rightly so; had he tried to get official sanction for this, they would have had him committed to St Elizabeth's long ago.

So he relied on unsuspecting experts in their respective fields. He trolled the Pentagon's Minerva Project—the boondoggle for impoverished anthropologists who were expected to conduct "anti-terrorism" research in Asia, Africa and the Middle East—looking for those with specialized knowledge of languages, cultures, religions. Cults. These were difficult people to deal with. Their intel could not always be trusted. They padded their reports to make themselves appear more valuable, to gain access to more Defense Department cash. And they were such prima donnas, to boot.

But one such specialist always stood out. He had no interest in Minerva, no expectations of wealth. He didn't play the political games every academic was supposed to play. He seemed to have no ego at all, at least not where academic standings and credentials were concerned. And he had the field experience they needed, coupled with an unparalleled academic background in the target languages and the people.

Even more attractive—and of utmost importance in this case—was his family's connections to Rhode Island, to Providence, and to its famous son: the eccentric author of pulp fiction, Howard Phillips Lovecraft. It was a double-edged sword, though.

Gregory Angell was a blade that could cut both ways.

Compulsively, Monroe once again looked at his watch.

"There's still time to catch the afternoon flight to New York."

"Sir."

"Do what you can. Promise what you have to. But we need Angell on the next available flight to Baghdad."

"We do this black?"

Monroe thought for a moment. He had the juice to authorize a military transport, but someone, somewhere would start asking questions. He did not need that distraction now.

"Arrange a commercial flight to Istanbul, and then take it from there. We still have assets at the border?"

"Yes, sir."

Monroe nodded, more to himself than to his agent.

"With any luck, then, we could have Angell embedded by this time tomorrow."

"What about Miller?"

Jason Miller was the remote viewer who had gone AWOL a few months earlier. No one knew why.

"Still no sign of him, sir."

"That worries me. Miller knows just enough to become a problem for us."

"We've had him put on the TSA watch list, and have notified the Brits, the Israelis and Interpol that he is a terror suspect. We've changed all the codes, anything to which he was exposed or privy. But he has not surfaced anywhere."

"Miller was good. He had Special Forces training and did a stint at CIA before coming to us. He had exceptional RV abilities." Monroe nodded to himself.

"Sir, maybe he went off the deep end, like the others."

Monroe frowned at the suggestion.

"He wasn't like the others. That's what worries me." He sighed. "We can't let that interfere with the schedule. Go to New York. Find Angell. Recruit him to our side and get him to the sheikh at once."

"Sir."

"And report back on the secure line as soon as you've landed in Turkey."

The agent nodded, and left the room quietly.

Monroe showed no sign that he was aware of the agent's departure. His eyes were focused on the locked cabinet and the world's only copy of the file he called the Lovecraft Codex. What had begun as a kind of hobby had turned into a passion, and then an obsession. He was aware of the danger of becoming too narrowly focused on an obsession. It was something that had ruined some of the best agents he had known, not only the field agents who could lose a sense of perspective after long periods in an alien culture, but even the office-bound analysts who could get completely side-tracked by a stray document, an old news story, a seductive idea. The glamour of intelligence work wears off rather quickly when bureaucracy, office politics, and the stupidity of elected officials interfere with the mission. There is the urge to come up with the earth-shaking revelation, the missing piece of the puzzle, the information no one else has but which everyone else suddenly needs. The urge to feel important. A need to stand out among the hundreds and thousands of others. It's what happens when the sense of community falls apart, when the common good takes a back seat to individual concerns and political ambitions.

Monroe knew all about this first-hand. It's what prompted him to conduct his investigation quietly, even when he felt he had to grab everyone by their collective lapels and shake them until they could see what he saw. Of course, paranoia was also part of his reluctance to discuss his findings with colleagues and superiors. He did not know how far the infiltration extended, and who might be in charge of protecting it.

He also could be just plain crazy.

At least, he used to think he might be. It was gratifying to realize that he had not been deceiving himself all these years. Gratifying, and now terrifying. Like a husband who has long suspected his spouse of being unfaithful and who now sees photographic proof.

All those years of intellectual isolation were still years of making his contribution to the defense of the United States of America, the only country he had ever loved, the only idea to which he kept faithful loyalty since before the Cold War began.

And now he had no choice but to extend that loyalty to the entire human race.

How easily treason had become ethical.

CHAPTER FIVE

WINGS

Magic can only be efficient if it has been transmitted without loss and without flaw from one generation to the other, till it has come down from primeval times to the present performer. Magic, therefore, requires a pedigree ...

—Bronislow Malinowski, *Myth in Primitive Psychology*

Brooklyn Heights Promenade
That evening

Gregory Angell sat on a bench and gazed across the East River towards the spot where the Twin Towers used to stand. Finally, after more than ten years, the towers were being rebuilt.

Like many New Yorkers, he was not entirely sure that was a good thing.

Of course, from the point of view of the peculiar sort of patriotism that New Yorkers feel—a patriotism that is inextricably linked to their City, which they identify with their country—it was inevitable that a new edifice would be raised in defiant memory of the old one. He remembered all those bumper stickers in the days and months after the September 11 attacks, the ones that said "We are all New Yorkers." At the time, he felt an incredible emotion well up within him at the sight of those gestures of solidarity, but he knew they would be short-lived. America did not really like New York City.

He was born in Rhode Island. Like many people living in the City he was from "out of town." But he had been in New York since his university days at Columbia, studying ancient religions and archaeology. Now he was a tenured professor of Middle Eastern languages, especially the dead ones: Akkadian, Ugaritic, Sumerian.

He was fluent in Biblical Greek and Hebrew, and could make his way in Arabic, Farsi, Pashto and Urdu. He was an anomaly, a lover of language and its nuances. He hated the way language had been used to divide peoples, societies, civilizations. He felt that the real motivations for most wars could be reduced to the famous quip from *Cool Hand Luke*: "What we have here is a failure to communicate."

He was idealistic once. That died, along with God, in Mosul. Now he knew that there was no hope for humanity. That people would never transcend their racial, ethnic or religious differences. God had become a source of cheap labor for politicians, demagogues, and terrorists of all religions, all races, all ethnicities; made to defend or oppose whatever they wished, whatever their vile, fever-induced fantasies delivered to them.

The New York City skyline had offered up an altar to this cheap labor. Angell's most famous relative had perished on September 11 when his plane flew into the North Tower. An important and hugely successful television producer and writer, responsible for the major sit-com hits of the 1980s and 1990s that were based in a Boston bar, a Seattle radio station, and even a small airport in Massachusetts; this particular Angell had died along with his wife and more than a hundred other passengers in a ball of flame that Gregory Angell had actually witnessed from the very spot where he was sitting now.

For him, it was Pearl Harbor. He was only an academic, but he wanted to enlist somewhere, join up to fight the amorphous "enemy." Even at the time he realized such a wish was futile: there was no enemy army, no enemy country. The antagonists were all underground, living in caves or melting through European, Asian, African, American landscapes with false identities and a network of safe houses, mosques, *madrassahs*.

So instead, he found himself embedded with a US platoon in Afghanistan in 2002, providing translation and "cultural" assistance to the young kids in their high-tech helmets and comm gear, who had no idea where the hell they were or what they were supposed to do, but who were all fired up to do it anyway. He did not have a commission, was not regular Army, but one of a corps of civilian advisors and experts called in at the last moment for their language skills and knowledge of the religion and the region.

It was an exhilarating time, to be walking in the footsteps of Alexander the Great and wallowing in the Kipling-esque atmosphere, all the while dodging bullets from the Taliban and Al-Qaeda. Kandahar—the city in southern Afghanistan that served as his base of operations, founded by Alexander himself in the third century BCE—was home to one of the oldest human settlements known, dating to a prehistoric period in the remotest past, with gods and cults of which modern scholars know next to nothing. He had no idea at the time how relevant this ancient religion would become to his own life.

He saw very little in the way of firefights or IEDs at first, and was used mainly to communicate with village elders in territories the Army had successfully pacified. Later, as the Army tried to hold onto the regions it thought it controlled, Angell's role became murkier. He found himself negotiating with frightened old men and women in small homes made of brick and clay, with the name of God written in Arabic on plaques hanging on their walls. He found himself performing a kind of ersatz intelligence role, collecting and analyzing information and passing it on to the officers in charge. He had crossed a line from trying to help the people he met to spying on them. It made him doubt his motivations, and he had a hard time connecting this mission to the one that had prompted him to enlist his abilities in the service of his government in the first place.

When he saw an opportunity to return Stateside after a few months in-country, he took it. For awhile he found himself lecturing CIA action agents on the local languages and religious customs of the northeastern region of Afghanistan: Waziristan and Nuristan, areas on the Pakistani border that contained a confusion of tribal conflicts and ancient rivalries. Then, after a few months of that, he was back at Columbia, his ethics and sense of purpose a little battered, but still intact. He found that he hated the Taliban, and especially Al-

Qaeda, but had developed a sincere appreciation for the people of Afghanistan, people who had never heard of the World Trade Center and who only wanted to be left alone to live in peace. He devoted the next few years to his academic work and fell back into the comfortable rhythms of the classes, the libraries, the museums, the collegial discussions with fellow professors and grad students.

But then his country called on him once again.

It was to be a simple field mission, this time in the northwestern part of Iraq, in Mosul, near the ancient city of Nineveh. He was to go there as an archaeologist, which was fine with him because it would give him the opportunity to visit some of the excavated sites as well as the museum in Mosul. There had been a steady traffic in stolen artifacts from Iraq's national heritage, an inevitable side effect of the war. The famous Baghdad Museum had been looted during the invasion, and while most of the priceless treasures had been returned—stolen by the museum staff themselves to save them from looters—there was a significant number of items that had never been returned and which had wound up on the black market. It was believed that some of the money obtained from these illegal sales was lining the coffers of Al-Qaeda. It was Angell's mission to ask around and get a feel for how the black market sales were being arranged. Posing as an archaeologist—which he was—he could gain entrée to the world of museums, antiquities dealers, and tomb robbers and pretend that he was interested in sourcing some choice items for museums and collectors back in the States.

That was when he found himself in a Humvee, stuck behind a crowded bus during what passed for a normal rush-hour in Mosul.

Mosul
February 20, 2007 CE / 1427 AH

The rusted claptrap of an old school bus made its way carefully from the Mosul Textile Factory to the small town of Bashika, in Nineveh Province. The workers were silent inside, tired from a long day at work in the hot and airless plant. The murmurs of some of the men were like white noise to the driver, who had driven that route more times than he could count. All he wanted was to finish the run and get home to his wife and children and maybe a hot meal.

Angell was in a heavily-armored Humvee that had just come from the archaeological site at Nineveh, the one excavated and explored by Layard in the nineteenth century. His mind was wandering, trying to accommodate the clash of eras—the ancient period when Babylon was at its height juxtaposed with modern, war-torn Iraq—as he sat next to the driver, a seasoned US Army veteran who now worked for Blackwater, the mercenary firm that was run by some kind of Christian Fundamentalist from America's Deep South. Angell's security had been farmed out to Blackwater as a matter of course: he wasn't on a tactical military mission but was working on the covert side for one of the many acronymic intelligence agencies. The driver didn't ask, and Angell didn't tell. They kept their eyes on the road and on the clattering bus ahead of them, Angell's reverie broken by the sight of some freshly-painted graffiti on the side of a building they had just passed.

Suddenly, two automobiles swerved out of a side street and slammed to a stop in front of the bus. The driver hit the brakes and tried to back up but was blocked by another car at the rear that had wedged itself between the bus and Angell's Humvee. The workers in the bus began standing up and shouting. To the driver. To their companions. To God.

"Stop! Stop the bus!" Armed men emerged from the cars and began screaming orders. The driver's hands were frozen to his steering wheel.

"Oh, no," he murmured to himself. A prayer, an imprecation, an invocation. There would be death today. The spilling of blood. *Inshallah*, it would not be his.

A few days earlier, a Yezidi woman had converted to Islam to marry her boyfriend who was a Muslim. Her parents found out, and dragged the unhappy woman back to their village, the same Bashika where the bus was now headed.

They then—her family and her neighbors—stoned her to death in the street.

As the video of the stoning circulated on the Internet, emotions and tensions ran high. Muslims vowed they would avenge the death of the woman who had converted to their faith.

The gunmen rushed into the bus. Automatic weapons are very convincing, especially at close range. It doesn't take a sharpshooter to cause heavy damage to property and flesh with an AK-47 at a distance of five feet. And most of the men on the bus had seen what these weapons could do during the American invasion and occupation—when Mosul had been turned into a war zone between Sunnis and Shi'a, Muslims and Christians, Al-Qaeda and the Coalition forces, and more subsets of these than anyone could remember.

One of the men, who seemed to be the leader, demanded to see everyone's identification cards.

And began splitting up the passengers into two groups.

As the groups began to form, the workers realized what was happening. All the members of one group were Christians. All the members of the other group, twenty-three in all, were Yezidis.

Angell shouted at his driver to do something, but the man merely shook his head.

"We have orders not to engage, and to fire only if fired upon. We are not getting into the middle of this, whatever it is. Your mission, Dr. Angell, takes priority. And, anyway, there are a lot more of them than there are of us." But in the end he picked up the radio and notified his commander of the situation, while Angell sat there, helpless as any academic when faced with real bullets, real violence, and a real historical event unfolding before him.

He watched in horror as the Christians were allowed to leave the bus. The driver was allowed to leave the bus. But the Yezidis were told to remain.

The bus was driven into eastern Mosul, as Angell's Humvee followed at a discrete distance. The bus stopped at a side street, as Angell and his driver watched from around the corner, helpless to intervene.

The twenty-three remaining passengers were taken off the bus.

And lined up against a wall.

And shot.

Gregory Angell sat on a bench on the Brooklyn Heights promenade, overlooking the East River and Lower Manhattan where the Twin Towers used to stand. He had watched the towers fall that day in September, not knowing that one of his relatives was in one of the planes. And then, years later, he had watched as twenty-three Yezidis were gunned down on a side street in Mosul.

That evening, as he sat in a building that was guarded entirely by Blackwater mercenaries, he came to the realization that the massacre of the Yezidis in Mosul and the September 11 attacks in the US were one and the same episode. The same force was working through both events, through both groups of crazed fanatics. The same innocent people were slaughtered. The same innocent blood was spilled. Even though the two events were removed in space and time, they were the same event. As an academic, he could parse through both scenes and come up with any dozen ways in which they were *not* related, in which there was no similarity in cause, in motivation, in the character of the perpetrators, the location of the attacks, the nature of the innocent people who died. And it would be pointless.

As a human being, he knew that all that violence, all that misery, was evidence of the action of an unspeakable force in the world, one that no one dared name, and which had existed since time immemorial.

It was God.

For a moment—a moment of blinding clarity—he saw how the entire run of human history was the chronology of wars fought over gods. God was the justification for all of it, for all that spilled blood, for all those mutilated bodies and minds. God.

The Great Absence.

And in that moment, Gregory Angell knew that there really was no God. That was the point. The whole thing was a kind of sick joke, perpetrated by some mad genius a hundred thousand years ago or more. God was the Black Hole around which the religions of the world since ancient times swirled in a slowly decelerating orbit. God was an Event Horizon towards which all humanity was moving in an endless parade of destruction. God was … Not Here.

God was murdered, along with faith and reason and love, that February day on a side street in the Iraqi city of Mosul, only a few kilometers from Nineveh in an area where the world's great religions were born. Fitting, then, that God should die there, confronted with his own perfidy. He thought of that famous aphorism of Nietzsche, "God is dead." God *was* dead and he, Gregory Angell, had discovered the body. The crime scene was Mesopotamia. The murder weapon was a much-delayed moment of enlightenment.

He returned to the States in a mood of profound depression. He began to drink, but that did not begin to fill the emptiness in his soul. What does a religious studies professor do when he has lost his religion? Well, as they say, those who can, do; those who can't, teach.

And teach he did. He got tenure, conducted seminars that were overflowing and the talk of the community, but resisted all attempts to have him go back to the Middle East, even for a talk or a conference. Even to Egypt, or Turkey. As he became well-known for his innovative approach to the study of religion, he became increasingly reclusive. He had a hard time sleeping, for he would frequently awaken to the sound of gunfire in his dreams, to the sight of blood pooling in the dust of Mosul. To the sudden extermination of human life, life taken by other humans in some kind of sick fantasy of cosmic justice.

He moved to Red Hook, away from the conviviality of Upper West Side Manhattan intellectual society, and into a basement apartment where he moved his books and papers and what oddments of his life mattered to him … or did not matter enough to jettison. He reduced his course load as much as he was able, and tried to find some meaning in his life, something to take the place of the giant Gorilla who had left the room. He became increasingly paranoid about his fellow human beings, and using his government connections managed to obtain a gun in New York City where the punishment for possessing an unlicensed firearm was a mandatory one-year prison sentence. He slept with it under his pillow at night, the oil staining his sheets. He carried it with him, illegally, through the streets of New York like a melancholy Charles Bronson or a slightly less-geeky Bernie Goetz. He ate in the Arab restaurants of Atlantic Avenue, where the cooks and the waiters took pity on this sad American scholar who spoke their language and read their newspapers, but who didn't share their faith.

And as for women, he avoided them. One might say, "religiously." As practical and realistic as most of them were in his experience, they accepted the existence of God quite naturally and without argument. The same way they accepted the existence of eternal love, or the fidelity of their husbands. They needed this unfounded belief in a fantasy world in order to survive everything from the rough advances of their lovers to the intense pain of childbirth and the bitterness of watching their infants turn into the sullen and angry children they eventually would become. Without God, and the promise of heaven, it would not be possible or even worth enduring. Mother's milk would turn poisonous in the breast.

This was the state of Gregory Angell's life in April of 2014, more than seven years after the Yezidi massacre at Mosul. A machine stuck in a neutral gear. A powerful engine with nowhere to go. A car with a disinterested driver. And a handgun he had never fired in anger, with ten rounds in the magazine and one in the pipe.

Which is when Dwight Monroe's agent sat down next to him on the bench on the Brooklyn Heights promenade, and looked at him, and smiled a cobra's smile.

CHAPTER SIX

A RICH UNCLE

… the sacred and the profane have always and everywhere been conceived by the human mind as a separate genera, as two worlds that have nothing in common. … This does not mean that a being can never pass from one world to the other, but when it happens, the way this passage occurs highlights the essential duality of the two realms. It implies a true metamorphosis. This is demonstrated particularly well in rites of initiation …

—Emile Durkheim, *The Elementary Forms of Religious Life*

When James Aubrey first set eyes on Gregory Angell, as the latter sat silently and still on his park bench on the Promenade like a gringo Buddha under a Bo tree, he had a hard time reconciling the man in front of him with the photograph in his file. While the dossier photo revealed a typical academic, albeit with a bit more physicality than one normally associates with the profession, the real Gregory Angell seemed to have withdrawn into himself to such an extent that his body appeared to have shrunk within its clothes. It was as if the scholar was trying slowly to disappear, and had begun by minimizing his affect. He would not have been surprised if Angell began speaking in a whisper, or with subtle twitches of his eye muscles.

He was of medium height, maybe five-ten or five-eleven, not quite six feet. About one hundred sixty pounds, or maybe less by now as he seemed to swim in his trousers and jacket. Dark hair, brown eyes. Regular features. He had a strong jaw, but it was usually obscured by a neatly-trimmed beard, also dark brown but with the beginning of some grey. His mouth was a little unusual, with the full lips one would expect of a woman rather than a forty-year-old man, but his moustache compensated. His fingers were those of a pianist, long and slender. In short, he could pass for almost any ethnicity from Central Asia to Portugal. A Pashtun tribesman, maybe. Or an Italian gigolo.

He knew from the file that Angell carried a gun, and that he was right-handed. That meant the piece was probably on his left-hand side to enable easy access. Thus, Aubrey decided to bear down on Angell from the right. He didn't believe the man was violent, but he wasn't taking any chances. The loose jacket Angell was wearing was large enough to conceal a weapon, and although Angell appeared to be relaxed there was no telling how far his paranoia had already taken him.

He sat down next to him.

Angell continued to stare out at the Manhattan skyline, as if totally unaware of the agent's presence. That was unusual for New York, and particularly so for a section of Brooklyn that had once been the gay cruising capital of the East Coast.

After a moment, Angell spoke.

"Who sent you?" he asked, still staring straight ahead.

"A mutual friend."

"A friend." The sarcasm was palpable.

"A rich uncle, then."

"You're not the first."

"I know."

"Then you know it's pointless to ask me. I'm not going back."

Aubrey let that sit for awhile, as if waiting for a soufflé to rise. His silence was a measured part of the conversation. He did not get up to leave, but he did not try to convince Angell to do anything, either. The pressure of the silence weighed on Angell, who tried to fill it with words that had little meaning for him but which he hoped would mean something to this man with the flat, burnt-umber aura of certain death about him.

"I've done all that anyone can ask of me. I'm not a spy, or a field agent. I'm a college professor. And I've seen all the action I ever want to see. There are other men just as capable as myself. Go ask them."

"We have," replied Aubrey.

"And?"

"And they all recommended you."

That was not entirely true. There were few other individuals Monroe's people could safely approach outside of normal channels and, anyway, Angell's value was something unique. It did not rest solely on his previous experience in the "region." It also did not rely on his knowledge of its languages and religions. For that, there were others who could be tapped, such as the anthropologists who worked for the Pentagon's Minerva Project, academics who were taking DOD money to create imaginative and sometimes wholly-invented profiles of terrorist groups and their celebrity leaders from Palestine to Papua. No, Monroe didn't need any more of those. They had their place, and were of some value in the total scheme of things, but they were too eager to please for Monroe's taste, and frequently exaggerated the importance of their data or just—in Aubrey's particular turn of phrase—"made shit up."

And then there were the lions of the field, men like Lawrence Schiffman, James Tabor, Tudor Parfitt … Dead Sea Scroll scholars and Biblical specialists who were rock stars in their profession, too well-known to send off into the wasteland on this particular venture. And in some cases they were not up to the physical demands that the mission required.

Angell wasn't like that. He was a loner, and even though he was respected he did not have the cachet of a Schiffman or a Tabor. And he didn't make shit up. He was too devoted to the pursuit of knowledge for its own sake, and that meant he could not afford to embellish or invent. He lived alone, had no bad habits anyone could discover, and thus was immune to blackmail, both financial and emotional. He seemed to have no need for money or, if he did—beyond his salary as a tenured professor at Columbia—it wasn't much. Angell wasn't out to make a fast buck, wasn't applying for grants or writing ambitious proposals, and that made him attractive to Monroe. At the same time, it also made him a loose cannon. Angell would do what Angell wanted to do, and to hell with the government. Ever since Mosul, Angell had become independent, and in the world of the Patriot Act, Camp X-Ray, and extraordinary rendition that translated as "eccentric."

But the upside was they didn't need him for long. Only a few days. A week, at the most. And then they could cut him loose. And if anything happened to him in the process, he had no ties in the States other than his classes and his students. In virtually every respect, Gregory Angell had the profile of an ideal field agent. The languages, the experience, the university cover, an anonymous appearance that enabled him to blend in anywhere, the lack of family obligations, even his recently acquired expertise with a firearm. He was driven, and did not give up easily once he had the bit between his teeth.

Problem was, he was just a little bit crazy.

Angell sighed, and made as if to get up and leave the agent there for the pigeons to anoint.

"Is there somewhere we can talk?"

For the first time Angell turned to look directly at his petitioner. Aubrey was shocked to see the expression in the professor's eyes. Deep sadness, mixed with a hint of desperation, and what seemed to be a chronic lack of sleep.

The professor was exhausted. For a moment, Aubrey was reluctant to proceed any further with the recruitment. Angell looked like a basket case. But the stakes were too high to get sentimental about his target's emotional state. Still, he could not shake a sudden bad feeling, an experienced agent's intuition that this would not end well for Angell.

"What do we have to talk about? I told you, I'm not going back."

"I understand, Professor Angell."

"Then?"

"I won't try to appeal to your vanity, Professor. I know that won't work, and I wouldn't want to offend you that way. I also won't appeal to your patriotism. You have already demonstrated that. But we are in a difficult situation, and only someone with your background ... your unique background ... can help us, help your country, and even help other people. Innocent people. Not only in America. I can't tell you more until I know you're with us, but I can say that this isn't a localized issue. It has implications far beyond our borders, and I can't emphasize enough how your specific profile is absolutely necessary at this time."

Angell almost smiled. "You want me to save the world, is that it?" When Aubrey didn't say anything, only stared back into Angell's haunted eyes, the academic turned his head in disgust.

"Give me a break, whatever your name is. I'm not a child, and this isn't an Indiana Jones movie. You don't need me. I'm just convenient and probably too needy, according to the psychological evaluation in my file, to turn you down. Well, you're wrong. You're all wrong. Go back to your masters and tell them you failed."

Aubrey had no choice but to play his trump card. As Angell had turned to go, he spoke to his retreating form, his words like gunfire shooting him in the back.

"Does the name Francis Wayland Thurston mean anything to you?"

Angell stopped dead, and slowly turned around to face his inquisitor. The look of shocked incredulity on the professor's face was impossible to misinterpret. "My ... *What*? What do my relatives, my ... *ancestors* have to do with ... with *anything*? Have you people lost your minds?"

He strode back up to Aubrey and stared at him, his fists clenched at his sides as if trying to keep himself from punching the older man in the face.

"Is this some kind of ... of *blackmail*? Have you all really stooped that low?"

"It's not blackmail, Professor. I know this is a sensitive issue with your family, and we would not bring this up if it were not relevant to the matter at hand. Urgently relevant, I might add."

"You know about Thurston, so you know about George Angell, his grand-uncle. George Gammell Angell, of whom I'm a direct descendant. You know this. So you know about the rumors, and the stories. You know how that libel has plagued my family for almost a hundred years now. And you're using it against me, just like every tinfoil hat conspiracy theorist and Sci-Fi conventioneer has been doing for at least as long as I've been alive. This is contemptible. It's below even the government's bar and that one has been set pretty damned low of late."

Aubrey finally stood up from the bench to face his accuser.

"Then it's time to put those rumors to rest, isn't it? Once and for all? And if we can't ... if the rumors have any basis in reality ... isn't it just as important for you to find that out? Once and for all?"

Angell was still gaping at the man in disbelief. A cold shudder had gone through him at the mention of Thurston, the family's black sheep. The one who told those tall tales about George Angell, the distinguished professor at Brown University, and the crank archaeological theories he came up with towards the end of his life. The ones that were eventually described in all their lurid detail by a deeply disturbed young Rhode Island writer of hack fiction. The ones that destroyed the Angell family reputation for decades.

But how this had anything to do with national security, or whatever it was this strange government agent had come to him about, was some bureaucrat's wet dream. It had to be.

"You can't ...you can't be serious."

"It won't take long, I promise," Aubrey insisted. "Hear me out. And if you still want out, you're out. We won't bother you again."

He held his hands out to his sides, either in supplication or to show that he wasn't armed. Or both. Angell held his gaze for another moment, and then nodded.

"This had better be good. If you're lying to me, I just want you to know that I'm carrying a weapon and will not hesitate to blow your fucking head off, government agent or no government agent. Are we clear?"

Aubrey smiled to himself, but said in a straight voice to the crazed professor, "Crystal. There's a place on Montague Street. It's quiet this time of day. Let's go there. It's only a few blocks away."

Angell didn't stop to consider how a G-man from DC would know about local restaurants in Brooklyn and their seating schedules, but allowed himself to be led out of the Promenade and down Montague Street as if he was Dante and James Aubrey was a pin-striped Virgil in black wingtips.

Spiraling down into the deepest circles of Hell.

Watching them leave, a man in a retro denim jacket and a floppy hat got up from lacing up his running shoes at a nearby bench. He was a professional, so he did not need to pat his pocket to be sure that his weapon was in its place. He did not need to touch his ear to ensure that his radio was intact and operative.

Slowly, he stood up and stretched, rolling his head around and seeming to get the kinks out of his neck and shoulders. And then he began walking, following the two men out of the park and into the streets of Brooklyn Heights.

CHAPTER SEVEN

THE LIBEL

They had come from the stars, and had brought Their images
with them.

—H.P. Lovecraft, "The Call of Cthulhu"

Montague Street in Brooklyn Heights is named after Lady Mary
Wortley Montagu, the wife of Britain's ambassador to Turkey in the
mid-eighteenth century, who resided briefly in the area. She is noted
primarily for her reporting on Islamic customs in "the Orient," one
of the first western women in history to do so. Her relatives, the
Pierreponts, gave their name to another Brooklyn Heights street.

Gregory Angell was not thinking of these connections at the
time, though if he had he might have taken some solace in them.
After all, there was a peculiar connection between this oldest of
Brooklyn neighborhoods and the Middle East. In addition to the
Lady Montagu link, there is also the fact of Atlantic Avenue which,
in that area of Brooklyn, boasts many Arab shops and restaurants. It's
an area that Angell knew well, for his own apartment in Red Hook
was close enough that he could walk it easily from Montague Street,
across Atlantic Avenue and through Cobble Hill.

Capriciously, a restaurateur once decided to open an establishment
named Capulet's on Montague Street. The popular bistro is long
gone, as is the Piccadeli and so many others that Angell knew from
his student days. Instead, Aubrey led him to a Hungarian restaurant
on the second floor of one of the older buildings on Montague,
close to Court Street. It was, as the agent had claimed, deserted at
that hour. The stock brokers had not yet returned home across the
bridge from lower Manhattan, and their wives were busy at home
with children, nannies, and the Food Channel.

Aubrey seemed to know the owners, and spoke to them briefly in Hungarian. They smiled, bowed, and disappeared into the kitchen as he and Angell took a seat at a table far enough from the window that they would not be observed.

"I know the owners," he told Angell, redundantly. "They worked for us for awhile. Before the Fall."

Angell merely nodded, and stared at his table cloth, playing with a fork while he waited for the agent to get on with it. The Cold War was before his time.

Aubrey sensed the man's impatience, and sighed. He leaned back in his seat and fixed Angell with a steady gaze.

"Okay. Thurston. Back in the day, he was close to George Angell, the professor, who left him some papers. At least, according to the information we have. Stop me if I am in error anywhere."

Angell looked up and shrugged.

"You probably know as much about this as I do, but go ahead."

They were silent for a moment as the owner's wife came out and placed some fresh bread and a dish of cucumber salad, seasoned with dill, on the table between them.

"You know that the Baghdad Museum was looted during the invasion."

Angell nodded. "I also know that most of the treasures were returned."

"That's true. Many of the so-called looters were actually museum personnel, saving the artifacts from danger. Some of them risked their lives to save these items. It was nothing short of heroic."

"What does this have to do with Thurston, or with George Angell for that matter? Or with me?"

The proprietor came over silently with a tray from which two glasses of Egri Bikaver—the deep red Hungarian wine whose name translates as "Bull's Blood"—were set down in front of the men.

Aubrey thanked him, and the man left without smiling.

"George Angell had in his possession one of the stolen artifacts from the Baghdad Museum."

"Now I know you're crazy. George Angell died in the 1920s. The Baghdad Museum was looted during Operation Iraqi Freedom. In 2003."

Aubrey's expression was difficult to read. He did not reply immediately, but instead lifted his glass of wine and urged the professor to do the same.

"It's really quite unique, this wine. No one credits the Hungarians as vintners—that honor usually goes to the French or the Italians, or maybe to the Spanish for sherry and Amontillado, the Germans for Riesling or the execrable *Liebfraumilch*—but this wine is actually quite good, in a heavy-handed sort of way. You should try it."

Angell humored the older man, and raised his glass in a mock toast.

"I imagine I will need every drop of this if I'm to believe a single word of what you're going to tell me."

Aubrey took an appreciate sip of the wine, and then set his glass down with an elegant gesture.

"Your ancestor, George Angell, was a revered scholar, was he not? A man who had gone on archaeological digs throughout the Middle East. He was a contemporary and a colleague of men like Layard and Woolley. He had published widely, and was known for his collection of ancient Babylonian artifacts, many from the area around Nineveh."

Angell sipped at his wine and held onto the glass, his elbow on the table and his eyes on the tablecloth, avoiding Aubrey's gaze. They were venturing into delicate territory, and Angell was intent on keeping his composure as the inevitable scandal was eventually— if carefully—brought up.

"At least one of those artifacts, however, did not come from your ancestor's own excavations. It was given to him by another man, an artist I believe. For identification."

And there it was. The story that had bedeviled the Angell family for ninety years. The libel that had nearly destroyed old George Gammell Angell's reputation long after his death, and which had resulted in at least three different university board decisions over the years to remove his name from the list of professors emeritus. Gregory's own decision to become a Biblical scholar was motivated, at least in part, by a desire to restore his family's dignity and its good name. Or maybe it was revenge.

"It never happened." Angell's voice was so low, Aubrey had to lean over the table to hear it.

"It never happened," he repeated, building up steam. "There was no artist, no sculpture of some alien being. No correspondence with my ancestor. It was invented, conveniently after George Angell had died and could not defend himself. There is no truth to the story and there never has been!" The last was said in a near shout. Fortunately, the restaurant was still empty except for the two men. The proprietor stuck his head out of the kitchen, looked around briefly, then returned to his pots.

"My God, you can't take seriously a ... a ghost story written in the 1920s! And what possible relevance does it have to anything having to do with national security?"

Aubrey looked up at his distraught companion who was now standing up over him, his fists resting on the table, his eyes boring into his own.

After a moment Aubrey said, "Please sit down, Professor. All will be revealed."

Angell took a deep breath, and then his shoulders slumped and he dropped back into his seat. He turned his gaze to the window, and looked down on the street without seeing it.

"I work for a man whose name you don't know, for a project you've never heard of. This man is very high up in the intelligence hierarchy. He's no fool. He's worked for our government since the Korean War era. He should have retired decades ago, but he refuses to do so until he has finished this one, final mission. Indeed, I doubt very much whether anyone else in government has the vision or the necessary intellectual chops to even conceive of this project much less carry it out.

"He has determined that you are the missing piece of this gigantic puzzle that he has been putting together since the 1960s. He knows your background. He knows what you've done for us so far. The mission in Afghanistan. The second one in Iraq. The briefings of our people in between those missions. He is sensitive to your reluctance to get involved in any intelligence work at this stage. And he also knows that you would resist any attempt to involve your personal family … connections … in this regard. But he knows things … things about you, about Thurston, things about George Angell … that even you don't know, or don't know that you know."

"That's offensive."

At this point, the proprietor and his wife brought to the table a very fine chicken paprikash with egg noodles and a side of potato dumplings. Angell suddenly realized that Aubrey had never actually ordered any food or even looked at a menu. The old couple silently returned to their kitchen, allowing the two men to resume their conversation.

Angell was silent. In his mind he was cursing Aubrey, cursing the government, cursing George Angell, and cursing especially the weird, anti-social and racist writer who started all this trouble in the first place. But he had to admit that Aubrey had him intrigued. Anyone would be flattered to realize that the government had taken a special interest in them and their family history. Flattered, or scared shitless.

Angell did not yet know which one he was.

Outside, on the sidewalk across the street, the man in the denim jacket and the floppy hat stood and stretched as if getting rid of a muscle cramp. But his eyes were fixed on the second floor window of the Hungarian restaurant.

Aubrey took a bite of the paprikash, closed his eyes in appreciation of the delicate yet faintly spicy flavor that was a hallmark of the restaurant, and then looked directly at Angell, waiting to get his attention.

When Angell looked back at him, he resumed his little speech. The one that had been prepared for him by his boss and mentor, Dwight Monroe.

"Once upon a time," he began, with a self-conscious wince at the cliché, "there was an esteemed professor named George Gammell Angell. He was murdered on the Providence docks on the night of December 21, 1926, at the age of 92.

"His killer was Carl Tanzler, an occultist and a man who later would be accused of grave robbing and necrophilia in Key West, Florida."

CHAPTER EIGHT

THE CODEX

The entry is an old one, dating from 1926. It contains official data on crime figures for Providence, Rhode Island.

There were no homicides at all in Providence in 1926.

But there *was* a murder and it took place at the dock where the Newport ferry gets in. It was not reported as a murder, because the man who committed it knew enough about medicine to make it look like a heart attack or a stroke.

The wording in the Codex is brief:

"Carl Tanzler, aka Count Karl Tanzler von Cosel, aka Georg Karl Tanzler. German immigrant. DOB Feb 8 1877. POB Dresden, Germany. Prisoner of war at Trial Bay internment camp, Australia, during WW I. Traveler to India. Occult leanings. Believed he could see spirits. Arrives US April 1926 after five years in Germany 1920–1925 and four days in Havana, Cuba. Settles in Zephyrhills, Florida; moves to Key West, Florida in 1927. Radiologist at US Marine Hospital. October 1940 arrested for robbing the grave of one **Maria Elena de Hoyos (DOD Oct 25 1931)** and stealing her corpse in 1933. Corpse was discovered in his home in October 1940. He had been involved in trying to re-animate it for nine years. Case was dropped due to lapsed statute of limitations. HPL visits Key West to see Tanzler in June 1931. They discuss Tanzler's occult ideas, specifically concerning re-animation of dead matter. Tanzler takes HPL to visit Elena de Hoyos who is terminally ill. Tanzler later dies in the arms of a wax effigy of Elena. DOD: July 23, 1952."

A more recent note, in Dwight Monroe's tiny, precise hand and appended to the file states:

"Tanzler in Providence RI December 1926. Eyewitness reports seeing Tanzler with hypodermic syringe in small leather case at the ferry pier. Eyewitness told by Tanzler that he is a doctor waiting for a patient. George Angell collapses at the pier thirty minutes later. Tanzler is back in Florida in time for Christmas. Then arranges move to Key West."

In the same file are some clippings. One set is from two 1939 issues of the *Rosicrucian Digest*, and concerns Tanzler's internment in Australia.

Another is a copy of an autobiography he wrote for the Raymond Palmer magazine, *Fantastic Adventures,* in 1947—the same year that Palmer published the Maury Island story about a flying saucer in distress raining debris on Puget Sound, the same year as the Roswell crash—with an illustration of Tanzler as a mad scientist attempting to revive his beloved Elena. 1947: the same year as Kenneth Arnold, Maury Island, the discovery of the Dead Sea Scrolls, the creation of the CIA, and the death of Aleister Crowley.

The full story is as remarkable as the intel summary. Carl Tanzler claimed to have been an intimate of German and Austrian paranormal investigators at the turn of the century, and to have been the descendant of a famous countess, an alchemist, whose ghost he would occasionally see. He traveled to Asia, visiting India and studying with gurus for a period of time before winding up in Australia and getting detained as World War One began.

After his release he makes his way back to Europe, and emigrates from there to the United States via Havana, Cuba in 1926. He meets a young Cuban woman, Maria Elena de Hoyos, and falls in love with her. She is a patient at the Key West hospital where he works. She has tuberculosis and will die in less than a year, and Tanzler begins various alternative remedies to try to combat her illness, but to no avail. She succumbs, and Tanzler builds an elaborate mausoleum to house her remains. What he does not tell anyone is that he has designed a special coffin to keep her body in as close a state to life as possible. In fact, he believes she is not entirely dead and that over time, with his careful ministrations and pumping her body full of nutrients and other material, she is gradually coming back to life. Her eyes open. She makes tiny gestures. He even hears her speak.

When Elena's family get wind of these strange affairs, the mausoleum is closed down, but not before Tanzler can steal the body and bring it to his house to continue his program of resuscitation, albeit much reduced in capacity. That is when he is finally discovered—and Elena's body, after having been dead for nine years, is taken away from him and reburied. He finds himself arrested and in prison.

Upon his release, he fashions a life-size wax effigy of Elena and, according to one version of events, this is how he was found in death in 1952, with the effigy in his arms.

The case made world headlines, and the Tanzler house is a tourist site to this day. What is not so well known is the fact that Lovecraft (the "HPL" of the Codex) visited Key West in the months before Elena's death. Lovecraft had been contacted by Tanzler after the latter read his famous story, "The Re-Animator."

This, anyway, is the story that Aubrey is relating to Gregory Angell in that Hungarian restaurant in Brooklyn Heights. What Gregory has so far not been told is the relationship between Tanzler and his ancestor, George Gammell Angell. The details of this relationship appear in no police file, no official record. They were uncovered during the course of Dwight Monroe's investigations, and these details made it imperative that Monroe somehow convince Angell to get onboard with his admittedly bizarre program. The only place the whole story appears is in the pages of the Codex, and there is only one copy of that file and it remains with Monroe. Aubrey must tell all of it from memory.

"A lie can be shouted, and if it's loud enough the people will believe it. Hitler knew this. So do talk radio hosts. But Kabbalists know that the truth must be told in a whisper, and then only to a few. Gregory Angell must be led slowly to the truth, otherwise he will assume it is a lie." This is what Dwight Monroe told Aubrey that morning, and it is the strategy he is using in the restaurant, a site chosen specifically to create the kind of atmosphere he needs to gently, but firmly, bring the professor around.

Tanzler claimed to have been an intimate of some of the most famous paranormal experts of the time, men like Johann Karl Friedrich Zöllner, Carl Kiesewetter, and Carl Freiherr du Prel. His autobiography—published in a pulp magazine that specialized in fantasy stories—specifically names these men and several others. Their names would mean nothing to you now, but at the time they were at the forefront of psychic research, mediumship and the whole panoply of the occult milieu in Leipzig and Dresden. The problem with Tanzler's timeline is all of these men died in the late nineteenth century. Zöllner in 1882, when Tanzler was only five years old. Kiesewetter and du Prel in the 1890s. It is doubtful that Tanzler ever met these men. Tanzler was inventing himself, creating what we in the trade call a "legend" and taking advantage of the distances of time and place to keep his secret safe. He claimed to have been mistaken for dead in a morgue in India, only waking up at the last moment to save himself from a premature cremation. He claimed to have experienced severe poltergeist activity at his ancestral castle in Saxony. None of this can be verified, of course. All we know for sure is that he did spend time in an Australian POW camp during the First World War, a claim that was verified by a famous Buddhist monk who was also imprisoned there, and that he did eventually make his way to America where he became a radiologist in Key West. The story of his obsession with the young Cuban woman is well-known and well-documented."

Aubrey paused to take another sip of the Egri Bikaver as Angell made an impatient gesture.

"What does any of this have to do with me? Or with my family for that matter?"

The agent set down the glass carefully, and smoothed the crisp white tablecloth before continuing.

"As I mentioned, Carl Tanzler murdered George Angell on that Providence dock."

Angell looked shook his head, and then a smile began to broaden his features.

"You're insane. You're all insane. That's a preposterous allegation."

"Bear with me for a moment, Professor. We know that Tanzler arrived in the United States from Cuba in the spring of 1926. Your ancestor was murdered that December. Tanzler moved to Key West the following year. Between April of 1926 when he is in Zephyrhills, Florida and when he heads for Key West in 1927, his movements are somewhat of a mystery. As is the reason behind his emigration from Germany in the first place. He came from a well-known, even prosperous, family. He had a noble bloodline, famous ancestors, even a haunted castle if anything he wrote was to be believed.

"At the end of World War One, he was repatriated to Germany, arriving—again, according to his autobiography—some two years after Armistice. In other words, around the end of 1920 and the beginning of 1921. He spent some five years with his family before leaving for America. We don't have much information as to what he was doing there all that time. Germany was in chaos then, its economy in shatters. This was especially true in Saxony, where the Tanzlers lived. Factories had closed all over the region. Tanzler's father had died while Karl was still in the prison camp. His sister had married and gone to America, but his mother and another sister remained behind in Germany. The Germans had lost the war, and were expected to pay enormous reparations to the Allies as well as give up some critical territories. Hitler had attempted the Beer Hall Putsch in 1923, representing the anger and frustration that many Germans felt over the way they had been betrayed by their leaders.

"Tanzler marched in that putsch. Tanzler was forty-six years old. Tanzler was a Nazi."

Aubrey said this last as if it should have considerable importance for Angell, but the latter was simply mystified.

"I still don't see ..."

"You're an anthropologist, Professor Angell."

"Yes, but …"

"Tanzler had pretensions to that field of study. He believed he had experienced psychic phenomena—visions, ghosts, poltergeists, hauntings of all kinds—as a young man, first in his native Germany and then later in India and elsewhere in his travels. He studied with gurus, experimented with a wide range of herbal concoctions designed to alter states of consciousness, talked to the dead. When he returned to Germany after World War One, with the memory still fresh in his mind of how he had been treated by the Australians, his disgust with the *ancien regime* propelled him to the streets to march with Hitler. After all, the symbol of the Nazi Party was the swastika, something he recognized from his time in India at the feet of mystic masters. He could relate to that, and to the whole *völkisch* ideology of racial memories and pagan gods. And he was something of a crackpot anyway, as history shows us.

"Tanzler first tried to get a position as a physicist or a chemist. He considered himself an inventor. But science was a hotly-contested field, becoming increasingly politicized, and the available positions were few. For instance Werner Heisenberg would take over the physics chair at Leipzig the year that Tanzler left for the States. But Tanzler had another love, and that was the study of the human race and most especially its psychic dimensions. At that time, in the 1920s, anthropology was a young discipline and it was populated by a lot of dreamers: men and women who speculated a great deal about ancient origins, dead civilizations, and the differences in races and cultures. Tanzler thought he had a place there, and after the failed putsch he contacted a professor he knew at the University of Leipzig with the idea of becoming an anthropologist. But Tanzler had no credentials in the field. In addition, the thrust of German and Austrian anthropological research at the time was towards the study of folk art, folk religion and folk culture with a view towards creating a kind of basic or primitive "genuine" German society that was based on its pagan roots. Tanzler's expertise was Asian.

"The university system was in danger of becoming an intellectual wasteland as more and more academics—many of them Jews—

found reasons to escape Germany for Great Britain, France, and the United States. The others, those that remained, fought long and hard to protect their positions in a time of tremendous economic and political uncertainty. But someone noticed Tanzler, understood his passion and his somewhat less-than-mainstream ideas about science, race, and occultism, as well as his long period of travel in the East.

"And so Heinrich Himmler gave him a job."

In 1925, two years after the failed putsch and when Hitler had just been released from Landsberg prison, the Nazi Party was being reorganized. Himmler had his eyes on a greater role than being a mere functionary in the SA, the infamous Brownshirts, and was agitating to head Hitler's special bodyguard, the SS or *Schutzstaffel*. Tanzler had not been arrested with the other putschists but had managed to stay at large and return to his family's home in Saxony. It was when Hitler, Himmler, and the fanatic propagandist Gregor Strasser came to Saxony to campaign in the upcoming election that Tanzler was tapped by Himmler for an important—yet very secret—mission.

Himmler's fascination with the occult was well-known. To Himmler, such subjects as ancient Indian scriptures, pagan rituals, and sacred artifacts were not the stuff of "occultism"—that repository of neglected, forbidden, or rejected knowledge—but the secret core of religion itself. He could foresee a time when occultism would replace the monotheistic religions of Judaism, Christianity and Islam and would empower the German people like never before.

It would be almost ten years before he would realize this dream in the formation of his notorious SS-Ahnenerbe, or the "Ancestral Heritage" Research Bureau of the SS, in 1935. But his circle of friends and colleagues already included some of the most influential German academics of the age. From them he had learned of the existence of a cult of powerful shamans in the East: men who were ageless, and who could call on terrible powers that other men had forgotten, powers from before the time of the Great Flood, before the construction of Solomon's Temple, before the exodus of the Jews from Egypt.

Himmler needed access to this power, both for Germany and—in a most special sense—for himself. While he admired Hitler, he did not respect him as his intellectual equal. To Himmler, Hitler was the front man for the Nazi Party and he, Himmler, was its brain. But Hitler had that indefinable power, that charisma, that Himmler lacked. It was raw spiritual energy, a kind of demonic possession, that came over Hitler during his speeches and his public appearances that was irresistible, even to foreigners who didn't speak a word of German. Himmler, with his owlish eye-glasses and his overall prissy appearance, looked like a bookkeeper or a minor bureaucrat. What he needed was access to the same kind of power—the same source of spiritual energy and divine fire—that Hitler had in abundance.

And he knew where to get it.

Dresden
1925

They sat across from each other in the Tanzler ancestral home. Tanzler's mother was hovering in the background, preparing a meager tea of some stale *küchen* and coffee bought at considerable expense from a neighbor.

Himmler was the first to speak.

"Count Tanzler, I remember you well from Munich in 1923. You marched with me and with young Walter Hewel, and stood up to the hooligans who attacked us. You are a dedicated National Socialist."

"Thank you, Herr Himmler."

"You have been baptized with the Blood Flag. You saw our brothers fall. And now, National Socialism is once again on the march and we need men like you to help us bring sanity and common sense to the German people."

"I am at your service, Herr Himmler." Tanzler was trembling, and was careful to speak slowly and deliberately so as not to reveal his nervousness before one of the most powerful men in the Party. He did not know the purpose of Himmler's visit, but he suspected that it had less to do with begging a donation than with something more sinister. Outside, in front of the manor house, Himmler's large black car was parked and two hard men in leather coats were pacing up and down, waiting for their leader to emerge.

"You have spent some time in the East, I understand."

It was not a question, but a statement.

"Yes, Herr Himmler."

"In India, I believe?"

"Yes, sir. And in the Near East and Central Asia as well."

Himmler was silent a moment, as if lost in a reverie of Oriental fantasy.

"The East may hold the secrets of our origins, my dear Count. The origins of the Aryan race. India, Tibet, even the fabled cities of Samarkand and Tashkent. Have you read Blavatsky?"

For a moment, Tanzler did not know how to respond. Was Blavatsky Jewish? Was her Theosophical Society one of those dangerous secret cabals he had heard so much about, like the Freemasons or the Golden Dawn? In the end, he decided on truthfulness, for he suspected that Himmler already knew the answer.

"Yes, Herr Himmler. Of course."

"If you can follow all that folderol about root races and sub-root races, you can see that there is a germ of truth in what she writes. Race is a spiritual thing, Count Tanzler. And the blood carries the spirit." He took a breath and his gaze settled calmly on Tanzler's face. The count found the gesture unsettling.

"There is a spiritual war taking place all around us, a war for the very soul of Germany, that involves races with very different characteristics, very different origins. We will have to employ methods that may seem strange or even obscene to the world in order to win this cosmic struggle. Blavatsky's major work is well-entitled, *The Secret Doctrine*. It *is* a secret: to the many, but not to the few. Not to us."

Tanzler did not know how to respond, except to listen intently and have the appropriate look of awe on his face.

Then his guest suddenly shifted gears.

"Did you know that Walter Hewel is now in the East Indies?"

"No, sir. I did not know."

"Yes. He is doing very good work for us there. He is building National Socialism among the expatriate Germans. He is very energetic, and very young."

"Yes, Herr Himmler."

"But the East Indies is far away. It will become crucial in the years to come, but at the moment we have more pressing concerns."

"As you say, *mein Herr*."

"We have enemies everywhere. Here, in Saxony. In Bavaria. Throughout Germany. And in other countries as well. International Jewry is a force to be reckoned with. There are conspiracies of Masonic lodges who work against National Socialism because they know we threaten their hegemony over the human race. And there are other secret societies, groups of evil men, who open their temples and their magic circles to those who would destroy our work."

"Then we must fight them, Herr Himmler. With everything we have."

"I am glad to hear you say that, Count Tanzler. I am happy to know that we can count on your support and your assistance." The future Reichsführer-SS got up abruptly from his chair and made for the door. "My associate will be in contact with you with further instructions. Please give my best regards to your mother." He turned once only to raise his arm and say, "Heil Hitler!"

"Heil Hitler!" responded Tanzler, mystified now more than ever. His mother stood in the doorway with a tray of tea things and was about to say something when she saw the bewildered look on her son's face and stopped. Himmler was gone, his boot steps clattering down the marble stairs to the front door and his waiting car.

On the table next to Himmler's chair, where she would have placed the tea tray, was an object that Tanzler had not seen before. It was a small idol, of uncertain age and identity, about four inches high. It seemed to have been made of clay, but Tanzler could not be sure since the surface was rough and pitted, as if it was some kind of stone. Volcanic in origin, maybe. Across the pedestal of the idol was a series of characters that might have been hieroglyphics. On the bottom of the pedestal was a small label that had been affixed not long before, judging by its clarity and the sharp, clean lines of the ink that was used to write the brief description, "Cutha, 1914."

What was disturbing, however, even more than the artifact's mysterious appearance on the coffee table, was the design of the thing itself. It seemed to show a half-man, half-fish sort of creature; and what Tanzler first thought was thick strands of hair turned, on closer inspection, to be … tendrils, or perhaps tentacles. Was it an octopus? A hybrid creature like those of the Egyptians, half human and half animal?

If so, what desert civilization would have worshipped a creature so obviously of the deep ocean? What was "Cutha" and what did it mean?

And what, Tanzler thought to himself, *does any of this have to do with the Party?*

What does it have to do … with me?

As Aubrey picked up the story, Angell sat and toyed with the paprikash on his plate. While the food was delicious, the conversation was ruining his appetite. He knew about a similar idol to the one Aubrey described, the one left in Tanzler's home. But how to connect the statue in a crazy count's castle in Saxony to the one that allegedly was given to his ancestor in Rhode Island?

He did a quick mental calculation. He wasn't sure of the exact dates, but according to the legend George Angell would have been given the item some years before Tanzler was given an identical one, thousands of miles apart. He suspected that Aubrey was either insane, or that he was not telling him the whole truth. In fact, he wasn't sure that anything he was being told was the truth and not some fantasy of a crazy element within the intelligence "community."

"Tanzler was later contacted by a man identifying himself as a colleague of Himmler's. He was given some cash, and was told he would be leaving on a ship bound for Cuba in four months' time. From there, Tanzler was expected to go to the United States and lay low until he was given further instructions. He would be contacted by a member of the Party in America and told what was expected of him. In the meantime, he was to determine as much as possible about the origins of the strange object that had been left for him by Himmler."

The proprietor came over and cleared away their plates, with barely a glance at the untouched meal on Angell's. He exchanged a look with Aubrey that took in the scene on the sidewalk where denim jacket man was still stretching. Aubrey nodded, almost imperceptibly, a gesture that escaped Angell who was deep in another world. The two diners remained silent until the cook was safely back in the kitchen, out of earshot.

"All anyone knew was that the idol had been uncovered in a dig in what is now Iraq, in the ancient city of Cutha, or Tell Ibrahim northeast of Babylon. It was a city variously known as Kuta, Kutu, or Gudua in Biblical times and sacred to the Babylonian deity of the Underworld, Nergal. It was also the site of a famous shrine to Abraham, the father of the three great monotheistic religions that came out of the region. The Germans had been busy throughout the Middle East, conducting archaeological excavations in Mesopotamia, Egypt, and the Levant. Often, these digs were covers for intelligence operations in the lead-up to World War One. The British were doing the same. T.E. Lawrence used his archaeological fieldwork as a cover, for instance. Nevertheless the Germans did uncover some interesting sites in the process.

"However, the Cutha artifact was unique. There was nothing like it anywhere in the Middle East, or in the world for that matter. Except in one place, of course.

"In your ancestor's study in Providence, Rhode Island. But you knew that."

CHAPTER NINE

THE HORROR IN CLAY

There had been aeons when other Things ruled the earth,
and They had had great cities.
—H.P. Lovecraft, "The Call of Cthulhu"

According to the timeline presented by Lovecraft in his famous short story "The Call of Cthulhu," George Gammell Angell, Professor Emeritus of Semitic Languages at Brown University in Providence, Rhode Island, had been shown a stone statuette identical in style and subject matter to the German idol during the annual meeting of the American Archaeological Society in St Louis, Missouri in 1908. It had been found a few months earlier at the site of a gathering of cultists in the bayous outside of New Orleans, Louisiana by a local police inspector identified as John Raymond Legrasse.

Seventeen years later, in Providence, Professor George Angell was presented with a bas-relief depicting an identical mythical creature by a young art student enrolled at the Rhode Island School of Design, or "Ris-Dee" as it is known to the locals. The student—Henry Wilcox—was not a member of any cult or secret society; rather, he had seen the creature in his dreams and fashioned it accordingly. He brought the art piece to the elderly professor because he needed an expert to interpret the design and place the object in a proper historical context ... since he was certain it represented some ancient civilization and the gods it worshipped, gods who were somehow visiting him in his tortured sleep, speaking to him in a language he did not understand and could not identify.

Unfortunately, Professor Angell died before he could record his conclusions concerning the strange juxtaposition of two such bizarre—yet identical—objects coming into his possession. That he took the event seriously is evidenced by the fact that he had amassed a large file of newspaper clippings and correspondence concerning the idol and the associated bas-relief, as well as a series of strange occurrences that took place around the same time that young Wilcox was having his bizarre nightmares. After his death, these fell into the possession of Francis Thurston, a grand-nephew of the professor, who was moved to continue his uncle's researches in a quest that would eventually take him around the world. At least, that's the story.

Dwight Monroe was certain that it was Professor Angell's wide-ranging correspondence with characters as disparate as distinguished academics in Europe to theosophists in Latin America, surrealist artists in France, and cultists in California that got him killed.

He was equally certain that Angell—as a professor of Semitic languages—would have recognized the mysterious word that Wilcox kept hearing and which was inscribed on the bas-relief as well as on the statue. The old academic knew exactly what the idol depicted, and he was searching—not for clues as to its meaning or identity—but for traces of the very cult whose worship it represented. He was conducting what was to all practical intents and purposes an intelligence operation.

Dwight Monroe could relate to that.

The years that followed saw the rise of the Nazi Party and the corresponding rise of Heinrich Himmler's sinister SS empire of racist occultism, crank scientific theories, = the unending quest for sacred artifacts, and the ransacking of archaeological sites around the world. Monroe considered George Gammell Angell to be one of the first casualties of the Second World War: a martyr to the rapacious greed of Himmler and his maniacal insistence that his occult Reich be protected at all costs. Angell's correspondence unintentionally revealed that he was in possession of a great secret: that an ancient cult of a pre-Christian, pre-Abrahamic era was being reconstituted in the twentieth century, with potentially dire consequences.

And Howard Phillips Lovecraft had inadvertently stumbled on the plot to kill Professor George Angell.

Lovecraft was friendly with the artist he called "Henry Wilcox" in his story, and knew of the strange dreams Wilcox was having and the fugue states to which he was prone. Lovecraft knew all about fugue states from his late mother's psychotic ramblings and rantings. It was Lovecraft who suggested that Wilcox visit old Professor Angell in an effort to decode the hieroglyphics on the bas-relief that the young artist had sculpted out of the stuff of his dreams. There was an ulterior motive behind his suggestion, of course.

Lovecraft was certain that there was some deeper cause, some underlying knowledge, behind his mother's insanity. He felt certain that there was some meaning to be found in his mother's rants. Perhaps she could not actually "see" the haunts that peopled her visions; perhaps they were not really "there." But to Lovecraft's scientific mind there had to be some sense to it all. If he could have divined the root cause of his mother's mental imbalance, he was sure that he could have cured her of her disease.

Wilcox provided an opportunity for Lovecraft to test his theory. After all, Wilcox was having very similar delusions. Wilcox was seeing things that were not there. Wilcox was to be found wandering the streets at night, shuddering at shadows and pointing at invisible beings. Lovecraft wasn't able to get his mother to see an analyst, and she died in hospital of complications due to gall bladder surgery, mad as a hatter to the very end. The specter of that hospital bed and his mother's tortured mind haunted him.

His last chance was to get Wilcox to see the famous Professor Angell. If there was any reason, any truth, to the dreams and nightmares that tortured poor Wilcox, then he might be able to use that information to understand his mother and salvage what was left of his life.

It was a desperate plan, but one that suited Lovecraft's nature. He would use Wilcox as a surrogate, and determine whether the Things that haunted the artist were the same Things that had troubled his mother. If the professor could provide a solution—at least insofar as an identification of the Things—then Lovecraft could move on to the next step in his program: a psychiatric cure of his own devising.

For while Lovecraft fancied himself a scientist and an atheist, insanity—with all its visions and hallucinations, auditory and visual—was a challenge to his worldview. If he could find the cause of his mother's insanity, then he could formulate a program that would cure the world of the excesses of religious fervor and ecstatic conversions. To Lovecraft, religion itself was a form of insanity, of mass hysteria and self-hypnosis. Why, then, was the vision of Wilcox one of a strange god and its obscene cult if religion was not at the root of his mental disorder?

At first, things seemed to go as planned. Old Professor Angell agreed to see Wilcox, and was intrigued by the sculpture as well as by the account of the young man's dreams and nightmares. In fact, over the next few weeks, Wilcox actually went from bad to worse, with Professor Angell keeping a careful record of everything Wilcox said and did. During this time Lovecraft had only the vaguest idea of what the two men discussed as Wilcox was often unreachable through his mental fog. Determined to get a better idea of what was transpiring between the two, he resorted to following Wilcox to the professor's home and trying to eavesdrop through a window or door.

And when that didn't work—and when Wilcox was taken to his family's home for observation due to his nervous breakdown, and was thus effectively out of reach—Lovecraft decided that he had to go to the professor and find out for himself what was wrong with the artist.

It was this bold move, so out of character for the reclusive author, that would result in the crisis that not only gave birth to what may be his most famous story but also to Lovecraft's lifelong feud with the entire Angell family.

It was late March, 1925. On the night of March 21–22, the vernal equinox, Wilcox had taken a turn for the worse. Several days later, his curiosity getting the better of him, Lovecraft decided to call on Professor Angell in his role as Wilcox's friend and confidant. He hoped he would be able to convince the academic to discuss at least some of the case with him. However, when he reached the Angell residence he was informed that the professor was out and would return shortly. Lovecraft was led into the old man's study to wait.

Lovecraft had always considered himself to be a gentleman of the old school. He was fussy that way, and fastidious in his manners and in his dealings with people in general. He fancied himself a kind of nobleman with intellectual pretensions. That is what makes the incident at the Angell residence so out of character and bizarre.

The study was like something out of a reader's dream. It was lined, floor to ceiling, with bookshelves and these were groaning with the weight of thousands of heavy tomes. The shelves themselves were of mahogany, polished to a high luster, and the books crowding them covered archaeology, anthropology, Biblical exegesis, linguistics, and ritual. There were books in Latin, Greek, and Hebrew, as well as in Arabic, Farsi, Urdu, and others Lovecraft could only guess at. There were records of excavations at Babylon and Ur, as well as others in Egypt, Ethiopia, and the Sudan. And there were artifacts from dozens of countries and countless historical periods. The study was the record of a life lived in the mind, but also a life lived in the field. For a man who would never leave North America in his entire life, it was like a magic carpet to a fabled Oriental kingdom.

And it was unfair.

Lovecraft had to drop out of school due to his own nervous ailments. He failed at his dream of becoming an astronomer because of that. His father had died when he was young, and his favorite grandfather died leaving Lovecraft in the care of his crazy mother and his spinster aunts. He was poor. His family was poor. Although he had married shortly after his mother's death, the marriage was—predictably, perhaps—not working out and his wife had left him for a job in Ohio. He was effectively alone. And he would never have a library like this, or travel to exotic places on the other side of the world. His brilliant mind would go unrecognized. His ideas would be ignored. There would be no "emeritus" after his name. No associations would honor his work, or praise his learning.

He gazed at the bookshelves with something like lust. The

knowledge of the ages was at his fingertips, but his reach exceeded his grasp. Before all that burnished leather and gold-stamped bindings, all that published erudition, he felt insignificant, almost unclean.

That is when he noticed the ornately-carved wooden desk with its throne-like, velvet-backed chair. The professor's desk.

Knowing that he would be alone for at least a few more moments, the nervous author could not resist sneaking a glance. There, at the very top of the central pile of documents and correspondence, was a large file marked "CTHULHU CULT" in capital letters.

Book Two

Tentacles

CHAPTER TEN

SUBMISSION

Thus I rediscovered what writers have always known ...
books always speak of other books, and every story tells a
story that has already been told.

— Umberto Eco, *The Name of the Rose* (Postscript)

Brooklyn Heights
2014

Gregory Angell stood up from their table and walked over to the
window overlooking Montague Street. Aubrey had turned silent,
and the restaurant itself was as soundless as an empty church on a
warm and dusty Saturday afternoon. Across the street, denim-jacket
man stood up suddenly from his stretch like a dog sniffing the wind.
There were rain clouds. Boat whistle sounds from the docks down
by the East River. And somewhere the click of a round being chambered.

Gregory broke the silence, in a voice close to a whisper, as if
out of respect for the solemnity of the subject matter or maybe just
because a gloom had descended on the table, the restaurant, the
street outside and Brooklyn itself with this evocation of dead souls
from the ancient past. Aubrey as magician; Gregory as medium.

"Yes, I knew about the Cutha artifact. It's a legend that's been
passed down from generation to generation in our family. The
legend, not the artifact itself. As far as I know, it never really existed."

A bizarre-looking thing, they said. Ancient. An anomaly.
Something that should not have existed at all, outside of a Marvel
comic or a madman's nightmare.

"So you knew about George Angell's visit to St Louis and his
talks with a police detective from New Orleans about a cult that

97

worshipped a statue like that?" Aubrey's tone was kindly, gently urging Gregory along a path he knew was strewn with landmines.

"Not everything in that story is accurate. Lovecraft made shit up. But the dates, the places are roughly the same. I researched it in grad school. There was a cult. Well, today it would be called something different."

"Such as?"

Gregory shrugged, and returned to the table.

"A *religion*. Voudon, Santeria, Palo Mayombe, Candomble ... whatever Afro-Caribbean belief system it represented. Calling it a cult is problematic. A throwback to colonialism and the 'white man's burden.' "

Aubrey smiled.

"You're talking like a professor."

Gregory was silent. Aubrey leaned over the table and passed a small photograph across to his guest.

It was an old monochrome photo, and there were notations on it from the New Orleans Police Department. It was marked "evidence."

It showed a statue surrounded by a small field, in the center of a circle of trees: palms, and banyans. The form and shape of the statue was hideous, like an octopus about to give birth to an elephant. Everything about it was repugnant, as if some sick psychopath had done his best to create something that would disgust everyone but some other sick psychopath.

"Look familiar?"

Gregory stared at the photo, not daring to touch it, but the hairs on the back of his neck stood up anyway.

"Where did you get this?"

"From the archives of the New Orleans Police Department. This goes back to 1907, 1908. There are others. Whatever could be saved during Hurricane Katrina. Not everything from that time period had been digitized."

They were both silent a moment, Gregory wracking his brain to come up with an explanation.

"This was photo-shopped."

"Excuse me?"

"You work for the government, right? You have the facilities to … to photo-shop something like this and make it look really old. You have … you must have … aged paper in stock…" his voice trailing off even as he lost the will to convince himself of his own theory. He stopped speaking because even he could hear the tremble in his voice.

Aubrey shook his head. "You know better than that, Doctor. You know this is genuine. You know that because you saw one just like it."

It didn't register at first. Just more graffiti on another shell-pocked wall in Mosul. A kid's drawing, maybe. Something vaguely sexual about it, though. More an adolescent fantasy than a small child's handiwork. They had just come from the dig, and were only a few streets from the place where the twenty-three Yezidis would be massacred in another ten minutes. Angell had been looking aimlessly out the window of the Humvee, lost in his own thoughts, and had noticed the splotchy-looking graffiti: wet as if it just had been painted, a dark and glossy black against the pale yellow of the plaster and the beige powder of the sand and dust all around them. It stood out for a brief moment, as did the scribbled Arabic word beneath it.

Al-Qhadhulu.

A word from the Qur'an. A word meaning "The Abandoner." An epithet for the Devil. But to some, the name of a God.

Angell had strained to see the drawing more clearly before they turned that fateful corner behind the bus full of Yezidis returning home from their work at a local factory. And then the world exploded, and Angell forgot all about the curious graffiti in the horror that ensued.

"A cult gathering in 1907 in New Orleans. A mural on a wall in Mosul in 2007. Death surrounding both events. And an Angell in the middle of each one. The same figure, Doctor Angell. The same weird, anomalous figure in both places, thousands of miles and a hundred years apart. Joined together by blood and fanaticism. What are the odds against that? Look at it. *Look at it!*"

Angell calmed himself and stared down once again at the old photograph, willing himself to see something different, some detail that would mean the two figures had nothing in common. But there could be no doubt: the two dimensional image of the statue in Louisiana looked as if it had been a photograph of the mural on the wall in Mosul. It was even from the same angle.

Angell looked up at the man across from him, trying to keep the pleading out of his eyes. Aubrey was having none of it.

"They killed people, Dr. Angell. They sacrificed human beings to this … this *thing*. And you want to give them the benefit of a doubt?"

The professor raised his eyes, feverish with the memory of so many murders, so much senseless suffering, to meet Aubrey's stare.

"What religion *hasn't* committed genocide in the name of God?" he hissed.

At that, Aubrey leaned back with a slight smile of victory.

"And there you have it, Professor. This is why we have come to you."

At that moment, on the street outside, denim-jacket man seemed to have had a heart attack. He pitched over and fell to the sidewalk. A small crowd began to gather. Gregory was oblivious to the scene outside, lost within his own history, but Aubrey noted the event and turned to face the kitchen door.

It opened, and the old woman leaned out and nodded. A faint smell of cordite lingered, then dissipated, mingling with the odors of paprika and dill.

Aubrey and the professor descended the steps to Montague Street. On the other side an ambulance was blocking the road as EMT's loaded a body onto a stretcher. There was a pool of blood where denim-jacket man had stood only minutes before. Angell remained unaware of the mayhem that had just been caused by the federal agent who had been speaking so kindly and patiently to him in the restaurant, the agent who had given the silent order to the cook. He was distracted, hearing Aubrey's words but seeing a massacre of innocent people in Mosul more than a decade ago.

"There is worse to come, Professor. Imagine a cult—a religion—that claims millions of followers around the world and that has a grudge against everyone, every other human being on the planet. This … religion … has been with us for thousands of years, suppressed, living underground on the scraps of society and civilization. Now, with the rise of violent fundamentalist sects everywhere on Earth, it sees an opening. A crack in the windshield of democracy, if you will. Ignored, this crack will widen and the windshield will blow apart, letting every evil thing you can imagine to come rushing in."

"There is no such religion, no such cult. I should know. I've been studying religion and religious movements for decades. That's David Icke territory. Alex Jones. An alternate reality created to entertain the economically and culturally dispossessed. You'll be talking to me about the Reptilians next, or the Illuminati."

"Have you ever considered that maybe the world's religions share a common mythos, an underlying set of facts that have been interpreted according to individual custom and context but which were always there, waiting to be understood? Missing only a key, a way to decode the original message?"

Angell was shaking his head. This was a philosophical discussion, at best. There couldn't be anything real behind it. Philosophy was a work of the imagination. It wasn't science.

"What if there is a key to this code …"

"Assuming it exists."

"Oh, it exists. What if there is a text, something in writing, that has been hidden or suppressed for centuries? More than centuries. For thousands of years, since writing first began? And if we had it, it would suddenly clarify everything because it would demonstrate once and for all the very origins of what we call religion? You know the drama over the Dead Sea Scrolls? The Nag Hammadi texts?"

"Yes, and nothing ever came of it. The Church didn't collapse."

"Because they were too recent. They didn't reveal the origin of thoughts about God itself."

The two men were walking in the direction of the Brooklyn Heights Promenade, speaking in low tones, Angell desperately trying to regain his composure as he realized he was talking to a master at manipulation. His head was spinning, and he just wanted time to think. To be left alone to think.

"I'm a professor of religious studies and Asian languages. I'm a member of most of the academic societies that deal with this sort of thing. I've been doing this a long time. If there was anything to this theory of yours, I would have heard about it by now. It's a small, incestuous little circle of specialists and we all know each other and are current on each other's work. What you're saying sounds like the kind of stuff paranoid schizophrenics write on subway walls." When he realized what he just said, he stopped himself. Walls. The flashback to Mosul was short, but intense.

"Yet, that same paranoid theory is what got your ancestor killed. And it's why you're carrying a gun today."

Angell was silent a moment. In his mind's eye, a row of Yezidis being lined up against a wall.

"Paranoia kills. It always has. That doesn't mean it has a basis in reality. People kill and die every day because of delusions. That doesn't mean we have to take them at face value."

"Fair enough. But if there was a way to defuse a particular delusion before it could grow and consume an entire generation, wouldn't you want to contribute? The weapon you are carrying can only defend *you*, and even then not for long. Not against a numerically superior force. But there is a weapon that can protect millions, or just as easily destroy them. You should appreciate the fact that it is a book. Your life's work is based on books, and books talking to books. This may very well be the ur-book, the original text that engendered all other texts. If you don't want what happened in Mosul to happen again, this time with a cast of millions, this is your chance."

As they approached the Promenade, a car pulled up slowly alongside them. A black SUV. Angell didn't know cars, but he thought it was a Ford Explorer. In the distance could be seen the new World Trade Center going up. A little further on, the Statue of Liberty.

Aubrey stopped next to the car.

"The Middle East is falling apart. We both know that. But the implications for the rest of the world are dire, and not because of the oil or even because of Al Qaeda or the Islamic State or any of the other violent factions out there intent on slaughtering each other. This has ramifications far beyond the borders of North Africa and the Levant. The same ... *religion* ... that was sacrificing human beings in the bayous and slaughtering on a massive scale in Iraq is operating in Central Asia, South Asia, East Asia, South America, and beyond. They were just waiting for a signal to rise up, all at once. And that signal is coming through, loud and strong. It's only a matter of time."

They stood facing each other. Around them swirled shoppers and dog walkers and tired investment bankers returning home from their jobs across the Brooklyn Bridge. There were baby strollers and mesh shopping bags and smartphones. A different world.

"We need you, Professor Angell. And we need you now. I wish it could be another way, a different person. Someone with a different background. But we don't have time to vet a dozen other men or women with your qualifications. It has to be you, and it has to be today."

"You said something about a weapon, something that could save or destroy millions…"

"Are you with us?"

The setting sun ignited the New York skyline aglow in reds and yellows. The site where the World Trade Center had stood—the site where an Angell had died on September 11—was conspicuous now, another massive construction in its place that would open in a few months. A gesture of defiance and a testament of survival.

How long would it stand?

If Angell didn't do the right thing now—whatever that was—how long would it stand?

The rear door of the SUV opened and before he could second-guess himself Professor Gregory Angell stepped inside and surrendered himself to his destiny.

Brooklyn Heights/Red Hook
1926

A short walk in space from where Aubrey and Gregory Angell were talking, but 88 years earlier in time, Howard Phillips Lovecraft closed the door to his tiny apartment on Clinton Street with a grateful sigh.

The peace and silence were luxurious. He was alone. Alone! No mother, no aunts, and most of all no wife.

His mother died in 1921, in the same hospital in Providence that had claimed his father's life, her husband. He married one Sonia Greene in 1924 after a rather lukewarm courtship that had begun shortly after his mother's death, but financial difficulties drove her to the Midwest in search of a job, leaving Lovecraft alone in Brooklyn. He was never able to tell her, not in so many words, but their separation gave him room to breathe. If it wasn't for the fact that he was in New York—a center of pestilence and depravity if he ever saw one—he would be as close as he had ever been to happy. He had some friends in the Kalem Klub—an informal group of writers that included his friends Frank Belknap Long and Samuel Loveman—and that served to pass the time and offered him a sense of collegiality, but the inspiration to write seemed elusive until he was left alone on Clinton Street.

He would return to the core experience of his life, the one he dared tell no one but which had been festering in his mind for years now. The distance from Providence was giving him the mental space he needed to create what would become his most famous tale, even as that distance was driving him slowly insane.

From the rooms next door in the apartment house he could hear the Syrians at it again, playing some indescribable alien melody on an instrument he could not identify. It put him in a foul mood, and he was fearful that the arcane chants of the diseased Levant would somehow act upon his mind the way the unheard music of her dreams drove his mother insane. Indeed, he had been having strange nightmares for weeks now which he attributed to the darkly hypnotic quality of the flute and the *oud*. He had written a story—"The Horror at Red Hook"—in a white heat, driven nearly mad by the nasal, atonal droning of the primitive harmonium and the arrhythmic thumping *doumbek* of the Yezidi family upstairs.

He sat on his narrow bed, little more than a cot, and reached under it for the box he had brought with him from Providence.

There, in among the notes for a dozen stories and some cherished correspondence, was the file he had stolen from Professor George Angell's office, the one marked CTHULHU CULT.

It was time to get down to business.

Providence
April, 1925

He had taken the Cthulhu file from Angell's desk and, not waiting for the professor to return he made his excuses and carried the folder back to the house his aunts were living in. He didn't know why he took the file, only that the name on the file brought back those early memories of dreams he had when he was a child, dreams of nameless cities with cyclopean architecture, and of a dead priest asleep in his sarcophagus beneath the seas. A priest dead, but dreaming.

There was a connection! There was an iron thread running between his mother's madness, Wilcox's psychopathy, and his own nightmares. The young artist had seen what Lovecraft saw in his dreams; and whatever that was, whatever was meant by *Cthulhu*, was somehow at the root of his mother's illness and his family's insanity.

His father, his mother … both driven insane. Lovecraft knew that there was no way to outrun whatever hereditary strain there was that he inherited from both his parents. So, instead of outrunning it, he would have to stand and fight it. The key was buried somewhere in the Cthulhu file.

So he had taken it.

There was a lot in it he didn't understand. References to cults around the world, strange phenomena, riots, surrealist art exhibits that seemed to hint at other dimensions and the beings—the entities— that dwelled there. Lovecraft prided himself on his pragmatic, scientific approach to the world. Science had replaced religion for him a long time ago. It had been his bulwark against his mother's hysteria. But as she descended slowly down a maelstrom of fevered hallucinations, getting worse and worse to the point that science could not help her, could not make sense out of the shuddering images that persecuted her every waking moment, he began to sense a dim outline of another reality beneath or behind the comfortable science of straight lines and chemical compounds. Insanity defied science. Maybe it also informed religion. Maybe there was even a kind of science that masqueraded as religion, a science so old and alien to this planet that it could stand right in front of us and we wouldn't even know it was there until it was too late. Didn't Einstein speak of strange geometries, non-Euclidean lines and angles that hinted at the vastness of space and time? Weren't we on the verge of discovering something—some power, some destructive force—that had existed all around us since the worlds began?

Buried in the file from the professor's office were references to Louisiana and a cult that practiced orgiastic rites in the bayous, including a report by an Inspector Legrasse and a statement from a witness called Castro. The site was raided by the police in 1907, and strange artifacts were recovered. Professor Angell was consulted on the case in 1908, and it was this initial consult that led to Angell making the connection between the bayou cult and the soul-bled dreams of young Henry Wilcox.

1908? The year had enormous significance for Lovecraft, for it was the year that he suffered a nervous breakdown and was forced to leave school for good.

"Oh, God," he said aloud in the silence of his small room. "The same year the devotees were calling upon Cthulhu in the swamps I was descending into my own pit of madness. Soon thereafter, my mother went insane. It's not … it's not possible. How can this be?"

He swiftly went through page after page of the professor's notes, some of it in a scrawl that was impossible to read as if the writer were in a desperate rush to get the words down on paper before something terrible happened. It was only by reading the professor's file and plugging in his own life story—the dates and sometimes even the places that seemed to match up so well—that he was able to see that what he and his family had suffered was only part of a much larger picture.

So Professor Angell was *not* trying to discover a cure for Wilcox's psychopathology but instead was investigating the extent to which a bizarre gaggle of devil worshippers in Louisiana could affect the consciousness of an art student in Rhode Island seventeen years later, and from there to a series of cult activities around the world.

He would try to digest the information in Angell's file and then perhaps pay a visit to the old man to get as much more from him as possible. This was suddenly no longer just about Lovecraft's mother but about something that was happening on a global scale. He didn't believe in astrology or any of the pseudo-sciences, but what if an alignment of the stars acted as a kind of cosmic clock, affecting gravity and electricity and the mysterious dark forces the ruminations of Einstein had only hinted at? A clock that was counting down to a date only the ancients would have known? How else to explain a worldwide increase in cultic activity that was directed towards one end only: the awakening of the Thing that had been drawn by Wilcox, worshipped in Louisiana, and haunted the dreams of Lovecraft himself?

The dead priest Cthulhu.

For the next several months in New York City Lovecraft spent hours in the Public Library's Main Branch on Forty-Second Street. He called for book after book from the deep stacks below street level, books that no one had looked at in decades. There was the Rare Book Room, and he lingered for days over ancient texts in Latin, Greek and Arabic with their elaborate designs of pentacles, magic squares, and drawings of demonic forces. He taught himself some basic Arabic, enough to learn that his childhood persona of *Abdul Alhazred* was not true Arabic, but that *Abdul Hazred* might be: the "Servant of the Forbidden," or so it was told to him by one of the room's curators.

"Is that me?" he asked himself when no one was around to notice his distress. "Am *I* the Servant of the Forbidden?"

Then there was the Brooklyn Museum, with its store of Babylonian artifacts. The Metropolitan Museum, with its extensive Egyptian section as well as rooms devoted entirely to the Greek and Roman gods. And there were other libraries, bookstores, and even curio shops specializing in the arcana of countries where the indigenous peoples prayed to goats, boars, crocodiles ... there was endless depravity to be found, certainly ... and no less in his own neighborhood of Red Hook, where the Arab hordes floated obscenely down Atlantic Avenue on nauseating fumes of sandalwood and roast lamb, fueled by hashish and hopelessness.

It took him nearly a year, but he finally put it all together. No one would believe him, of course, and he was not going to commit the whole truth to paper lest he be considered completely insane. He had to report the danger, reveal the darkness that was closing in on the Earth, without showing his hand. He was no one. He had no credentials, no degrees after his name. He was not part of the academic elite or the scientific establishment. He wrote stories, that's all. If no one listened to him, if Professor Angell somehow rebuffed his petition, he would do this the way he always did: with fiction, with story-telling. He would bury the truth in the fertile ground of language and suggestion. He would let readers come to the truth slowly, as he had, but with all of the essential facts in one place. All it would take would be someone clever enough to read the signs, to notice the dates, and put the pieces of the puzzle back together. This was not a thing you shouted from the rooftops, no matter how imminent the threat. This was a thing that had to be whispered, from one to another, until that whisper became a murmur and from there an alarum.

In another fifty years or so, his discovery would go mainstream. Erich von D niken, Pauwels and Bergier, Robert Temple, Graham Hancock … reinterpretations of ancient history and religion (especially those of the "ancient alien" genre) would make the best-seller lists and enrich a generation of writers and historians. Lovecraft, though, would remain virtually penniless for his entire life.

For now, however, it was of utmost importance that he return to Providence to confront Professor Angell with what he had found and to enlist his aid to avert a disaster that was rapidly forming on the outer edges of the galaxy.

He had to convince the old "emeritus" that he had discovered the key to the Cthulhu Cult.

CHAPTER ELEVEN

THE CODEX II

There is more in the Codex than the biographies of either Love-craft or the crazy old Count Karl Tanzler would reveal. Context is everything, and the quiet travels of Lovecraft back and forth to Providence, New York City, and Florida bear much more investigation than has been revealed. The same with Tanzler, who made his way from Germany to Cuba and then to Florida, at a time when the Nazi Party was growing in strength and influence. Tanzler's connections with German occultists and psychics would have been of intense interest to many in the Party, and his strange voyage to Cuba and then to Key West suggests the itinerary of a man who wanted to slip into the United States unnoticed.

Tanzler's brief was quite specific. Based on his research concerning the Cutha artifact and what was known about the academic career of Professor George Gammel Angell, it was obvious that the old professor knew much more about the mythology of Cutha and its mysterious ancient inhabitants than did even the German archaeologists who were embedded deep within the digs of Babylon and Nineveh. Himmler's instructions were clear: obtain a copy of the professor's research on Cutha and anything having to do with the civilization of Sumer.

But then, even as Tanzler had just arrived in Florida, a bombshell: an unknown writer of fantastic fiction had written a short story in which the entire scenario was played out, for all the world to see.

The story was "The Call of Cthulhu," and the writer was Howard Phillips Lovecraft.

From the Codex:

The Cthulhu File was stolen from HPL's apartment on Clinton Street in May 1925. His rooms were entered by someone who possessed a key. Suspects were many, and HPL suspected the perpetrator was one of his Arab neighbors. HPL returned to Providence in April 1926. He made overtures to Professor Angell immediately. He did not reveal that he had stolen the Cthulhu file from his office. The elderly Angell, by then ninety-two years old, did not put together the appearance of HPL and the disappearance of his file. He answered questions about Henry Wilcox as best as he was able without violating confidence. He was somewhat more reticent about discussing the cult. He did, however, mention the existence of a mysterious "black book" that was said to contain secrets of the cult. He mentioned a tribe of Kurds in northern Iraq called the Yezidi who, it was claimed, were devil-worshippers and who had access to the volume.

Lovecraft remembered the Arabs who lived in Red Hook, and who had persecuted him with their music and their chants. Now they had a name. Yezidi. They were the ones who had stolen the Cthulhu file, he believed. And now they knew what he was up to. Devil worshippers! His life was very probably in danger.

During the summer of 1926 he quickly wrote down all that he knew in a story that would become the touchstone for all his later work, "The Call of Cthulhu." It was encoded, so that only those "in the know" would recognize the essential elements and see how it was all put together. He sent a copy of the story to friends of his from the Kalem Klub back in New York City, before it was finally published in *Weird Tales* in February, 1928. By then, of course, it was too late and the cat was out of the bag.

One of those friends—even now, no one knows who—leaked the existence of the manuscript to a German literary figure living in the City: George Sylvester Vierick. Vierick worked for the German government during World War One as a spy in New York, and later worked closely with the Nazi Party in the same capacity. He had also been an intimate of famed British occultist and magician, Aleister Crowley, who worked for Vierick during World War One as a contributing editor and who also had excellent connections back in the Fatherland through a number of German secret societies. In fact,

Vierick had published his own vampire novel as early as 1907, as well as a collection of poems entitled *Nineveh* that same year, had been friendly with Sigmund Freud, as well as Albert Einstein, and in 1923 had interviewed Adolf Hitler himself. With that background, Vierick immediately saw the value of the Lovecraft manuscript to people like Himmler and Rudolf Hess, and sent word back to Berlin where it eventually made its way to Himmler. The short story had contained the words "CTHULHU CULT" in connection with a secret file on the subject. Many of the details in the story were already known to Himmler, which meant that the original file existed in reality and had to be of extreme importance. Himmler then sent a coded cable to Tanzler with the simple command: "Angell. Cutha File. At once."

But the file was gone.

Tanzler had no way of knowing this, however. He made his way to Providence in December of 1926 and surveilled the home of Professor Angell. Unfortunately, Angell was not in residence at the time but was visiting friends in Newport. Tanzler waited until the house was asleep and then broke into Angell's study. He went through the professor's desk and bookshelves, but found nothing on the Cthulhu cult. However, he did see a notation in the old man's diary that revealed his trip to Newport and the fact that he would be returning that night on the ferry.

Providence
December 21, 1926

The strange-looking gentleman with the goatee, dressed shabbily but somehow elegantly in a threadbare coat and scarf against the bitter cold blowing in from the harbor, was carrying a small leather satchel by his side. He was tanned a dark brown, result of some months spent in the unrelenting sun of South Florida. He appeared to be waiting for the ferry to come in from Newport. There were two others on the pier that night, one a man already celebrating the upcoming Christmas holiday, the fumes of alcoholic bliss billowing about his face like a drunken halo, and the other a slight woman with a worried expression who might have been his wife. Tanzler took note of their appearance and condition and felt he had nothing to fear from the couple. Just in case, though, he moved away from them and further down the pier.

A cold night, a quarter moon hanging in the air above the harbor, the spray of stars overhead like a jury of its peers. Tanzler shivered slightly in the salty breeze coming off the bay and heard the sound of the ferry making its way to the dock. A rustle of movement all up and down the pier and Tanzler held his position, far enough away from the off-ramp that he would not be seen in the light from its lamps.

He had killed a man once before, in India. It had been necessary. A thief who had come at him from behind with the knotted scarf of the thuggee. The man was not a real thug, of course, for they traveled in groups and attacked according to ritual requirements. This was on a side street in Calcutta. The thief had misjudged Tanzler's height, and the scarf did not make it around his neck as intended. Rather, Tanzler turned and grabbed the now-frightened man by the shoulders and slammed him up against a wall of masonry. There had been an iron nail in the wall, protruding just enough that it penetrated the man's neck, severing his spinal column. The thief slumped and hung there, an astonished expression on his face.

Tanzler turned and ran. He had been seen, however, by one of the thief's brothers who had been keeping a lookout on the street while his brother went to kill and rob the foreigner. A day later, and Tanzler was having tea in a shop a mile from the alley where he had defended himself when he felt sick and collapsed.

His body was picked up and taken to the morgue, for it was thought that he had died. He had no vital signs, and did not respond at all to any kind of stimuli. It was only while awaiting cremation that he came to, awoke from the drug that had been administered to him in the café, and frightened the staff to the point of hysteria.

The thief's brothers had underestimated the dose they would have to give Tanzler to kill him, and the effects wore off after a day.

Now Tanzler stood at the dock of the Newport ferry with a syringe full of the same exotic drug. It would mimic a heart-attack. But this time, the dose was enough to kill an elephant.

The ferry docked, with much bumping and knocking, and the ramp lowered for the passengers to disembark. The couple with the drunken husband and the forlorn wife staggered to the ramp and embraced who appeared to be their child: an uncomfortable-looking teenage girl in a hooded coat and muff.

The passengers were few in number. Tanzler watched out of the side of his eyes, as if more or less disinterested in the ferry and its occupants. Finally, an elderly man walked carefully down the ramp, holding a cane in one hand and a small case in the other. His steps were agonizing slow, especially considering the wintry cold air blowing all around him.

This had to be Professor Emeritus George Gammel Angell, of Brown University. Whatever was in that case had to be the document Tanzler was sent to find. For a moment he thought that he could simply snatch it from the old man and make his way in a hurry before anyone was the wiser, but he couldn't take the chance that the old man would cry out and alert any passersby. Himmler would not tolerate any mistakes.

The old professor began a slow shamble away from the pier. His snail's pace made it easier for Tanzler because that meant that the other passengers had long since passed him by. The professor had a long, uphill walk ahead of him along darkened streets, but Tanzler did not want to wait until he hit any of the main thoroughfares for that meant a likelihood of other witnesses.

He had to do it now.

Professor Angell was lost in his own reverie. He had just come from a meeting at the brand-new Hotel Viking in Newport where he discussed the latest findings on his investigation. It had begun the previous year with the case of poor Henry Wilcox and the painting of the strange demon which so closely matched the statue that was at the center of the Cthulhu Cult in Louisiana seventeen years earlier. The investigation had expanded considerably since then, and the involvement of Howard Phillips Lovecraft the past few months had only complicated matters. What did Lovecraft know about the cult? He said he was a friend of young Wilcox. Was it possible that it was Lovecraft that had influenced the fevered dreams of the artist with his own macabre imaginings?

He didn't know much about Lovecraft. He came from a good family, one with a long pedigree in Providence, but there was scandal there, as well. His father was a traveling salesman—not a particularly acceptable occupation—and possibly had contracted syphilis which led to his insanity. His mother, from the esteemed Phillips dynasty, had similar mental problems. Everyone in town knew the story. And Howard himself? A recluse. Unstable, certainly. Chronically unemployed. Bright, but uneducated. A scribbler of some kind. Stories, poems. Lovecraft's presence in his library made the professor distinctly uncomfortable. The young man had looked around at all the books on their massive shelves with something like hunger, or lust. Or even, strangely enough, fear.

But the Newport meeting had been profitable. He had with him now a copy of a document that the others suggested he might be able to translate, for they believed it held the key to the operations and ideology of the Cthulhu Cult. The man who discovered it, a Sunni theologian from Sana'a, mentioned a forgotten library in the Hadrahmut. He was rather vague about it, and his poor command of English made it impossible to get any more information concerning its provenance. Angell was not sure he agreed with his colleagues as to the relevance of the text but decided he would take a close look and give them his conclusions. Legrasse had introduced him to the other investigators, some of whom came from great distances: India, in one case. Singapore. The Hindu Kush. Mexico City. The others from the United States and Canada. A total of twenty-three very serious men, some of them police investigators, the others academics like himself. It was an unusual, perhaps a unique, gathering.

And the document itself. A handwritten manuscript on hundreds of pages. In Greek, it would seem, but with long passages that were indecipherable. Reminded him of some of the Gnostic writings with their long chains of glossolalia, of *voces magicae*. Mumbo jumbo, probably, but it was not important that he and his colleagues believed in it, but just acknowledged that others did and were prepared to kill to further its demonic message.

He switched the briefcase from one hand to the other, for it was heavy and he was ninety-two years old. He saw his breath cloud the frozen air before him as he took another tentative step, always aware that the ice could be deadly.

The cloud separated for a moment and as it did the old professor saw a face materialize out of the bleak night before him.

Tanzler quickly jabbed the syringe into the side of Angell's neck and hit the plunger. The poison shoved its way into the old man's parchment-thin skin. He held him for a moment to steady the flow of the drug, and then slowly let him down onto the sidewalk. He withdrew the needle and grabbed the case from the dying man's grasp.

He heard a shout somewhere along the pier behind him but could not afford to look back. Instead he made his way at a careful run over the icy streets. He was supposed to hand the case over to a German agent waiting at the train station and then make his circuitous way back to Florida on his own.

The agent was late. Probably due to the weather. Tanzler looked around and saw there was no one else on the platform. A weak light spilled out from the ticket office, and he held the case close to his chest and tried to open it.

It was a simple leather case with brass fittings. There was a lock, but it was largely ornamental and no match for a determined thief. Tanzler popped it and looked inside.

All he saw was a pile of old paper with writing he could not make out. It was handwritten, and as he riffled through the pages he saw arcane symbols. He recognized none of them, but he did recognize their character. These were magic signs, occult seals of some kind. From his background in the occult arts he could sense the value of the manuscript. If nothing else, it was the private diary or record of a sorcerer long dead. Who knew what secrets it held?

For a moment, Tanzler thought of keeping it. The specter of Himmler and his black-uniformed thugs hovered in the background like an unspoken threat, but he was in America now and far from the reach of the Nazis.

He lifted out some of the pages, trying to see if he could make out any of the cursive script, when he felt a pressure in his back.

"Herr Tanzler?" The voice was quiet and soft, but the knife at his back was hard and sharp. He dropped the pages back into the case, and turned.

It was Vierick.

With a last longing look, Tanzler surrendered the case to the German agent who put his knife back in his pocket and turned on his heel without a look back. Tanzler was annoyed, not least because Vierick had not acknowledged his title. He was, after all, *Count* Karl Tanzler von Cosel.

George Sylvester Vierick, darling of the Prussian elite and of Herr Hitler himself, disappeared into the darkness and in a moment Tanzler heard a car's engine turn over. Vierick was probably returning to New York City in the warmth and comfort of a luxurious automobile, leaving Tanzler alone to catch the train. Another little instance of one-upmanship. Very well. Vierick—and Himmler— would have need of him again. That much was certain. And then we would see who had the upper hand.

CHAPTER TWELVE

Ahl al-Kitab
"PEOPLE OF THE BOOK"

Books are not made to be believed, but to be subjected to
inquiry. When we consider a book, we mustn't ask ourselves
what it says but what it means.

    —Umberto Eco, *The Name of the Rose*

A Refugee Camp
The Syrian-Turkish Border, near Kobani

There were no streets, no pavement, just mud. Hundreds of gray
tents, squatting like toads, all up and down the makeshift avenues.
Women huddling around a water pump with plastic bottles to fill.
Men sitting on woven mats or on plastic sheeting in the tents to
keep dry, talking, smoking, or drinking tea. Children everywhere,
their mothers doing their best to keep them clean and fed. Fami-
lies of six, ten, twelve members or more. Some had been there for
months; others for a year. A mélange of languages: Turkish, Arabic,
even French and English, and Kurdish. But mostly Kurdish.

It might be Turkish land but it was Kurdish territory. Across the
border, in Syria, a new group calling itself the Islamic State had been
shelling Kurdish positions up and down the border with Turkey and
at times infiltrating saboteurs and assassins into the camps and towns.
Kurdish resistance fighters, including the famous Peshmerga in
Iraqi Kurdistan, had organized themselves into a variety of credible
militias—each with its own political ideology and allegiances—
and were striking back (supplied with weapons by various foreign
governments who were using the Kurds as a kind of proxy army
against the Syrians, the Turks, the Iraqis, what remained of Al-Qaeda,
and the new Islamic State). The northern part of Syria, from Kobani

in the west to the Semalka border crossing with Iraq to the east, was all under Kurdish control: a tenuous hold on territory that had been Kurdistan for centuries even though it was unrecognized—first by the Ottomans, then by the British and French after World War One, and finally by the Iraqi and Syrian regimes, not to mention the Turks—and existed in a kind of virtual reality outside the normal functioning of governments, borders, and custom. And, hidden within the Kurdish landscape like a system of caverns underground, were the Yezidi.

It was the Yezidi that Gregory Angell and his minders had come to find.

Angell had only asked that they stop at his apartment in Red Hook so he could pick up a change of underwear and a few reference materials. Aubrey went with him to the apartment, and looked around at the small quarters with its stack of books. The titles on the spines were indecipherable to Aubrey, written in alphabets or ideograms that meant nothing to him. There were a few in French, German and Latin that he could make out, but Angell avoided all of those and instead brought a few tattered paperback dictionaries in Kurmanji, Farsi and Urdu and stuck them in a backpack.

There were few ornaments or signs of a personal life other than the books. On a small table in the middle of the room that served both as dining table and as desk there was a Syrian incantation bowl, also called a "demon trap." It was clay, and had an inscription in Aramaic inside running from the rim down to the center of the bowl in a neat spiral. It looked to be at least a thousand years old, if not older: a memento of Angell's archaeological period in the Syrian-Iraqi border towns. Other than that, there was not much there to give someone a clue as to Angell's family or friends.

Angell pulled the gun from his waistband, reluctantly, and raised an eyebrow at Aubrey.

"You can't take that with you, and you shouldn't leave it here. It might be best if I held onto it until you return."

Angell emptied the automatic of its cartridges, remembering the one in the chamber, and handed it over to Aubrey who pocketed it without a second glance.

"Ready?"

The SUV took them up the Brooklyn-Queens Expressway to the Van Wyck in Queens which brought them to Kennedy Airport. They were taking a commercial flight that evening for Frankfurt, after which they would take a connecting flight to Istanbul. After that, the itinerary was a little … well … murky.

As he sat in the waiting room next to Aubrey, Gregory Angell asked himself what he thought he was doing, and why he had agreed so quickly. Did Aubrey realize that he was only going through the motions at the university? That the joy had gone out of teaching once he understood that there was a gaping hole at the center of his worldview that was left behind when God had abdicated his throne at Mosul? He felt like he was teaching alchemy to chemistry majors. The entire basic premise was wrong.

And yet … that gaping hole in his worldview was matched by the gaping hole in his own heart. There had been nothing to rush in to fill the emptiness. Nature, they say, abhors a vacuum. You couldn't prove it by Gregory Angell. Alcohol, drugs, sex … he had tried them all, and nothing worked. There was always the next morning, and that thundering Absence. And his beloved Glock.

On the one hand, the last thing he wanted to do was to go back to the place God died. He had no interest to go over the crime scene, like an FBI profiler looking for clues. He had no need of those memories, no desire to relive the anguish of that horrible moment, his own, personal 9/11, because he lived with it every day—and especially every night—of his life. Going back would prove nothing, solve nothing.

On the other hand, shouldn't someone stand up for the dead?

It was all overwhelming, and that is when Gregory realized that the reason he went along was because he simply had lacked the will to resist. Aubrey had come into his life with a mission and an agenda, and Gregory had had neither. He wasn't looking for redemption; nothing quite as trite as that. He needed a purpose, a distraction, and almost anything would do. He needed something that would delay as long as possible the moment Gregory knew was coming, when he would raise that nine millimeter to his head and create his own gaping, existential hole.

And then Aubrey had come along, with his soft-spoken delivery, his patience, and his insistence. Aubrey already knew all about Gregory's past, his demons, even his family history. All the things that made Gregory, Gregory. It was like an hour with a really good therapist. And in spite of himself Gregory was hooked.

They were calling his flight. He looked up to see Aubrey standing there with a folded newspaper under his arm.

"Time to go, Professor."

The newspaper had been full of bad news, and they were flying right into the story. As they sat in their assigned seats and waited for take-off Aubrey pointed out a headline about a surge of radicals into Kurdish territory north and west of Mosul. They had already taken Fallujah and Ramadi.

"We are not a minute too soon. The people we need to see may not be around for very long. They will be moving across the border into Syria and then to Turkey. A massive wave of migration is starting and our contacts could very well be lost in the flood of refugees."

Angell scanned the story and looked at the map that was printed in a sidebar next to the columns of text.

"That's Yezidi territory. Sinjar is their ancestral homeland, their religious and secular capital."

Aubrey nodded and, with knowledge gleaned from classified DIA reports, said "And they're about to be slaughtered."

Angell shuddered at the coincidence, synchronicity, whatever you wanted to call it. He had left all of that behind because of the slaughter of Yezidis in Mosul so many years ago, and now he was about to face another genocidal attack on the same people. He began to tremble with a nameless dread. There was something waiting for him there, something intrinsically evil in a way that transcended everything he had learned about ethics and morality. This was evil in a way that most humans did not understand it. Evil as a force of its own, something greater than the humans who were its pawns and willing servants.

As the Boeing 777 made its ascent Gregory looked outside at the landscape of New York City passing below their wings and wondered, briefly, if he would ever see the city again.

Angell had looked over a file Aubrey had handed to him on the plane once they were over the Atlantic Ocean and no longer in American airspace. It contained some transcribed cell phone chatter as well as excerpts from emails, Facebook entries, WhatsApp and Telegram messages, and the like. It was a celebration of social media, and much of it was incomprehensible to Angell who tended to avoid leaving a digital trace if he could.

But there was something intriguing about the messages, taken in the aggregate. Individually, they didn't seem to mean much but when they were seen as pieces of a larger puzzle an image began to form.

Part of the file consisted of the drawings that Aubrey had shown him in the restaurant on Montague Street, and there was another sheet of paper that had some sentences in what Angell knew to be Kurmanji: a Kurdish dialect, and one spoken by members of the Yezidi ethnicity. There was also an inventory of sorts in Arabic from the Baghdad Museum, a nondescript listing of shards and tools and ancient implements that was relieved only by the mention of a manuscript that supposedly dated from the ninth century in a line item that was highlighted in yellow. A manuscript that old would certainly be valuable, to a collector if not to an academic. The title was bizarre, to say the least. *Al Azif:* the buzz of insects. A work on entomology? He briefly wondered if it had been sold to raise money for terrorists. And then he realized that this was what they were looking for. A book. *Al Azif*? What the hell?

"Do you know the fragments of writing on that paper?" Aubrey pointed to the single sheet.

Angell nodded.

"It's in Kurmanji, the same language that the Yezidi *Black Book* is written in. It's classical Kurmanji; dating from ... I don't know ... the tenth century? Earlier? It's an Indo-European language, not a Semitic one like Arabic or Hebrew."

"Can you translate it?"

Angell frowned. At that moment a flight attendant appeared to offer them beverages. Angell accepted only water; Aubrey treated himself to a glass of red wine.

"It's ... poetic. I suppose it would be, if it was old. Something about long lengths of time, death, and dying. Flowery stuff, but somehow also sinister. As if it represented a threat, or a dire prediction. Without a larger sample, it's difficult to say what it means."

Aubrey sipped the Chilean cabernet thoughtfully, a half-smile on his face. Monroe had been right, he thought. This timid, half-mad little professor is just the right person for the job.

"When we get to Diyarbakir we will be met at the airport by our escort."

"Escort?"

"Turkey is relatively safe for foreigners, but we are heading towards the border with Syria and will need security. It will be rough going once we leave the metropolitan area, and there is always the danger of bandits, highwaymen, and the odd terrorist. Al Qaeda is not the threat it used to be, but the new group is. You've heard of it. The Islamic State..."

Angell nodded, "What they call ISIL."

"... or ISIS."

Angell shook his head.

"I prefer not to use that acronym. These murderers have nothing to do with the gentle Egyptian goddess of the same name. ISIL is just fine; or just Islamic State, or even Daesh, which is how they are referred to in Arabic."

"Well, however you want to call them, they are building up a force to attack Sinjar, the Yezidi capital. They have already been slaughtering Yezidi in Iraq and Syria, and not even the Kurds seem willing to extend themselves to help them. They consider the Yezidi to be devil worshippers, as you know."

Angell turned in his seat to look Aubrey in the eyes.

"And you mean to tell me we are going to walk right into that crossfire?"

"Easy, Professor. This is just a fact-finding mission. We will proceed to a refugee camp—I'll tell you where later—and ask a few questions, and then return to Istanbul for a flight back home. I have no intention of being anywhere near a military offensive. I'm much too old for that sort of thing."

Their connection in Frankfurt was mercifully brief, and they landed in Istanbul in the late afternoon. It was morning in New York City, and Angell wondered if anyone had noticed he was missing.

The two men headed over to another area of the airport where they would catch a domestic flight to the regional airport at Diyarbakir. From there they would be met by their security escort and begin the drive to the Syrian border.

Diyarbakir is sometimes called the "unofficial capital" of Kurdistan, and it has been a center of violence between the official Turkish government and the Kurdish resistance movements that are based in that ancient city on the Tigris. The airport is both civilian and military, and in another few months it would become the base for the American anti-ISIL efforts known as Operation Enduring Freedom. In April of 2014, however, it was the Turkish Air Force that dominated the region from the skies, and the PKK—a Kurdish resistance movement declared a terrorist organization by the US—from the ground.

The flight to Diyarbakir was uneventful, which is the best one can hope for under the circumstances. Having already gone through Immigration and Customs in Istanbul, the men simply walked out of the terminal onto the pavement in front of the arrivals area where they were met by two of the largest men Angell had ever seen.

They were not especially tall, but they were muscularly broad with close-cropped hair and hands the size of hams. They were Americans, in their late twenties, and spoke with the accents of East Texas. Aubrey nodded at them as if they were old acquaintances. They were led to an idling Humvee at the arrivals area where another man, just as broad and just as young, sat behind the wheel and looked straight ahead.

As the car took off, heading out of the airport to the main road that would lead them south to the Syrian border, Angell noticed the automatic weapons stacked behind them. The sight was not comforting.

The men hardly spoke at all. The driver kept his eyes on the road, and the other two escorts watched the surroundings carefully as they drove, alert to any possible threat from any direction. Angell wanted to call them Tweedledum and Tweedledee; they seemed like twins, cookie cutter-spooks with assault rifles and hair-trigger reflexes.

The sun was going down just as they reached a vast camp made of tents near the Syrian town of Kobani (also known as *Ayn al-Arab* in Arabic) on the other side of the border. Cooking fires could be seen everywhere, like votive lamps in a pagan landscape. Kobani itself was under control of Kurdish forces and had been since 2012, a situation that began with the onset of the Syrian civil war, but refugees had begun moving across into the Turkish side for quite a while as Kobani was subject to bomb and mortar attack from Syrians, Islamic radicals, and God only knew who else. As the capital of the putative Kurdish state of Rojava, Kobani was a target for everyone.

Angell knew that there were at least three main Kurdish political groups, each with its own militias and the territory they had won by force of arms. He had not stayed current on the situation and, anyway, his interests did not include either the internecine wars of

Kurd against Kurd, or the struggle of the Kurds against the Iraqis, Turks, or Syrians. He was looking for the man Aubrey said would be in the camp, a Yezidi leader with important information about the book that seemed to be at the center of the whole operation. It was Angell's expertise—not just with the language but with the religious and cultural background of the Yezidis—that was critical to the mission's success.

Anyway, that was what they told him. Somehow the statue and drawing of the weird deity and that crappy short story by Lovecraft had something to do with all of this. He didn't like what he was feeling: that the events of Mosul and the short story and the statue were all related in some way. He felt a kind of doom descending on him even though he couldn't put it all together. Not yet.

He found himself longing for his Glock and the comfort holding it had given him.

The three men who had escorted them thus far got out of the Humvee first. They had no trouble in the drive down to the border, and had been stopped only once on the way by a Kurdish roadblock a mile outside the camp. Angell had remained silent most of the way down, leafing through the file Aubrey had given him and from time to time refreshing his knowledge of Kurmanji. He would look out the window at the passing landscape of armed men, wandering children and goats, and the minarets of mosques in the towns they passed and old memories came flooding through him like a familiar poison in his veins.

They had brought food and water with them, but Angell had no appetite. His mind was trying to accommodate two conflicting streams of thought at once: the reason for his being in Kurdistan on the one hand, and his memories of the Yezidi slaughter on the other. At the back of all of this, like a deep bass beat just below the surface of human hearing, was his own family's background and that inescapable suspicion that there was *much* more to this operation than he was being told.

Lovecraft—his family's tormentor—had hated the Yezidis, even though he probably had never met one in his life. The popular imagination at the time associated the Yezidis with devil worship and even the local Kurdish and Arab populations continue to harbor the same ideas about them. They were closed off, isolated. One could not convert to Yezidism: you were either born into the sect or you were an outsider. Their religion seemed like an amalgam of Christianity, Judaism and Islam with various pre-Abrahamic elements thrown in for good measure. They had a "black book"—that no one had really seen, despite claims to the contrary—and lived in an area of northern Iraq close to Mosul. Their coat of arms boasted a peacock, and writing in cuneiform that hinted at a Babylonian or even Sumerian origin. Indeed, their God was referred to as the "Peacock Angel"—*Melek Ta'us*—even though peacocks were not native to Mesopotamia but to India. Go figure. And then, they also revered a figure known as *Shaitan*.

Satan.

The theology was complex, but in simple terms the Yezidi believe that Satan, the Fallen Angel, will be the first to be welcomed back to heaven at the End Times. Satan was the first sinner; he had refused to bow down before Adam, even though God had ordered him to do so. This much is consistent with the Qur'an. The Muslims believe that Satan refused to bow down to Adam due to the sin of pride. But the Yezidis believe that the reason he gave was that he would bow before no one in all creation except God himself, for it was only to God that he owed his loyalty and obeisance, and he had promised God since the beginning that he would be loyal only to him. For this sin of obedience/disobedience, Satan was cast out of heaven. Eventually, Satan would return to heaven and the first to follow him through the pearly gates would be the Yezidi themselves. For that reason, they never even speak the word *Shaitan*.

The Yezidi believe they are the first people, the most ancient of all peoples on the Earth, the inheritors of the Sumerian civilization. In fact, it is possible that the name *Melek Ta'us* is a corruption of the ancient Mesopotamian deity Tammuz, or *Tawuz*. This would reinforce the idea that they are descended from an ancient civilization. They are non-Semitic, are not ethnically or linguistically related to the Arab populations of Iraq or Syria, but have more in common with their neighbors in Iran. They are also not Muslim and that fact has led to repression and oppression from Muslims both in the Sunni and the Shiite areas. While the Kurds are despised by Turks, Syrians, Iraqis and Iranians equally, even the Kurds discriminate against the Yezidis.

What would happen to them in the next few months, however, would far exceed anything Saddam Hussein, the Syrians, or the Turks had accomplished in the past centuries. In fact, it would be the genocide of the Yezidis by the Islamic State beginning in June of 2014 that would bring the United States into open warfare with the terror organization.

In April, however, things were still relatively calm in the refugee camp. They parked their vehicle at one end and walked back towards a small wooden building that seemed to be the main office.

Their driver walked in front, his Glock conspicuous in a shoulder holster under his left arm. Aubrey and Gregory, unarmed, followed him, and were in turn followed by the two other security officers, one of whom held an AR-15 assault rifle.

So much for discretion.

Before they reached the building the door opened and a middle-aged European woman in khakis stepped out to greet them. She was of medium height and pleasant appearance, with a light coloring of hair, skin and eyes suggesting Dutch or perhaps German ethnicity, and was holding a satellite phone in her left hand. Her right hand was outstretched.

Aubrey stepped forward and grasped her hand in his.

"Doctor De Vries?"

"Yes. You must be …"

"Anonymous, if you please. As is my associate here, who has come a long way to talk to Fahim. You have been contacted by my people?"

"Yes. They have been on the phone to me. As have my own people. I gather this is an important mission you're on."

The driver went inside the small building first, ahead of the others, to ensure it was secure. Then he stepped outside and nodded. Aubrey, Gregory and Doctor DeVries went inside and shut the door while their security contingent took up posts outside and around the building. There was no point in trying to be inconspicuous in that place. If you were not a Kurd or an aid worker, you were a foreigner of some kind and everyone in the camp knew you were there and what you were doing.

"You know I can't discuss our purpose here, other than to say it is urgent we speak with Fahim."

She nodded.

"The Daasin—that is what the Yezidi call themselves, by the way—are very cautious when it comes to bringing attention their way. They have their own section of the camp but I am afraid that their numbers are due to increase, perhaps exponentially."

She moved some papers around on her makeshift desk and pulled out an old reconnaissance map of the area that had many penciled-in notations and large sections blocked off with striped lines.

"The Islamic State has its eye on Mosul. There are rumors that they will start a major offensive in the next six weeks or so. If they take Mosul, that puts Mount Sinjar right in their crosshairs." She pointed to Mosul on the map and then drew a short line with her finger to the west, to Mount Sinjar. "The holiest site in all of Yezidi religion and culture will come under direct attack. It is only a matter of a month or two at most, maybe even weeks. Thousands of Yezidi are already making their way on foot across Syria to this border and to areas in the north under Kurdish control. The rest are determined to stay and fight."

Aubrey nodded if he had been aware of this all along.

"Do you mean to say that this way is blocked?" He pointed at a road that snaked across the border into Syria and which led to a border crossing on the other—the Iraqi—side.

"You surely don't intend to cross Syria by land?"

Angell looked up, startled.

"No," replied Aubrey, thinking. "No, that was not the plan. But if Mosul falls and Mount Sinjar is next, then we are really running out of time."

She looked at Aubrey with an expression that was both wistful and angry.

"I wish the rest of your government felt the way you do about the plight of the Yezidis," she said. "I doubt anyone in your State Department has even heard of them."

At that moment there was a knock on the door. It opened, and the security officer filled the doorway with his bulk.

"There is someone here to speak with the doctor. He says it's urgent." He added, "He's clean."

De Vries looked at Aubrey, who only nodded.

"It's okay. Let him in."

The security man stepped aside, and a much smaller individual entered the room. It was a Kurd, by his appearance and speech. He spoke rapidly to the doctor, who responded in the same dialect. Angell listened to every word, but said nothing.

The man bowed in the general direction of everyone, and then left the building.

"There are some vehicles coming this way. A Turkish Army patrol, most likely, but we shouldn't take any chances." De Vries began rolling up the map with the other papers on her desk, shoving them into a battered leather briefcase as she talked. "We need to hide you for an hour or so."

"The Turkish government knows we are here," Aubrey protested.

"That may be just the problem," she answered. "There are a lot of special interests in Turkey these days. Many want Assad of Syria to be deposed, and are helping the Syrian resistance. Others support the Assad regime for reasons of their own. Still others are sympathetic to the jihadists. And almost all the Turks hate the Kurds and resent their presence here. We don't know which of these groups is coming and where its loyalty may lie. It may even be a Kurdish patrol, or a terror cell. We can't take the risk. My people told me to provide you with every manner of support and cover, and that is what I intend to do."

As she ushered them out of the office Angell whispered to Aubrey: "It's a trap."

"What do you mean?"

"The doctor. She told the man to warn Fahim, to get out of the camp and hide until we left."

Aubrey raised an eyebrow. "She must know you speak Kurmanji."

Angell nodded. "She didn't speak to him in Kurmanji, but in Farsi. The Iranian language. No time to explain. If we want to find Fahim we have to lose the doctor."

They left the building, Aubrey following the doctor with two of his men, chatting loudly enough so that she thought they were all together. Instead, he made a signal to the driver and he and Angell split off from the rest and headed toward the Yezidi section of the camp where they saw the strange little man from before darting down a passageway.

The driver pointed in one direction and Angell went in the other, attempting to catch the little man in the middle. Angell jumped over a puddle of foul-looking water that had been produced by a leaking water pump in the middle of the virtual street and almost slid in the mud before righting himself and turning a corner in the street of tents.

He heard a shout behind him, which was probably due to Doctor DeVries realizing that he had gone walkabout in her refugee camp. He kept running when he saw before him what had to be the most beautiful woman he had ever seen. Maybe she wasn't beautiful. Maybe it was only the juxtaposition of the squalor of a refugee camp and the unexpected bright, knowing blue eyes set within the angelic features of a Flemish painting with a half-smile that was pure Da Vinci, but nevertheless the vision was a shock. Distracted, he tripped on something and fell flat on his face in the mud.

He struggled to his feet, which is when he noticed that what he had tripped over was another man's outstretched leg.

A voice spoke to him in Kurmanji.

"I am Fahim. I understand you are looking for me. Strange, for it is I who have been looking for you."

They were all sitting in Fahim's tent, on woven rugs that had been laid over plastic sheeting to keep out the damp. There was thick, hot coffee in tiny porcelain cups for which Angell was grateful since he had eaten little since leaving New York. He was also aware of the importance of this meeting, for it resembled a *Diwan*: a formal Yezidi community meeting. There were other men in attendance, sitting around the edges of the tent, silent and watchful. There were Kalashnikovs in evidence as well.

Once Angell had realized that the man who tripped him was the man he sought, he stood up and grasped his hand with his own. The others had come running and soon Angell and Fahim were surrounded by Aubrey and the security escort, as well as Doctor De Vries who was noticeably upset.

They sat and waited for the coffee to be poured, and then Fahim—seated farthest from the door as befitting his position—began to speak, first in Kurmanji for the benefit of the Yezidi elders and then in English for the benefit of his guests.

"You honor us with your visit, American friends. I am the *mukhtar*, the headman, of this community. I know the time is short, so I will dispense with formalities." He looked around at his community and the men nodded, solemnly.

He then continued in English.

"We of the Daasin are an ancient people. We trace our origins to Sumer, a land that was older than Egypt, older than any other on the face of the Earth. Our capital was the city of Cutha or Kutu, the city of the Sumerian Underworld. Today that city is an archaeological site south of Baghdad.

"I worked at the Baghdad Museum at the time of the American invasion of 2003. I was one of the workers who rescued our priceless heritage by bringing artifacts to our homes and burying them where the soldiers and the rebels would not find them. Once the fighting stopped, we returned those artifacts to the museum. Many objects were lost. Those too big to carry off and some that simply didn't survive the bombings."

He was silent a moment, his eyes filled with sadness at the memory of ancient statues and cuneiform tablets turned to dust after having survived for more than four or five thousand years only to succumb to twenty-first century weaponry.

Aubrey was sitting a little behind Gregory Angell, and to the side. This was going to be Angell's show for awhile, and Aubrey thought it best to sit it out and let the professor handle the questions. Doctor De Vries had joined the meeting initially, but decided the camp would be better served by her work elsewhere.

Outside Fahim's tent the security detail stood guard.

"Our world is in danger of being destroyed, Professor. Not just the world of the Daasin, of the people you call the Yezidi, but the whole world. I was a curator at the Baghdad Museum. I was a student of history, like you. But what I see now is something very different. There is an uprising taking place throughout the Middle East, and its origin is in Mesopotamia.

"This is not a Muslim uprising, or a Kurdish uprising. It is not Sunni or Shi'a. It is not Yezidi or Nestorian or Assyrian or Alawi. Everyone is involved. Druze, Sufis, Samaritans, Hezbollah, Hamas, Al-Qaeda, Daesh, al-Nusra, the Peshmerga … these are groups that have serious differences with each other, separated by centuries of hatred and violence. Yet now they are united as one and no one in the West seems to understand that."

Aubrey was paying very close attention to every word out of Fahim's mouth. This was further confirmation of the chatter that had been detected the past several weeks or months. They were getting close to the truth, to the source of the problem, and he wondered if the Yezidi leader would give it a name.

Angell, for his part, thought the old guy was half-mad.

"What do you mean they are united as one?"

"I don't mean they have buried their differences. No. That will never happen. What has taken place is something I have never seen before and which has only taken place once in our history, going back to the glorious days of Sumer and Babylon. No. What is happening now is that there is another group, a terror *clan*, operating underneath all of the others, inciting each one to greater and greater excesses of violence and bloodshed. These are not Muslims or Christians or any kind of religion or denomination we understand. They are more ancient than any of these, and yet perhaps the root of all. They glory in the torture and mutilation of women and children. In the execution of old men and young boys. They are idolaters and blasphemers.

"They are worshippers of the Lord of the Underworld, the Lord of the ancient city, Kutu.

"They are followers of the priest of the Underworld. In Arabic, his name is *Al-Qhadhulu*. In the old language: *Kutulu*."

The spoken name hit the tent like a bomb. The old Yezidi men began murmuring among themselves as Aubrey sat back and breathed in the word like a confirmation of everything he and Monroe had been working on for decades.

Gregory Angell, however, was not amused.

"What the hell is this?" he asked Aubrey, turning to face him. "What *bullshit* is this?"

Aubrey simply shook his head, a sad smile on his face like the memory of an old foe.

"It's no bullshit. At least, not to the men sitting here. And not to the millions of people who are now on the verge of changing the whole world, pawns of this underground—under*world*—cult."

Fahim noticed Angell's disbelief and apparent distress, and reached over to touch his arm.

"You are Professor Gregory Angell. Of Providence?"

Angell nodded.

"You are of the same family as George Angell, also a professor, a century ago?"

"Yes, I am a member of the Angell family. I am a descendant of George Angell."

Fahim bowed his head, and then looked up.

"George Angell knew my grandfather. They spoke together many times, in the old days. Before the Great War. Before I was born. He visited my family at Lalish. He was welcome."

Fahim managed a smile, gesturing at his poor tent and shabby furnishings.

"And now you are welcome."

"I didn't know George Angell had visited your people. He would have been … what, in his seventies by then?"

"Oh, yes. He was here at the time of Woolley and Lawrence. My family helped them to find the old places, the buried cities of our ancestors. Carchemish is near here, near the town of Jarabulus, in Syria, which attracted many archaeologists in those days. Famous names, like Hogarth and Thompson. Your ancestor knew them all. But it was while he was at Ur with Woolley in 1922 that he learned of the existence of the Book."

The Book. The reason he was there in the first place. Maybe he would find out what the old man knew and then he could get out of Turkey and back to his apartment in Red Hook. But what he had said just now did not ring true. If George Angell had visited Iraq in 1922, that would have made him eighty-eight years old, only four short years before his death. What was the old professor doing traveling around the world at that age?

As if sensing his guest's disbelief, Fahim tried to explain.

"Your ancestor had been consulting for a police department in your country. There was a forbidden religious ceremony of some kind in your state of Louisiana. I believe this was before the Woolley expedition to Carchemish. There were artifacts found at the site of the ceremony, including an idol. George Angell recognized them as Mesopotamian in origin. The Sumerian tablets had been discovered not long before, and there was a great deal of excitement over them. Professor Angell was one of those who were involved in the translation efforts. He came to understand that there was a Sumerian connection to the idol and the other artifacts from the Louisiana site. He knew we trace our origins to Sumer. He visited my grandfather to see what could be learned about that culture."

Angell shook his head vigorously, as if trying to dislodge a mosquito or a bad dream.

"Do you mean to tell me that the people worshipping in the swamps outside New Orleans were Yezidis?"

Fahim looked startled at the suggestion.

"Oh, no. Of course not! That is what I am trying to explain. We of the Daasin are protectors of the ancient knowledge. We are guardians. We are servants of God. The others ... those whom you seek ... they are demoniacs. They worship the Lord of Death. Our people have guarded the entrance to the Underworld for thousands of years. To keep it sealed. Closed forever, until the Last Days when the dead will rise and smell the incense."

He leaned forward, his forehead almost touching Angell's own, as he whispered:

"The others want to *open* that entrance. They want to open the *Gate*. That is why they want the Book."

While the Yezidis had a reputation as devil-worshippers—an idea promoted by travelers to the region and, in the twentieth century, publicized by such adventure authors as William Seabrook in a book published in 1927 that claimed there was a chain of "seven towers of Satan" stretching across Kurdistan and as far as Tibet and Mongolia—the association was ill-founded. There were those who disagreed, of course, and who would see their reverence for a "Peacock Angel" as de facto evidence of idolatry or some other form of satanic practice. And then their shrines, with their bas-reliefs of a serpent rising up from the ground at the entranceways, gave rise to more speculation.

And then there was the Black Book.

The sacred scripture of the Yezidis has never been seen by those outside the sect. There are writers who have claimed to have seen it, and there have been several published versions of it, but it is generally understood today that none of these "sightings" and publications represent the actual Black Book.

What Fahim was talking about, however, had nothing to do with the Yezidi Black Book.

The Yezidis are divided into clans or tribes. Some of these are hostile to each other, reflecting old grievances. Others are more geographically-based, with some clans native to Turkey, others to Syria, Iraq, and even Armenia. The clan represented by Fahim was a group that was formerly based in Mosul, near Nineveh, but which now floated between Mosul, Baghdad, Lalish, and Sinjar. This focus on moving between the ancient sites is a key characteristic of Fahim's clan, which is seen as an anomaly among the Yezidi tribes that have stronger ties to a specific place. The geography of Fahim's clan was, in a sense, multi-dimensional. They represented a line of priesthood that extended back into the mists of history, back to the original Sumerian city-states, and their development was a response to a hideous threat that had the potential to destroy every human being on the planet.

The stories are hinted at in the Sumerian religious and historical corpus, those fragments that have survived. Texts like the *Enuma Elish* and the *Atra Hasis*: broken tablets in cuneiform, pieced together by myopic wizened researchers in the cramped basements of the world's universities, texts missing beginnings, endings ... the Epic of *Gilgamesh* with its humanoid hero and its battle with *Humwawa* ... and muttered tales of the ponderous, monstrous being that desired nothing but the slaughter of innocents on the Earth, and especially of the priesthood that was created to deny it victory; the imprisonment of its agents in the Underworld: a cavern deep beneath the Sumerian city of Cutha...

... and the Book that was written by an apostate, a man who had divined the secrets of Cutha and of the Being that dwelled in the vastness beneath it. The spy from Yemen who found himself trapped in Mesopotamia when the armies under the Prophet arrived to

destroy the temples and smash the idols. The Prophet, whose tribe
had its origins itself in Cutha. The tribe that had been in charge of
the temple complex in Mecca, the great stone Ka'aba: the tribe of
the Quraish.

"The Book you seek is the one that was written in haste by Abdul
Hazred, a man who called himself the 'Servant of the Forbidden.' He
was an Arab, not one of us. He was not a Muslim, at least not when
he came to us in the seventh century, although it is said he converted
later under threat of execution. They say he was a Sabaean. He was
a worshipper of the god they called *Yaghuth*, who is mentioned in
the Qur'an. Their Prophet had ordered the idol destroyed, but there
were those who maintained its worship even unto modern times,
often at risk of their lives. We understood this, since we were also
threatened by the armies under the Prophet. The Arab came to us in
those days to learn what he could of the old faith, the religion from
before the Prophet, before the Christians, before the Jews. One of
our priests took pity on him, for the Arab was half-mad.

"As the armies of the Prophet moved on Mesopotamia, to the
original land of the Quraish their ancestors, my clan picked up and
moved farther north. The Arab went with us. He told us of his gods,
Yaghuth and Al-Qullus and Hubal, of A'ra and Azizos and Manat.
He spoke to us of the cult of Qos of the black basalt shrine of Wadi
Hesa, and of many others. We could understand from his descriptions
that these gods were those we had defeated in ancient times, and this
made our elders afraid. Perhaps the followers of the Prophet were
right in destroying these idols, if the Arabs of Sana and Mecca and
Medina were still praying to them, trying to rouse them from their
slumber in the Underworld.

"Our priest instructed the Arab, telling him that these gods
must be kept in chains below the Earth. He gave him the formulas
for restraining them, in case the clan was captured or killed by the
Muslims. These the Arab wrote down in his own hand and preserved
them secretly so that our people were not aware, for we never
commit these sacred things to paper or to stone."

In spite of himself, Angell found he was fascinated by the old man's account. He had heard many tales told by Yezidi headmen in the past, but had never been close to any of them. They kept to themselves and were suspicious of outsiders since they had suffered at their hands so many times over the centuries. But now, in this moment of desperation, Fahim was saying things that Angell knew had never been uttered aloud before in front of a non-Yezidi. Even then, they would not have been revealed before anyone who was not one of their priesthood. Thus, Angell was acutely aware of the unique situation and even of the honor, but that sentiment was sidelined due to the imminent threat.

"Our people moved north, as I said. To Mosul. And then to our homeland in Sinjar. The Arab went with them, even as far as Lalish and the tomb of our Prophet, Sheikh Adi. The armies of the Muslims were already as far as Baghdad. They were trampling on the ground over the lost city of Cutha. We could feel it in our bones. We could feel the great imprisoned Lord of the Underworld moving about in his dreary palace under the Earth, shaken by the tremors of so many feet and horses.

"Thus it was in fear that our priests revealed some of the secrets of our faith to the Arab, for it was necessary that the Old Ones not be roused from their slumber. The Muslims would not know the formulas, would consider such things unclean. So, as has been told to me by my father, and to him by his father, back for countless generations to the time of the Muslim invasion of Mesopotamia, the Arab learned the essential methods for keeping the Old Ones chained and the Gate between our world and theirs forever closed.

"And he wrote all of this down in a book. As our ancestors fled to the safety of Mount Sinjar, the Arab went further east with our secrets. It is said he went to Persia, and from there perhaps to Afghanistan where some of the old people had fled centuries earlier and where the old gods were known and their incantations preserved."

Fahim stopped to take a sip of coffee. Angell decided to jump in at that point and ask, "And the book? What happened to it?"

He could sense Aubrey stiffen behind him. This was what they had come for.

"The book was never out of the possession of Abdul Hazred, the 'Servant of the Forbidden.' He took it with him to Persia. It disappeared after he died, a crazy mystic more than one hundred years old in the streets of Damascus. Then it surfaced somewhere in Europe after the Crusades. Then it disappeared again. Later, much later, after the Second World War, the book was deposited in the Baghdad Museum where I was archivist. I don't know by whom, or why. I only know that I kept it out of the hands of Saddam's men and then escaped with a young Yezidi girl and the book to Syria.

"It was known as *Al Kitab Al Azif*, an Arabic expression meaning the buzzing of insects. This means the cicadas that eat our grape vines. Their sound is unusual and, to someone of Abdul Hazred's sensitivity, extremely … suggestive. He believed the sound was made by the cicadas reacting to the presence of the Old Ones. Of course, by that time he was completely mad.

"The book was written in Abdul Hazred's own hand, in Arabic, but was translated into Greek shortly after the Arab's death by an Assyrian priest. The priest felt that the buzzing of insects was a reference to the strange words that are found in the book, words that are not Arabic or Farsi or even Kurdish but which come from the ancient tongue of the Yezidi: Sumerian. In Europe they would have called it the 'language of the birds' instead of insects, a coded language understood only by the initiated. As the book is concerned with the dead gods of the old times, and the means to ensure they remain dead, the priest gave the book the title in Greek by which it is best known.

"*Necronomicon.*"

The silence in the tent was palpable, a living thing that sucked the spirits dry of all the men squatting there. There was no movement. Not even an intake of breath.

Angell was stunned. A fantasy had become reality. Two worlds had suddenly encountered each other, clashed, fused, and created a third: the one he now was living in.

The Necronomicon was a joke, a running literary gag, an invention of his family's sick, twisted tormentor. Yet here were Lovecraft's despised Yezidis, telling him it was real. And there was nothing more real than sitting in a tent in a refugee camp on the Turkish-Syrian border, surrounded by armed men, and with the ever-present threat of a mortar attack or a suicide bomber to sweeten the pot. He knew they weren't *lying*, but they couldn't be telling the truth either.

He turned to look at Aubrey.

"You're buying this?"

But before Aubrey could answer there was a penetrating, high-pitched scream coming from somewhere outside the tent.

The sound of men running brought everyone out of their reverie. Angell and Aubrey jumped up, uncertain what to do. Fahim pushed through them purposefully, as if he knew what had just transpired.

Strangely, none of the other men in the tent made any move to retrieve their weapons and join the crowd outside. Instead, they looked at each other with meaningful glances and remained in their places along the tent walls. Aubrey noted that, but did not comment.

After all, this is what they came for.

The two Americans followed Fahim out of the tent and onto the now darkened pathway between the tents. The scream came again, more insistent. It was the voice of a woman, or a child. Angell noticed that his security minders were nowhere to be seen, and this—more than the screams—terrified him.

He raced after Aubrey who was now at a full sprint towards the source of the screams. A small crowd of men and some women had formed in a clearing ahead of them, making a kind of rough circle around someone in its center.

Angell pushed through behind Aubrey and stopped dead.

It was the beautiful, blue-eyed woman from earlier that day. Only now she was disheveled, her glistening black hair in Medusa-like coils damp with perspiration around her face, staring straight at him. Her mouth stretched unnaturally wide as yet another scream burst forth like a hand grenade tossed into the crowd.

"*Qhadhulu!*" she screamed, without seeming to move her lips or tongue.

Qhadhulu. Angell knew what that meant. But to Aubrey it sounded like *Kutulu.*

Fahim stroked the girl's hair and spoke softly to her. One of the men brought a jug of water and Fahim poured a few drops onto her forehead while speaking in a dialect Angell could not identify. All he could make out was the occasional use of the girl's name. Jamila.

Aubrey spoke briefly to Fahim, who handed him a scrap of paper that Aubrey immediately put into his pocket without looking at it.

Angell, shaken, stood apart from the crowd, trembling. Aubrey walked over to him.

"You okay, Professor?"

Without looking up, he asked him: "What has this been all about? What am I really doing here? Why are you ... *showing* me all of this?"

"I haven't lied to you, Angell. It's about finding a book before the bad guys do."

"And just who are the bad guys? There are too many players. I can't keep them all straight anymore."

"The bad guys are the ones who want to create worldwide hysteria and panic. They're the ones who want to overthrow civilization itself, and replace it with something unholy and unspeakable."

"And *who* are they?"

"That's the thing. Today it might be the Turks; tomorrow al-Nusra or one of the other Syrian resistance groups. The next day, the Islamic State. Or the Iranians. The day after that? Who knows? If all we do is look at the uniforms we'll never figure out who the generals are. They work through existing groups, and when they have no need of them or when the tactical situation changes, they switch alliances and work through someone else. Everything we see, everything we hear, is pantomime. It's a mummer show, a costume party by invitation only. The rest of us are just pushing our noses against the window, trying to get a peek."

"So this is not about ideology, or religion ..."

"Religion itself is part of the charade, Professor. It's what you realized long ago, at Mosul. Religion—for want of a better word—*is* the game. It's the way we see the conflict being played out. But it's got nothing to do with God."

"Who was ... who is that girl?"

"It's a distant relative of Fahim's. From the same clan. Her name is Jamila. She was with him when the Iraqi security services tried to seize the Book. They were neighbors in Mosul in 2003, during the invasion. It is said she saved his life."

"What's wrong with her?"

Aubrey shook his head.

"Epilepsy, maybe. Some kind of nervous disorder. She keeps to herself mostly, and has not been married off yet. Fahim says the men of their clan are afraid of her, and since Yezidis cannot marry outsiders ..." he let that thought trail off.

"You heard what she said, what she screamed." It was a statement, not a question.

Aubrey nodded. "I did."

"What the hell is going on? I have a right to know. First those drawings in the file, then that history lesson about old George Angell, and now a young woman screaming 'Kutulu' while a Yezidi headman tells me about the *Necronomicon*? Seriously?"

He grabbed Aubrey by the shoulders, but lowered his voice when he noticed some men from the crowd staring at him.

"You were there, Professor. You saw what I saw. How do you explain it?"

At that moment there was a strange, crunching sound coming from the edge of the camp and then a blinding light.

Rocket attack.

Aubrey pushed Angell down on the ground, covering him with his own body while he quickly assessed the situation. The attack was probably just a feint, to test the camp's defenses (if any). The panic it caused, however, was considerable.

"Stay down!" he told Angell. There was a sound of answering small arms fire, men from one of the Kurdish sections opening up with AK-47s on full auto with their unmistakable sound like a dozen crazed woodpeckers on crystal meth. Aubrey had no idea what they were shooting at. The rocket, or maybe mortar, attack had to have come from the hills outside the camp and was probably out of range of the Kalashnikovs.

He looked up when heard a car's engine and saw the Hummer pulling alongside them. His security escort. About time.

Two of the men jumped down and shielded the bodies of Aubrey and his charge as their eyes—and weapons—swept the area for threats, the driver calm and unemotional behind the wheel.

"Angell! Professor! Let's go!"

The men bundled the shaken religious studies professor into the back of the Humvee as they took off down the mud road to the camp's exit. They passed Doctor DeVries standing next to the gate, a look of fatalism mixed with anger distorting her features making her seem like a hungry Valkyrie. She made no effort to stop their escape. She knew they had what they came for, and she was glad to see them go.

Outside the camp, on a small rise overlooking the firefight, was another American. A man in dark clothing, watching the scene unfold through a pair of military grade binoculars.

The missing remote viewer and one of the most wanted men in the world, Jason Miller, was back in business.

Chapter Thirteen

The Horror at Red Hook

A thing is consecrated when it is put into contact with a source of religious energy …

—Emile Durckheim, *The Elementary Forms of Religious Life*

May, 1925
Brooklyn

He has gone to bed hungry, as usual. He is surrounded by some brooding pieces of heavy furniture shipped to him by his aunts in Providence and they form a fortress of memories around his bed in the cramped room. Under a heavy comforter he tries to sleep, luxuriating in the ponderous warmth of Brooklyn on a spring evening. In his apartment building on Clinton Street there are unsettling nocturnal sounds from the other rooms. Lovecraft pulls the covers up to his ears to block out the sniffling, snuffling sounds of Syrian sex from one room and the hideous screech of Egyptian music coming from another. They seem to meld into one noxious incantation of all the darkest elements of the human condition.

Doumbek and depravity, the rhythm of the jinn.

He is the most miserable he has ever been in his life. Alone in this city seething with foreigners and their imported nightmares, as if his own Anglo-Saxon dreams were not enough, abandoned by his wife who has left him for some backwater Midwestern burg in her quest for money and acceptance. She should have known that when she married him, a gentleman after all, that such pathetic pursuits as employment and intercourse were not priorities in his life. He came from delicate English stock, a family heritage that traced it roots to the earliest settlers of the New England frontier. The proper occupation for a Lovecraft (and a Phillips, don't forget) was literature, the arts, music, and travel. His aunts were positively horrified by his choice of spouse: a tradeswoman! A ... a ... *a hat maker!* A milliner! They didn't understand that *he* hadn't done the choosing.

After the death of his mother from a botched surgical operation—a merciful death, for all that, for she was quite mad—Sonia Greene had come into his life as if sent to pick up the slack. She ordered his life and took charge of everything. She understood his special needs, his sensitivity to the things of this world.

Or he thought she did.

But when her business went bad and they were suddenly broke, everything changed. *She* changed. It was a disruption to his life—to the thirty-year-long train of thought that had come perilously close to being broken—and he could not have that.

To make matters worse, a few months ago he had stolen that file from old Professor Angell.

He didn't know why he had done that. It was completely out of character for a Lovecraft to do something so ... sordid as stealing. But there was something about that library. It reminded him of one he had lost so long ago, with the death of his grandfather. His beloved grandfather. The only human being who had ever understood him, and the only one of his relatives with a massive and excellent library. By stealing from Angell's library he was recovering his own past.

He spent hours among those books as a child, immersed in Burton's *Thousand and One Nights*, and books on ancient cities and lost civilizations. It was his refuge from a world that had mocked him, even as a child. His own mother thought he looked freakish. And he was sickly. Stayed home from school. Lay dreaming, like now, in bed and listening to the sounds of life taking place all around him like a blind man divining the time of day from the noise of the street and the passage of birds and the buzzing of insects.

Then his grandfather died, and they sold off his estate.

And all his books.

He was not sure, some days, which he missed more. The grandfather who loved him, or the books that he loved.

If only he could find a book that could love him back.

Sleep came slowly, but surely. When Lovecraft slept, it was like a stone lost in thought. His dreams were his entertainment, and he looked forward to them. At times he would fall asleep giddy, in anticipation of what that night's offering might be. Would it be a voyage to the wastes of unknown Kadath? Would it be a mysterious search in the bowels of some abandoned church? Would he commune with alien beings from some distant galaxy? Or would it be that damned Arab again, Abdul Alhazred and his cursed book of black magic and alien contact? With that music pounding from next door, he feared it would be the latter.

He drifted. His mind loosed its grasp on his mortal sheath and began to wander. He saw things in distant places, could make out cyclopean architecture in cities sunken beneath the waves of the Pacific Ocean. He walked among creatures that had been dead for aeons, creatures he could see and hear but knew that when he awoke they would be impossible to describe in human terms.

And that is how he liked it.

It was while deep within the embrace of an eldritch temple in a country he did not recognize that someone came into his apartment *with a key* and stole his suits, a suitcase, some odds and ends of radio equipment he was storing for a friend …

… and, to his waking horror, the Cthulhu file.

When he awakes the next morning, it seems as if he is not completely awake. His eyes seem to be open, but the room around him has changed while he slept. Things have been moved. Things have been changed. Things are missing.

He gets out of bed gingerly, as if afraid to jostle the dream from his head. If it is a dream. If it is, it is truly one of his least impressive.

The door to his wardrobe is open. He would never have left it that way. He reaches over to close it but at the last moment looks inside.

It's gaping blackness greets him, and it is more horrible than he could imagine. His suits are gone. His overcoat is gone! How will he survive a Brooklyn winter without it, especially in that apartment with a landlady who denied him heat?

A box is missing. Oh, no. Loveman will be quite upset. A suitcase is missing, too. The thieves evidently packed all their stolen property in his one and only suitcase.

It is only then that he thinks of the file marked CTHULHU CULT.

He has hidden it, cleverly he thought, under his bed. With the duvet draping down to the floor, he was certain no one would think to look there. He was conscious of the fact that it was the only object he had that anyone might conceivably want to steal, and the sight of it reminded him of his guilt anyway, so he took pains to make sure it was well-concealed.

Taking a deep breath, he bent down and lifted the heavy duvet and was greeted by the same yawning darkness as he was at his wardrobe.

Lovecraft screamed.

The visit by the police was perfunctory. The interview with the landlady even more so. No one liked Lovecraft in the building. The thief could have been anyone, including even the landlady herself. Whoever had entered his apartment had done so with a key. There was no sign of forced entry, and anyway they had come in and robbed Lovecraft clean while he slept in the same room. It was obviously premeditated and executed with assistance from someone in the apartment building.

Nothing could be done. Lovecraft would have to save money and buy another overcoat. It would take months. In the meantime he had another very real problem.

He couldn't tell the police about the missing Cthulhu file, obviously. The stain of it would have to stay with him for a very long time. He had stolen it, and now someone had stolen it from him. In fact, they seemed to know where to look and he wondered if the theft of the other objects was merely a way to disguise the real object of their crime.

Consumed with a growing sense of panic, Lovecraft decided he had to write down everything he remembered from the file. This would be important, and later might even help to figure out who stole the file back from him. It could not have been Professor Angell. The man was quite old and one could not imagine him as some kind of cat burglar. Then … who?

He had no time to waste. He would write down all the data from the file and include with it his own story about the visit to Angell and the situation with Wilcox and how it reminded him of his own mother's insanity and the possibility that he, too, would suffer the same fate as his parents.

Maybe he would find some way to make amends to Professor Angell. That thought warmed him and gave him the energy to complete his task, writing feverishly in his now somewhat roomier apartment. He would go to Providence and interview old George Angell soon. He would find out what he knew.

But Professor Angell would be dead within eighteen months, murdered by a Nazi agent on the Providence docks. An agent who was looking for the stolen Cthulhu file.

April 2014
Brooklyn

Gregory Angell's apartment in Red Hook has become something of a mystery. There are sounds of chanting coming from the rooms in the middle of the night, but no one has seen Angell in days. No one has come into or out of the apartment since he left with James

Aubrey. Yet, every night since then, the chanting begins in a language that his Syrian neighbors do not recognize as Arabic or Farsi.

Finally, the disturbance has become too much. Mrs. Abadi from upstairs decides it is time to call the police.

An officer from the seven-six showed up at her door at 3:50 am and introduced himself as Detective Wasserman. He was nearing retirement, and his wavy gray hair and handlebar mustache were grown out enough to signal that he just didn't care anymore. He had a gold shield and thirty years on the job, in every department from vice to homicide. He would put in his papers in another few weeks and the only reason he was answering this call was because he was in the neighborhood at 3:50 in the morning having just come from some junior officer's bachelor party in the Heights. He had not been drinking; he gave that up years ago, as well as smoking, red meat, and the missionary position, but he liked to show support for the younger guys who would become cynical on their own soon enough.

"Please, sir, officer …"

"Detective, ma'am."

"Detective. He has been gone for several days but there are strange sounds coming from his apartment." She was about forty-five, wearing a headscarf, but that might have been to hide her curlers rather than her hair. He couldn't tell anymore. Couldn't keep it all straight. She was plump and earnest and not a little fearful of dealing with the cops, even this long after 9/11.

From somewhere in the back of her apartment he could hear someone else moving about.

"Are you alone, Mrs. Abadi?"

"That's my husband, Detective. He doesn't sleep very well at night. And this just makes it worse."

Wasserman paused for a moment, holding up his hand to silence Mrs. Abadi.

He heard a kind of soft pounding, a vibration that came through the floorboards, and then something that sounded like Gregorian chant. But in a weird sort of minor key. Hell, what did he know from Gregorian chant? Last time he heard anyone chant, it was at his son's bar mitzvah.

"Is that what you mean?"

"Yes, but now is more quiet. More soft. Before it was very loud and … and sharp."

Wasserman nodded. He wondered what he had gotten himself into.

"Did you try to knock on the door, Mrs. Abadi?"

"Yes, of course." She nodded, wringing her hands.

"And?"

"And it became worse. More noise. More … singing."

"What language is that? Arabic?"

"No," she shook her head vigorously. "I never hear that language before." But there was something about her denial that didn't ring true. When she said that, her eyes darted away and back, like she was trying to hide something.

"Do you have a key to the apartment?"

"Yes. I mean, no. I mean I have a key but it … is not … workable."

"You mean he changed the locks?"

"Yes, I think so."

"But you're the landlady, right? You have ownership of this place?"

"Yes, sir, Detective."

"Okay, well, that's all I need. If you give me permission I will try to force the door."

"Yes, of course. Yes, please."

For a moment he wondered if he should call it in, ask for backup. But that sounded stupid even as he thought it. What would they think? The old geezer had lost his touch? It was a radio or something, maybe on a timer.

A *timer*?

He stopped halfway down the stairs to the apartment and turned. The landlady was a few steps above him.

"Mrs. Abadi. What is the tenant's name?"

"He is a very nice man. A professor. His name is Angell. Gregory Angell."

Didn't sound Arab. But it did sound phony. An alias, maybe. *Angel?*

"Professor? What does he teach?"

"Um, at the Columbia University. He teach religion."

Religion?

A timer?

Yeah, better call for backup.

A patrol car parked half on the curb, lights flashing, radio squawking, and two officers walked up the tenement's steps to meet Wasserman in the doorway, adjusting their belts and batons, one of the men carrying a crowbar.

It was just after shift-change so these guys were wide awake and alert.

"What've we got, Detective?"

"I don't know what we have. You hear that sound?"

They listened, and could vaguely make out the chanting from the street.

"It's a lot louder inside, right by the door to the tenant's apartment. Landlady says he hasn't been seen in days. Could be he's lying on his kitchen floor dead from a heart attack. But the guy teaches religion and his landlady is Syrian or Egyptian or something. And the music only comes on late at night. Like on a timer."

"Detective, if you're thinking what I'm thinking, you should maybe want the bomb squad."

"I thought of that. But if it was a bomb, it shoulda gone off by now. The music has been coming on every night for days. And if it was a bomb, why announce it with the whole MTV routine?"

"The what?"

"Never mind. I just want backup in case there's something squirrely going on in there. I'm gonna knock on the door, and if

the mope doesn't answer I'm gonna ask you two nice gentlemen to
open the door. You have the crowbar I asked for?"

"Right here."

"Okay. Follow me."

Mrs. Abadi had used her landline to dial the police. Dispatch had
put out the call on the radio and Wasserman heard it in his car
and responded. When Wasserman called for backup he used his cell
phone to contact the precinct. Then dispatch used the radio to send
a patrol car to Angell's Red Hook address. Between the landline, the
cell phones and the radio the address raised a discrete flag which
roused Monroe from a fitful sleep. Monroe knew Angell's address
but no one else would suspect anything or, if they did, it would be
hours or days before they put anything together. Still, Monroe had
to know why NYPD was being called to Angell's building.

He sat on the edge of his bed and thought for a second, then
reached for his own phone.

Wasserman led the way to Angell's door. The two patrolmen were
standing behind him, one with his gun drawn and aimed at the door,
the other with his crowbar at the ready.

Wasserman heard the chanting clearly through the apartment
door. He knocked.

"Mr. Angell! Open up, please. Police!"

The chanting continued.

"Angell, we're coming in!"

The chanting continued.

Wasserman turned to the patrolman with the crowbar and
nodded, stepping aside but keeping his gun drawn on the door.

The crowbar easily slid through the jamb and the door, and the
cop slowly pried the door open. It had been locked, but there was no
chain so there was a good chance there was no one inside.

Just as the door was pried loose, the patrolman stopped.
Wasserman changed position so that he was on the right side of the

door. The other patrolman, gun raised, stood on the left. Wasserman looked up and down the door jamb, trying to see if there were any trip wires or booby traps, but it was too dark. Instead, the sound of chanting only grew louder.

He motioned to the other patrolman for his flashlight. Aiming it through the slightly opened door he could see inside the entire apartment. It was bleak, barely furnished. No sign of a trip wire, timer, or anything vaguely electrical or mechanical. It could have been a monk's cell on Mount Athos. But there was movement.

Something was spinning on the tabletop.

Monroe got through to one of his network, an FBI agent in New York City who worked in counter-intelligence on the China desk. After a few minutes of waiting on the line he found out that the call had to do with noise coming from an apartment at that address. Strictly a nuisance call. Nothing vaguely terrorist or intelligence related as far as could be seen. There were three officers at the scene, one a detective and two patrolmen. The agent promised to let Monroe know if there were any developments, but that it was probably a radio playing too loud or a party getting out of control.

Monroe thanked the agent and hung up, but he was worried. He didn't believe in coincidences. Someone was sending a message. Or some*thing*.

"Bomb!"

Wasserman and his two patrolmen dropped to the floor and covered their heads and necks with their hands. And waited.

Nothing happened. The chanting started to wind down just as it was getting light outside. The sound of an object spinning could now be heard along with the chant, and it was slowing down as well.

Wasserman raised his head and peered into the room. He got up and motioned to the two men to follow him into the apartment.

As they stood there, guns drawn, the Syrian incantation bowl, the "demon trap," began to end its spin in a wobble on the table. As it did so, the sound of chanting also dissipated. The bowl wobbled … wobbled … and then came to a stop.

The chanting stopped.

And then the spirit bowl cracked right down the middle.

It was a loud report, like a rifle shot, and the three police officers stood there, dazed. They had no idea what had just happened. But behind them, Mrs. Abadi stood in the doorway to the apartment and stared at the cracked bowl, a look of absolute horror distorting her features into a Halloween mask.

"*Allahu akbar*," she said. "*Allahu akbar*."

Wasserman turned at the sound of her voice.

"What is it, Mrs. Abadi?"

She pointed at the bowl.

"What is this doing here? I don't ever see this before."

"What is it?"

"From the old country. From Syria. This is very old, it is not … it is *haram*. Forbidden. You understand?"

Wasserman smiled in spite of himself.

"You mean, it's not kosher?"

She either did not get the reference, or the joke, or was ignoring it.

"It is for black magic. *Sihr*. It is for holding the … what you call it … the bad spirits. The jinn."

One of the patrolmen made a quiet remark, something to do with *Ghostbusters*.

Wasserman ignored him, and instead asked the Syrian woman:

"So, what now? Is it okay now? It seems to be broken."

The woman simply shook her head, back and forth, saying over and over again "*Allahu akbar*." God is great.

Then she broke out of her reverie and told the old detective, "It is not okay. It is *broken*. The trap is *broken*. The spirit has escaped.

"Poor Professor Angell …"

CHAPTER FOURTEEN

THE GATE TO THE UNDERWORLD

There are vocal qualities peculiar to men, and vocal qualities peculiar to beasts; and it is terrible to hear the one when the source should yield the other.

—H.P. Lovecraft, "The Call of Cthulhu"

Tell Ibrahim
South of Baghdad
April 30, 2014
"The Day the Bear Hangs from its Tail in the Sky"

It had been a harrowing journey from the refugee camp on the Turkish-Syrian border to Baghdad, in Iraq. Turkish troops had arrived at the camp, alerted by the rocket attack and the return fire from the Kurds, which led to a stand-off between the two groups. The relationship between the Turks and the Kurds was problematic, to say the least. Some Turks favored working with the Kurds against both Assad's Syria and the Islamic State. Other Turks favored removing the Kurds completely from Turkish territory. It was a mess, and represented a constantly shifting political and military landscape that only someone with years of experience in-country could hope to understand, let alone anticipate.

Unknown to either Aubrey or Angell at the time, the identity of the attackers was a mystery. The assumption was that they were Islamic State soldiers, testing the security situation at the camp, but that was by no means a safe guess. It could have been anyone, for any reason at all.

Only Jason Miller knew the truth, and he was already on the move.

Aubrey calmly led their little mission back to Diyarbakir, which still was largely under Kurdish control. There were no flights back to Istanbul that night, but Aubrey had no intention of returning there now that he knew where his prey was heading. In his pocket he held the scrap of paper that Fahim had given him just before the attack started. It gave him the name and location of a Yezidi contact in Iraq living underground, a member of a network of Fahim's clan that was spread from Turkey to Syria, Iraq, Iran, and all the way to northern India.

Angell was silent in the car on the way back along the road to the city. As far as he knew, they were going back to the airport and taking a flight home. Aubrey would have to disabuse him of that notion, and he was not looking forward to it. The mission, however, took precedence over everything else, and they were running out of time.

Oddly, it was Angell himself who suggested that they continue in their search for the book.

The lights of Diyarbakir were coming up. The minarets of mosques could be seen in the distance, while along the dusty road there were small shops, cafés, and newsstands. Motor scooters and minivans were everywhere, and it seemed like a semblance of normal life. Angell found himself staring out the window, not believing that only a few hours earlier there were people shooting at them.

"We're not going back, are we?" he asked Aubrey, who had been silent, too, up till now.

"Do you want to go back?" Clever, Aubrey. Very clever.

Angell turned back to the window and the street scene before answering.

"Yes. Fahim, Jamila, gunfire, that file in your briefcase … everything I've seen and heard the past … what? Six hours? Twelve? … tells me I ought to get the hell out of here. We have no real allies here. We can't trust the Turks, and we sure as hell can't trust the Syrians or the Iraqis. Even the Kurds … even the Kurds …"

He turned to face Aubrey.

"I don't want to see any more bloodshed. I saw enough of that in my life. I know you ... all of you ... you ... that's *your* job. You're used to it. You're trained. You're calm under fire. You're warriors. I'm not. I'm a college professor. I've seen enough of this part of the world to last me a lifetime. I don't need to see more sand, more marsh, more broken cities, more spent cartridges, more crazed prophets. I'm not Lawrence, or Woolley. I'm not CIA. I'm nothing. But I have something you want. Something you need.

"You guys walk through real mine fields like you're tip-toeing through the tulips. But I walk through theological and archaeological mine fields, where a wrong word said the wrong way can ignite a holy war. You need me to finish your job. I get that. I even get why your job should be *my* job. There's too much at stake. I can see that now. Someone wanted to kill us over this thing. This *book*. This book that doesn't even ... that can't really exist. Back there, at the camp, the real world and the imaginary world collided. Right in front of my eyes. That's religion, isn't it? Some kind of religion, anyway. Some kind of fucked up psycho-spiritual bullshit. There's something deeply sinister taking place here, something sickeningly *wrong*, and not just here but on the whole friggin' planet.

"So, yes, I want to go back. I want to go *home*. Lucky for you, I don't know where that is. So until I find out, I'm with you for the duration."

So there they were. Using Monroe's networks and his own expertise, Aubrey got himself and Angell from the airport at Diyarbakir to a military airfield in the south of Turkey. Diyarbakir serves as both a commercial airport and a military one for the Turkish Air Force; they were able to hop a transport for Incirlik where the US Air Force had a base. From Incirlik they flew to Baghdad where they were greeted by members of an American mercenary group that would serve as their Iraqi security escort. Aubrey bid the first three men goodbye at Incirlik from where they would proceed to other destinations, other missions.

Angell never even knew their names.

It was afternoon when they landed in Baghdad. Aubrey had shown Angell the paper that Fahim had handed him the previous day. It gave the name of their contact and a location: Tell Ibrahim, an archaeological site south of Baghdad on Route 8. The road was somewhat safe, according to their escorts. The group known as the Islamic State had taken Fallujah and Ramadi, to the north and west of the ancient city of Babylon, in January but the road as far south as Hillah was secure at the moment. It might not be for long, however. Mosul was being threatened, and it was not clear how long it could hold out. There was dissension in the Iraqi Army leading to a general consensus among the mercenaries that the army would not put up an energetic resistance. If Mosul fell, then the Yezidis were in danger of extermination, not to mention the Assyrian Christians who were their neighbors.

The mercenaries were employees of a private American security corporation that was hired to provide both protection and intelligence for foreign missions in the region. The men were wearing Kevlar vests and helmets and carried a variety of weapons, most of which Angell did not recognize. The only member of the security detail who did not wear a helmet was their own driver, who was dressed like a local.

They passed Kevlar vests to both Aubrey and Angell, with the instruction to put them on immediately. Attached to each was a lapel mike and commset which linked all the members of the team together. The mercenaries looked like rock stars with their earplugs and mikes, about to give a concert in hell.

As the men bundled into their armored vehicles for the trip down Route 8, the leader of the escort passed a secure satellite phone to Aubrey.

It was a call from Monroe. Aubrey stepped outside the car, out of earshot of the others and especially of Angell, to take the call.

"Angell's apartment was broken into last night by NYPD. There were sounds that frightened the neighbors. They found nothing, but the situation is worrisome."

"Should I tell him?"

"No point. Nothing was taken. We'll have the door fixed, and the place watched. What do you know about the girl?"

"Jamila? She disappeared after the rocket attack on the camp. Fahim told me."

"So now?"

"To Kutha." It was practically a code-word. No one called it that anymore. Not in the last two thousand years, anyway.

"It's a war zone."

"Should be okay tonight. We won't be there for long."

"Is the book there?"

"No. Well, I don't know. But we have a contact waiting for us. It's possible Jamila went there as well. That's what Fahim is hoping for, anyway."

Monroe was silent a moment, thinking. Aubrey was used to it, and waited.

"Jason Miller was sighted in Turkey a few days ago."

"Confirmed?"

"No. But it seems likely. No one else has claimed responsibility for the attack on the camp. He might have been trying to flush you out. Or the girl."

It was Aubrey's turn to keep quiet. Then:

"The girl. Or the book. We have to assume he's after the same thing we are."

"Then … you're a stalking horse. He's going to use you to get to the book."

"But can he use it without Jamila?"

"The bigger question is: can he use it without Angell?"

"By the way, he's on board. Officially."

"We knew he would be. What choice does he have?"

The armored car carrying Angell and Aubrey followed a lead car containing more mercenaries as they made their way down Route 8 from Baghdad, through a region dense with burned-out vehicles by the side of the road, mosques with the call to prayer loud and insistent from tinny loudspeakers, people walking aimlessly around looking like zombies in caftans. There was a risk of IEDs—Improvised Explosive Devices—and the escort was prepared for the eventuality. The road was busy with trucks and cars and they followed carefully behind the traffic. If there was a bomb planted in the road they would not be the ones who triggered it. However, if the device was more sophisticated—controlled by a cell phone or other device—then the lead car would probably take the hit. It had better armor plate than anything the American troops had, and was specially constructed with a steel reinforced undercarriage designed to resist a blast from a typical IED. It was a very visible Humvee, whereas the car Angell was in looked nondescript even though it was heavily armored as well. Their driver was wearing Arab dress—kaffiyeh and agal—and boasted a thick, black beard. If there was an attack, it would most likely be directed towards the Humvee (symbol of foreign presence) rather than the old Mercedes following it.

The region was largely Shiite, and it hugged the contours of the Euphrates. The place they were going was about 23 miles northeast of the ancient city of Babylon, and Angell was aware that they were in the very thick of Mesopotamia. The town that was their target was Tell Ibrahim, formerly known as Kutha or Gudua. The Gate to the Mesopotamian Underworld.

It was an archaeological site that had been excavated in the nineteenth century and not much was found there. It had been turned into a kind of park, and its ancient associations were largely forgotten in a land that was in the middle of a war zone. But the modern modifications to the site were lost on Angell, who had the sinking feeling they were walking into a trap.

He was second-guessing himself on the way down to Kutha. Why did he agree to stay with the mission? How the hell did he get himself into this? The view outside the windshield was nightmarish. There was the veneer of normalcy over a deep terror that flowed

like a subterranean river beneath the sand, the dust, and the cordite. The region had seen a lot of combat during the second Gulf
War as the Marines fought their way up the Euphrates all the way
to Baghdad. Route 8 itself was known as the "Highway of Death"
during the first Gulf War. And now Iraq had splintered into Sunni
and Shi'a factions, pro-government forces and rebel groups, and
with the addition of the latest iteration of violent extremism—the
Islamic State—the country was on the verge of collapse. The area to
the west of Baghdad—including the infamous towns of Fallujah and
Ramadi—were now in ISIL hands. Iraq was as divided as Syria, and
there was no end in sight for anyone.

And they were all Muslims. They all spoke the same language.
Shared the same customs. And they were slaughtering each other
with a kind of manic joy mixed with desperation, like people trapped
on a roller coaster with no way of getting off.

Angell knew that the key to this mystery was here, somewhere,
in this ancient land that gave birth to the world's three monotheist
religions: Judaism, Christianity, and Islam. They all traced their
origins to Abraham, and for whatever reason the old city of Kutha—
Gate to the Underworld—was now known as Tell Ibrahim. Ibrahim:
the Arabic for *Abraham*. Abraham and the Underworld. Abraham and
the Quraish, for this was their ancestral home.

They made it to Tell Ibrahim without incident. It was already dusk,
and they inched their way as close as they were able to the site. It
was a new moon, so the stars were visible. In the north, the Dipper
and the Pole Star. There were streets on all sides, and there was some
light foot traffic. Aubrey noticed that the pedestrians all seemed to
be walking towards the park.

And they were all armed.

The mercs didn't like what they saw. They muttered among themselves. An enclosed area, filled with armed men, in the gathering
gloom of twilight passing to night. Their leader decided they should

split up, with one team going to the far side of the park while the other would stay with the client.

The night was closing in on him. Tendrils of shadow were reaching around the armored Mercedes, slithering beneath and above the chassis, growing in size and daring in intention. Angell felt his heart pounding and he didn't know why. It was peaceful here. There was no sound of gunfire, no roadblocks, nothing that would suggest this was anything other than a sleepy Iraqi town. But Angell was terrified.

He was having a panic attack, like he would have back in his apartment in Red Hook when exhaustion was not enough to put him to sleep. There were sounds out there, sounds he could not identify. Animal sounds. The sinister buzz of nocturnal insects. And something else.

"Do you hear that?" It was Aubrey who broke the silence in the car.

"What?" Angell could hear the terror in his own voice, and he was afraid everyone else could hear it for miles around.

"That sound. Like women singing. Or humming."

The mercenary escort exited the two vehicles, the Humvee and their own Mercedes. They arranged themselves around the cars and sniffed the air like a pack of wolves. As they did so, the sound grew louder and Angell could identify it, even though the realization was like a knife to his heart. He stepped out of the car, his attention drawn to the source of the sound, his legs weak with fear.

"It's ululation," he explained. "It's common in this part of the world."

"Why are they doing it?"

"That's the question. It can be heard at weddings, but also at funerals. Sometimes as a greeting. I think it's safe to say it's not a wedding."

Of course it's not a wedding, Angell thought to himself. He recognized the setting. The arrival of armed civilians from all over the town, converging on the site of Tell Ibrahim itself.

It was the same ululation that the Martians had made in that H.G. Wells novel, *The War of the Worlds*. There, it was the sound the aliens made as they went into battle.

To Angell, it was all of those things. But mostly it was a greeting. "They are welcoming … something," he said aloud, without realizing it, the sound of his voice strange to him in the Mesopotamian darkness. "Calling it. They're *calling* it."

"That's our signal," Aubrey said to Angell and to the men.

As they approached the clearing in the middle of the darkening park the sight that greeted them was like something out of a horror movie or a snuff film. There were dozens of armed men: Shiite pilgrims with Kalashnikovs, stoned-looking teenagers sharing a joint and a rifle with a folding stock, heavily-painted transvestites with mascara and machine guns, and some kind of religious leader in their midst. An aged Imam.

Heavy weaponry was evident everywhere they looked, from home-made armored cars—old banged-up jalopies souped up with turbos and sheet metal patches—to rocket launchers, new-looking and shiny assault rifles, and at least seven curved scimitars that were older than Adam's sin. It was like something out of *Mad Max*, Iraqi style.

One of the transvestites was dressed in a yellow halter top and orange hot pants, and she was holding an M-16 between her legs like a witch riding a broom. Her movements were both pious and obscene, like a naked priest celebrating Mass in a blasphemous frenzy.

And in a rough circle around the wacked-out warriors were the women.

They were all dressed in black burqas, their hands raised to their faces as they ululated in ebbs and flows of trilling, moaning wails like a chant they had learned as crack babies in their mother's womb. Angell could see them everywhere, standing straight up like soldiers, all facing the center of the park where, he noticed, the grass was smoldering with an odor like the sickening incense from a thousand massacres.

And the Imam, wandering among the players like a sheikh among the satanic *semazen*: whirling dervishes spinning like tops on an axis that plunged straight as an arrow to the deepest parts of Hell, the Devil—Iblis—furiously shaking their stems and causing them to spin even more manically. The Imam was a tall, grey-bearded man in a long black robe and a black turban, his chest crossed with bandoliers like a Mexican Zapatista. He held a carved wooden staff in his hand that was in the shape of a serpent coiled around someone's spinal column. He had a sleepy but dangerous look in his eyes as he maneuvered effortlessly among the crowd, mumbling some sort of prayer under his breath with saliva dripping out of the side of his mouth.

And the players—all of them, Shiite pilgrims and transvestite terrorists, teenage dopers and black-robed wailers—were spinning now in the ritual that was banned in Turkey under Ataturk, the mystical rite of contact with the Unspeakable, the Ineffable. But this was not Rumi's dervish dance. This was not what the tourists came to see in Istanbul, high on Turkish coffee and black market *kif*. No; these were demonic dervishes, their dizzying spin designed to drag them *down*, to open the buried, rusted-over portal to Gehennna, Gudua, the Underworld.

Kutha.

And in the god-abandoned center of that accursed chapel or charnel house or whatever it pretended to be was a small statue on a tall wooden base. As Angell set his eyes on it, the alarm in his heart growing by the second, the ululations reached a frantic pitch and he could finally make out something more than just a sound. The light from a hundred tiny fires lit up the hideous features of the statue: a thing that was not a god, not a human, yet some kind of hybrid of the two; but only if it was a god wracked by disease and madness that had mated with a human teratoma if that teratoma had elongated

fingers and teeth like rusted razor blades. It was the same figure as
the one in Aubrey's file; the one that polluted the desk of George
Angell and the nightmares of Henry Wilcox.

And the ululation. It grew to a drumbeat, a chorus, a strangled
shout. It was an imprecation, a curse, a prayer to the spirit and soul
of all the filth that ever soiled the planet Earth. It was that one word,
that entreaty from a doomed prisoner to his torturer to end it all, to
stop the pain, to just get it over with and kill him, and by so doing
purge the entire planet of all life:

Qhadhulu

They were spotted. One of the stoned-out teenagers was not so
stoned he didn't see heavily-armed American mercenaries gazing
down at them. Or maybe he thought he was hallucinating on some
fucked-up hashish. No matter. He nudged his friend, who poked his
other friend, and the three of them looked up.

The drooling Imam felt the change in the current and looked,
first at the teenagers then in the direction they were staring. A
deranged smile sharpened his features and he raised his serpent cane,
pointing directly at Angell as he did so.

Those who were armed raised their weapons and began firing in
disorganized but nonetheless lethal fashion at the spot where Aubrey
and Angell now took cover as their escorts provided covering fire
from two sides of the park. Bullets pinged and sparked off some
ancient stonework behind Angell's head. A second front opened up
on the opposite side of the park as the other mercenaries started
pouring disciplined fire into the crowd. They knew who they were
looking for, and wanted to do as little damage as possible but in a
firefight like this—with crazed cultists firing automatic weapons and
rocket launchers—it would be difficult to get to their target and
keep him alive.

This was the first time that Angell found himself in the middle
of combat rather than simply a spectator, as he had been at Mosul,
and he felt strangely calm. The threat of physical danger didn't seem

to bother him. Instead, his eyes were focused on the obscenity in the middle of the clearing and the efforts by some of the cultists to surround it and protect it.

Aubrey's hand was on his head, keeping him down, while he spoke into the commset to the mercenary commander.

"Do not shoot the Imam! We need to talk to him!"

At that moment, one of the oddly-dressed transvestite guerrillas raised his rocket launcher and aimed it directly for the spot where Aubrey and Angell were hiding, as if sensing their presence and knowing that they were the real target. Just as his eyes—heavily ringed with kohl—met those of Angell his head exploded into a red mist as a round from one of the mercenaries met its mark. The cultist dropped his launcher and fell to the ground, headless. Angell ducked behind his cover and started gasping in great heaves.

"Head shot," said Aubrey, calmly and dispassionately.

Chaos had erupted with the first rounds fired. The cultists were scattering all over the park, some making for the streets that ringed the site. The mercenaries were not looking to stop them. They were not there to engage in a bloodbath, but to locate a man they had to interrogate as quickly as possible.

As they started to sweep the park and make their way to its center a fine mist grew up around them. It was gray, with what appeared to be fireflies or fairy lights sprinkled around it. It was surreal, almost pretty, until the men noticed the smell that accompanied the mist. It was an odor they knew all too well. The scent of burned flesh and rotting corpses. It was as if someone had opened the door to an abattoir, one that had been shut up for centuries.

Covering their noses as best they could, but with their focus still on their mission, they crept closer to the central area of the site where once ancient Kutha had flourished. There were weird, small fires burning everywhere. Strange that the mist did not ignite from all the open flames, the flying ordinance, and abject terror made flesh. They were about to stop a crowd of the burqa-clad women on the suspicion that one of them might be their quarry in drag—after all, the transvestite terrorists were the most lethal of the group anyway—when a shout from one of their comrades drew them to the center of site, next to the column with the evil-looking idol on top.

"That's it," Aubrey said, grabbing at Angell's shoulder. "Let's go down."

The professor looked at the spook as if he were insane.

"They're still shooting down there! The place is in chaos!"

"Nonsense. They're just mopping up now." He turned to Angell and said, with a wink, "It's safe to surf!"

With that, he practically picked Angell up off the ground and dragged him down the small rise they were on to the center of the action. This is where the professor would earn his salary.

Behind a small outcropping of ancient stones, an Iraqi teenager—mind clear now since he was so totally stoned out of it—raised his old Armalite with its multi-colored barrel and its stock adorned with cartoon stickers and pink graffiti and took aim at the academic. Angell was the one person there who did not seem to belong at all, and therefore had to be the most important person in the place. If he killed him then the Imam would be pleased and their Grand Mahdi—the priest of all priests, the one the Imam said was lying underground at Kutha, the Lord of Kutha, *Kutulu,* just waiting for the right moment to call his people together—would rise and smell the incense.

"*Qhadhulu shay altheemon,*" he whispered to himself. "*Qhadhulu* is great." Then, growing bolder, he added "*Qhadhuluhu akbar,*" his voice a little higher, almost a shout, the blasphemous, artificial construction instantly condemning him to a Muslim hell.

And pulled the trigger.

Jason Miller stood on the roof of a building over a thousand yards from the epicenter of the firefight. He watched the proceedings through his binoculars, and then reached down for his sniper rifle, a customized version of the MK 21. Laying the rifle on a sandbag rest, he chambered a .338 Lapua Magnum round and took aim through the telescopic sight at the head of the drugged-out teenage shooter pointing his piece-of-shit gopher gun in the direction of the professor.

Miller took a breath, and let it out slowly.

There was no wind.

He fired.

The teenager did not know he was dead. He thought he was just stoned. He saw … well, nothing. Something was wrong. He had no eyes, no sight, but he … saw … something. He felt it, too. Felt its fingers probe his brain and then make a grab for his heart muscle. It squeezed. His heart exploded like a water balloon.

But it wasn't his heart.

He was already dead.

Angell started at the sound. A shot had been fired from the teenager's rifle but it went up into the air. Did the youth think he was shooting at God?

At Angell's feet lay the wounded Imam, a sucking chest wound, blood pooling all around his waist and groin and chest. The man's eyes were glazing over. There was almost no time.

"Talk to him!" shouted Aubrey, above the sound of small arms fire and the cries of the wounded.

Angell was looking into the eyes of the aged Imam who was breathing his last. He wasn't sure the man could see him, even though his eyes were open. He was looking, but what he saw wasn't in this world or even this dimension.

He spoke to him first in Arabic, then in Kurmanji. The old man answered in Farsi. He was Iranian. And delirious.

"I came here for the Ayatollahs," he whispered, with a wistful stare as if he was recounting his autobiography. Or entertaining his grandchildren. "I was sent to infiltrate the Shiite resistance against Saddam. Then the invasion. Then I saw … impossible things."

He seemed to be drifting. Once he did, the oceanic tide would carry him away forever.

Angell shook him gently by the shoulder. Around them, the sound of gunfire was diminishing as the darkness deepened.

"The book? Who has it? Where is it?" he asked in Farsi.

The old man smiled, then coughed.

"They call him the First Priest, the King of this World. The one who speaks to the Old Ones. They were waiting for him. Calling him. They don't know anything about a book."

Angell nodded.

"But you do."

"In Arabic, the *Kitab al-Azif*. Yes. It means the sound of the *jinn*. You understand? *Jinn*?"

Angell was growing impatient, but he was moved by the fact that this old man was dying in his arms. The old Iranian's mind was wandering, and he was mixing Arabic with Farsi and even some Urdu. He was obviously educated and had lived for years underground, a spy in Saddam's camp, living one step ahead of the *Mukhabarat*.

It suddenly dawned on Angell that this man had known Fahim. They were both strangers in a strange land, each with their own reason to be afraid of Saddam's secret police.

On a hunch, he spoke the name.

"Fahim? Yes. My friend. Fahim. And the beautiful Jamila."

He raised his head, with a great deal of effort, and his eyes cleared for a moment as he looked around at the carnage that surrounded them. He grasped Angell's hand.

"Where is she? Where is Jamila?"

"She was *here*?"

"Yezd," he said. For a second, Angell thought he said "yes" in English, but then realized he meant a city in his native Iran.

"Yezd?"

"They will go … yes, Yezd. They will go to Yezd. To Arad. The book must be taken to the People. The People of the Book." At that he started to laugh, but his body went rigid.

Angell closed the old man's eyes with the palm of his hand, and looked up at Aubrey who had been watching intently the entire exchange.

"He says the group here didn't know anything about a book. But they did know about the … that thing on the column. They were trying to wake it up, or something. But he said that Jamila was here, but left to go to Iran."

"Iran?"

"To the city of Yezd. It's in the middle of the country. They have a large Zoroastrian temple there. Eternal flame. The whole thing."

"How the hell …?" Aubrey started thinking aloud.

"Zoroastrians. Iran. Shiites. Yezidis. Yezd. I suppose there is some logic to it. I just wish I had more proof that what the Imam was saying was true."

Angell gently pried the dead man's hand from his own and realized that there was writing on the old man's palm in ink.

"Will this do?"

Someone had drawn a map, using the hand's own contours and lines in the palm as if they were hills and roads, with a small dot and a word in Farsi: *Dakhmeh.*

"What is that?"

"It's a map. Of Yezd. Well, of one place in Yezd. *Dakhmeh.*"

"*Dakhmeh?*"

"The Towers of Silence."

CHAPTER FIFTEEN

THE TOWERS OF SATAN

Of the cult, he said that he thought the centre lay amid the pathless deserts of Arabia, where Irem, the City of Pillars, dreams hidden and untouched.

— H.P. Lovecraft, "The Call of Cthulhu"

Baghdad Airport
Iraq

Incredibly, to Angell, they had managed to leave Tell Ibrahim without encountering any more militants. After a hurried conversation with their escort and an encrypted call to Monroe, arrangements were made to ferry Aubrey and his charge to the Iranian border. This was a hazardous affair, for Iraq was falling and the Iranians were sending troops in a constant stream across their mutual frontier to prop up the Shiite faction in its struggle with the official Iraqi (i.e. Sunni) government as well as the new force in the area, the Islamic State. They had good intelligence on where the safest place to cross would be, but then they would be on their own in getting to Yezd.

Angell was not even sure they should be going there. This whole thing was getting out of hand. If it wasn't for the totally bizarre experience of the ritual that took place at the site of ancient Kutha and the old Iranian Imam with the map on his palm, Angell would not even credit this mission's purpose at all. But he had seen the conviction and the fear in the man's eyes as he lay dying, and it was that dying declaration that convinced Angell to give it another try.

He could not get the image of that sickening idol out of his mind, either.

Aubrey had the foresight to photograph the entire site with his phone, and to take close-ups of the idol as well as of the Imam. He

172

was scrolling through the images on the ride back to the Baghdad Airport. As he did so, he came across another photo: one that he did not remember taking. It was of the teenage sniper having his head blown off.

"Incredible," he muttered, mostly to himself. "Not many could have pulled off a shot like that."

Angell stirred from his reverie in the relative peace and quiet of the back of the old Mercedes and asked Aubrey what he meant.

"The kid who was going to shoot you was shot instead, from behind it looks like. That means someone was in one of the buildings across the road from the park. Another sniper. A guardian angel, or a guardian for an Angell." He smirked to himself. "You have friends in 'high' places," he added.

"Very funny. So what does it mean? Who would it have been?"

"Not one of ours, actually. I know all our assets in theater, and this wasn't one of them. You know the expression, the 'god spot'?"

"No. What does that mean?" He absentmindedly looked at the road outside the window. Their driver was quiet, intent on watching the lead car and following in its tracks precisely.

"It's the sniper's nest. It's the highest terrain around. He sits up there—in a tree, on a rooftop, somewhere like that—and gazes down at humanity. He picks out his target from there, and then fires a single round and ends a life. Like God, in almost every respect. If he's lucky he has a spotter with him, but that is not always the case."

"So this ... this sniper. He was sitting in the god spot?"

"Sure. And he saved your life from there. Also like God."

"Why?"

"Well," Aubrey thought for a moment. "I guess 'God' has other plans for you."

In the back of his mind, Aubrey was entertaining another scenario entirely. One that involved Jason Miller, the AWOL remote viewer. He knew that Miller was after the same thing he was, and suspected that Miller was dogging their every move, as Monroe had suggested.

This last incident only served to reinforce that idea. Jason Miller would protect them just as long as they served his purpose. After that, they were on their own.

Angell appreciated the irony. He had stopped believing in God; or, at least, had stopped loving God, which amounted to the same thing as far as he was concerned. Like when you stop believing in a lover and stopped loving them at the same time, the betrayal poisoning love like a drop of a nasty bacillus in an otherwise limpid pool of clean water. He had devoted his life to studying religion, to traveling to distant lands and learning new and ancient—living and dead—languages just in order to understand God better. And now he figured he *did* understand God, all too well.

Yet … the belief that burned in the old Iranian's eyes as he lay dying in Angell's arms. That Imam had loved God. Some kind of God, anyway. And he had seen far more death and destruction in a single month than Angell had experienced in his entire life. Maybe God was a sociopath, a sophisticated charmer who could make anyone believe anything. And then, when it suited him, would leave you high and dry. Would … would *abandon* you.

Al-Qhadhulu. The one who abandons, who leaves. Who disappears.

Shit, he thought. Was *that* what Lovecraft was trying to tell everyone?

They arrived at Baghdad Airport in the dead of night. They passed checkpoints and drove to a hangar in the military section where a modified (for stealth) MH60-M Black Hawk helicopter was waiting for them. Its rotors were still, and Aubrey told him that they would get something to eat first and refresh their supplies for what might be a long trek inland from the border. They would leave in an hour or so, after he had a chance to talk over the mission with the team leader.

As before, their mercenary escort simply disappeared into the background, anonymous and sober in their black uniforms and blank expressions. As before, Angell never learned their names.

Angell was desperate for a shower and a nap. He could get the shower, and one of the members of the new team showed him where everything was. He was told not to shave, however, as the growth of beard would help disguise him and allow him to blend into his surroundings. Angell had a change of clothes with him but not much else. He had not expected to be out of the country as long as he had been, and now he wasn't sure when he would be allowed to return. He thought of himself as almost a prisoner, of Aubrey and the mysterious Monroe and the ever-shifting cast of military experts who accompanied them everywhere.

The shower was surprisingly modern and efficient, a modular affair at the officers' quarters at the base. He switched from hot water to cold and back to hot again, just to open his pores and massage his tired muscles. As he stood in the steady pour of clean water he noticed that there was a pool of pink water forming around the drain. Startled, he looked at himself to see if he had been hurt, but there was no wound, no scratch that he could see. The blood had to be someone else's.

Gregory Angell, Professor of Religious Studies at Columbia University, New York City and resident of Brooklyn, New York was suddenly very alone and very, very far from home.

He rejoined the group at a conference table in an office just off the large aircraft hangar. Arrayed around the table was a bizarre sight: Starbucks coffee cups and McDonald's cheeseburgers, along with packages of French fries and bottles of Coke.

The man in charge of the team gestured at the spread.

"Help yourself. If you want KFC or Pizza Hut, we have that, too."

He was serious.

Noticing Angell's confusion, he clarified as best he could.

"We had one of the largest fast food installations in the world here, before the rollback. Right now, there's just us and whatever mercenary group is the flavor of the month. Blackwater, of course, in all its iterations. Halliburton. All sorts of corporate security teams. And us.

"Welcome to the temporary home of the 160th Special Operations Aviation Regiment, or SOAR. We will be your tour guides this evening. I understand that Iran is lovely this time of year. Or not."

"You're the ones who flew Seal Team Six into Abbottabad a few years ago." Angell was stunned. This had been all over the news in 2011. In fact, this was the third anniversary of the attack on the Osama bin Laden compound and the execution of the mad leader of Al-Qaeda.

Another "Mad Arab." Something about the phrase nagged at Angell's mind. He knew that it was the creation of his nemesis, H.P. Lovecraft, but there was something else, too.

Aubrey reached over and snagged a single French fry, dipping it daintily into a pool of Heinz ketchup in a small paper cup, before inserting it in his mouth.

"The team doesn't use proper names here," he explained to Angell. "That's for security reasons. And they do not carry identification, or show their rank in any way. It's all by the numbers, or the colors as the case may be."

"That is correct," added the officer from SOAR. "You can refer to me as 'Black.' Yeah, I know, quite a stretch, right?" The man was indeed African-American.

"You will meet the others, and they will have colors for names as well. You will probably not have to engage with them very much, anyway. We are taking you in that helo out there to a location across the Iranian border. We will be flying low to the ground, in stealth mode. We will drop you off, and then return to base. You will have forty-eight hours to make it back to the drop off location to be extracted. It's a tight schedule, I know, and I can't discuss with you the reasons since you're not cleared for classified, compartmented details. Nothing personal. It's just our orders."

"I understand," said Angell, although he really didn't. He picked up a cardboard cup of coffee and added enough cream and sugar to make a cake. He figured he needed all the caffeine, lactose and glucose he could manage.

"You will be met by one of our people who will infiltrate you into a group of tourists that are heading to Yezd. When you get close to your target location you will be separated from the group and will be guided to your final destination. Our operative will then escort you back to the LZ."

Aubrey was oddly quiet during the whole exchange. Angell had the uneasy feeling that something had changed.

The man from SOAR continued.

"Yezd, or Yazd as it's officially spelled by the Iranians when they use Roman letters, is not an easy place to get to from Iraq. For one thing, you have an entire mountain range between here and there. For another, there is no direct highway that cuts across the interior from the border to the city. There are smaller roads, but they are not secure and would take much longer anyway. So you have to take highways that circle around the wasteland in the middle. We can't get you further than about four to five hours' drive to Yezd. Those five hours could get hairy. You have the Revolutionary Guard to deal with, checkpoints everywhere. A good thing is that Iran actively seeks to attract foreign tourists, so there are tour bus operators going from Isfahan to Yezd. They are all, of course, in the employ of the government and should be regarded as informers and spies. Hopefully that won't be a problem because you will have your own car and driver."

There it was.

"You're not going with me, are you, Aubrey?"

The old spy shook his head.

"This is as far as I go, Professor. I would never pass as an Iranian. I don't speak Farsi and I don't know Islam well enough to pass as a

Muslim from Iraq, for instance. I will be waiting here for you to get back, of course. If your mission to Yezd is successful, then we should be able to return Stateside in a few days."

Although Angell had never cared very much for James Aubrey, he had gotten used to relying on him. Now he was going into the lion's den without a whip or a stool.

"You'll have full communications, courtesy of your escort and guide. You'll be fitted with a GPS tracking device so we will know where you are every step of the way. Once we know you are on your way back, these nice gentlemen from SOAR will send an extraction team and you will be on your way to this hangar. It's less than an hour's flight from Baghdad to Yezd itself, of course, so it takes about half of that for us to get you from the extraction point to base."

"We can't take a shorter route from the coastline inland, because that area is heavily monitored by Iranian security forces," added the SOAR commander. "We considered bringing a dhow or sambuk close to the coast and dropping you off from there but the whole thing is too risky. Flying a helo over the mountain range at its lowest point and setting you down outside of Isfahan or Shiraz seemed like the best option. Either way, it's a good five hour drive and that's without checkpoints and other hazards. So you'll have an hour or so at Yezd and then an immediate return. All things being equal, and figuring for unforeseen delays, you should be in-country for only about twenty-four hours, max."

Angell was not convinced.

"An hour at Yezd? How do you figure? I have to find the contact there, get him or her to talk to me, and then figure out the location of the book. It could take hours. Or days."

"Days is not an option," Aubrey replied. "We don't have days. You don't have days. If it is not going well, you're going to have to return without the book."

"Then this was all for nothing?" Angell was thinking of the old man. And the exploding teenage assassin.

"The longer you stay in-country, the greater the chance you

will be discovered. The penalties for espionage—and you will be considered a spy without a moment's hesitation—are harsh. And that's if they let you live."

"But if I don't find the book, then we have no way of stopping this scheme from going forward."

He leaned forward, forgetting the fast food, the smell of French fries, the allure of fresh coffee. Forgetting even his exhaustion.

"I saw what happened at Kutha. I saw what happened in the refugee camp. There is something very strange going on and it involves people who don't care if they live or die. It involves a religion or a cult or something that is as dangerous as anything we have faced out here in a long time, and I'm including Al-Qaeda. This is the worship of Death. And worse.

"It's reaching a fever pitch. I know religion, and I know religious movements. This is a religious movement on steroids. That idol, that obscenity in the center of the ritual at Kutha, can only be an object of veneration by people who have lost all sense of humanity. They keep using the word *qhadhulu*. It's from the Qur'an. It's a demon, a jinnee. An evil spirit. It's an imprecation. A curse. *And they are worshipping it.* And not just Sunnis, but Shiites, too. And maybe some Kurds. Iranians. God knows who else. This could be something that unites all of these warring factions into one movement, something so crazy that it attracts the psychotics of entire nations.

"Look. The old man, the one who died at Kutha, told me they were waiting for the First Priest. This is like the Mahdi, a kind of warrior-Messiah figure. Every time a Mahdi is declared there is widespread violence. Warfare. Bloodshed. But the Mahdi is a subject of controversy and disagreement between the Sunnis and the Shiites. The one they were calling at Kutha was a *universal* Mahdi. One who would satisfy the requirements of *both* Sunnis and Shiites.

"You understand? There is no such thing! It doesn't exist, not even in the wildest imaginations of Islamic theologians. The Mahdi only comes at the time of the Second Coming of Jesus, and together they both cleanse the world of evil. That's the idea. But this ...

this Mahdi … is evil. Satanic. No! More than that. *Other* than that. Like the figure of the Mahdi among the Twelve Shiites, this one is 'hidden.' A Hidden Imam. Dead and buried, but not really dead. They want to summon it, call it back from the dead. They think they can hear it speak. It's … it's *talking* to them."

Aubrey was silent but extremely attentive to everything the professor was saying, for it only reinforced the chatter that had started this whole process going. The remote viewers in their employ had seen the same thing, had *communicated* with it. And now Angell was saying that there were others—many others—who also were communicating with it. Young Jamila was one.

Jason Miller had been another.

"How do you know this, Professor?"

Angell rubbed his eyes with the palms of his hands.

"It was there. During that ritual in Kutha. It was like a revival meeting. Everyone was in synch, from the guys in makeup and halter tops and machine guns to the women in burqas. They all knew their roles. They moved like a single organism, thought like a single organism. The Imam was the ground, like in electricity. He was grounding the energy being raised by the … the worshippers. Except that it really *was* a grounding. Literally. The energy was being sent *into the ground*. Underground. Into the *Underworld*. The rhythmic dancing, stamping of feet … the fires lit everywhere … I mean, that's the whole point of Kutha, right? Why else would they have chosen that spot?

"And it *was* a revival. A *literal* revival. They were reviving a dead god."

There was silence around the table as his words sunk in.

"So it was an act of necromancy, in a way?" This from Aubrey, who knew more about this than he let on.

"Yes. Necromancy. *Necronomicon*, right? Dead names. It's all about reviving the dead. Dead gods. Dead religions. It's like those Tea Party true believers back in the States who are always talking about 'taking their country back.' Except that in this case it's the dead gods who want to take their planet back."

The words flowed out of him. Maybe it was the exhaustion. Maybe it was the experience of being in his first firefight. Maybe it was all the death around him. Or watching the slow implosion of the world and everything good and beautiful in it. But he found himself saying things he would never have thought about so clearly, not in the privacy of his own brain anyway.

"It doesn't matter if *we* believe any of this, or not. They believe it. That's what's so dangerous. *They* believe it. And ... look! Look at the state of the world. All those apocalyptic predictions look like they're coming true. It verifies what they think they know. Validates it. Gives it a voice.

"All they need now is the ultimate validation. These are all People of the *Book*. They need the text, the scripture, to give their darkest emotions form and function. Without the focal point of the text, it all dissipates and withers away. The book is not just a text. It's a roadmap. A circuit diagram. A contract with zombies. It's the social network of demons, a telephone for talking with Satan. It's all the protocols they need to navigate the Pit. That's what they believe, anyway. It was written on their faces, on their foreheads like the Mark of the Beast.

"Imagine a cult, a secret society, that didn't need to be secret anymore. Look what happened when Christianity came out of the catacombs and became a state religion under Constantine. Now imagine something a lot darker than Christianity. Something a lot older. Imagine an Inquisition where a Church is at war with all of humanity.

"Susan Sontag once wrote that white people are a cancer in the world. Later she walked that back, but imagine that there is something ...someone ... who thinks that *all* people are a cancer on this planet, a cancer to be eradicated."

Aubrey stopped him there.

"It doesn't make sense. Why would human beings go along with an agenda like that? Why are there cultists, devotees, whatever you want to call them, of this hideous philosophy and this savage Being?"

Angell took a deep breath, and let it out slowly before replying.

"Because they are in contact with It. It's *real*. Somehow it's real. It talks to them. And because they are dancing to his music. Because they have already lost their souls and their minds. They are just vehicles for It. Puppets. Pawns. Whatever you want to call it. But they still need the Book. Without it, they are just a weird, violent and deeply unsettling road show of suicide bombers and sociopaths, playing the small towns and summer stock. But with it, with that *script*, that *scripture*, they are ready for the big time. They are ready to open on Broadway."

The SOAR commander, who had been listening to it all and not sure what to believe, checked his watch.

"It will be dawn in another two hours. We have to go now, Professor."

The old spy and the religion professor met in front of the Black Hawk helicopter and shook hands. The rest of the Night Stalker team was already on board and the rotors started to turn.

"Best of luck, Professor. I'll be here when you get back. I wish this was the type of mission where we could just send in a covert action team, locate the missing object, and get out quickly. But this is not that mission."

Angell smiled in spite of himself. "You mean you wish you didn't have to rely on somebody like me. I get it. I wish things were different, too. To be honest, I'm scared shitless."

"You're with the best right now, Professor. There are no more highly trained commandos in the world."

"I have no doubt about that. But I lose them at the border."

"You'll be met by someone equally experienced and capable. Your expertise and knowledge are essential to the mission's success.

We wouldn't risk that if we didn't know for a certainty that you will remain safe."

The rotors picked up speed and the two men found themselves ducking from the wash. Aubrey shouted over the racket:

"Good hunting, Professor Angell."

Sitting in the state-of-the-art helicopter, holding on for dear life, Angell watched as the lights of Baghdad twinkled out below him. He had the sinking feeling he would never see James Aubrey again.

Ahead of them, to the east, Angell thought he could make out the faint light of dawn over the Zagros mountain range. Perhaps it was a trick of the imagination, for otherwise the entire scene outside the helicopter was pitch black.

Once they were airborne, one of the SOAR team handed him a small bundle. The man tapped on his ear to signal that he wanted to talk over the communication system. Angell nodded and put on the headset that was handed to him.

"These are clothes. Some of those baggy trousers they wear, and a kind of vest, jacket-type thing. And a cap. Before we arrive at the insertion site you're supposed to change into them. They're to help you blend in. You can keep your other clothes with you in your backpack, or you can leave them with us and we'll get them back to you when we pick you up."

Angell thought a moment and considered. He would need his backpack. He had his reference materials in there. But he was worried that any scraps of paper, notes, and even the books themselves might give him away.

"The GPS locator is sewn into the trousers we provided. Anything else you might need will be in the car at the insertion site."

Angell simply nodded. He would leave his clothes and his backpack with the Night Stalkers. He began to change out of his Western clothes and into the Kurdish trousers.

It was all suddenly becoming very, very real.

The area they were flying to was located just over the mountains, about an hour's drive south of the city of Isfahan but far enough away from that city's air defense batteries and radar systems to enable a quiet insertion with no fanfare. Iran's defense systems were largely Russian and Chinese made, but with newer Iranian-manufactured systems nearing completion. The major cities—like Tehran—had substantial radar operations as well as deadly SAM (Surface-to-Air Missile) batteries. The coastline from the Persian Gulf to the Indian Ocean was also well-defended.

The particular border region east of Baghdad was a favorite of smugglers as well as of Kurdish nomads. Iranian military personnel guarding the border were few and far between in that area, and there was even a certain level of cooperation between the Iraqis and the Iranians when it came to border security. The growing threat of terror cells entering Iran from Iraq was one concern; the surreptitious movement of Iranian troops coming from the other direction was another. Angell's mission was aided by the covert support of a clan of Kurdish *Ahl-e Haqq* adherents operating up and down the mountains: another strange religious sect in a region replete with strange religious sects: Alevis, Yezidis, Nabataeans, Assyrians, Mandaeans, and Zoroastrians to name only a few. The man he was meeting was an American operative who had been trained as a Navy SEAL but who was ethnically a Kurd, born and raised in the Kurdish community in Nashville, Tennessee: home to America's largest Kurdish population. He spoke not only fluent Kurmanji but was also at ease in Sorani and Hurami (sometimes called Gorani), dialects spoken by Iranian Kurds.

The flight across the mountains and to a small clearing somewhere near the town of Shahreza was fast and uneventful. The air was cool, the vast central Iranian plateau—largely inhospitable desert—was looming up before them as the helo touched down gently and Angell jumped off, although with less enthusiasm than he demonstrated. He gave the obligatory thumb's up to the Night Stalkers, who returned the gesture, and then the Black Hawk seemed to ascend straight up as if levitated. It disappeared almost immediately, with only the barest minimum of sound.

Now he simply stood there, in the darkness, and waited.

This was grassland, the mountains rising up in the distance behind him. He shivered a little in the cold. He knew the days would be blisteringly hot as they crossed the desert towards Yazd, and he had no idea if the car coming to pick him up was air-conditioned or not.

Or if the car was coming at all.

At the airbase in Baghdad, James Aubrey was on the sat phone with Monroe, who never seemed to sleep.

"He's in theater now?"

"Yes. The ride is returning to base as we speak."

"And the others?"

"He'll be met by one, but we have assets all around him and on the way to target. He'll be protected."

"He's as important as the target, you know that. We need them both. And the girl, if possible."

"She's not a girl anymore, chief. She's a little disoriented and … off … but that could be the result of what she's been through the past ten years and her peculiar mental capabilities. She's the joker in this deck, and it bothers me."

"ETA?" Monroe changed the subject.

"He will be at the target in about eight hours, maybe less if our luck holds up."

"Keep me posted." He rang off.

Aubrey put down the phone and looked around at the ad hoc conference room they had set up for the mission. There was one officer manning the comms gear and tracking the GPS in a corner of the room. The conference table itself was still littered with coffee cups and the remains of fast food wrappers and cold French fries. It looked a little sad. Like all the cool kids had gone somewhere else without him.

Yes, this was an unconventional mission—the most unconventional in his entire career—and no one was following the rules. Nothing about this latest incursion into Iranian airspace was by the book. The whole thing had the atmosphere of a prank by college kids, frat boys maybe, running some underwear up a flag pole. It was jerry-rigged, put together at the last minute using whatever assets they had, wherever they happened to be, and poaching others on the sly. If they lost that Black Hawk, that was millions of dollars down the tubes not to mention lives. Not to mention an international incident of no small proportion.

And in twenty-four hours, if they were lucky, they would do it all again as they brought Angell back.

Then there was Angell himself. The poor bastard still didn't have a clue as to what was going on. He was half-starved, sleep-deprived, and totally disoriented. He was rushed into this project and when it was all over he would be rushed right back out again. What they were doing was unethical and immoral. And if anything happened to Angell—if he was captured or killed—it would weigh heavily on his conscience. For about a week. That's all it would take for the whole world to fall into the crapper if they failed.

Aubrey needed a shower and a shave. He looked around, got up—his knees creaking with the effort—and headed towards the officers' quarters. You got sleep when you could in this business, and he was overdue.

The sound of a car's engine tickled the edge of his hearing. Angell turned in its direction and saw an old Paykan—an Iranian-made automobile that had been discontinued seven years previously—wind its way up the dirt road to where the drop had been made. This one had to be at least twenty years old, with spots of rust and different color paint that had been worn away by the abrasive sands of the desert winds. Had the car been left parked in that spot, in about a week it would have looked like it grew there.

The car stopped but the engine kept running.

"*Milyaket?*"

Angell got the reference immediately. *Milyaket* is the Kurmanji word for "angel."

"*Ereh*," he answered. Yes.

"Hop in," the driver said, in English.

"You can call me Adnan." He reached over to Angell in the passenger seat and offered his hand. Angell shook it.

"I'm from Tennessee originally, but my parents are from here. That's about all you need to know about me, and that's already too much. I know I am supposed to take you to Yazd, which is a bitch of a drive but at least it's not summer yet when it would be worse. You speak Kurmanji?"

"Yes, I do. And Farsi."

"Okay. Kurmanji is not really the lingua franca around here but I guess you knew that if you speak Farsi. You probably know something about Iranian demographics too, which you will agree are as clear as mud. There are a lot of ethnic minorities, and minorities within minorities. There are a lot of Kurdish dialects, too. So try not to speak if you can help it, and if you have to speak, speak Farsi. You can pass for Iranian, maybe. Depends on your accent. If you have to speak, speak in monosyllables. Yes, no, like that. Don't make any speeches because that's where they'll trip you up."

He looked Angell up and down as he drove.

"You have any paper on you?"

"Pardon?"

"Any ID? Anything at all with writing on it?"

"No. They took all of that back at base."

Adnan nodded, gratefully.

"Okay. So here's the story. We're going to join up with a bunch of pilgrims heading for Yazd. I understand we're not to go into the city but head instead for the Towers, right?"

"Correct."

"Good. They're on the hills south of the downtown area. Not

much goes on up there anymore. I mean, they don't use them for
sky burials like they used to. But tourists go there, both foreign and
Iranian, so we will just be part of the general population."

"Who are these pilgrims?"

Adnan smiled.

"That's the beauty of it. They're all our people. They're family,
you could say."

Angell stared at him, and Adnan—seeing it—laughed out loud.

"Don't worry about it. Sit back, relax, and enjoy one of the
hairiest goddam rides you'll ever experience."

They drove through the town of Shahreza and headed south, towards
Abadeh. It was still quite early, but there was already some traffic.
Adnan was worried that the helicopter had been caught on radar or
by sight, but there was no activity on the road that would suggest
there was a military presence in response.

"There are SAM installations around Isfahan, which is why we
are not going in that direction. Too big a military presence.

"After Abadeh there is a turn-off and we get on another road to
Yazd. It's the long way around, but the roads here are better. If we
try to go direct we will have to cross the plateau and that would
be dangerous, if not impossible in this vehicle anyway. We will be
met at Abadeh, and that will provide us some cover. There's bottled
water in the back seat and some figs, dates, that sort of thing if you
get hungry."

"I'm good, thanks. How long have you been here?"

"Iran?" He smiled. "All goddam day."

The heat began shortly after they left the outskirts of Shahreza and
were on the road driving south to Abadeh. Adnan began speaking
in Farsi to see how well Angell could manage the accent as well
as the grammar. Angell's background had been in classical Persian
but after spending time in Turkey and Iraq he had managed to find
Farsi speakers among some of the Kurds and perfected a colloquial

rhythm, although his accent was tinged with a distinctly Kurdish tone. Adnan did not find that too problematic, for it enabled Angell to pass as an Iranian Kurd. So they chatted amicably for a few hours as they made their approach to Abadeh.

The road passed through some fertile lands, with green fields and vegetation that relieved the rust- and sand-colored lands they were driving through, the mountains still in the distance sometimes giving the impression that they had not moved at all in two hours.

There were the remains of what appeared to be fortifications in places, going back twelve hundred years to the Sassanid times. Crumbling edifices in dusty white stone. Angell felt he was in a mysterious landscape that was no longer really on the Earth. He could understand how so many of the world's most extreme religious views came out of regions like this. The land seemed to float between this reality and some Other.

"There is our connection," Adnan pointed out the windshield of the aging Paykan.

Angell saw a small village with low, white-washed houses scattered on either side of the road.

"Abadeh is another few miles, but here we will meet our escort. They're *Ahl-e Haqq*. You know what that means?"

"It means they're not Muslim, and they're not Yezidis."

"Right. The Iranians put them in the same category as Yezidis, though, which pisses off the both of them. They have a secret book, too." Adnan winked at him.

"You know about that, huh?"

"A few months ago we were told to be on the lookout for any indication that people were talking about a secret book or looking for one, or that some new kind of scripture was making the rounds. When we started getting intel on that, mostly from Kurdish circles, it went right up the chain of command and suddenly here you are. I know you're not a cowboy, but this isn't your first rodeo, either."

"We?"

"Say again?"

"You said 'we were told' … who's 'we'?"

Adnan smiled.

"Why, we in the 'community,' that's who. More than that would be telling."

He pulled over behind one of the squat white houses and put the car in park but did not shut off the engine and did not get out.

"Stay in the car until we are greeted," he suggested to Angell.

"Are there people living here?" He didn't see anything suggesting life in the village. No vehicles, animals, cooking fires, or anything else.

"Just wait. They're checking us out."

Somehow Angell felt relatively secure with the Kurdish boy from Nashville. Maybe because he was an American, like him, in a strange land. Maybe because he was an American who knew the local culture and spoke the local languages, something that always impressed Angell who usually saw so little of that.

Adnan was tall, not yet thirty, with a round boyish face sporting a wispy growth of light brown beard. Dressed in baggy brown trousers (called *rank*) and a brown vest of the same material (called *chogha*) over a white shirt, and a kind of turban, he looked the part but when he opened his mouth and a Tennessee drawl came out Angell could not help but be amused.

In moments, there was the sound of an engine and an old bus could be seen pulling out of one of the squat white buildings. The house evidently served as a garage, and once the bus was all the way out, two men—dressed similarly to Adnan—came out from nowhere and pulled a wooden screen over the opening in the house from where the bus had driven out.

And what a bus. It was belching smoke and fumes and was painted in a bilious shade of yellow with geometric designs in different colors. The emblem on the front of the bus said it was a Mercedes, but Angell had his doubts.

It was smaller than the usual run of tour buses operating in Iran which were usually more commodious and had the painted name of the tour company covering half of the windshield, but it would do. This one could seat about twelve passengers and was little more than a van.

Adnan got out of the car and walked over to the two men who had covered up the garage and they were joined by the driver of the bus. They stood around, speaking quietly, and Angell could not hear a word. He knew they were talking about him, for every few seconds one of the men would glance in his direction.

Just as Angell was about to get out of the car himself and join them, Adnan walked back and got into the driver's seat.

"Change of plans."

"What's going on?"

"There's a roadblock after Abadeh, between Surmaq and Abarkooh. That's the route I was planning to take to Yazd. I don't know the reason for the roadblock, and it probably has nothing to do with you, but it would be better if we avoid it."

"So what do we do?"

Adnan rubbed his eyes wearily, and stared out the windshield at the bus.

"We go as far as Surmaq. From there we get off the highway and go around Abarkooh, pick up Highway 78 a few klicks after it and then it's a straight run to Yazd. But we have to be careful. There may be more roadblocks on the way to Yazd. Good thing for us it's a famous tourist area and there will be a lot of busses on the road."

Adnan put the car in gear and started driving back onto the highway. From the rear, the tour bus followed with its driver and two passengers.

"We're going to pick up more passengers in Abadeh. They'll take the bus. We'll follow once we leave Abadeh and go off road. This may add another hour or so to the drive, but safety first, you know?"

"What if we're stopped?"

"Well ... depends on who stops us. If it's the *sepah*—the Revolutionary Guard—it could be a problem. If it's the *basij*, the militia, we can bargain our way out of it. The key is not showing them you're a foreigner. To the *sepah*, a foreigner is automatically a spy under these circumstances. You have no papers, no suitcase, no visa for Iran. To the militia, a foreigner is a commodity. They'll try to get as much out of us as possible—money, maybe the car—and then turn around and sell you to the Guard anyway."

Angell's heart sank. None of these were good options, especially since they all ended up with him in Guard custody and a certain death sentence. After the appropriate show trial, of course.

"We're not about to let that happen. I don't know what kind of juice you have but I have orders from 'the highest level' as they say to make sure that nothing bad happens to you. My guys back there in the bus are Kurdish smugglers. They do this sort of thing for a living, but usually a lot closer to the Iraq border. We are way inland now, and getting deeper into the heart of the country. They have a network of smugglers all through Iran, but they're usually moving medicine, food, like that. Stuff in bags and boxes and secret compartments. You … well, you present a unique opportunity to diversify their business model, let's say."

"Well, then at least it won't be a total loss."

"That's the spirit. We should be in Abadeh in a few minutes. If I were you, I would look like you're sleeping. Pull that cap down over your face a little. That's it. Don't worry about a thing. We got it covered."

Angell closed his eyes and tried not to feel fear. Adnan was reassuring, but then he had to be. Angell went through all the possible scenarios in his mind, imagining each eventuality. It was true he had no identification on him. There wasn't time for that. They had not known he was going into Iran until that night at Tell Ibrahim. He couldn't use his US passport in Iran, not without the appropriate visas. So he was a stateless person in a country whose leaders constantly called for America to be destroyed.

What could possibly go wrong?

As he mulled over the pros and cons of this approach or that approach, he found himself falling asleep. He had not slept in days, and running on coffee and adrenaline was taking its toll. On top of that it was getting warm in the car, and the motion and heat conspired to lull him into what had started as a cat nap and then evolved into a full-bore slumber.

He was back in his apartment in Red Hook, but it wasn't the same. It was somehow vast, as if the tiny studio had concealed more dimensions than could be seen with the naked eye. His desk, which doubled as his dinner table, was large and dominated the center of the apartment. On it was his incantation bowl, his "demon-trap." The writing was in Aramaic and it spiraled down from the lip of the bowl into its center: a center that kept retreating from sight until the sheer vortex of it drew Angell's eyes down into the maelstrom of its depths where the ink of the script merged to become an extended blackness, a gateway to another world. The writing had begun as an incantation but had degenerated into gibberish with each successive spiral until it had become a scream, a moan of despair that Angell could hear as well as read.

It was a demon-trap, and now Angell was trapped inside it himself.

Adnan was shaking him by the shoulder.

"Look alive, man."

His consciousness stumbled from sleep to wakefulness like a drunk after a three-day binge. He opened his eyes and looked around.

"How long was I out?"

"An hour or so. No big deal."

"Where are we?"

"We just left Abadeh and are heading off-road for a little bit. How are you doing?"

"I guess I was more tired than I knew."

"No shit. Okay, here's the drill."

Angell looked outside the windshield and saw an expanse of

hills in the distance on the left and the main road retreating on his right. The tour bus was on the highway, still heading for Yazd. They were alone on what appeared to be a dirt track of some kind, cut through some low brush and with a stretch of sandy soil and rock after that.

"We're going to go as fast as we can, but that won't be much. The terrain around here is hairy. We don't want to throw a rod or blow a tire, so we are going to be careful. This path is sometimes used by smugglers, and it curves around to the east about ten, fifteen klicks from here and reconnects with the highway."

He reached into the back seat with his right hand for a large duffle bag, his left still holding the wheel as they bumped along the road.

"Open that, will you?"

Angell unzipped the bag and saw a small collection of weapons. He recognized a Sig Sauer, a Heckler & Koch, an Armalite assault rifle with its 30-round magazine, an old Bulldog revolver. And boxes of ammunition.

"What's this for?"

"Like I said, this road is used mainly by smugglers. Nice guys, some of them. Some of them, not so nice. Better to be safe than sorry, right?"

"Jesus."

"Don't sweat it. They're mostly for show. When we come upon a jeep or a van we just keep them in plain sight and they'll leave us alone. They'll figure us for fellow smugglers and violence is bad for business. Well, unless the outcome is guaranteed in your favor. But even then you don't know whose clan you'll piss off if you waste a guy on the road. That leads to blood feuds, and there have been plenty around here. So easy does it, just remain calm, and we'll be back on the highway in no time."

The sun was high overhead now, and there was a reflection shimmering off the rust-colored terrain in front of them. Except for the sound of their engine there was absolute silence, as if they were driving through someone's living room and there was no one home. The dream still bothered Angell, who remembered it clearly on awaking.

"We'll get a call on this burner phone when the bus has passed the checkpoint." Adnan waved a small cell phone in front of him. "They'll let us know how serious it is and what they're looking for. They're probably just looking for smuggled goods and baksheesh. But we need to be sure."

A question had been bothering Angell, and now was the perfect time to ask it.

"You're Kurdish, right?"

"Yep. My parents were from a town closer to the Iraqi border, up north of here, called Kermanshah."

"Muslim?"

"No. I mean, there are Islamic elements. Some people associate us with Twelver Shia, since one of our principal … well, we call them assistants … is Ali, who is an assistant to God for us but the rightful heir to the Prophet's throne, as it were, for the Shia. We're a minority sect, pretty much everywhere we go. As I said, the people helping us are Kurds of the *Ahl-e Haqq* religion. I was brought up in that, sorta."

"Sorta?"

"It's not like we had a support group out there in Nashville, son. We were on our own. We didn't have a *sayyed*, you know, a religious leader. Each group within our sect is called a *khandan*. It's like a tribe or clan. The leader is the *sayyed*. Our *sayyed* is here in Iran, in Kermanshah. Still is. But you see only the leader knows all the rituals, the theology, and like that. And has the book."

"The book?"

"Yeah. It's called the *Saranjam*. Well, the main one is called that. There are others, and they're secret. We're pretty much like the Yezidis that way. In the west, people think they know about the two main Yezidi scriptures, but they really don't. What they have is like summaries or abbreviated versions, designed for outsiders. We're the same."

"So how do you get along with the Muslims?"

Adnan snorted.

"Out here, they're mainly Shiites. You know that, right? Now Shiites can be pretty out there when it comes to how most people understand Islam. They have some different holidays, and they accept more variation. Like I said, sometimes they consider us a weird branch of Islam, because of Ali. And we have reincarnation, which is problematic for Islam. But everyone hates the Kurds anyway, right? They leave us alone for the most part since we are not really 'People of the Book' but we have these, like, crossover elements. Other times, they persecute us. That's why my parents left Iran around the time of the first Gulf War. They took advantage of all the confusion and crossed over into Iraq, and from there got themselves to the States. It took a while, but they managed it."

Angell had the distinct impression Adnan wasn't telling him everything, but he let it slide. He didn't want to know too much, anyway. You never knew when some information became too much information.

"They kept the language and what they knew and remembered of the religion. They met up with some other Kurds, not all of them *Ahl-e Haqq*, and managed to hold onto an identity of sorts. I grew up half American and half Kurd, like a lot of us."

Angell decided to dive right in.

"You noticed weird shit happening out here lately. That was the intel you mentioned earlier. What was it, if you can tell me? I mean, as far as religion and new religious movements are concerned?"

Adnan thought a moment before answering.

"I guess you must be cleared, since you're the one on the mission and I'm just logistical support. But if they didn't tell you, I shouldn't be. You know what I mean?"

Angell nodded. "Yeah, I know."

They passed in silence a few moments.

"Well, I can't read you in but I can tell you whatever is open source on the subject."

"Open source?"

"Yeah, some of it has made the papers around here. You would see it if you were here long enough. Which you won't be. But anyway. There were some reports of a violent extremist group operating in the central part of the country, and then an outbreak on the border with Afghanistan. Yeah, it was crazy."

"But doesn't that just mean another terror group, or some Islamic fundamentalists?"

Adnan looked over at him and shook his head.

"Not these guys. It wasn't like they were agitating to overthrow the ayatollahs or anything like that. It wasn't quite that sophisticated, if you know what I mean. The Guard came down hard against them, though. Calling them infidels and blasphemers, even idolaters. It doesn't get much worse than that around here."

"Idolaters?"

"Yeah. That's what's got everybody's panties in a twist. I mean, we got the Zoroastrians here and they've kept that flame alive in their temple at Yazd for like three thousand years. They're tolerated by the ayatollahs. But this … this was worse. Much worse. Some kind of orgy, with dancing, music, and all around an *idol*. In Iran, you're just asking for an execution if you are into that shit. A slow execution, after a slow torture. From what I hear, the Guard beheaded like twenty of these guys. Some of them were even Kurds."

Angell thought back to the eerie night at Tell Ibrahim, ancient Kutha, and shivered.

"The location? Where did this happen, exactly?"

"Exactly?"

"Yes. If you can tell me."

"Oh, I can tell you. But I don't think you wanna know."

He looked over and smiled a big, toothy smile that was somehow sinister for all its apparent friendliness.

"It's where we're going, my friend. The ritual was at Yazd."

Renegade remote viewer Jason Miller has stopped to rest at a small village south of Shiraz. He is dressed like an Iranian sheepherder with a full beard and a turban, and carrying a walking stick through the dusty landscape. In the distance he can see a plume of dust and smoke signaling the presence of a motorized army patrol. He judges the distance as about five kilometers. He watches for a minute, and sees that the patrol is heading away from his location. He nods to himself, satisfied.

Sitting on a rock in the hot sun, he closes his eyes and slows his breathing. His mind sees a screen in front of him, empty, blank, but full of a humming presence. Like space itself, a total darkness permeated by invisible particles no one suspected were there.

These particles coalesce on his screen and begin to form images. His breathing has slowed to the point that it is barely there, and the images grow stronger. He sees a crowd of people. He can't make out their faces. He sees a circle, ever expanding outward from the center of the crowd.

The index finger on his left hand is scribbling furiously in the dirt, making circles, mandalas, complex geometric designs, which are then erased and new drawings, new scribbles replace them as his vision continues.

The particles break apart, coalesce again, form patterns, images, icons, symbols. All language is symbol, is ritual, is art. A train of thought. He hitches a ride on a train of thought. It's older than civilization, older than the Earth. It's a train of thought that spirals outward from the center of time, embracing everything, preserving nothing.

Scribble. Scribble. A helix. A moebius strip. A tower.

A tower rising from the desert sands. A minaret. A mosque. No. Not a mosque. But a minaret nonetheless. A wind-catcher. Spirit catcher. Dream catcher.

Train of thought. A long, ancient train of eldritch thought by a creature, a Being, a God … but not of this Earth. A train of thought spiraling … spiraling … now running straight as a laser … running parallel … no, perpendicular … perpendicular to the planet …

The tower again. A spiral rising from the Earth with its roots deep underground. An artesian well of sinister power, drawing on the fetid ichor of a buried coffin, a sarcophagus, and the Being floating within it. A circle. In the center the tower.

His eyes still closed, he is writing in the sand.

Finally, he opens his eyes and reads what he has written.

Arabic letters. *Al- liha al-ahy ' as-sarmadiyya al-qad ma.*

"The living, the eternal, the ancient gods …"

Jason Miller now knew where the American professor was going. He was linking to a string of temples that cut across all of Central Asia and to the ends of the Earth. A network that has been maintained since time immemorial for just such a moment as this.

Alhamdullilah, he said aloud, softly, ironically. *Thank God.*

He stood up and erased the writing, stretched, and looked around. He would have to hustle if he was going to get to the site before the professor and lie in wait for the drama to play out. But at least now he knew more than the professor and his entourage.

He knew the endgame.

Chapter Sixteen

The Towers of Silence

The most merciful thing in the world, I think, is the inability
of the human mind to correlate all its contents.

—H. P. Lovecraft, "The Call of Cthulhu"

The drive back onto the highway was blessedly uneventful. The tour
bus that was their escort stopped to wait for them, letting its passengers stretch their legs and the driver tinker with the engine as cover
for their delay. As Adnan drove up onto the highway from the dirt
road alongside, the passengers quickly got back on the bus and they
all started off for the straight run to Yazd, but not before Adnan got
out and had another confab with the others.

Angell got out of the car to stretch and look around. It was a
bleak landscape, even in the shimmering light of the sun. All around
were dung-colored hills and grey rock. There were towns that
hugged the highway, but once off of it there was nothing. Nothing at
all. It was beautiful in the way a ghost town is beautiful: the absence
of any living presence forces the mind to populate the scene with
ghosts of one's own.

He took a swig from a plastic water bottle and let a few drops
fall onto his hands so he could scrub some of the dust off them. He
wiped his face with a paper tissue he had dampened with the same
water, and looked up to see Adnan coming towards him.

"We better leave now," he said, heading for the driver's side. "We
got word there is a militia patrol coming up from Abadeh. There
were rumors of a plane or helicopter violating Iran's sacred air space
this morning. There are always rumors like that, but for some reason
they are taking this one seriously."

The sound of the bus's engines preceded them. Angell got back
in the car and they pulled out behind the bus.

"What if they notify the checkpoints ahead of us?"

"There shouldn't be any checkpoints between here and Yazd, but you never know. Should they set up a roadblock our people ahead will let us know and we will take evasive action while they create a diversion. It's okay. We've done this before, many times."

Angell opened his mouth but was stopped by Adnan.

"Don't ask," he said, with a smile.

On the way up the highway Angell asked about the cult activity in Yazd.

"You know we have many religious minorities here, as there are in Iraq, Jordan, Lebanon, and throughout the Middle East and North Africa. We're used to them. Hell, I'm a religious minority. But these guys … they were something else. Suicidal too, if you ask me. No one has any illusions about what life is like in this country if you're not a member of the Shi'a majority. Even the Shiites themselves are persecuted for minor violations of the laws set down by the ayatollahs.

"Iranians thought they were free once they got rid of the Shah. The Savak, his secret police, were hated and feared. The people thought that having a country based on religious law instead of secular law would be a relief. It wasn't. It was just the exchange of one set of tyrants for another. And everyone knows the Shah was propped up by the Americans. Hell, we even installed him here. You know about that, right?"

Angell nodded, gloomily. "Yes. The CIA overthrow of Mossadegh."

"Yep. Once we got rid of that old bastard we brought the Shah out of mothballs and had ourselves an ally in the Middle East. But it was a two-edged sword. The Shah treated his people like enemies. The Iranians knew that he was a puppet of the United States, and they figured once they got rid of him they would be okay. But they were wrong."

"So … what does all of this have to do with a cult in Yazd?"

"That's just it. Their leader turned out to be a wanted man. One of the Shah's own bad guys. Savak."

"Jesus. After all this time? What's it been, like … thirty-five years?"

"Yes, sir. The guy was an interrogator, and you know what that means. He's pushing seventy … or he was when they caught him."

"Was he one of the ones they …?"

"Beheaded? No. As far as we know he was taken to Evin Prison in Tehran. That's pretty much where all the political prisoners wind up. There are still some there who were arrested in '79 when the ayatollahs came to power. It's notorious. A hell on Earth."

"Why would they keep him alive?"

"Well, I figure, to give him some of the same treatment he gave them back in the day."

Angell shivered, even though it was at least 80 degrees Fahrenheit in the car.

"Most likely, though, they'd want to know how he was able to stay on the lam for so long. You know, who his networks are, that sort of thing. And why he got involved with that weird-ass cult. Makes no sense, really. Unless the guy just lost his mind."

"Sounds like it."

"But the Guard. You know, they gotta figure that the cult was part of some wider network of terror cells or something. The line between cultist and terrorist is mighty thin in these parts."

Something occurred to Angell. "Wouldn't they be turning Yazd upside down right about now, looking for other members of the cult?"

Adnan shrugged.

"Well. Ordinarily you would be right. But they got some actionable intel that said the surviving members had fled to Isfahan."

"Really? How do you know that?"

"*I'm* the source for that particular intel. So just sit back and enjoy the ride. In another few hours we'll be at the Towers of Silence."

When they arrived at the outskirts of Yazd, Angell saw immediately why the tour bus was so essential to their mission. He had been wondering about that the whole way, since it didn't seem to do anything except precede them on the highway. Here, as the road signs told them they were approaching the city, the bus slowed down and Adnan slowed down behind it on the shoulder.

Two men exited the bus and started walking away, down the road in the direction of the town. The bus started up again and they were on their way. Adnan followed.

Angell was mystified by the maneuver.

"They're gonna reconnoiter. We've got only another klick or so to go before we reach the Towers. These guys are gonna make sure there isn't a welcoming committee."

"But ... they're walking. We'll arrive long before they do."

"Not to worry, my friend. We know what we're doing."

They drove along for another few minutes and saw the signs for the Zoroastrian burial ground, the *dakhmah*: the famous Towers of Silence.

The approach was eerie. It was part tourist attraction, part cemetery. Angell was reminded of the Recoleta in Buenos Aires, the place where Evita Peron had been buried which was now a tourist attraction as well. He had once walked among the mausoleums with their broken sarcophagi, bones of the dead clearly visible through the wrought iron gates and doors.

The Towers of Silence, however, did not have the claustrophobic feel of the Recoleta. It was an open plain, dotted with small buildings that had served as shelter and chapels for the Zoroastrian priests who maintained the site and which were now in disuse. In front of them were two hills, and at the top of each were stone, clay and brick towers. On top of those towers—until about forty years ago—the Zoroastrians placed their dead in the open air so that the vultures could consume their bodies. It was a practice that could be found throughout the Zoroastrian world as far as Mumbai in India, which also has its Towers of Silence. In Tibet, open-air burials are also to be found although the Zoroastrian influence there is debatable.

As they drove up to the parking area behind the bus, Angell saw in the distance the two men they had left by the side of the road only a few minutes earlier.

"They're already here?" he asked.

"The road to the Towers goes around a little from the highway. They took the direct route. We wanted to be sure there were no militia on the side away from the road, so that was their function. Now the rest of the passengers from the bus—all our people, you understand—will fan out around the Towers. They look like tourists and they will act like tourists but they are our bodyguard. They will blend in with everyone else and not be noticed."

It was true. There were other tourists in the area, walking quietly among the low, white-washed buildings and staring up at the towers around them. Some were Europeans or Americans, in carefully-chaperoned groups by government-approved tour guides. Others were local Iranians. In a moment it was nearly impossible to tell who their escorts were from the real tourists.

They passed one group, and Angell heard Americans speaking English. He almost turned around but Adnan grabbed him by the arm.

"Careful," he whispered. "You're not an American here. Remember that."

Angell swallowed and nodded.

Adnan looked over to him and winked.

"It's showtime."

There was a low, squat building with five domes and open archways. It was separated from the other buildings, towards the edge of one of the two hills with the towers. Adnan and Angell walked towards it but without seeming to do so. They wandered in a circular pattern, sometimes separating from each other, at other times wandering closer until they both arrived at the entrance to the building at about the same time. Adnan was alert to any possibility that their presence was being noticed, and he made eye contact with one of his people who looked back, expressionless. So far, so good.

Angell found himself trembling a little at the realization of where he was and what he was doing. If the Iranian security forces found him, he was either dead for sure or would wind up in Evin Prison and be tortured ruthlessly. At the same time, if he did not follow through then many thousands—if not millions—of people would suffer and die as the result of this crazy cult. The weight of the responsibility fused with the sense of imminent danger, and it made him lose his breath.

"You okay, man?"

Angell just nodded.

"Let's do this."

The light was dim inside the building, refreshing after the glare from the sun that reflected off the white structures all around them. It was not exactly cool, but there was a sensation of death in those dark rooms that made the two men shiver.

The room they were in was the main part of the building, directly under a small central dome. There was nothing but sand and grit and broken bricks on the floor. No decoration on the walls, and no furniture. There were open windows on the sides that had never had glass. There were three smaller rooms at the rear of the building that seemed similarly empty.

"We're supposed to wait here. Someone will contact us," said Adnan.

"How do you know?"

"Once your people understood where we were going they made some contacts, me being one of them. We analyzed the name you were given, Arad, and made contact first to be sure it wasn't a trap."

They heard a sound, and from the gloom at the central area at the rear of the building a figure began to emerge from the shadows.

It was a small boy with startlingly blue eyes and hair the color of a desert night. He held up a finger to his lips, the gesture of silence amid the Towers of Silence, and pointed up.

Towards the Tower.

"I guess we're going up," said Adnan. The boy smiled and ran off on some other mysterious errand.

There are two Towers at Yazd, towers of death where thousands of corpses have been placed over the centuries to decompose in the open air and be devoured by vultures. Angell could not help but think of those other two Towers, the ones that claimed members of his own family on that September morning thirteen years before.

What was the connection between those two, lightning-struck, towers and the ones before him in this remote part of Iran?

The way up was a winding road that went partway around the hill and ended in a few stairs carved out of the rock. They passed tourists coming down from the tower, women in black veils from Iran and women from Europe and America in windbreakers and carrying cameras, men from many countries in jackets and hats against the sun, and could not imagine that their contact would have chosen so open and public a place for such an important meeting.

As they climbed higher up the hill they could see the city of Yazd in the distance. All around the site were roads, small buildings, what appeared to be a modern-looking housing complex, and the signs of everyday life. A brick wall separated the parking area from the site itself. As they walked up the path to the top of the tower they noted graffiti here and there, a lot of broken masonry and crumbled stones, and a dryness about the place that tickled their throats with its dust. This was a cemetery of a cemetery, a graveyard for a graveyard.

On the wall of the tower, near the narrow entranceway, was more graffiti. This time it looked obscene at first until Angell got a better look. It was some kind of animal, almost cartoonish. Like a talking fish. He stopped briefly, its design reminiscent of another he had seen, the one at Mosul just before the massacre. He thought no more of it at the time, but the memory of it would come back to haunt him.

When they finally reached the top and walked through a narrow entryway to the burial area itself they found themselves strangely alone. The tourists had all gone down ahead of them, as if on cue. Suddenly they were back in the open air, under the direct sun.

They were standing on the edge of a giant circle. In the center of the circle was what used to be an ossuary pit for the bones of the dead but which now was filled with stones. From this vantage point they could look down on the site below and on Yazd itself in the distance, but the view was lost on Angell as he realized that so many dead bodies had been left where he was standing, to rot in the sun and feed generations of vultures. It was like Ground Zero, desert version. It was while thinking about this that he jumped at the sound of a voice coming from somewhere behind him.

He was tall, and gaunt. Although he wore a long black robe over what appeared to be a white tunic he looked rail-thin. His hands had long, boney fingers that seemed preternatural, almost feral. A beard that reached down to his waist was the most impressive part of the old man's appearance. Gray tinged with black, at first Angell thought it was an article of clothing. A trick of the light and the strange circumstance of their meeting.

"*Salaam*," came the raspy greeting in Farsi by way of Arabic. Peace.

"*Salaam*," Adnan replied, his hand over his heart in a gesture of greeting.

"*Khosh amadid*," the old man offered. Welcome. "I am Arad."

He then turned to Angell, who so far had said nothing.

"You are *al-malak*?" he said in English, but using the Arabic word for "angel."

Angell smiled at the usage in spite of himself.

"Perhaps *al-malak al-din saqatu*," he said, using the Arabic for "fallen angel."

The old man was not amused.

"Be careful, my son. These are not subjects for levity."

"My apologies, sir."

"You have come about the book." It was a statement, not a question. It seemed everyone and his brother knew about the book and Angell's quest for it, no matter how far he traveled or under what circumstances.

"Yes, this is true, *mobad.*" Mobad. A priest.

The old man nodded.

"I am a priest of the prophet Zarathustra, whom you call Zoroaster. It is the oldest monotheistic religion in the world. I have lived all my life here in Yazd, except for two years abroad to study before the Revolution. Your name was given to me by a friend who lives in Mosul, who was contacted by a man from Tell Ibrahim. They are Yezidi, I think you call them. They are Yezidi, but they are not from Yazd," he said, with a slight smile at the pun.

Angell nodded. "Yes. We were told to look for you. Here. We were told you would be expecting us."

The old man expelled some air, and then relaxed.

"I would ordinarily offer you some tea and some hospitality. Unfortunately the circumstances require that we be brief. There were some difficulties here a little while ago. You have heard about this."

"Yes, sir. We have."

"These people ... these demoniacs ... they also came here looking for the book. But they were confused."

Angell looked at Adnan, who shrugged as if to say, "I don't know, either."

"Confused?"

"These are called the Towers of Silence in English, yes?"

"Yes."

"But there are other Towers. Our Towers can be found wherever there are members of our faith, as far away as India. But the other Towers, they are not part of our religion. The other Towers are of Angra Mainyu, the evil Spirit, the one called Ahriman. They form a network that stretches from Iraq to Mongolia. Ours are Towers of death, it is true. We lay the bodies in circles at the top of each Tower, here," he pointed to the circular area in which they were standing. "Men on the outside, women in the middle, and children at the very center. We return our physical forms to the World. But the other Towers, the Towers of Shaitan, are edifices built to resurrect dead gods. It is blasphemy. Criminal. A system of channels that runs through the Earth, connecting the putrefaction of corpses and consolidating it as the material basis for their High Priest to return."

The old man had run out of breath and held up a hand to support himself against a wall as he spoke.

"You must stop them," he gasped. "You must not let them get the book."

Angell went up to him then, and touched him on the shoulder.

"You need to rest," he said. "Do you need water? We have some …"

"No, no," he interrupted, holding his head erect with some effort. "I am old, that's all. I used to prepare burials here, back before the Revolution. Now we bury our dead underground, like the Muslims. But we use concrete blocks, all around. *We seal them in so they do not touch the earth.* So they are not … how do you say … grounded. We cannot let them use our dead as … as batteries, or, or, food … for their High Priest."

"But who are they? Who are those who seek the book? Yezidis?"

The old man looked startled. "Yezidis? No."

"But they have towers, outside Mosul, Lalish, and at Sinjar …"

"Yes, yes," the old man said, waving his hand impatiently. "Those are shrines of their faith. Because they are said to worship the Devil, they are accused of maintaining the Towers of Satan. But this is not true. The Yezidis are guardians, since ancient times."

"So, then, who …?"

Adnan interrupted to say that his cell phone was ringing and he was going to take the call outside, in the entranceway. He left Angell there with the old man, who then pressed him for an answer.

"We Zoroastrians are an ancient people. We are older than

Christians, Muslims, even the Jews. But the people who seek the book are even older. They have harbored a resentment against all humans for thousands of years. Since the rise of human civilization, which they abhor. Our brothers, the Yezidis, may be just as old. They know the old words, the ancient rituals, from Sumer and Babylon. The Yezidi towers are a fortress against the evil of the worshippers of the Ancient Ones. We call the leader of the Ancient Ones by the name of Ahriman. But the old word for their High Priest is known to every culture in the world by the same name: *al-Qhadhulu*. Kutulu."

That name again.

"Who are they? How can we tell …?"

"They are everywhere. They play with religion the way politicians play with politics, the way bankers play with money. They have no name, none that is known to us. They operate through other groups, even other cults. When a religion sheds human blood as part of their rituals, they are revealed. Their gods need human sacrifice."

Adnan came rushing back in to the circle.

"We have to move. Now."

"What's happening?"

"My people got word over the radio that militia have been alerted to the presence of enemies of the state at the towers. We don't know how, or why the Guard isn't involved, but we can't take any chances."

The old man grabbed Angell by both shoulders with a strange gesture. For the first time Angell realized that the old man was blind, with cataracts clouding his vision.

"Their priest speaks to his followers in dreams. Dreams while they are awake. He is dead, but not dead. He sleeps and dreams in his death and sends dreams to others. They follow his commands."

"Let's go! Now!" Adnan ran to the entrance and looked in all directions, waving at Angell as he did so.

Angell tried to wrest himself away from the man's strong grasp.

"Kafiristan! The book is in Kafiristan. Find it before the others do! Seek the Katra in Kamdesh!"

Angell got out of the grasp of the old Zoroastrian priest, but could make no sense of the words he said. But their alliteration— Katra of Kamdesh—stayed with him. And as for Kafiristan, he knew very well where that was.

It was in Afghanistan.

He walked quickly behind Adnan who signaled his men with a gesture. He could see people returning purposefully to their bus, walking quickly but not running. Their car was parked alongside, but before they could get to it they saw two jeeps slam on their brakes just outside the brick wall.

"Wait." Adnan stopped in his tracks.

"What's wrong?"

"We're not going to make it to the car in time. Let's walk back up to the tower and see what happens."

Slowly, Adnan and Angell turned and started walking back up, hoping they would not be noticed from the street. Behind them, their tour bus passengers began getting back on the bus as if nothing was happening. One man did not join them but instead walked over to the car driven by Adnan.

"Good thing I left my keys in the car, as always," he said.

"Why?"

They had just made it to the top of the stairway and were looking down from the darkened entryway.

"If everyone left the parking lot and that car was still there, it would have alerted the militia that there was still someone on-site.

"We might be safe up here if we need to lie low. Let's just wait a spell and see what happens."

Angell was by now quite nervous. It looked like the worst possible scenario was about to play out.

"Hey," he whispered to his companion. "Where's the old priest? Wasn't he in the tower when we left?"

They were strangely alone in the tower. Adnan looked around. "Didn't see him leave. He would have been right behind us."

"He didn't look well. If the militia finds him, questions him, he won't stand up. He'd have to talk, and it wouldn't take much. We need to be sure we're not compromised. Is there another way off this tower?"

Angell began walking around the perimeter of the circle, looking for a hidden exit or a fake wall. Like something from the movies. *Indiana Jones and the Towers of Silence*, maybe.

The sun was low on the western horizon. Shadows, long and menacing, were everywhere, stretching out from the hilltops and the towers like the old man's long fingers.

From the side of the tower opposite the entrance came a sound.

"Did you hear that?"

"What?"

"From the back of the tower. It sounded like a cough or a rattle."

Adnan said something in Farsi, just loud enough to carry to the rear of the structure. There was no answering call.

"He's not here. He got out somehow. There's a bad section of the wall back there," he pointed to where some bricks had come loose and were littering the floor of the circle.

Angell walked quickly in that direction, hugging the wall as he did so. And he heard the sound again as he got closer to the breach.

"It's the old man."

Angell looked through the broken masonry to see the old priest sitting against the tower wall. At his feet was a straight drop down the hill. If he moved another few inches he would fall and probably be killed from banging against the shards of rock and brick in the way down. Angell reached over to get Arad's attention, and his hand came away with blood on it.

Adnan rushed over to where Angell was trying to revive the priest. He was more interested at the moment in what was happening to his people on the ground, but Angell was his reason for being there in the first place. The two of them lifted the man up and brought him back inside the tower. There was no way he was going to make it down the hill on his own.

"He was already wounded when he spoke with us. I wondered why he was holding onto the wall. Thought it might have been a heart attack, or something. But it was this."

He moved the old man's robe aside and showed Angell a slash that looked like it was made by a large knife or machete. It had gone through the robe and tunic and they hadn't seen it against the black color of the robe.

"Someone tried to kill him. He's still alive, but barely."

Angell already knew that they weren't taking him to any hospital. It would be suicide for all of them.

"Is there anything we can do?"

Adnan just shook his head.

"We can bind him up the best we can, but that's about all. I have a little water left in the bottle." He handed the plastic bottle to Angell who unscrewed the cap.

"If we don't do something soon, the old man will die."

"*I know that*," hissed Adnan. "You think I don't know that?"

The dying man tried to speak. Adnan and Angell both leaned down to hear him. His voice was weak and his last conversation with them took everything out of him.

"Leave me in the Tower," he said, in Farsi.

Outside there was a gunshot. And then another.

"Let me die where I belong …here, as a priest of Zoroaster."

Adnan was clearly agitated. The gunshots told him they had only moments before they would be discovered. And … he worried about his men outside.

"There's no time. I have to see what's going on out there. Be ready to move when I say. Sit the old man down and get ready to run for it."

Without waiting for an argument Adnan slid across to the entrance and peered out at the commotion.

The militia had blocked the buses from leaving and were rounding up the tourists. The shots he heard must have been warning shots, intended to herd the gaggle of tourists into a single place in the parking lot. No one seemed to be paying any attention to the buildings in their direction, at least not yet. He could see his car parked where he left it.

One of the militia men was talking to the tourists, one by one, asking them questions. The others were spread out around the lot, their weapons hanging loosely at their sides. They were not expecting trouble. Maybe it was only a spot check. Most of the tourists would be foreigners, mostly from those countries which still allowed travel to Iran.

Or maybe it was something far, far worse.

"Who did this to you?" Angell asked the priest in his own language. "Was it the Guard, the militia …"

He could barely speak, and his tongue kept moving over his lips as if seeking some drop of moisture. His breath was coming in shallow gasps and Angell knew there was not much time. Angell tried to get him to drink, but instead he took the water in his hand and made a sign with it over his face.

"*Daghaneh* …" he whispered then in Angell's ear. "*Daghaneh.* Their priests…"

He was obviously delirious, thought Angell with tremendous sympathy for the man. Although Angell had no use for religion or God any longer, he could see the tremendous humanity in this man who risked his life for what he believed.

Blood was still pooling around his body. Angell gently tore a piece of the robe to use as a bandage to staunch the flow and bind his chest the best he could. The pure white tunic was now half scarlet. Angell knew that the Zoroastrians hated impurity of any kind. And this old man, thought Angell, must be one of the last of the *mobad*, the priests. There were not many left in all of Iran.

He looked up anxiously, expecting Adnan to appear at any moment. It was growing a little darker as the sun stretched out over the western hills. He wondered if there was a fast way down the tower behind them. He hoped the militia would be superstitious enough that they wouldn't climb up to see if anyone was hiding there.

The militia was a civilian group, as opposed to the more tightly trained and official Revolutionary Guard. There were criminal types among the militia, including smugglers. He didn't know from first-hand experience if they included violent psychopaths among their ranks but he wasn't about to find out.

"*Daghaneh*," he said again.

That's when it hit Angell. The old priest was using a word he hadn't heard in years, not since he taught undergrad classes in Sumerian and Babylonian religion. *Daghaneh* meant Dagon, one of the oldest deities of Mesopotamia. Dagon was sometimes depicted as a fish god, or half-man, half-fish. He was associated with death and even murder. The old man was saying that priests of Dagon had attacked him. Presumably that was his name for the cult that slashed him looking for the book.

Terrific, thought Angell. *Dagon. Another friggin' fairy tale.*

That was when the gunfire started in earnest.

From the top of the other Tower of Silence came the first shots, aimed in the general direction of the militia guarding the group of tourists. Everyone hit the ground, with the militia trying to return fire but not certain which of the towers was being used as a sniper's nest. Angell heard the staccato rapid fire of what was probably an AK-47 or a Chinese AKM. He had heard them often enough the last time he was in Iraq. He left the priest by the side of the building and crept around to get a better look and to find out what happened to Adnan.

He found the agent huddled in the doorway, talking on a cell phone. He seemed to be directing the operation from there.

He looked up as Angell approached and held out a hand to stall him.

"Keep them pinned down," he shouted into the phone. "They'll call for backup any minute but it will take a while for it to get here," he said in the local Kurdish dialect.

"What's going on? Who's doing the shooting?"

"Our guys. The two who left the bus earlier. They're creating a diversion so we can get out of here."

"But they're calling attention to us."

"They're calling attention to the *other* tower."

"Why couldn't we just sit it out and wait for the militia to leave?"

"Because they're not militia. And they're not the Revolutionary Guard."

Adnan looked at Angell with something like pity mixed with fear.

"Somehow our communications were compromised. Someone either got to the contact in Tell Ibrahim or the one in Mosul. Whoever was responsible, it doesn't matter now. It's the cult, whatever members survived the purge by the Guard, and god dammit they're here looking for you."

Behind them, Arad—the aged Zoroastrian priest—breathed his last.

On the plain below, the cultists belonging to the same group they had encountered in Tell Ibrahim were taking cover behind the old adobe buildings on the ground and trying to return fire to the tower, but they were out of range. They would have to get closer, but they were essentially pinned down. The two shooters in the second tower had the advantage. Adnan was unarmed. His weapons were all in the trunk of his car. He hadn't wanted to be caught with a firearm for it would have meant a certain death sentence if he was caught. Instead, he relied upon his team to provide firepower when necessary. Now, however, he wished he had his pistol, if nothing else.

"We can go down the hill unseen if we don't use the path. This way," he said, pointing to a perilous-looking section of the hill facing away from the parking area. "From there we can get picked up by one of our team. The cultists are not paying much attention to the tourists now, figuring the shooters are their target. If any of them can get away they'll drive the bus into Yazd. This way the bad guys will follow the bus, and not us."

Angell just nodded. He was too frightened to be of much use as a conversationalist.

"Did you get what you needed? From the old man?"

Angell swallowed, then answered.

"Yes. He told me where to go next."

"Don't tell me. I don't have a need to know. Save it for the debrief. My mission now is to get you back to the extraction site."

Angell looked down the hill in the direction Adnan had suggested. It was not going to be easy.

"We were set up, weren't we?"

"Not exactly. Someone got turned somewhere along the line. It would have been after you got the intel about Yazd. They got to the priest first, interrogated him, and stabbed him once they realized they weren't getting anything out of him. They probably figured he was dead by the time we arrived. To make matters worse, our feint in sending the Guard looking for us in Isfahan gave the cult some room to go after us here. Best laid plans, and all that."

This was all getting to be way too real for Angell, but there was no backing out now.

Adnan spoke a few more words into his phone, then dropped it into his pocket.

"Okay. Let's go."

The two men crawled out of the back of the tower, where Arad's body lay. The sight of the old man exposed to the elements saddened Angell, but then he realized that was exactly what Arad had wanted. With the takeover by the ayatollahs, the traditional Zoroastrian burial practices had been forbidden. For the first time in memory, the Zoroastrians now had to bury their dead in the ground. In order to survive under the fundamentalist regime, the priests had to accept the ruling. At least, they were still allowed to keep their eternal flame lit in the temple in Yazd where it had been burning for more than three thousand years.

Adnan went first over the side, finding handholds and places that were level enough to crouch or crawl down the hillside. With a last look at Arad, dead in the place he longed to be, Angell followed.

They could hear the crack of gunfire but it seemed far away now. They scrambled as best they could until they came to an outcropping of rock that was large enough to conceal them. They were only about ten feet above the surface, but they waited to be sure there were no surprises.

The two men, dressed like locals, did not look as out of place as one might imagine. They could have been from any of the small villages they had passed on the highway. They were tired and dusty from the climb down the hill. On top of that they were emotionally drained from the visit with Arad and completely wired by the danger they were in.

Adnan was the first to notice an anomaly in his field of vision. "Three o'clock."

Angell turned to his right and saw something moving in the distance, behind a line of trees.

"What is it?"

"One of ours, I think. But let's just wait a minute to be sure."

It was not as if Angell was planning on taking a walk.

The cultists were firing back at the two shooters in the tower, and one peeled off to try to approach them from another angle. He was spotted, and shots from the tower kicked up dust in front of him so he dropped to the ground and crab-walked back to his original position. Angell could see puffs of smoke as bullets hit the wall of the tower, but the shooters were so well-placed that it would take an army—or a drone strike—to bring them down.

They could wait there for hours, but time was running out. Soon all of Yazd would be on-site. From the first shot to the most recent was only about ten minutes, but they were pushing it.

Adnan heard the bus start up before Angell did. He craned his neck around and saw that his people were already on board. The other tourists—the real ones—were running for the brick wall that separated them from their transport and the cultists simply ignored them, too.

Another bus, and then another started up. All three entered traffic and started heading towards Yazd on the main road. The sun was going down and the lights were coming on in the city. Darkness came with its own special set of problems, but it would also provide cover.

Adnan risked another look at where the buses had been.

"Good," he said, relieved. "My car is gone. That means everyone is okay and they are coming back for us around the other side."

Just as they were getting up to make a run for it, Angell heard a sound that made the hairs on the back of his neck stand straight up.

From the building where the cultists were pinned down came a kind of howl. Like the cry of "*Allahu akhbar!*" that had become so familiar to television audiences around the world. Except the first sound was not *Allahu* but *Kutulu*.

The howl rolled around the desert floor and up the sides of the hill to swirl around the Towers of Silence like the lustful mating call of a zombie in the last stages of decomp.

"What are they saying? It sounds like *Kutuluhu akhbar* or something like that. It's not Arabic, it's not Farsi, and it sure as hell ain't Gorani."

"Adnan, my friend, you don't want to know. You really don't. Let's just get the hell out of here because things could go very dark very fast."

He didn't need to be told twice. They crept out from behind their outcropping and scrambled down the rest of the hill to the flat desert floor. Adnan pointed to a spot away from the firefight, an open expanse of dirt and sand that led to a road running on the other side of the Towers. It was a road with very few buildings on the other side, so they would not be noticed. That was where he expected to meet his pick-up.

The howl came again, this time even stronger. They could hear their two shooters increasing their fire down the hill at the cultists but it sounded like panic-firing. The thought made Adnan's blood run cold.

The two shooters left the safety of their tower fortress and were walking calmly down the circuitous path, firing and reloading, firing and reloading. Something had possessed them. The weird screams from the cultists that had so terrified Angell had acted to solidify the shooters' convictions. This was not a political battle, and it wasn't even a religious one. Not in any conventional sense. They knew they were facing something much deeper, much more frightening and enormously more lethal than any modern weapon or ancient form of torture could inflict.

The two shooters—their names were Bahadur and Firooz—shot straight and true. The man who had tried to outflank them earlier was the first to die. He was followed by his friend who tried to use the dead body as a tripod for his rifle. He was taken out by a head shot that penetrated his forehead and destroyed his pineal gland. The wound looked like Edvard Munch had painted him a Third Eye.

Bullets sang and danced around Bahadur and Firooz but they took no notice. The other cultists, armed with a depressing variety of weapons, decided to charge them. Bahadur smiled. Firooz frowned. They started firing their Chinese-made AK-47s from the hip.

They didn't see cultists. They saw devils. They didn't see men. They saw fictional characters from horror stories and nightmares. Freddie Krueger in a turban. Jason with a scimitar. "*Heeeere's Johnny* …*" These were Kurds, Bahadur and Firooz, men of Ahl-e Haqq, and they would show these depraved eunuch sons of pederasts and whores how real men dealt with the scum of the universe.

Angell and Adnan were running for their lives across the flat, open plain to the road. It was full-on twilight now, the lights coming up all over the city: a jewel of an oasis in the middle of the desert. They could still hear the firefight taking place behind them. For Adnan, not knowing what was going on was torture.

He fumbled for his phone and called the man who was driving his car. He spoke a few words and then saw a pair of headlights signaling him from the road. Okay, he was already there. One less thing to worry about.

The driver told him the bus had made it to downtown Yazd. Everyone was okay. *But what about Bahadur and Firooz?*

In the movies, the heroes laugh at danger. Here, in the Iranian wasteland, there was no laughter. The shooters respected their work, and they were pious men who knew what death was all about. They took no joy in slaughter. But they were Kurds. They were born fighters.

So … like … fuck that.

Bahadur and Firooz stood side by side. They each were down to their last clip. They exchanged a glance that said goodbye, it was great. See you on the flip side.

And they walked into an abattoir.

Six cultists were down, and another four were still in the building they were using as a fort. The two Kurds calmly walked up to the entrance, then split up, each taking a side. Bahadur went left, Firooz went right.

In the distance they could hear sirens. They thought that was funny.

One of the cult members—a twenty-something in camouflage pants, flat on the floor inside the doorway—raised an automatic pistol to blow a hole through Bahadur but Firooz was faster and rammed a NATO round through the kid's mouth that took out his jaw and whatever he had for a brain. Bahadur fired blind into the open space inside the building, just so he could catch a glimpse of what was waiting for them by the light of the discharge. He saw a pair of eyes and felt a round from some kind of piece-of-shit handgun whiz past his ear. He pulled his trigger in the general direction of the eyes and the gun. He heard a scream.

Two down. Two to go.

They made it to the car. Adnan jumped in the front passenger side and Angell took the back seat. The car peeled out into traffic just as a squad car, all lights and sirens, raced past them.

"Where to, boss?" came the oddly accented question, in English.

"What's our chance of getting back to Abadeh tonight?"

The driver shook his head. "Not good. Not now. Maybe if *that* hadn't happened ..." he said, gesturing in the general direction of the firefight.

"We can't stay in Yazd. They'll be tearing the city apart soon."

They were all silent for a moment. Angell looked out the window at the passing street scene, his mind on the two shooters and the old priest. How much death was he leaving in his wake? He had never wanted to see death again, not like this, and now he was *causing* it.

"What if we go south?"

The driver looked over at the crazy Kurdish American.

"What do you mean, south?"

"Well, we can't go north. Yazd is hot. And we can't go west, back to Abadeh. What if we head for Mehriz?"

"Won't help you, boss. You'd be pretty far away from where you have to be. You gotta get back to the mountains, right?"

"I don't know. Maybe not."

"What do you *mean*?" This time it was Angell's turn to be surprised.

"It's going to be hard getting an extraction done now. We weren't supposed to start a firefight, get noticed. Now the Iranians will start sealing off the borders to keep us inside. There were those rumors about a plane or helo coming in over the mountains from Iraq. They start putting two and two together and ... you see what I mean?"

"What choice do we have? How do I get out of here? You guys can blend back into the population. They'll never trace any of this back to you. You're the professionals. But they'll be looking for *me*. Especially if any of those killers back at the Towers are captured and start talking."

They continued this way for another twenty minutes, arguing about the best options. Their driver took them to a friend's house on the outskirts of town where they would not be noticed so they could rest and clean up. As they did so, Adnan's phone rang.

One of the cultists had been hiding outside the building. He came in fast, like he was in a gangster film, guns blazing from both hands, firing wildly into the space before him. Bahadur shot him in the stomach. He dropped to his knees and tried to return fire, but Bahadur shot him again, this time in the face.

He was out of ammunition.

One down, one to go.

There was a rustling sound from the back of the building. Had Adnan and Angell been there, they would have recognized the place. And the sound.

The small boy from before walked over the blood and the dead bodies, through the haze of smoke and fumes from the firefight, careful not to trip on the broken bricks and the gore, a smile of wonder on his face. Firooz almost shot him, but stopped just in time.

"What are you doing here, boy? Go away!" he hissed.

The boy reached up with his finger and touched his lips. Silence.

Firooz just stared at him, at this strange apparition who seemed so calm and self-contained. He started to smile.

And the last crazed cultist blew him away.

Bahadur leaped over to Firooz's now lifeless body and snatched up his weapon. He spun around in the darkness and the filth, looking for his target. Outside, he could hear the sirens get closer. He knew they were already in the parking lot.

Now or never.

He stood up, as if to draw the last shooter's fire, and saw

movement out of the corner of his eye. He opened up, firing steadily in that direction, and as he did so he heard that howl once again. That depraved oration or incantation or invocation or whatever the hell it was. And he fired once more in its direction, and it stopped. The howl stopped. In mid-shriek.

He had one bullet left in the magazine. He saw a glow on the floor. It was a cell phone. It belonged to Firooz, his brother in arms, his warrior friend. He picked up the phone as he heard voices coming from outside the building. The authorities.

He looked at the phone and hit a speed dial number.

A mile or so away, Adnan's phone was ringing.

He picked it up when he saw who it was.

"Firooz?"

"Bahadur. Firooz has left this Earth behind."

"Oh, my …"

"Do what you can. These must be stopped. *They* must be stopped."

And then there was the sound of a shot, loud and angry over the tinny speaker of the cell phone.

Bahadur had shot the phone to splinters and dust. He didn't want it to fall into the hands of the Guard. They were using burner phones, but he didn't know if the Guard had ways of retrieving information from them anyway.

He sat with his back against the wall of the broken building, one hand resting on the head of his fallen comrade, the other holding his Chinese-knock-off piece-of-shit Kalashnikov. As the men made to enter the building, guns drawn, shouting, flashlights, sirens, lights … he raised the empty weapon as if he had a full clip and one in the pipe.

They riddled his body with ammunition bought from a Russian arms dealer who got it from a French arms dealer who got it from an American supplier.

His body danced, and jumped, and then was still.

Silence.

Adnan looked up to meet the gaze of the two other men in the room, and shook his head.

The driver muttered a curse and left the room, leaving Angell to ask the question.

"Both?"

He nodded.

"What about the others? The cultists?"

"If my experience is any guide, they're all dead, too."

Angell started tallying the list of those who had been killed since he was enlisted in this mission, and then gave up. It was too overwhelming, and he felt considerable guilt for his role in their deaths. He was not military; he had not been trained to deal with death in any kind of professional way. Yet there was a sense that this roll call of the dead was the core of a community of souls in which he, involuntarily, had been included. The dead would stay with him, just as those slain Yezidis in Mosul were still with him. Just as his relatives were still with him, those who died in those other towers on September 11, 2001. There was a chain of connection between all of these events and he was the central link. Without him, many of those might still be alive.

He wondered how soldiers lived with it, with all the death they witnessed and even caused. At least they were fighting in a battle with a determined enemy who desired their destruction. Angell didn't know what his excuse was. Sure, he had been enlisted by the government. He had been told that he had a unique and irreplaceable skillset to offer. He had also been told that the fate of many innocent lives was at stake.

But so far he had not seen any of those innocent lives spared. Instead, the pile of corpses was growing higher all around him.

CHAPTER SEVENTEEN

THE CODEX — III

Autumn, 1927. HPL writes "The History of the Necronomicon." William Seabrook publishes *Adventures in Arabia*, with account of the Seven Towers of Satan, i.e. Yezidi.

February, 1928. "The Call of Cthulhu" published. Also this year: first Byrd expedition to Antarctica begins (1928–1930).

April, 1929. "The Dunwich Horror" published.

May 1, 1930. Newly discovered planet is named Pluto, after the Lord of the Underworld.

Spring, 1931. HPL writes *At the Mountains of Madness*.

Summer, 1931. HPL to Florida. Meets Henry St. Clair Whitehead, minister, expert on voudon in Dunedin, FL. Meets Karl Tanzler von Cosel, who discusses with him the reanimation of a corpse, in Key West, FL. Tanzler, an agent for the German government, is a contact for German spies entering the US from Cuba and elsewhere in the Caribbean. Tanzler tasked with finding the Cthulhu File. Believes HPL has it. Tanzler enamored of Cuban woman dying of TB (or sees her as disposable test subject for experiments on reviving corpse).

May, 1932. Respected journalist Pierre van Paassen reports the existence of a cult of devil worshippers conducting a Black Mass in Paris and connects them to a satanic cult outside Baghdad. It is believed this is a reference to the Yezidi. Yezidi however do not celebrate Mass of any kind.

August, 1932. International Eugenics Conference held in New York City. Ernst Rüdin, president. Later interned for Nazi war crimes related to genocide.

October, 1932. Cuban woman, Elena Hoyos, dies of TB. Tanzler begins attempts to resuscitate her corpse.

It's been five years since Tanzler had stabbed the needle into Professor George Angell's neck on the Providence docks, killing him, and stealing his briefcase. In the intervening period a man called Lovecraft published a story that contained so many elements of the tale that Himmler already had told him in Germany—a story that included direct references to old Professor Angell himself—that Tanzler grew increasingly nervous that the American writer had beaten him to the Cthulhu File. The story was entitled "The Call of Cthulhu" and was published in a fringe magazine with lurid covers that specialized in fantasy and science fiction tales by unknown authors. That was in 1928.

He begins to take an interest in Lovecraft, believing that the American was using fiction and the pulp press to communicate military and other secrets to unknown contacts, possibly to a network of occultists and astrologers in Europe. After all, George Sylvester Viereck was doing just that for Germany in his own newspapers, such as *The Fatherland* and *The International*, while based in the United States. He had even written a book on rejuvenation! If he could figure out what Lovecraft was doing, Himmler would be pleased. He would be pleased even more if he could locate the Cthulhu File.

So he began scouring bookstores and magazine stands, libraries and archives, for more of Lovecraft's work and came upon a series of stories about the re-animation of dead matter. "Herbert West—Reanimator" was one such series, published ten years earlier, but there were others that treated of the same theme. Reviving corpses. It seemed to be an obsession of Lovecraft's.

And now it was his.

He began writing to Lovecraft, telling him how much he admired his work. Lovecraft eventually replied, polite and generous, and Tanzler had invited him to come down to Florida some time, perhaps for a few days of vacation. When Lovecraft actually replied that he would be coming down—to visit another correspondent of his, one Whitehead—Tanzler was delighted and signaled Munich at once.

The previous year he had met the love of his life, a beautiful Cuban-American woman named Elena Hoyos. He found work in a US Marine hospital in Key West, as instructed by Himmler. This was necessary in order to maintain a network of German operatives entering the United States from Cuba. Tanzler's modest home would become an ersatz safe house. Not that anyone would have noticed the arrival of yet more immigrants from Cuba in those days.

Elena had come in due to some troubling symptoms. Tanzler, as the x-ray technician, knew that he was dealing with tuberculosis but was optimistic that—with his help, experience honed by years of dealing with the esoteric literature on health and healing—he would enable her to beat her illness and they would marry and fly off to some tropical paradise together. His feelings for Elena were not shared with the Nazis back in Germany, but remained fiercely his own.

He noted the day he met Elena, and claimed it was the day when his life changed forever. It was April 22, 1930. A few days earlier, Charles Lindbergh set a new continental US record of flying from Los Angeles to New York in under fifteen hours. Lindbergh, he knew, was one of theirs: a patriotic American who would never let the United States enter into another war against Germany.

But these things were far from his mind, even as Munich signaled demanding more and more information. How was he supposed to run an intelligence network on such a small expense account? He was getting money wired every month from Himmler via the Reich Credit Bank in Germany under the cover of a pension for his military service during the last war, but it was not enough. Neither was his paycheck from the US Government for his work at their military hospital. It was ironic, really. He was getting paid by the armies and governments of both sides and it was peacetime! He was aware that a new war was coming soon; it was inevitable. The Jews had shown their true colors, first in Moscow and then in Berlin, and now in the United States where Jewish immigrants were flooding the cities and towns and displacing loyal American citizens from their homes and jobs.

At least, that was what Henry Ford was saying. And how can you argue with such a successful businessman?

If he had Ford's money, or Lindbergh's, he would be able to perfect his medical system: a system so advanced it would revolutionize science. He understood about electricity and x-rays, and about the subtle psychic forces that wove the web of reality, of life and death, all around us in glittering strands of possibility. In the meantime he was doing his best to care for young Elena with the paltry tools at his disposal. The raven-haired Latin beauty was the incarnation of a spirit he had seen years earlier, first in Europe and then in Asia. At those times she was only a vision, an apparition, like a photograph in a magazine. Seeing her in the flesh, as an actual physical woman, was as if that magazine picture had suddenly come to life. The effect on him was astonishing. It was more than love or lust; it was what one would feel if God himself had appeared without warning and, like a genie, offered you three wishes. No; more. It was as if the Virgin Mother had descended from her throne and pulled aside her veil and loosened her blue and white robe, and asked him to take her there, right there, on the altar of the church.

He was overwhelmed with emotion.

Her full name was Maria Elena Milagro de Hoyos. The message was there, right there in her name. Tanzler the occultist, Tanzler the Kabbalist, broke it down with dictionaries, pen and paper, scribbling furiously in his secret notebook.

Maria was Mary, the Virgin Mother. Milagro was the Spanish word for "miracle." Hoyos meant "holes" in the vernacular, but it also indicated "sepulcher." A mausoleum. A hole in the ground. But he called her Elena: his Bright Star, his Shining One.

Taken altogether: she was his miracle, his bright shining miracle, his virgin and his final destination. He was not yet aware how apt her family name, Hoyos, would become. Womb to Tomb. Hoyos.

Using Himmler's money, he rained jewels down on Elena from his open palms. Tanzler bought her clothing, more jewelry, a constant march of flowers, even a bed, and brought medicines he created himself in feverish midnight labors under a dim electric bulb in his ramshackle laboratory in the sticky Florida heat.

But now, in 1931, she was dying.

He applied more techniques, using electrodes on her body to cauterize the disease. He brought in a Tesla coil and vacuum tubes. Even inserted one of the tubes down her throat and increased the voltage until it burned. Everything worked briefly, and then the symptoms would return, relentless and mocking.

He was going to have to face facts. Her body would succumb to the disease, there was no other way.

But maybe that was a good thing. Maybe—with his knowledge of esoterica and electricity—a dead body was easier to cure than a living one. He knew that no one really died. He had seen the shades of the dearly departed so many times in his life that physical death held no terrors for him. He was an alchemist of the life-force, a man with medical training who was also an initiate of the great mysteries.

And besides ... what would Himmler give him if he, Count von Cosel, discovered the key to reanimation of dead matter? If that secret could be found and if it could be employed on a massive scale—something a Henry Ford would design—then the German army would never have to suffer a humiliating defeat again as it had in the last war. Imagine it! An army of the Undead! Or, at least, the Recently Dead.

Then, as if in answer to his prayers, he received a letter from H. P. Lovecraft saying he would be in Key West that very summer.

Lovecraft was back living in Providence where he was happier than anywhere else on the planet. He still enjoyed traveling, however, and visited Quebec, Savannah, Georgia, and New Orleans, and even went back to New York City on a number of occasions, but now the time had come for him to visit Florida.

He had a number of correspondents down there, including a man who was an expert on Caribbean religion. There was one aspect of the Cthulhu File that had disturbed him when he read it, the convocation of voodoo worshippers around the statue of that alien god. He didn't understand the connection between a bunch of deranged and murderous savages in the Louisiana bayous of 1907 and the ancient cult of Cthulhu that had its origins in Mesopotamia. Perhaps Reverend Whitehead could clarify that for him. There might be a secret buried in that detail that the good man, an Episcopal minister who was schooled both in the Bible and in voodoo, would recognize at once.

Whitehead lived in Dunedin, outside Tampa on the Gulf Coast of Florida, but he had another correspondent he intended to visit: a man of European origin living in Key West. He would try to visit both. The European correspondent seemed to understand a great deal in his writing that was unstated or only hinted at, and he found that compelling. Whitehead was obviously a well-traveled and cultured older man, and he reminded him somewhat of his own beloved late grandfather. The letters from the European, a man by the name of Tanzler who said he was a German nobleman, were articulate and profound. These two men had qualities that Lovecraft admired.

So, in late May of 1931, Lovecraft embarked on this fateful trip to Florida. He had no idea that this visit would generate repercussions for decades to come.

His visit with Whitehead from May 21 to June 10 was very helpful. The 49-year old Anglican minister cleared up a great many mysteries concerning the weird rites of the African and Caribbean religions and did so from an educated point of view, which Lovecraft approved. Whitehead had lived in St Croix, in the Virgin Islands, in the 1920s and had observed first hand the hideous incantations

of the notorious voodoo worshippers. He began publishing stories
about what he saw in *Weird Tales*, the same publication Lovecraft
graced with his own prose, and the two became friends, eventually
including another writer, Robert H. Barlow, in their circle. To make
matters more interesting, Whitehead was also a personal friend of
the soon-to-be President of the United States, Franklin D. Roosevelt, and had photos of himself and Roosevelt in his comfortable
home. Lovecraft was interested in this strange connection between
an Anglican minister who was also a specialist in voodoo—as well as
an author of horror stories—and the American president. It was not
the sort of relationship that would occur to most people.

Whitehead, however, was sick from a variety of illnesses, no doubt
contracted during his lengthy sojourn in the Caribbean. He was not
the dry, dignified sort of clergyman but a rather more outgoing type
who reveled in the company of young boys that he would take on
camping trips to the Adirondacks. He availed of Lovecraft's visit to
convince the author to do a dramatic reading of one of his stories
to just such a group of boys. And in that manner Lovecraft passed
almost two enjoyable weeks in Dunedin.

His visit to Key West, however, was rather more intense.

Count Karl Tanzler von Cosel met Lovecraft at the Florida East
Coast Railway station, and the two men walked along the streets
for awhile as they approached Tanzler's dilapidated residence, Tanzler
apologizing for the lack of transport by telling Lovecraft that his car
had recently been stolen. The Count had a brief moment of déjà vu
as he realized it was on a similar train platform that George Viereck
had taken from him the bizarre manuscript he had stolen from the
man he murdered, Professor George Angell: a man known to his
guest.

For his part Lovecraft was amused at Tanzler's weird appearance:
the gaunt figure with the jutting beard, bald head and heavy
spectacles. The old German's accent was also amusing to Lovecraft,
who did not like foreigners generally but who found Tanzler's

intensity fascinating. The "residence" however, was another story. A ramshackle building with no running water or other conveniences, it looked more like mechanic's workshop than a home. Lovecraft knew he could not stay there, but did not have the heart to tell his host just yet.

Tanzler introduced himself as a nobleman from Dresden. A former soldier in the Kaiser's army, he was now practicing as a medical man in Key West and an expert in radiology. There was a frisson of something that passed between the two men as Lovecraft mentally connected his old creation, Herbert West, with Key West and radiology with the strange and forbidden experimentation of Herbert West in the reanimation of the dead. Key West, after all, is the Anglicization of the Spanish *Cayo Hueso*, or "bone cay," an island that was littered with the bones of the ancient people who originally inhabited the site. This idea appealed to Lovecraft, even as the presence of so many Cubans on the streets appalled him.

Tanzler put Lovecraft's suitcase in a corner of his home, and the two men went in search of refreshments. Neither was very wealthy; in fact, both were counting pennies, so Tanzler suggested an open air café where they could eat simply and cheaply and plan the next few days in pleasant surroundings. Before they left, Lovecraft noted the unusual medical apparatus everywhere, including what looked like a Tesla coil and other, very heavy, electrical equipment for purposes he could only guess, including a rather massive organ with a moldy stack of sheet music. Had he actually met a mad scientist?

The pleasantries completed, the two were sitting at a small table on Duval Street drinking iced tea. It was hot, even for June, and they welcomed the arrival of their drinks with pleasure and anticipation. Tanzler liked his extremely sweet, a fact Lovecraft noted with some distaste. He watched the condensation form on his own glass as he took moderate sips, letting the bitterness and the cold adjust his mental processes to something approaching normal. He wondered if he could catch a ferry to Havana.

Instead of discussing the tourist attractions of Key West, however,

Tanzler brought the subject around almost at once to the theme that obsessed him.

"My dear Lovecraft," he began. "I have read your stories with fascination and appreciation. As a man of science, with a specialty in the field of the electrical stimulation of the life processes, I wonder if you are aware that there are those who are working on precisely the type of resurrection techniques hinted at in your work."

Lovecraft looked up at Tanzler, not quite sure what he was getting at.

"Forgive me, but my little stories are works of fiction and the imagination. The resurrection—or, should I say, reanimation—of dead matter is something horrible, of which no sane man would consider himself guilty."

"*Nein, mein lieber Freund.* There are those even now who, on a pleasantly sunny day such as we enjoy, are concentrating intently on this very goal."

"But my dear Count, that is not possible. Once the body dies it begins to decompose very quickly. Its internal systems collapse. The brain, deprived of blood and therefore of oxygen, shuts down and with it all consciousness disappears. There is nothing left to reanimate, I assure you. In fact, I understand that Tibetan monks, in that savage and inaccessible part of the Himalayan wasteland, carve up corpses with laughter and glee and quite sharp cleavers as they do not believe the dead body has any relationship any longer to the soul that inhabited it. They throw the severed cadavers on the snowy mountain tops like the detritus of a squalid restaurant and let the vultures consume them." A strange gleam flicked briefly across the writer's eyes at the thought.

"I would have to disagree, good sir. The ancients tell us of the portability of the mind, that it can travel out of the body and even, under certain circumstances, inhabit or possess another body. The phenomenon of possession and exorcism surely suggests as much?"

"Nonsense, Karl. May I call you Karl? Thank you. It is nonsense to believe in any of this superstitious claptrap about spirits and ghosts and demons and such. There is simply no scientific basis for any of it. Religion is a curse upon humanity, Karl. It distorts reality at the hands of vain and venal men who wish to use fantasies to control the masses. It is way to lie without seeming to lie; in fact, it is a way to lie that demands no proof that the lie is, in fact, the truth. In that, it is the perfect lie!"

The German spy and occultist waited a moment before responding. His mind went to his beloved Elena, even now in the last few months of her life, and the cruelty with which Lovecraft denied all possibility of post-mortem existence was depressing him.

Then he thought of a way to bring the conversation around to the subject with which his superior was most interested.

"Would you be surprised if I told you that, even now, there are those among us who not only believe in the existence of ghosts, gods and demons but who actively seek to make contact with them?"

Lovecraft was a little startled at the intensity in the German's gaze. What had he gotten himself into?

"The foolishness of humanity is no surprise to me, my good Count."

"Do you, then, deny the value of psychology and psychotherapy in the treatment of mental disorders?"

This was a bolt that struck home as surely as if it had been fired by William Tell himself.

"Are mental disorders then to be considered spiritual disorders? Is this what civilization has come to, applying scientific-sounding terms to superstitious beliefs?"

"Ah, then you do not believe that mental disorders exist?"

"Oh, but I do. I am surrounded in this world by morons, idiots, and the criminally insane. One only has to read a newspaper, or visit Congress, to be assured of that!"

It was a slick reply, one that Lovecraft had made before in other contexts, but the tone and direction of this conversation was cutting a little too close to home.

"Agreed, *mein Freund. Aber* consider the populations of our asylums. These are individuals who would have been cured of their disorders in the old days by the ritual of exorcism. But since we now live in a scientific world, exorcism is no longer employed as a remedy and thus the poor individuals must live the rest of their lives untreated and undiagnosed. A diagnosis of demonic possession would relieve one of their medical license, *nicht war?*"

"What you are characterizing as either a spiritual or a mental disorder may be nothing more than an organic condition, treatable by medicines and other appropriate methodologies. It is to the body we must look for both the cause and the cure of disease, not to the invisible and intangible spirit!"

As they were arguing, one of Tanzler's agents—a German spy on his way to the shipyards in Virginia—went into Tanzler's home and found Lovecraft's suitcase. He opened it easily and rummaged through everything he could find. There was the usual collection of clothing and toiletries, and a notebook.

Thinking this might be the Cthulhu File, the agent opened it and flipped through its pages. Sadly, it turned out to be nothing but descriptions of places visited, snippets of conversation, and other ordinary scribblings. There was nothing about the Cthulhu Cult in the file, no references to arcane events or satanic conspiracies.

With a sigh, the agent put everything back in its place and quietly left the house. On the doorjamb he scratched a single line with a piece of chalk, indicating to Tanzler that the file was not there.

After having had two large glasses of iced tea each, the two men paid and got up from their table, still talking. Tanzler had a restaurant in mind for their dinner, one that would certainly cheer up his guest and perhaps make him more amenable to discussion about the things that mattered most to him: the Cthulhu File, of course, and the process of reanimation.

They walked down Duval Street to a restaurant that specialized in fresh seafood as well as more pedestrian fare. Tanzler had no idea what his guest would eat, so he chose a place that would have a little of everything. If Lovecraft was not a picky eater, he would order some Caribbean seafood delicacies. He felt certain that the New Englander would not turn down a conch chowder, for instance. It was still Prohibition so finding a bar was out of the question.

Lovecraft pronounced the place acceptable, and he and Tanzler took a table in a corner away from the noise of the other diners. The checkered tablecloth and the candles in wine bottles seemed a little too ... romantic ... for Tanzler's taste but his guest had no apparent objections to either the décor or the menu.

At another table on the far side of the room, Ernest Hemingway and his wife, Pauline, relative newcomers to Key West, were dining on swordfish and salads. They had just bought a house only a few blocks away and were planning to settle there for the foreseeable future. Neither Tanzler nor Lovecraft were even aware of Hemingway at the time, and so would not have been star-struck at the proximity.

Having made a little small talk over the menu and the restaurant itself, Tanzler returned to business.

"You are familiar with some of the Latin traditions in this part of the world?" he asked Lovecraft.

"You are referring to the Cubans, who so seem to proliferate here?"

"Yes. The Cubans and some of the people from the other islands."

"Well, I am familiar with voodoo. Perhaps more than most. I have just come from a very interesting visit with a man who is an expert on voodoo. We had many an enjoyable conversation on the subject. He, too, is an author of stories of the imagination and horror, and his time among the savages of St. Croix has afforded him much material for his work."

"Ach, that is indeed interesting! You have many interesting friends, Herr Lovecraft. Perhaps he has told you about one such cult, one that has been operating in this part of the world for more than a century, at least. A cult that is as evil and degenerated as anything a civilized man could imagine."

"Surely you mean voodoo, or some version of it?"

"Not at all. This cult is to voodoo what the Black Mass is to the Catholic Church. It is ancient, and widespread. It has been underground, in all meanings of that word, for centuries now. Perhaps millennia. But now it is threatening to reemerge and threatens us all with its depravity."

"Communism?"

Lovecraft could not help himself. He was making jokes because the content of the conversation was now circling around his own life and making him very nervous. Tanzler was an odd duck; virtually everything he said in the past few hours had something to do with Lovecraft's own concerns and the dark mysteries he had been keeping within himself. It was as if Tanzler was reading his mind and rummaging through the contents like a matron at a jumble sale.

"You may joke, Herr Lovecraft, but this is serious business."

"Perhaps too serious for this delightful chowder?"

Their dishes had arrived and both men, who each spent their lives in an almost continuous state of hunger, dug in.

The conch chowder was excellent. It was creamy, with an orange tinge of paprika. Not too heavily spiced, which would have bothered Lovecraft's delicate constitution, but nevertheless flavorful.

The two men were silent awhile as they enjoyed their meal.

As their waitress cleared the plates and offered them tea or coffee, Tanzler returned to the subject at hand.

"Herr Lovecraft …"

"Please. Call me Howard."

"As you wish. Howard, have you heard of a cult named after its leader, a high priest called … how does one pronounce it … Cah-thu-lu?"

And there it was. It had dropped on the table between them like a vile imprecation. There was no going back from this now.

"Count von Cosel, you know very well that I have. I published a story with that name."

"Yes, of course. But you did not take the contents of that story seriously. You published it in a magazine devoted to the most vulgar form of literature."

"How else should I have treated such an outrageous theme? Monsters, strange idols, orgiastic rites in the bayou …"

"Let us be frank, please. We both know the cult exists. We also know where you derived your information about it."

Lovecraft leaned back in his chair, as if to put as much distance between himself and his memories—incarnated in this horrible little man—as possible.

"You named your source. You revealed all the basic contours of this cult. You were quite specific as to dates and places. You held nothing back, not one detail no matter how insignificant. This was not the work of a fantasist, *Mister* Lovecraft. *Howard*. It was not a short story, a horror tale or a fantasy.

"It was *an intelligence report*."

After the theft of the Cthulhu Cult file from his apartment in Brooklyn, Lovecraft wrote down as much as he could remember from the file. He included the information about George Angell but did not mention his visit to the old professor or, of course, his own theft of the Cthulhu File from the professor's desk.

What he read in the file had amazed him. He was not given to conspiracy theory or wild speculations about international cabals of Satanists, but the news clippings and other data in the file provided a rare glimpse into a world of underground rites, exotic locations, and bizarre people. He realized that the file was selective in its inclusion of data and that there might be other ways of interpreting the same facts, ways that were not so terrifying or suggestive of supernatural causes. Yet, he could not deny the multiplication of coincidences that seemed to accrue around the events of the spring of 1925 that led the professor to some unsettling conclusions.

Lovecraft remembered that there had been a serious earthquake around that time in the region of the St. Lawrence River in Canada.

The effect of the earthquake was severe enough that it caused buildings *to rotate*. In fact, it caused *the monuments in cemeteries to rotate*. Lovecraft spent time researching the event and came upon an article in *The Journal of the Royal Astronomical Society of Canada* entitled "The Rotation Effects of the St. Lawrence Earthquake of February 28, 1925" by Ernest A. Hodgson that attested to this fact and noted its peculiarity. This rotation would seem to indicate a re-orientation of the affected tombs, as if the monuments over them were keys being turned in a series of locks. The implication of this fact unnerved Lovecraft, and he tried to push it out of his mind.

Then he came upon a notice from April 2, 1925 and thus only a month after the earthquake and two weeks after the psychological crisis suffered by young Henry Wilcox on the vernal equinox that year. This was a meeting of the French Surrealists that took place on that day in which they struggled with the direction of their movement: Surrealism or revolution. The first point, as reported in their Memorandum, was:

Before any Surrealist or revolutionary preoccupation, that which dominates their minds is *a certain state of fury*.

This state of fury was partially attributable to their support of a revolt in Morocco against the French colonial authority. Mad Arabs.

Lovecraft researched the Surrealists because artistic movements were expressly mentioned and documented in the Cthulhu File as being somehow linked to the massive, subterranean tensions that were rising as a response to the "call" of the impossible, or at least improbable, Cthulhu. He found that the Surrealists traced the origins of their movement and their art to the unconscious mind; that is, they considered themselves mediums (in all senses of that word) for the eruptions of unconscious material that were splayed across their canvases and their texts: the *ejecta* of psychosis, neurosis, nightmares and forbidden fantasies, and all the impedimenta of the new science of psychology. This was exactly what Professor Angell had been tracking, and how this being—this construct of demented vision—called Cthulhu communicated with its followers on the Earth. The artists were the first to feel the effects, and they were followed in turn by the cults.

Cults. A concept difficult to describe or identify. Lovecraft went through all the usual sources for an understanding of this term, going back to the vicious attacks of Leo Taxil on Freemasonry to the slightly more reserved approaches of Arthur Edward Waite as well as the ravings of the French cleric Eliphas Levi. It would seem that, for all their apparent diversity, these groups shared a common origin, the same as the Surrealists, the *fons et origo* of psychic phenomena, artistic genius, and every sort of diseased invention: the unconscious mind.

This, this thing, this Cthulhu—"High Priest of the Old Ones"—existed in some kind of real relationship to the unconscious minds of human beings and was able to communicate with them. Perhaps the word "Cthulhu" was just a literary or scientific convenience, a term of art to describe the mechanisms of the process, a word culled from some obscure volume on mental hygiene perhaps. Yet, in addition, there was a demonstrable connection between the messages being sent and physical phenomena taking place on the planet, such as earthquakes and other natural disasters that seemed to be epiphenomena of these unconscious contacts.

The implication of this was not lost on Lovecraft. Had his mother been in contact with this loathsome creature? Had her rantings been nothing less than the *actual speech* of Cthulhu, straining to be heard and understood through the poor woman's own weakened vocal chords? Had his mother been a *medium* for this evil Being?

And who was to say that he, Lovecraft himself, was not just such a medium? Had he not also an unconscious mind, subject to the same forces and machinations as his mother's? As those Surrealists in Paris? As the masses of colonized people who were every day revolting against European civilization and their white masters, threatening to destabilize the world order?

How does one protect oneself against the possibility that one could be just such a medium for evil? An unconscious tool in the hands of sinister forces lurking behind every random thought, every unsettling dream, every uncontrolled emotion?

He had to know if there were others in the world who were tracking the same events, seeing the contours of an invisible threat beneath the surface dimensions of cult, religious fanaticism, political revolt, and artistic transgression. He had to know that he was not alone in this realization, and he had to know if others had developed any strategies for counteracting its effects. Most of all, he had to know if he was going down the same dark path as his mother and father, both of whom were driven insane. Was this the reason? Was manipulation by some heretofore undiscovered phenomenon of matter, some unseen physical force, some power that operated through the nervous systems of human beings which were—after all—like transmitters and receivers in a radio set, was this manipulation recognized, suspected, or even understood by other researchers in the field? Perhaps researchers who were afraid to publish in the peer-reviewed literature for fear of being ostracized or ridiculed?

And did this phenomenon have a name?

And was it *Cthulhu*?

So he published. As quickly as he could. He wrote down all of it—all that he could remember—and it became his most celebrated effort. "The Call of Cthulhu" was his plea to others to contact him, to validate his research and that of poor murdered Professor Angell. It was his notice to those who worked in the shadows that he was one of them, and that he was afraid. Not only for his own life and sanity, but for civilization itself.

In Key West, Lovecraft was silent. This was the first time that another human being had decoded his story and recognized it for what it was. There was no longer any profit in maintaining his skeptical façade. This man, this unlikely German count, had seen right through his pretense.

"What do you want?" Lovecraft asked.

"I want to know what you know. And in return, I will tell you what I know."

Lovecraft looked around at the restaurant. The bull of a man with the thick black mustache and the slight, dark-haired woman with him—Hemingway and his wife, Pauline—had already left, but Lovecraft was still a little uncomfortable being out in the open and discussing forbidden topics.

"Let's find somewhere else to talk."

Tanzler was reluctant to go back to his place until he was sure he left enough time for his colleague to enter his home and search Lovecraft's suitcase. So he decided to lead his guest on a circuitous walk around Key West which would eventually take him to his shack.

They wound up on Whitehead Street, which seemed to amuse the taciturn writer from Rhode Island.

"*Was geht?*"

"Oh, it's just that I was visiting with a Reverend Whitehead before I came here. I merely noticed the coincidence."

"This was the voodoo expert, *ja?*"

"Yes, as a matter of fact."

"Was he able to assist you in your, ah, researches?"

"What is it you really want, Count von Cosel? Why am I here?"

They stopped at an intersection of two sleepy streets. The beach was close by, and there was a growth of ferns and palm trees that suggested the savage jungle of primitive tribes, the womb that gave birth to all humanity, was not really all that far away. The two men glared at each other for a heartbeat, and then the Count decided on the direct approach.

"*Ach*, so. You have written about the Cthulhu cult, and you have mentioned the existence of the Cthulhu File. No, don't deny that it exists! We both know it does. My question to you is, where is the file now?"

"Why does this matter to you? What could you possibly gain from the file?"

"That is my business, Herr Lovecraft."

The evening was pleasant enough. The moon was in its dark phase, so the sky was lit with stars. With the palm trees in the background and the sound of the ocean within walking distance, it seemed as if they were two actors on a stage with a magnificent backdrop. How often is the setting at odds with the set!

"I no longer have the file."

"Then, who does?"

"I have no earthly idea."

"Then how did you write the story?"

"From memory."

"Do you have perfect recall?"

"No. The file was stolen from me. Immediately I sat down and wrote all that I remembered. Then I turned it into a story."

Lovecraft sighed, and looked around for somewhere to sit, but there was nothing. Instead, he started walking again and Tanzler followed.

"I wanted to talk to Professor Angell about it. I wanted more information. But before I could convince him to talk to me he was murdered."

"Was he? Murdered?"

"What do you mean?"

"Curious, that you would say he was murdered when a search through the records of Providence, Rhode Island for the month in question reveals that *no murders took place at all during that time.*"

"You must be joking! It was common knowledge ..."

"Common knowledge and truth are not always the same thing, are they?"

"Spoken like a man who practices deceit on a regular basis."

"And why did you suggest that it was a 'nautical-looking Negro' who committed this alleged murder? What proof was there of that?"

Lovecraft was fuming. What did this irritating immigrant from a vanquished country know about his personal life, his motivations? How does he challenge the story Lovecraft wrote and published in all sincerity?

Tanzler grabbed his arm.

"Do you know *why* there was no reported murder of Professor Angell? Because there was no evidence of murder. He had a heart attack, as you wrote, which is a natural cause. Or, perhaps, unnatural, as the case may be."

"What are you saying?"

"A heart attack is an easy thing to arrange, once you know the science. I predict that heart attacks will become the assassination method of the future. Not so obvious and messy as poisoning. Certainly not as immediately suspicious as a gunshot or a stabbing."

"Why are you telling me this?"

"Consider, Herr Lovecraft. You know your own country. Would Professor Angell have allowed a Negro to come close enough to him to kill him? And what motive would he have?"

"I don't like where this is going."

"*Scheisse*, man! Open your eyes! He was killed for the briefcase he was carrying."

"Briefcase …"

"And for the document in the briefcase. The one that was never discovered. The one entrusted to him by a group of colleagues at a secret meeting in Newport that day."

"What secret meeting? And how do you know so much about this?"

"I have been following your work for a number of years now. You have to know that you are not alone in this. That there are others, many others, influential people, who are aware of the activities of this Cult of Cthulhu. Professor Angell only became aware of it through a series of accidents. When it became known that he had stumbled upon the truth, he was taken into confidence by others. He perhaps knew more about it than was good for him. That is why I need to locate that file."

"I told you. It was stolen from me."

"By whom?"

"How should I know? A thief in the night. Arabs, maybe."

"Arabs?"

"Whoever it was had a key to my rooms. The tenants were all Arabs. I don't know. The police never …"

"You brought the authorities into this?" Tanzler was shocked.

"No, no. To the theft of my clothes, only. I never mentioned the file."

"And how did you become the owner of the file? I thought it was part of Angell's estate?"

"That part was made up. Invented. I couldn't say that I had the physical file, and be dragged into a possible lawsuit by the Angell family. They are very powerful in Providence. No. I wanted to throw the authorities off, but still get my message to the right people."

Tanzler patted the distraught man on the arm.

"And so you have, Herr Lovecraft. So you have."

By this time they had reached the shack where Tanzler lived. He noticed the chalked note on the side of the door, and knew that his agent had gone through Lovecraft's suitcase. There was no electricity in the wooden structure so Tanzler lit a few candles and an old hurricane lantern. Lovecraft simply stood there while the Count moved some papers off of a chair and bade him sit.

Lovecraft was by no means willing to spend more than a few moments in that hideous edifice, but he needed to know what Tanzler knew.

"You still have not told me how you came into possession of the Cthulhu file."

"I don't feel the need to go into details on this with you, regardless of what you already know. Let us simply agree that my possession of it was not entirely legal. And that it was taken from me in a manner that was also not legal."

"How long ago was that?"

"In 1925. In May."

Tanzler did some quick calculations. He had not murdered Angell until fully eighteen months later. And Angell had only been involved in the case beginning the spring of 1925. Wilcox was still seeing him in March and April of that year, yet Lovecraft was saying he had the file in his possession in *May*.

"And 'The Call of Cthulhu' …?"

"Written sometime in the summer of 1926. August, maybe."

"When Professor Angell was still alive."

"Yes, precisely. I went to visit him earlier that year, to see if I could discover more about the cult."

"And …?"

"My dear Count, you are asking all the questions and allowing me none."

"In time, *mein lieber Freund*. Tea?"

One look at the crapped cups and filthy teapot decided that question for him.

"No, thank you, Count. Now, what was your question?"

"I was asking about your visit to Professor Angell."

"Ah, yes. The Professor was most kind and generous with his time, but he really had little to add to what I already knew. He did mention a group of what he called 'devil worshippers' who held rituals of a completely blasphemous nature in the land south of Baghdad, near the ancient city of Gudua. He mentioned also a tribe known as the Yezidis. I think he intended me to know that they were one and the same."

"Ach, the Yezidis. Nasty business, I understand." Tanzler was paying extreme attention to everything his guest was saying. There were some missing pieces in his understanding of the cult and now Lovecraft was supplying them. What he said next, however, indicated that the lantern-jawed New Englander was on the same page as Tanzler himself, and his superiors.

"There were enough of them in New York City when I lived there. Arabs, anyway. But Yezidis, I think, are Kurds? Well, it matters not to me. New York is a cesspool of non-Aryan types, including a population of Jews that will certainly bring this country to destruction. There is no possibility of assimilating people into our civilization who have a culture and a belief system so wholly antagonistic to our own. If you want to see devil worshippers, I suggest you consult your nearest synagogue."

The vehemence with which Lovecraft uttered these infamous lines surprised even Tanzler, no stranger to anti-Semitism and theories of eugenics and race science. Lovecraft was obviously tired and a little uncomfortable in Tanzler's humble lodgings, but that did not explain the articulation of a worldview so parallel to his own.

"Are there many Americans who feel the way you do?"

"Some of our greatest leaders feel this way. Henry Ford, Charles Lindbergh … but we were talking about Professor Angell."

"Are you sure you don't want any tea?"

"Quite sure, thank you, Count," he said, without a tinge of sarcasm.

"Then, you were saying …"

"The Professor intimated to me that the cult was in possession of a document, a text of some kind. A book. And that this book contained all their rituals and their methods for contacting alien forces."

"The Yezidis have a mysterious book that no one has seen. It is called the Black Book."

"I am not certain it is the same document, or the professor would have mentioned it. He was something of an expert on Middle Eastern religions, and this … cult was something new to him."

"I see. What was the book called?"

"According to him, he heard of it while consulting on a case of satanic ritual murder in Louisiana. The informer told him it was called *Necronomicon*."

"My knowledge of Greek is rusty, but I believe that word means 'names of the dead' or something like that."

"It refers to their High Priest, Cthulhu, who is dead but dreaming. He communicates in dreams to his … devotees."

"Dead, but dreaming …"Tanzler's voice trailed off as he thought of his beloved Elena, so close to death herself.

"So I am afraid I can't help you. I don't have the Cthulhu file, and I don't know more about it than what I published in my story."

"And the book?"

"The *Necronomicon*? I have no idea."

A few months earlier Tanzler's boss, Heinrich Himmler, had risen to prominence in the Nazi Party by crushing a revolt against Adolf Hitler by the SA, the *Sturmabteilung* or "Storm Troopers." His SS had become the *de facto* elite military arm of the Party. At the time Tanzler and Lovecraft were talking in Key West, Himmler was creating the *Sicherheitsdienst* or Security Service, the SD. Hitler would not become Chancellor of Germany until January of 1933, but the machinery of what would become the Third Reich was already in motion.

And on the last day of 1931—six months after Tanzler and Lovecraft's meeting—Himmler would create the Race and Settlement Office of the SS, which was concerned with racial purity and the requirement of potential SS recruits to prove their pure Aryan blood as well as that of any potential mate.

All during 1931, however, Himmler's orders were sent on a regular basis to Tanzler. Most of the memoranda concerned local intelligence operations, the running of Tanzler's network based in Key West and extending towards Havana in the south and up to the Carolinas in the north. Tanzler was performing basic housekeeping duties for the network and was not distinguishing himself in the process, but there was one function in particular that Himmler was paying for and for which failure was not an option: obtaining the Cthulhu File.

There was a very specific reason for this, and Tanzler was unaware of its significance. Quite simply, Himmler needed the File in order to make sense of a very important—albeit almost incomprehensible—manuscript in his possession, the one delivered to him by Viereck in New York.

The *Necronomicon.*

The document stayed on Himmler's desk until the creation of the SS-Ahnenerbe, the "ancestral heritage" research foundation that numbered many crank anthropologists and fringe academics in its ranks. Himmler also recruited the fascist philosopher and mystic Julius Evola, and put him to work researching material in the SS archives on secret societies, occult manuscripts, and the like, with a special view to finding out anything he could about the mysterious *Necronomicon* and its incantations that were not in any known language. Subhas Chandra Bose, the pro-Nazi, anti-British leader from India, was summoned to assist as well, in Himmler's belief that the book had an Indian or perhaps Tibetan component. It was Bose who had once seen the manuscript first-hand, during a visit to the Hadrahmut in 1919 when it was in the possession of a merchant of ancient manuscripts, who told him it was obtained from Jeremiah Shamir, a well-known purveyor of antique texts from Mosul. Shamir was the one who actually composed what became known as the Yezidi scriptures: clever forgeries that were sold as authentic to those Orientalist Europeans of the *fin de siècle* who sought genuine Yezidi texts. This conflation of the Yezidi "Black Book" with the *Necronomicon* would bedevil researchers for decades and confound efforts to locate either one. It was Bose who alerted the future Reichsführer-SS of the existence of the manuscript; and it was Himmler whose contact with German archaeologists had resulted in the discovery of the obscene statuette from Gudua (Kutha). He understood that the Book, the Cult, and the Idol were all part of the same underground movement, one that threatened the hegemony of the colonial powers over Africa, the Middle East, and Asia. Himmler knew he could exploit this cult to his advantage in the coming war.

The *Necronomicon* then made its way to Newport, Rhode Island from Kurdistan when the latter was overrun by British troops in 1924. How the book managed to get from Yemen to Kurdistan remained a mystery. It was removed for safekeeping by a scholar of ancient astronomy who was working in Mosul at the time. He was taken by a translated portion of the text that referred to the constellation *Ursa Major* (the Great Bear) and its asterism, the Big Dipper. He noted the connection between this constellation and a cult's activities that seemed to be timed to the position of the Great Bear in the sky at certain days and times of their infernal calendar. He brought the manuscript with him to the meeting in Newport that was attended by Professor Angell—a meeting hastily arranged when reports began coming in of the activities of this bloodthirsty cabal all around the world—and it was openly discussed and even marveled at by all those present. Part Greek, part Arabic and some other tongue that could not be identified, it was decided that only Professor George Angell of their group could decipher it.

And then it was stolen by Tanzler on the Providence docks, handed over to George Viereck, and from there made its way to Berlin.

Thus, the cursed tome that was being discussed by Tanzler and Lovecraft had been in Germany all along. Himmler, however, had reached an impasse. Instinctively he knew that the book contained secrets that were just as valuable, or even more valuable, than the Holy Grail, the Ark of the Covenant, and the Spear of Destiny: all of which were the subjects of secret missions he would authorize in the years to come. Now, however, his resources were not as great as they would be when the Reich was consolidated. He was working on a shoe-string. The *Necronomicon* was useless to him without the File.

When he first sent Tanzler to America it was because of the evidence of the Cthulhu Cult and the rumors of its unimaginable power. Now he had some of the pieces in his hand, but not everything.

He would have to lean on Tanzler even more.

As they talked, the sky outside the shack began to lighten. Dawn was coming, and the singing of birds could be heard outside. Lovecraft had not realized how long they had been speaking, and now he felt fatigue begin to wear him out.

They had discussed ancient cults, Eastern spirituality, Tanzler's trip to India and Southeast Asia, his time spent as a prisoner of war in Australia ... and eventually the subject of reanimating dead matter. It was this interest of Lovecraft's that had added a special interest to the mission for Tanzler, and he would get as much information from him as possible. He could already report back to Himmler on Lovecraft's loss of the Cthulhu file; Viereck in New York could follow up the story and maybe locate the police report on the theft. In the meantime, he would wheedle out of his guest the secrets of resurrecting a corpse. He suspected that Lovecraft knew more than he thought he did on the subject, and time was running out.

Perhaps a little shock therapy?

"Have you ever seen a Tesla coil?" he asked.

Tanzler powered up a gas-powered generator and in moments a naked electric bulb that Lovecraft had not noticed before began to flicker on. He adjusted some dials, and soon a large metal globe on top of a tall cylindrical column in the rear of the room began to buzz as little lightning bolts were created all around it. The buzzing of the coil was eerie in the pre-dawn silence of the room, and Lovecraft felt his hair standing on end. Whether that was from some effect of the electricity or his own paranoia, he didn't know.

Lovecraft was a man of science, and ordinarily this spectacle would be pleasing to him. But he was in a strange town in a strange state, far from home, in the company of a German immigrant who was some kind of wizard, and who knew all about the Cthulhu cult and the missing file. He suddenly felt that he was out of his depth entirely, and wondered briefly if a Tesla coil could be used as a weapon. His knowledge of science said no, but for once science was not a comfort.

The surge of plasma seemed to form a satanic halo around the head of his host, a man already weird in appearance. Tanzler's tiny eyes were hidden behind a perpetual squint and those thick eyeglasses, but his beard seemed to take on new life. His glasses reflected the dynamic discharges so that it appeared his eyes were emanating rays in all directions.

After a few moments, Tanzler powered down the device and turned to his guest.

"You are familiar with Nicola Tesla and his work?"

"Yes. Of course."

"Then you are aware that he has been in contact with extraterrestrial forces?"

"I understand that his wireless receiver has picked up anomalous signals from space."

"Precisely. There must be a source for those signals, an intelligence that is broadcasting them to our planet."

"What is your point?"

Tanzler checked to make sure that his equipment was properly shut down and that there was no damage to anything in its vicinity due to the electrical arcs.

"The intelligence that Tesla discovered may, in fact, be the same intelligence that the Cthulhu cult claims to contact."

This was getting out of hand. Lovecraft had come at this problem with a desire to find the root cause of his family's insanity. He had stolen a file that contained clippings and reports on the existence of a group of people who believed themselves in contact with a fantastic and unbelievable creature who was a medium between the Earth and some stellar race. They believed this contact was in the form of telepathy, dreams, and the like, and could be accelerated or amplified through the bizarre, orgiastic rituals they employed. It was possible, only *possible*, that this had something to do with his family's condition in ways that so far were not understood. If the cult was exhibiting some of the same symptoms then it was possible there was a psychological basis for the phenomenon. So far, so good.

But now this crazy German was telling him that there was a scientific basis for their beliefs: that instruments and devices might exist that would prove there was an intelligence lurking in the stars that was communicating with an entity here on Earth. He was getting too deep in the swamps of fantasy and paranoia, and longed for the common sense approach of Whitehead who saw arcane rituals for what they were: exhibitions of mental disorder. There were no gods, no demons, thought Lovecraft. And quite possibly no Martians, either. There was only Man, in all his hideous brutality and stupidity.

But Tanzler was still talking.

"Your story about the reanimator. Herbert West. He used some of the same techniques that would be familiar to those who follow Tesla. You wrote about reviving a corpse, infusing life back into lifeless matter …"

"It was only a story, a tale of fantasy, my dear Count. And not one of my most successful, I am ashamed to admit. I meant no scientific claims, no assertion of superior knowledge. It was a work of the imagination."

"As are all scientific discoveries, at first. Hasn't Herr Einstein shown us the fantastical realms that exist in our natural world?"

"I am not sure I understand the point you are trying to make."

"It is time I returned to my job at the hospital. Perhaps you would like to accompany me? You have not slept, and there are a few beds available. I can arrange a small room for you, if you like, for a few hours of sleep."

That sounded acceptable to Lovecraft, under the circumstances, and it would save him some money that he would otherwise have to spend on a hotel.

The two men left the shack with Lovecraft's suitcase in tow and made their way to the Marine Hospital where Tanzler worked. Lovecraft was wired, but exhausted. The spectacle of the Tesla coil in full operation was still with him, the spiny fingers of the arcs still glowing in his eyes.

They made their way to the hospital, but before they entered Tanzler gestured him to the rear of the structure where there appeared to be a disassembled aircraft of some sort with enormous wheels.

"This is one of my projects," he told the startled writer. "I am fixing the plane so that one day I may be able to fly away from here. I am thinking the South Pacific. There is an island there I remember from the old days. A real paradise on earth!"

Lovecraft could only stare at the bizarre contraption, which looked as if someone lived in it. It was missing its wings, but the fuselage seemed relatively intact. There was no rear wheel, however, so the whole contraption basically was immoveable. Now he knew that Tanzler was truly insane.

They entered the hospital from the rear entrance. The presence of military insignia here and there reassured him somewhat; the Marines were the best of the best, in Lovecraft's estimation, and he remembered how they had pacified the tiny nation of Haiti. That was one way to deal with savage cults, he thought at the time. This idea was now reinforced after the unsettling evening spent with Tanzler.

True to his word, the German "doctor" found Lovecraft a room and a narrow bed, for which the latter was exceedingly grateful. He collapsed onto it, and was asleep before he knew it.

Tanzler, who seemed not to need any sleep at all, was back at work in his radiology lab. When no one was around, he opened a drawer in his desk and withdrew a copy of a *Home Brew* magazine from almost ten years earlier. He opened it to the first installment of the Lovecraft tale, "Herbert West–Reanimator":

> …West had already made himself notorious through his wild theories on the nature of death and the possibility of overcoming it artificially. His views, which were widely ridiculed by the faculty and his fellow-students, hinged on the essentially mechanistic nature of life; and concerned means for operating the organic machinery of mankind by calculated chemical action after the failure of natural processes. In his experiments with various animating solutions he had killed and treated immense numbers of rabbits, guinea-pigs, cats, dogs, and monkeys, till he had become the prime nuisance of the college. Several times he had actually obtained signs of life in animals supposedly dead; in many cases violent signs …

This was the paragraph at the very start of the story that alerted

Tanzler to the fact that Lovecraft was aware of the same theories of reanimation that he, Tanzler, had been espousing privately for years. As he read on, he knew that Lovecraft was writing an instruction book for him if he knew how to read between the lines.

> Holding with Haeckel that all life is a chemical and physical process, and that the so-called "soul" is a myth, my friend believed that artificial reanimation of the dead can depend only on the condition of the tissues; and that unless actual decomposition has set in, a corpse fully equipped with organs may with suitable measures be set going again in the peculiar fashion known as life. That the psychic or intellectual life might be impaired by the slight deterioration of sensitive brain-cells which even a short period of death would be apt to cause, West fully realised.

This was the key point. While Tanzler did not agree with West, the famous German biologist Ernst Haeckel, or Lovecraft that the soul was a myth, he did realize that the body had to be kept from decomposing if reanimation was to take place. One cannot play a melody on an organ if the pipes are broken. Certain nutrients and other chemicals had to be injected into the body both to retard decomposition and to counter the effects of dehydration and lack of life-sustaining vitamins. But there was an aspect of the treatment that neither Lovecraft nor his fictional creation Herbert West had included, and that was electricity.

The labors of Tesla, whom Tanzler fervently admired, had demonstrated the link between light and energy on the one side, and life itself on the other. Obviously, without that spark of energy there could be no resuscitation of dead matter, no matter how many elixirs or chemical nutrients were pumped into the body. Thus his use of electrical instruments in the attempt to cure his Elena of tuberculosis.

Her family, however, had other ideas. They did not trust him, in part because it was obvious he had romantic designs on the young woman and in part because his methods were … unsound. They were strange and horrifying, an affront to civilized medicine. Ironically, it was civilized medicine that admitted it had no cure for Elena's condition; they just looked better at failing.

The combination of Lovecraft's approach to revivification, Tesla's electrical principles, and his own knowledge of modern instrumentation coupled with training in the occult arts meant that he had a greater chance of curing Elena or, failing that, of keeping her body viable long enough after death that he would be able to apply the full range of his medical powers to her in order to cleanse her body of the disease and then bring her back to him. How could she resist the man who had brought her back from the dead?

And how could Himmler resist one of his own agents who had demonstrated to the world that German science and ingenuity were superior to anything else on the planet?

As for the Cthulhu cult, they understood what Tanzler already knew: that even a god can be dead and alive at the same time. There is an invisible network of electrical impulses, insisted Tanzler, which connects human beings not only with each other but with beings and entities on other planes, on other planets. Those human beings who realize this and who exploit it will overthrow the established world order and replace it with one in harmony with the mysterious, telepathic instructions of the Ancient Ones.

Those who do not will be destroyed.

In his room, on his hospital bed, Lovecraft dreamed a dream of demons from space. If there are demons on the Earth, his dream seemed to say, then why not demons on other planets, too? If one can summon a demon with a book and a candle, which one actually appears? The demon of Earth or a demon from Elsewhere?

In his fitful, unpleasant sleep he saw a great, groaning Gate studded with the nails that had crucified the Savior of the Christians and it was being pushed open from the other side, even as a horde of small, dark men struggled to open it from this side. He knew the answer lay on the other side of that Gate.

As the Gate budged open the slightest amount, he could hear a sound from the other side.

"Help me!" spoke the strangled voice, one he knew so well. "Help us all!"

Lovecraft awoke with a start, wild-eyed and perspiring profusely. He tried to calm himself in the broad light of day, but it was no use. That sound … that hideous, croaking sound.

It was his mother's voice.

CHAPTER EIGHTEEN

THE EIDOLON

Finally, the point is not to exercise a kind of physical constraint on blind or even imaginary forces but to touch minds, reinvigorate them, and discipline them.

—Emile Durckheim, *The Myth of Primitive Psychology*

Dwight Monroe was getting worried.

The old spy sat in his office outside Washington, D.C. and scanned the dispatches. The GPS chip was still sending out its signal so he knew Angell's location to the city block. Unfortunately, the reluctant college professor was nowhere near a city block. He was in the back of beyond.

He didn't make the extraction rendezvous as scheduled. The helo team would try again in twenty-four hours and again twenty-four hours later, as per pre-arrangement. If Angell didn't show up for any of these scheduled pick-ups they would have to find an alternate way to make contact. The fact that his GPS was still sending a signal was only minimally reassuring, because his location seemed to be nowhere near the western border of Iran. It was, in fact, heading in the opposite direction.

Intelligence had come in from several sources on the ground reporting a firefight at the Towers of Silence in Yazd. That had to be Angell and his team. But that was twenty-four hours ago. Since then, no one knew what had happened. Worst case scenario was an interception by the Revolutionary Guard, but if the GPS was any indication Angell was on his way in the opposite direction from Evin Prison in Teheran. In fact, he was headed for the Afghan border.

He had been on the sat phone with Aubrey every few hours. The exhausted agent could report nothing of substance. He had no way of getting in touch with the agent known as Adnan. As per Adnan's training he and his team of Kurdish rebels used burner phones and they destroyed them after every mission. If Angell was making his way towards Afghanistan it could only mean that he was travelling with Adnan. Nothing else made any sense.

To make matters more interesting there were UFO reports coming in from the Iran-Iraq border region, right in the heart of Kurdistan. Monroe felt these had to be related to the super-secret stealth helicopter being used by the SOAR team in Baghdad, which had already made two trips across the border: one to insert Angell and the second to (unsuccessfully) extract him. Iranian jets would be scrambled the next time these reports came in, of that Monroe was certain. Iran had had its share of UFO sightings, one of which—in the 1970s—resulted in a general flap among their military. There were those in Iran, however, who believed that these "sightings" were really of American spy planes and drones.

Monroe shuffled through the papers of the Lovecraft Codex, brittle as some of them were with age, and consulted the gazette. The gazette was a simple chronological breakdown of the salient points that were covered in the Codex, and it helped him sometimes to refresh his memory of the timeline in order to apply it to the current situation. Events that occurred decades ago could surface in ways that only someone schooled in the peculiar tradecraft of remote viewing, PSI, and ancient divination systems could deduce. There was a symbol stream flowing beneath the surface of everyday events, and Monroe was particularly keen on taking its pulse.

If Angell was going to Afghanistan there had to be a very good reason. He had not found the Book yet, but he was moving fast to the place where it was being held. He only hoped that Adnan was unharmed and providing the kind of tactical support needed for this new deviation from the plan. Aubrey had assured him he was, but the stakes were so high Monroe didn't know who he could trust anymore.

Afghanistan. Monroe didn't wish that tour on anyone. He knew from personal experience that the Afghan people were heroic, brave and courageous fighters with a tremendous sense of honor and dignity. That wasn't the problem. He was worried about the Taliban, about remnants of Al-Qaeda operating in the region, and even about what was left of the Northern Alliance. There were tribal feuds and rivalries going back centuries, and they were a minefield for outsiders. Add to that the increased trade in opium and you had all the elements of a failed state being run by criminal gangs and terror groups. He wasn't feeling guilty yet about sending Angell into that shitstorm, but he knew that eventually he would. He only hoped that when it was all over he could make his apologies in person, to a living, breathing Gregory Angell.

The news coming in from his sources as well as the general media increased his growing sense of despair. A group calling itself *Boko Haram* had just kidnapped hundreds of young girls from a school in Nigeria. Intel described the group as Al-Qaeda wannabes who were going to sell the girls into slavery to raise money for their operation. He sensed there was something deeper at work there. It was all part of the overall picture, a picture some insane artist had begun to paint decades earlier in tints of blood and tears.

Boko Haram. Al-Qaeda. Al-Qaeda in the Maghreb (AQIM), Jema'ah Islammiyah, Lashkar-e-Taiba. And now this group claiming to be the Islamic State of Iraq and the Levant: ISIL. List all these groups and try to draw a line connecting their ideological and religious positions and you would see that none of them agreed with each other on anything. But they were all vicious, all murderous. On the surface they were different; below the surface, Monroe knew they were being guided and controlled by something no one could see but which was lethal for all that. He could see it. And eventually others would, too, once they had opened their minds up to the possibility.

Something occurred to Monroe as he sifted through the pages of the Codex. Iraq. Kutha. Kurds. Yazd. Zoroastrians. Yezidis. Afghanistan.

Oh, Christ, he said to himself. *Afghanistan. That could only mean one thing: Kafiristan.*

The new name for this region in the east of Afghanistan on the Pakistan border is Nuristan, the "land of the enlightened." For more than a hundred years, however, it was known as Kafiristan, the "land of the unbelievers," or *kafirs.* That was because it was the last place in Afghanistan to accept Islam. It remained animist—what some call "pagan"—until the end of the nineteenth century when they were finally converted at the point of a sword. Many Nuristanis today are devout Muslims; but many retain the old ways, as well. Across the border into Pakistan there is another group of "kafirs" with whom the Nuristanis have much in common and to whom they are, in fact, related: the Kalasha people. Prior to 1895, the people of Kafiristan and the people of Chitral—the Kalasha people—were both members of the same polytheistic religion. The Kalasha are called "Black Kafirs" and the Nuristanis "Red Kafirs" to distinguish them. In a situation similar to that of the Kurds, they found themselves divided by arbitrary boundaries set by foreign powers, and in 1895–1896 the people on the Kafiristan side of the border were forcibly converted to Islam, while those on the Indian (now Pakistani) side remained as they were.

From the Yezidis of Iraq, to the Zoroastrians of Iran, to the Nuristanis of Afghanistan, and the Kalashas of Pakistan, there exists deep within the Muslim world a network of cultures with pre-Islamic beliefs and traditions that doctrinaire Muslims consider "satanic." These are also people who are different in appearance from their neighbors. The Yezidis and Nuristanis often have blue eyes and even blonde hair, characteristics that they ascribe to being descendants of the soldiers of the armies of Alexander the Great as he marched through the region on his way to India.

Kafiristan (or Nuristan) is located in the Hindu Kush: a dangerous and inhospitable part of the world at the foot of the Himalayas. One of the reasons for the late conversion of the people to Islam could very well be the inaccessibility of the region. When the snows come, Kafiristan is virtually cut off from the rest of the world.

At one time it was believed that Osama bin Laden had retreated to Kafiristan, based on remote viewing sessions by none other than Jason Miller. By the time American and Coalition forces could reach the area during Operation Red Wing in the summer of 2005 it was believed that OBL had dug himself in and was being protected by loyal Al-Qaeda operatives in the region north of Kunar. It was never determined whether or not Miller's RV sessions had been correct, for the terror leader disappeared once again only to turn up in Abbottabad, Pakistan not long after. A look at the map shows that Abbottabad is a short distance (as the crow flies) from Nuristan, and less than 300 miles if using the Islamabad-Peshawar Highway. Once across the border, bin Laden would have been able to rely upon an Al-Qaeda and ISI (the Pakistani intelligence agency) network to get him across Pakistan at that narrow point where he would set up his residence and live quietly until taken out by Seal Team Six a few years later.

This was the region where Gregory Angell was headed, in the company of his contact Adnan and two of his men.

"We can't drive all the way. It would take days, and the danger of running into patrols of militia, regular army, and even the Taliban once we get close to the Afghan border is enormous. No way, Professor. We have to go back. If we *can* go back."

This argument went on for more than two hours after the firefight at the Towers of Silence and after Angell had a fitful nap on a threadbare couch, listening to the sounds of Iranian pop music coming from a radio in the kitchen.

In the end, it was decided that they would drive to the Afghan border once they got the word from their people that there was no one looking for them. The two dead Kurds closed the case as far as the authorities were concerned. The fact of a dozen dead cultists threw panic into their colleagues, causing them to go underground for awhile to see if there would be any blowback. They had not achieved their objective, but it was too dangerous to continue the operation immediately. Nonetheless, word went out through their networks that it was possible their targets had escaped, and to keep an eye out for ... well, anyone. They had no idea who they were really looking for. Had they kept the old Zoroastrian priest alive they might have had more luck.

Adnan was not happy with the change to their mission. At the same time, he knew it would be dangerous to go back the way they came. He wanted to make contact with Aubrey, but he knew he could not call him at once. He had to use burner cell phones; if he was caught with a sat phone or something equally sophisticated his whole network could be blown. So he sent the driver out to source a few more phones, and he and Angell waited in the apartment, not speaking, with a lot on their minds.

There was nowhere to get online, and even if they could the Iranians were blocking a lot of sites and generally censoring Internet access. Any suspicious web activity could be traced back to them, especially as they would be forced to use an internet café or some other public access point. Adnan went over all the options in his mind, but he was a professional who had been in-country for more than a year and knew what he was up against.

On the plus side, there was probably no one looking for them on the road to Birjand, which was their do or die point. After Birjand, they had a decision to make: north to the official crossing at Taybad, or south to the more questionable crossing at Zaranj. With a sinking feeling that he didn't let Angell see, Adnan knew which one they had to take.

The Zaranj crossing was dangerous; it was used by smugglers (mostly of weapons and drugs) and bandits. It was often said that no foreigner ever crossed into Afghanistan at Zaranj and came out alive. In addition it was Taliban country. One could not imagine a more potentially lethal spot in all of Central Asia, made more so by the fact that the US Marines who had been deployed to Zaranj were on their way home after the Afghan elections, leaving the whole place in the control of the Afghan National Army, the ANA. Yet, it was a crossing where not having the right identification papers, visas, or passports might be seen as an asset rather than a liability. It was also a busy border station, with the newly-constructed two-lane Highway 606 leading from Zaranj to Delaram in Afghanistan with a proposed connection through Iran to the port city of Chabahar. Even though the region was in turmoil, commerce was still in full swing.

Once across, he could make contact with a local clan that would get them close to their destination. If they tried to cross at Taybad, they could easily get detained on either side of the border if the fake papers he was hastily arranging for the professor didn't hold up to scrutiny.

This entire operation was going sideways, and so fast it made his head spin. He was deep undercover, a NOC in a country that had no diplomatic relations with the United States and which could use his presence there—and Angell's—as an international incident and bargaining chip in whatever fucked up plot the ayatollahs came up with.

But he understood Angell's insistence that he get to Nuristan as quickly as possible. He had to hand it to the guy. He was obviously nervous as hell, on the verge of a panic attack every hour, and he still pushed Adnan for a way to get to the other side of one of the most dangerous countries in the world. It wasn't just Afghanistan; it was Nuristan. Nuristan had to be the darkest spot in the country. Hell, they lost a Chinook in there back in 2005. Not to mention some very good men. They thought OBL was in there, too, but didn't find him. No surprise there; the guy had been slippery as hell and had a lot of on-the-ground support. You could hide a 747 in there and no one would ever know.

Adnan was comfortable in Iran. He knew his way around. He passed easily for a local, and he had solid tactical support. He could drive them to the border and get them across. As for Afghanistan, they would have to cross the entire country to get to Nuristan. He gave their chances there about 50-50.

And after Nuristan, then what? They would be in an inaccessible border region between Afghanistan and Pakistan. They could try to make it to Kashmir, and from there to an Indian military base. It would be tricky diplomatically, but he was sure Aubrey could arrange transport for them in India.

But ... how? Cross the Hindu Kush? The Himalayas? This wasn't something out of Kipling or the Great Game. They were working against the clock.

Jesus.

He had to get a hold of Aubrey.

As an ethnic Kurd, and a member of a minority religion to boot, Adnan had a unique perspective on the conflict in the Middle East. But he was also a loyal American, and belonged to the elite intelligence community. He was proud of who he was and what he had accomplished in his life. His parents were equally proud, even though they didn't know much about his work. They only knew that he was working for the American government.

His languages and knowledge of Kurdish clans and cultures made him one of those agents that got loaned out for special ops. There were few people working for US intelligence—domestic or international—who had that kind of expertise. Languages did not come easily to most Americans, and those who could speak Kurdish dialects as well as Farsi without a noticeable accent were few and far between. That meant he spent a lot of time in Iran, Iraq, Syria and Turkey: territories that include what used to be called Kurdistan.

Afghanistan, however, was a little outside his comfort zone and way above his pay grade. But what he witnessed at the Towers of Silence hardened his heart. He lost two good men that day, and his last call from them was chilling:

They must be stopped.

They were strong men. Warriors. Passionate about few things in this world outside of their people and their struggle for survival. They were not given to exaggeration or hyperbole.

They must be stopped.

If Bahadur took the time to call him as he was looking down the barrels of a dozen automatic weapons and certain death, it was to give Adnan a message that he felt had to be delivered regardless of the cost to himself. Regardless of the fact that he would use the last moments of his life on Earth to deliver that message.

They must be stopped.

His brain told him to pack it in and find a way back to the extraction site. But the ghosts of his comrades had other instructions and he began to realize he was really taking orders from them.

In the middle of that night, about two hours before dawn, Adnan, Angell and the driver were back on the road. They were making for the city of Birjand.

Adnan would wait to phone Aubrey about their new mission until they were far enough away from Yazd. He would use one of the burner phones and then smash it by the side of the road. He had two more, provided by his faithful driver Sangar.

They were provided with more bottles of water, flat bread and dried food to eat along the way. They were not intending to stop for any reason, except to get gas if necessary. The trunk had two spare jerry cans of gas, but the drive ahead to Birjand was more than 400 miles. From there it was another 250 miles to the border. Once they got to Afghanistan, they would leave their car behind in Iran as they were going to be met by Adnan's contact. Sangar would drive the car to a town close to the border crossing and wait in Iran for instructions.

All proceeded without any problems all the way to Birjand. The 400 mile trip took almost ten hours, and by the time they reached the city Adnan decided it was okay to call Aubrey using a special number and coded system for communicating key information that had been provided to him for emergencies.

PETER LEVENDA

They stopped outside a small market on the outskirts of town, legs shaky and rattled from the long drive in a car with questionable suspension, and Sangar went inside to get more bottled water and the lay of the land. Adnan made the call to Aubrey with Angell in the seat next to him.

A series of clicks replaced the usual ringing sound, and Aubrey was on the line.

After an exchange of codes Adnan said, "Blue. Package sent airmail to the east coast." Blue was Adnan's coded designator, and "airmail" meant they were traveling by land. East coast meant Afghanistan.

The "package" of course was Angell.

The rest of the conversation was unintelligible to the "package." Angell understood all the words, but not the sentences made up of those words. It was like a page from some Surrealist's novel. It was totally out of context for what was happening. And in the end Aubrey did not ask to speak to Angell. He couldn't, for Angell didn't know the "language" they were using, a fact that was not lost on the multi-lingual professor and which made him smile in spite of the fact.

"Aubrey sends his regards," Adnan finally told him. "He regrets not being able to speak with you personally. He thinks you're very brave to continue with this mission in view of everything that has happened so far."

"I don't really have a choice, do I?"

Adnan smiled a little ruefully. "I guess not. It's not like you can pick up your toys and go home," he said, gesturing around at their environment.

"So, what's next?"

"They've been monitoring our progress through the GPS chips. They know where we are, they just didn't know why. Now they do. They're going to do their best to provide ground support and arrange for an extraction team when we're ready. We still have bases in Afghanistan, and they are contacting them now to see what options are available.

"When I told him what crossing we're going to use, Aubrey about shit his pants."

"That's comforting."

"No worries. It's all good."

Somehow those pleasantries did nothing to assuage Angell's anxiety.

And rightly so, as it turned out.

A few miles away, Jason Miller sat in his car and got a phone call from one of his spotters.

"They are outside Birjand. Still heading east. Still the three of them."

"Do not engage. Just keep me informed if they change their itinerary."

He rang off, and then sat and thought awhile.

They were obviously heading for a border crossing into Afghanistan. But which border crossing?

He pulled out a map and studied it for awhile. There were a few possibilities, legitimate crossings, some of which were hairier than others. And then, of course, there were the unofficial crossings: smuggler's routes through dangerous terrain. They wouldn't be able to take their car into there. Even a jeep would have problems negotiating some of those passes. They would have to walk. Did they have that kind of time?

He didn't think so.

They would use a regular crossing, and there were only two within striking distance of Birjand.

Miller closed his eyes and began the deep breathing exercises that he used to initiate the remote viewing process.

He began, as always for this mission, with an image. The image was a kind of *eidolon*, a word he picked up during an informal meeting with Umberto Eco in Turin a few months earlier. Eidolon was Eco's suggestion as a term for the meditative symbol Miller used in his remote viewing sessions.

Miller had presented his government credentials to Eco's assistant with a request for an urgent meeting. This was shortly after his desertion from the remote viewing team when he traveled to Europe incognito to begin researching secret societies and obscure religious denominations in the Levant. He came across Eco's work in semiotics and realized that this was the type of perspective he lacked. Eco had introduced the science of symbols to a wide audience with his novels, but he was at heart a philosopher who understood the relationship that exists between symbols and the things they represent, as well as symbols taken in and of themselves. This opened Miller's eyes to the possibilities of remote viewing taken to a whole new level, a transcendental plane where the symbol stream flowed beneath the surface world of material reality. It was the missing link, as far as Miller was concerned, and he wanted to talk to Eco directly. Hence the subterfuge, since Miller was no longer an employee of the federal government.

At first, Miller tried to convince Eco that he was there because he was tracking a terror group and that Eco's knowledge of secret societies—especially those with a political motivation—would be of assistance. Eco, however, saw through the charade at once and became impatient.

"Mr. Miller, I am an academic and a writer. I do not consort with the type of individuals I write about in my books. You understand that, I think?"

Eco's English was impeccable, if highly accented and a delivery that was sometimes halting. Miller replied by saying "Yes, Dottore. It's in the realm of the information you have already gathered on secret societies and cults that I need your help."

Eco sighed.

"*Foucault's Pendulum*, you mean? Young man, that book is about a hoax. It's about the careful cultivation of a hoax, a fantastic story about a secret cult that *does not exist*. It's fiction, and even in the novel it is revealed to be fiction, almost from the beginning. Do you know how many people write to me every day from all over the world with more information on this non-existent cult? Do you realize how many people take it seriously, believe in the existence of something *I made up*? And now, here is a member of the American intelligence community asking me for … I believe you call it 'deep background' … on something that has no substance whatsoever and therefore cannot have even a shallow background much less a deep one. It's insane."

"Doctor Eco, I am not here about the specific secret societies mentioned in your book, but about a genuine cult. One that we have reason to believe …"

"Is about to destroy the world? Something like that?"

Miller was silent in the face of Eco's irritation.

"This obsession with cults and secret societies is one of the first steps towards fascism. You understand that, don't you? Conspiracy, paranoia, secret enemies, hidden plots … *The Protocols of the Learned Elders of Zion* … I mention that text in my novels … that was a hoax, too, and people believed in it so strongly they invented the Holocaust."

"Sir. What if there was another such text, one with the power to inspire thousands … no, millions … of followers worldwide. Another *Protocols*, but one that deals specifically with a kind of religion. One that is at the heart of all religions, all belief systems, and has the capacity to produce another Holocaust, but one of even greater proportions …"

"Then I would say it doesn't exist," the philosopher said, interrupting him.

"Perhaps. But for the sake of argument, say there is a text that not only includes religious concepts and images but which goes beyond that to embrace modern ideas about consciousness, genetics, space travel …"

"Like von D niken? Zecharia Sitchin? Pauwels and Bergier?"

Miller nodded.

"Yes, essentially. But those were non-fiction accounts …"

"Just barely."

"Agreed. But imagine a scripture, a religious text, a received document, which incorporated all this material in a coherent, or at least consistent, fashion?"

"Well," said Eco, leaning back in his leather chair that creaked under his weight. "There have been inventions of this type. All sorts of 'space gospels.' Insipid things."

"Yes. But the one I am describing has an ancient pedigree."

"Such an origin would argue heavily in favor of its being accepted by a great many people, unfortunately."

"This is what is happening now."

Eco leaned forward with renewed interest. "Do you have a copy of this text?"

Miller just shook his head.

"I am looking for it. Which is why I need your help."

The old novelist looked at Miller for a long time. He was a large man with a round face, mustache, and glasses, and dressed in a fine suit of European cut. His novels had all been bestsellers, which argued for his competence where the manipulation of images and symbols was concerned. In a sense, his novels were proof of the power of semiotics, demonstrations of that discipline in very tangible forms. Eco was a conscious practitioner of the art, and this was the type of expertise that Miller wanted to access.

But he was no dummy.

"Who are you really, Mr. Miller?"

"Sir?"

"Who do you work for? It isn't CIA I don't think. It must be one of the other ones, the ones that get very little publicity and hence no novels written about them."

"Sir."

"I thought so. Are you one of Hal Puthoff's boys? Over at SRI?"

Eco had put it all together: Miller's intelligence credentials, his interest in secret societies and cults, and especially his direct approach to Eco himself. This was not a regular CIA dangle; he had been through enough of those before. This man, this Jason Miller, had an intensity about him that suggested something even darker, more clandestine. All his talk about a terror group and then suddenly an esoteric text … the name of Hal Puthoff came immediately to mind. Science, the military, intelligence, and the paranormal.

Puthoff was one of the pioneers of research into PSI back in the 1970s, out of his office at what was then known as the Stanford Research Institute in Palo Alto, California. He, Russell Targ and many other luminaries of the time were investigating paranormal phenomena, including even Uri Geller (the famous spoon-bending Israeli psychic). But their chief program, the one that got all the CIA funding, was remote viewing.

You couldn't make this stuff up. Eco knew all about the program, and its continued existence for decades indicated that some of what he had written about government involvement in occultism had a basis in reality, which made the whole story at the heart of *Foucault's Pendulum* even more delicious. At least, to him.

"I did not work for Puthoff, sir. That was before my time."

"Of course, of course. But I am on the right track, correct?"

Miller nodded, swallowing.

"Very well. I have a proposition for you. You tell me how remote viewing works and I will tell you everything I know about whatever it is you're asking me. Do we have a deal?"

And there it was. Miller explained how it worked, how he was taught and then the personal modifications he made, and Eco suggested the use of an eidolon: an image, an idol or a two-dimensional symbol, which contained within it the "spiritual" aspect of the thing represented by the symbol. He cautioned Miller not to be too literal-minded about his choice, but instead to let an accumulation of ideas and images form to create a perfect gateway to the part of the brain that controlled remote viewing. And, most importantly, to share the eidolon with no one else. Not even Eco himself.

In return, Miller spoke about his personal mission to find the mysterious book before the terror groups did.

"It was composed, according to what we have been told, sometime in the eighth century by an Arab who may or may not have been a Muslim. It is not a particularly Islamic text; in fact, it was written in Arabic originally but contained much that was not in that language, suggesting an earlier composition. Its philosophical context is definitely pre-Islamic and polytheist."

Eco raised an eyebrow. Something was nagging at his memory.

"And what does this text actually say? What does it do?"

"Well, we don't really know. We only have bits and pieces. We know from the chatter ..."

"Chatter?"

"Intercepted communications, mostly between members of various guerrilla and terror groups that we collect from phone calls, text messages, emails, social media postings ..."

"Yes, please. I understand. Go on."

"Well, the chatter indicates that the book contains a set of instructions for, ah, making contact or communicating with, ah, forces that exist ... well, elsewhere. It posits the existence of a gate, which we assume to mean a theoretical construct that would permit access to other modalities of ..."

Eco, by this time, was smiling incredulously.

"What?"

"I'm very sorry my American intelligence operative friend, but what you are telling me is very funny."

"Well, I admit that it strains belief but we *are* talking about a kind of religious or occult text ..."

"No, no, no. You don't understand. I know the book you are talking about. I know it very well!"

"Seriously?"

"Certainly. There is even an obscure reference to its theme in *Foucault's Pendulum*." He began pulling out books and papers from a stack next to his chair. "This is not my office, unfortunately. I am only here for a short while. Ah, here …"

"But … I read that book. Carefully …"

"Not carefully enough, I am afraid," he said, passing a copy of the book over to Miller with his finger pointing at a passage. It was a reference to the word *Cthulhu*.

"What is that?"

"Ah, you have never heard of it?"

"I don't think so."

"It is a reference to the stories of an American writer, Howard Phillips Lovecraft. He created what is sometimes—erroneously—referred to as the 'Cthulhu Mythos' and …"

"Wait! What did you just say?"

"Lovecraft, he …"

"No, no. The other word. How did you pronounce it?"

"Oh, you mean Cthulhu. Ku … tu … lu."

Miller sat back in his chair and looked away. There was a window with a view of the old city of Turin. In the distance, could be seen the church known as "Granma," a weird round-shaped edifice about which many strange tales were told. Turin was where Nietzsche went insane. It was also, briefly, a town where the French sage Nostradamus resided.

"Kutulu," he whispered, half to himself. "I didn't catch that before. I saw all those consonants and my eyes just passed over the word."

"Lovecraft himself suggested that the sound made by the letters was a sort of blurting noise rather than a word we could pronounce using human speech apparatus, but the link between Cthulhu and the word chthonic is so close that …"

"I heard that word. Not that long ago. In a different context."

Not understanding, Eco plowed on.

"But that is what I am trying to tell you! There is no Cthulhu. There never was. It was a fictional device, an invention!"

Miller looked away from the window and directly at the philosopher.

"And the book?"

"The book! Another fabrication! It doesn't exist, Cthulhu doesn't exist …"

"The book," Miller insisted. "Where is it? *What* is it? What was it called?"

Eco sighed in frustration.

"You are wasting your time, and your government's time. The book doesn't exist. The *Necronomicon* doesn't exist!"

Miller paused, and looked down at his shoes. His heart was racing, and he felt half-in, half-out of the room he was in, the city, the country, and the world. Without realizing it or intending it, Umberto Eco had just put the pieces together for him.

He had just fallen down the rabbit hole.

In Iran, Miller opened his eyes.

"Zaranj," he said to himself. "They're going to Zaranj."

CHAPTER NINETEEN

KAFIRISTAN

They call it Kafiristan. By my reckoning it's the top right-hand corner of Afghanistan, not more than three hundred miles from Peshawar. They have two and thirty heathen idols there, and we'll be the thirty-third.

— Rudyard Kipling, *The Man Who Would Be King*

They stopped short of the Afghan border.

They were outside the village of Milak, on route A-71. They could look across the border from where they stood. They parked by the side of the road to consider their next move.

Adnan and Sangar got out first, telling Angell to sit back and wait. The two men walked up and down outside the car, talking in low voices and glancing over at the crossing at Zaranj.

"This could get hairy," said Sangar.

Adnan nodded, slightly, with a look back at Angell still sitting in the car.

"We'll be met once we get through."

"It's the getting through that'll be tough. I don't like it."

"There is a US Marine base, FOB Delaram, up a little ways north of Zaranj."

"Used to be. After the Afghan elections they're ready to redeploy Stateside. They may have already gone. Even if they left a small contingent here you know they'd pretty much stay on base. And the smugglers practically run the place under the noses of the Afghan security forces—the ANA—and the Marines. I can't see anyone coming out here to save your ass."

"If we can manage to get to the Zaranj airfield we might be able to hitch a ride to Kamdesh. It's just north of the town."

"Seriously? Look around you."

The area was pure desert. It was hot, dusty and dry, with a temperature north of 90 degrees F. The land was flat, and a paved road led the way to the checkpoint with a caravan of trucks and cars choking it: the pride of the brand-new Highway 606. From a distance the city of Zaranj looked like something you would see on an Etch-a-Sketch, faint straight lines that would be erased if you just shook the sand a little.

"The Zaranj airfield is a major terrorist target. The ANA has to patrol the tarmac every day to make sure there are no IEDs. Getting past the guards and hopping a flight to Kamdesh ... man, there is no such thing, anyway. You'd be lucky to get a ride to Kabul, and from there you're pretty much fucked. There's no one you can trust to get you the rest of the way to Kafiristan."

As they stood there talking, they could see a plume of dust about three kilometers from their position.

"You see that? It's nothing. A car, a truck. But you can see them from miles away. Just like they'd see you. The ANA won't give a shit until you get close enough to border control, but the Taliban and the smugglers will."

Sangar looked up and around, as if he couldn't believe what he had to say.

"Man, we have a job to do here in Iran. It's what we're trained for, and what we know. This ... this is not in our job description. You know what I'm saying? This is a suicide mission. And not in a good way."

"We came all this way, and you're just now telling me not to go?"

"I did my part, man. I got you this far. I wanted you to see what you were up against. If the smugglers don't kill you, the desert will. This place makes Yazd look like Vegas. You see what I mean? Just look. The land past Zaranj is all desert. Pure desert. It's isolated and desolate. Taliban nation, man. They bring bodies out there and leave them to die. They don't have to kill them. They just leave them there, dug halfway into the ground. They aren't found again for years, and when they are they're just rags and bones."

The plume of dust was getting closer. Adnan could just about see the silhouette of the car that was causing it. It was headed their way. Probably an Iranian making his way to the border town to trade bootleg CDs, or something.

"If we don't go now, Bahadur and Firooz would have died for nothing."

"This is war, man. People die in war. They knew what they were getting into when they signed up."

"Yeah, well, then I guess I do too."

Adnan was irritated, but not at Sangar. He knew his friend was right. Sangar had spent three years in the States getting his master's degree in engineering and learning to speak English like a surfer from the beaches south of LA. But there was no way he could abandon the mission at this point. His orders from Aubrey were clear, and when you talked to Aubrey you were talking to the highest levels of the American intelligence "community." You might as well be talking to the President. Even better: presidents come and go, but people like Aubrey remained from administration to administration and got things done.

The approaching car appeared to slow down as they were arguing. Angell noticed it in the rear view mirror and then turned to watch it. He saw the car slow but it didn't stop. He caught a glimpse of the driver who did not seem to take notice of them at all. The car continued on and joined the line behind the traffic heading into Afghanistan.

Angell turned back around to face Adnan and Sangar who were still talking by the edge of the road.

WHUMP!

A flash of light preceded by microseconds the sound of the explosion as the car that had just passed them detonated on the highway into Zaranj.

Adnan and Sangar hit the ground as a reflex and Angell simply stared out the windshield at the plume of dark smoke that erupted near the border control point.

This is where we are going? he asked himself.

"This could work in our favor," said Adnan when he got back in the car. "The border guards are probably cowering somewhere and not watching who comes in. There's chaos at the checkpoint, damaged vehicles, broken bodies. Small fires. All their attention is focused on survival right now."

"You still have to get through that mess," offered Sangar, getting behind the wheel. "You could probably walk through, if you can sidestep the blast site. But the road looks completely torn up there. No vehicle is going to make it through now, not until they clear that away and do some repairs. Could be days. If you're going to go, it had better be now while everyone is still shaken up."

"Agreed," Adnan replied. He looked over the backseat at Angell. "You ready to go?"

Angell looked out at the devastation caused by the suicide bomber, and could only nod.

The look on his face caused both Adnan and Sangar to laugh out loud.

Sangar drove them as close as he dared, then stopped the car. With the engine still idling, he held out his hand to Adnan.

"Good hunting, my friend."

"Give my best to everyone. I plan to be back here in seventy-two hours. After Kamdesh we should be able to hop a military transport back to Zaranj or maybe a ticket out of here. I'll keep you informed along the way."

Angell and Adnan got out of the car, carrying nothing but the clothes on their backs. Sangar waited until he saw them get onto the highway and make their way towards the border, then made a U-turn in the sand and drove away, back towards the heart of Iran.

He would hole up in one of the towns they had passed and wait for a signal from Adnan.

Or, failing that, news of his death or capture.

New Orleans
Same day

Half a world away, in the devastated Ninth Ward of New Orleans, police officers make a gruesome discovery.

The aftermath of Hurricane Katrina in 2005 left many parts of the city under water and destroyed homes, shops and churches. The Ninth Ward was disproportionately affected, and a number of condemned structures still dot the Lower Ninth all these years later. When a Vietnamese real estate developer decided to build an Asian supermarket and restaurant on one block, he hired a bulldozer to come in and level one such structure.

As the dozer rolled over the building, wood planks and sheetrock shattered under its massive tracks while people from the neighborhood stood on the streets and watched. When the dozer was finished and pulled away from the debris, workers came in and started breaking up the larger pieces and piling the refuse into dumpsters.

When they reached the ground level, a scream was heard that penetrated the hearing of anyone within a two block radius of the site.

An iron trapdoor was discovered that workers thought was part of a safe that was left behind. Thinking they would find a treasure, or at least some water-damaged currency, they lifted the door whose lock was long since smashed by the bulldozer rolling over it. But it wasn't a safe.

The door was pulled open with some effort, and all anyone could see for the first minute was what looked like a pipe pointing straight up to the sky. Shining a flashlight down the open entrance and around the pipe that seemed to be lodged in a concrete slab they found the remains of two human bodies. They had been shackled to the pipe with heavy chains.

The stench of dead flesh billowed out of the open hole like a cloud of damnation.

The pipe was ten feet high. The basement of the doomed building had been reinforced with concrete slabs for floors and walls. New Orleans has a water table that defies most attempts at building basements or cellars; the people who build this one must have had professional assistance and support. Once police officials were able to get down into the underground area, they found a kind of temple. There were strange symbols painted onto the walls and floors, and experts in Afro-Caribbean religions pronounced them a kind of vévé: the symbols used in Haitian *voudon*; except these symbols had nothing in common with traditional Haitian vévés. It was obvious that the two human beings who had been chained to the pipe were sacrifices of some sort, and the word began to spread throughout the community that an evil *poteau mitan* had been discovered in the Lower Ninth as the centerpiece of a *hounfort* that was dedicated to some very evil, very ancient gods.

In Haitian religion, the hounfort is the temple area and the *poteau mitan* is the central column that rises from the center of the hounfort. It provides a channel whereby the *loa*—the African gods—ascend from the earth to the surface in order to communicate with the worshippers. The gods are said to come from Guinée, i.e., Africa itself, through the center of the earth and up the *poteau mitan*.

An underground central column, however, in an underground temple was anathema to Haitian *voudon*. Someone went to a great deal of trouble to reverse the usual architecture.

If, as one local expert opined, the traditional arrangement is to call the loa up from Guinée to visit the worshippers, then placing the entire temple underground must have had the opposite intention: to call something else *down* from the stars.

The police detective in charge of what had become a homicide investigation with cult overtones stood in the basement after they had installed a ladder to enable access. He couldn't see how those who created the temple had gone in and out, since the underground chamber was nothing more than an airless concrete block. His officers had hung electric lights from a generator on the street and the photographer and coroner had completed their work, removing the bodies finally and taking them off in a mortuary van to be identified at some later date. Somehow.

The detective made note of all the drawings and symbols, carefully copying them down in a notebook. He knew the photographer already had a complete still and video record, but he liked to do his own work whenever possible. Sometimes the human eye saw something that the equipment missed. Now that the bodies had been removed he could get a better idea of the layout of the place.

It looked like a perfect square, a cube really. He was inside a cube made out of concrete except for the ceiling which was lath and plaster. At first it looked like concrete and was probably intended to match the rest of the structure. He wondered how it had withstood the weight of the bulldozer.

Shining a pocket flashlight up towards the ceiling and walking slowly around the *poteau mitan* he saw that there were steel rods running the length of the ceiling, like narrow beams, criss-crossing. That might account for the strength of the ceiling as well as provide a solid platform for the heavy iron trapdoor.

As he followed the line of the steel rods across the ceiling he saw how they connected to the walls on either side. This was intriguing.

He pulled the ladder away from the entrance hole and dragged it over to one of the corners of the room, propping it up and testing that it wouldn't slide across the floor when he went up. Satisfied, he climbed the ladder to the point where he saw the steel rods go into the corners.

Chipping away at a little of the concrete with his fingers and then with a pocket knife, he saw that the steel did not run straight across to the rest of the house as he had initially surmised, but that it hung a ninety-degree angle and went straight down the wall.

That didn't make any sense.

Poking a little more, he saw that the steel beams or rods were welded to steel rods of the same dimension that came up from the floor. Why?

Stiffly, he got down from the ladder and dropped to his knees on the floor, looking for a place that was weaker than the rest, a place where some of the concrete might have chipped away, but he could find nothing. He called up for a hammer and a large nail. He had to move the ladder back to its original position to allow the officer to give them to him.

"What do you have, Detective?"

"Damned if I know."

He went back down to the floor and crept along where the wall and the floor met, scraping the nail along and looking for a weak spot. Still finding none, he sighed and stuck the nail in one likely place at the join and started hammering, using the nail as a chisel. After a few minutes the concrete began to give way. He put the hammer down and started removing the concrete chips by hand, gingerly.

There. Just as he suspected. The metal rods came straight down from the ceiling where they were welded to other rods that went underneath the floor.

The entire structure was a kind of metal cage encased in concrete.

He stood up, knees creaking, and looked at the confused officer with wonder in his eyes.

"It's a Faraday cage," he said. "A fucking Faraday cage."

The New Orleans Homicide Division has only about twenty detectives. The police department has gone through a tremendous drain of active officers and detectives since Hurricane Katrina. Detective Anthony Cuneo was originally from New York City before he was picked up by NOPD a few years earlier. Cuneo, an American of Italian and African-American ancestry, had relatives in the New Orleans area and one day during a visit fell in love with the city. Well, with the Quarter, anyway.

One thing led to another, and he found himself a position as a homicide detective in the Big Easy.

One thing he couldn't get used to, though, was the voodoo. He knew it was an Afro-Caribbean religion and that Hollywood versions of it were nothing short of slander, but coming across the shops that sold herbs and talismans to the tourist trade was one thing; the occasional crime scene replete with arcane statues and dead chickens was another. Cuneo, as a good Catholic from Arthur Avenue in the Bronx, could never get used to the altars and candles and emblems of death that he came across from time to time. And never the idols.

This case, though, was something else. Like a mad scientist got together with a priest of the Petro cult (see, he knew his Petro from his Rada) and decided to make a science-fiction hounfort. At his desk, he started going through the digital photos of the temple that were taken earlier, paying special attention to what he thought were vévés and what he now thought were nothing like traditional Haitian religious symbolism. In fact, they didn't look Afro-Caribbean at all to him.

One image in particular was unsettling. It was a kind of weird half-anthropoid, half-cephalopod thing. It would be comical if it wasn't executed with a grim precision, including what appeared to be letters on certain areas of the creature and lines connecting some of the letters to other letters or other features of the image. It was like a map, or maybe an electrical diagram, which is why Cuneo's mind went right to "Faraday Cage."

"What is that, Detective?"

"Hmm?" He looked up from the laptop that had the images he was flipping through.

"Faraday cage. What's that?"

"It's a way of isolating something from electrical waves, or something. Like a SCIF."

A SCIF—Sensitive Compartmented Information Facility—is a room that has been electronically sealed against eavesdropping. They can be found at FBI offices and various other secure locations to prevent enemy agents from listening in to conversations.

"Oh. Who would do that underneath a house in the Lower Ninth?"

"Beats the shit outta me."

He kept going through the images and symbols, but something else was nagging at the corner of his mind.

"This wasn't used as a SCIF, so what was it for?" He knew he was talking to himself, but that was okay. Intelligent conversation and no arguments, as his mother used to say. "It wasn't used to keep something out, but to keep something in. But what?"

His mind went back to that iron door. Who would put an iron door in the middle of the wire grid that was the Faraday cage?

Unless it was there to complete a circuit.

He swept through the digital files again, looking for the photo of the ceiling of the concrete temple. There it was: the edges of the iron door made contact with the wire frame surrounding the opening. If you lifted the door, you broke the circuit.

The bulldozer, in smashing the locks on the door, probably shifted it enough that the circuit was broken before the cops arrived. The central pillar of the temple, the by now infamous *poteau mitan*, was made of metal, which itself was strange since they're usually made of wood or are actual trees.

"Do we have a prelim on the bodies yet?" he asked the room in general. No one responded. It was probably too early. It could take days before that mess was analyzed.

What if the bodies were in good shape until the circuit was broken?

What if, when Katrina passed through, they were still alive?

Cuneo's captain passed by his desk and looked down at the

photo on his laptop, the one of the strange creature with all the letters and connecting lines on it.

"Looks like that thing they pulled out of the bayous back a hundred years ago," he said to Cuneo.

"What's that, Captain?"

"You don't know the story? It was before your time. Hell, it was before my time and my daddy's time. But it was famous around here for awhile. Crazy-assed cult in the middle of nowhere, carrying on, having orgies and whatnot, around this statue of some kind of octopus god or some damned thing. Got written up. A lot of arrests, but few convictions. Nothing much came of it, but it made a lot of papers at the time. I'll ask Ti Frère to pull the file."

Ti Frère was their pet name for an unpaid reserve officer who just liked to hang out around cops. They used him for the grunt work that no cop likes to do. The Captain found him next to the coffee machine and had a word. In a moment, the young man was out the door and heading for the archives.

The Captain winked at Cuneo.

"Hey, when you have a minute, you can ask him to get the file on Lee Harvey Oswald, too!" And with a loud guffaw and exaggerated wink, the Captain walked away leaving Cuneo speechless.

Zaranj

Adnan and Angell began by helping some of the Afghan troops move debris as if they had lived in Zaranj all their lives. No one bothered to ask for papers. The checkpoint was in chaos, and no one was in charge. Slowly, the two men walked past and made for the town itself.

As they walked along the hot and dusty road, a man approached riding a donkey. He was dressed in typical Afghan attire, the long tunic over the baggy trousers, a vest, and a turban. His beard was thick and black, and the donkey looked like it had seen better days.

"*Asalaamu aleikhoum,*" he greeted them.

"*Wa aleikhoum salaam*," Adnan responded.

The man passed them, but as he did so they could hear him softly singing.

"The Son of God goes forth to war, a kingly crown to gain; his blood red banner streams afar: who follows in his train?"

Adnan turned to him and sang:"Who best can drink his cup of woe, triumphant over pain, who patient bears his cross below, he follows in his train."

The donkey rider stopped and rode back to them with some difficulty.

"I understand you're headed north. To become kings. Of Kafiristan, as I remember." A broad smile split his face in two.

"My God, is it Peachey?" Adnan's smile was the equal of the other man's.

"The same. But we best not hang about here. Follow me back to Zaranj. No one pays attention to a man on a donkey."

"Or the two fools who walk beside him."

Peachey was a British SAS officer who had served with Coalition forces back in the day. He knew Adnan from a clandestine operation at the southern Iraq-Iran border, near the Gulf. They had bonded over the film *The Man Who Would Be King*, based on the Rudyard Kipling story of the same name. They were also probably the only two men in all of Central Asia who knew the lyrics to the Kipling version of the song better known as "The Minstrel Boy." Peachey— his moniker also came from the Kipling tale—used it to identify himself to Adnan who didn't recognize him in his Afghan getup.

Or his beard.

Peachey would be their contact in Afghanistan and the man who would arrange for the two to get to Kamdesh.

Zaranj was a small, flat town with small squat, whitewashed buildings. There were shops and cafés, but the overall impression the two visitors had was of a Wild West town moments before the shoot-out at the OK Corral. Peachey led them to a nondescript structure with slits for windows. Adnan wondered if they were rifle ports, or were just small to keep out the heat, the punishing sunlight, and the dust.

Inside there was virtually no furniture. Carpets on the floor, a small wooden table holding tea cups and plates, and a slow-moving fan completed the décor.

He bade the two men enter and make themselves at home. He produced a bottle of boiled water from an old but ornate wooden armoire and some glasses.

"You'll need this," he said, pouring the water. "Have to stay hydrated out here, you know."

They took the glasses gratefully and drank. It had been a long walk from the checkpoint and they had brought nothing with them that would arouse suspicion or interest, not even bottled water.

"It will be nightfall soon. We can't go anywhere until then. I got a signal from your uncle," he said, addressing Adnan directly. "Uncle" was the generally-accepted spook term for the US government, as in "Uncle Sam."

"That's comforting," he replied.

"He says you're really going up north. You do realize that between here and there you have to cross Taliban country. They control huge swaths of the country in the south. The Northern Alliance has a lot of friends in the north, but they are not to be trusted, either."

"What do you suggest?"

"Your best bet is to find a way to cross over the area between here and there."

"Plane? Helicopter?"

"They're each problematic, of course. We can get you on a military transport as far as it's safe to go, but that means announcing your arrival to every informant and undercover operative in the region.

"How long do you need in Kamdesh?"

They both looked at Angell, who until now had been ignored.

"A few hours, if we find the man I was sent to find."

"Kamdesh is not very big, but it will still take awhile if you don't have any more information than that."

"I need to find someone called the Katra," he replied, remembering the old man and his crazy insistence.

Peachey looked at Angell strangely.

"The Katra? Are you sure?"

"It's what the old priest told me, just before he died."

Peachey made a face and looked over at Adnan.

"Katra is the Nuristani word for dagger, a kind of ceremonial dagger like the Indonesian kriss. But I've also heard the word used to refer to a kind of priest or shaman of the Kalasha people. They're the ones who gave Kafiristan its name. It was a pagan country until the Muslims arrived." He winked at Adnan. "You know, Imra and all that."

Adnan remembered the giant idol of the Kafiris from the movie with Sean Connery and Michael Caine.

"What did the old priest say, exactly?"

"He said, find the Katra of Kamdesh."

"The Katra of Kamdesh," Peachey repeated. "Terrific. It's an old title, obviously. An honorific. Pre-Islamic. But that doesn't mean he's not either Taliban or Northern Alliance anyway. If it's *the* Katra of Kamdesh, and it means what I think it means, then I know who it is."

In the end, they decided that taking a military transport plane as far as Kabul was going to be the way to go. They would have to find a way to minimize the presence of Adnan and Angell on the way up, and to do that Peachey arranged for them to look like real Afghans. He organized some clothes and warned the two not to shave. They were already pretty scruffy, but beards were a necessary accessory in that part of the world. They didn't have time to grow long ones, so whatever they had would have to do. Peachey even went so far as to search for fake beards, but was coming up empty.

They would leave the following morning from the Delaram airbase. It was a ride of some miles north of Zaranj but it was the safest alternative and would attract the least attention from the locals. It was relatively secure, and the idea was to have Adnan and Angell look like they were working on the base. They would get aboard the transport at the last possible moment.

Once in Kabul, Peachey had his people ready to pick them up and take them as far as Kamdesh. Ordinarily they would go as a full-on military escort, replete with Humvees and heavily-armed Marines. But the idea was to keep everything low key. Had they arrived in force, their contact would be scared off and there would be no way to find him if he didn't want to be found. They had precious little time, so they had to employ the tactic of surprise.

"You know the Nuristanis were the first ones to go up against the Soviet invasion back in the 1970s? They are fiercely independent people, which is why they were the last to convert to Islam, and even then it was at the point of a sword. There are those who say they are still pagans at heart, and that they still observe a lot of the old customs."

Peachey was holding forth. It was evening, and they were sitting around the low table with the tea cups, eating flat bread and some kind of lamb dish. Angell was dead tired, but knew he had to pay attention as any little detail might prove valuable in the days to come. Adnan and Peachey had been talking over old times for an hour, but then talk came around to the mission ahead.

"They're pretty much the same people as the Kalasha, right across the border in Pakistan. The Kalasha have retained their old ways and are entirely pre-Islamic. The Nuristanis—and whatever you do, don't call them Kafiris or they will cut you for sure—talk about the old ways in a kind of nostalgic tone, even slightly embarrassed by their past. But if you scratch a little deeper beneath the surface, you'll find that they still hold a lot of the old beliefs. One of their gods, Gish, is a warrior deity and when they went into battle against the Soviets there were still men who called on Gish to give them victory."

"How are they with the Taliban?" asked Angell, trying to make a contribution.

"They hate the fuckers. The Nuristanis were pretty much Northern Alliance all the way. The Taliban have been trying to make inroads there, but they haven't been successful. The Nuristanis hate outsiders generally. Any outsiders. So be careful. Be respectful, and take it slow. Observe the niceties. You'll be okay."

The flight to Kabul International Airport—soon to be renamed Hamid Karzai International Airport—was blessedly uneventful. Adnan and Angell were dropped off at Delaram which still had a contingent of Marines. Peachey—dressed in his Afghan clothes— walked them through security, and they puttered around the tarmac until their flight was ready at which time they disappeared into the body of the aircraft, leaving Peachey behind.

The plane dropped down through the clouds and the mountains to Kabul. It would land at the north cantonment of the airport which was reserved for military use. Adnan and Angell were both quiet during the entire flight, each occupied with their own thoughts. Adnan wasn't really worried about security so far. There was a network of US and Coalition operatives throughout the country he could call upon for assistance, and he knew that Aubrey and his people were aware of every step they took. But the mission in general worried him because it was so nebulous and had everything to do with religion and cults and that kind of scene was always trouble. Weird religious groups were harmless in and of themselves; when they got their hands on guns and territory, though, it became a different story.

As for Angell, he was haunted by the scenes of violence and the faces of the dead. He was running on autopilot, but he knew that once he crashed after all this he would crash badly. It didn't matter he was doing this for the greater good, or saving more lives in the process. He knew that in the end it would be his own culpability that would drive him back into that corner of his mind where the light never quite reached. That place he was at after the massacre of the Yezidis in Mosul.

God, how he hated religion.

And now he had crossed all of Iran and all of Afghanistan in order to fulfill his mission to get a book—a simple text, a collection of words—out of the hands of some mysterious enemy that everyone seemed to know about and no one knew what to call it or who its members were. The old Zoroastrian had mentioned Dagon. What Angell knew and what he hadn't mentioned to anyone was the fact that the Kalasha people also had a god named Dagon. There was a Dagon cult in ancient Mesopotamia, too.

For a region that was considered by Western media and its consumers to be nothing but hordes of crazy Muslims—Mad Arabs—there sure was a lot of cult activity under the surface. Nabataeans, Mazdaeans, Sabeans, Alawis, Nestorians, Druze, Sufis, Yezidis, Nuristanis, Kalashas ... the list was endless. They didn't know or appreciate this in the West. A legacy of centuries of colonialism had produced an attitude that they were all the same, all "Arabs" or all Muslims; like saying there was no difference between Chinese and Japanese. Try telling that to a young woman in Nanjing. Or an old man in Kyoto.

The Iranians aren't Arabs. Neither are the Afghans. Or the Kurds. But what difference did it make in the end? This blindness to ethnic, cultural and religious differences handicapped US foreign policy in a region that stretches from North Africa to China, and including the Balkans. There were some really astute people in the State Department—Angell knew some of them—but if they tried explaining these things to the American people they would lose their audience within the hour.

And now the dreadful had already happened. These disparate cults were being used by some other Force to manipulate the status quo, to destabilize not only the political and geopolitical map, but the religious map as well. This ... whatever it was ... was weaponizing religion in a way that the old Crusaders and the Moors before them had only dreamed about. The fascination of people all over the world with religion, spirituality, esoterica, and the like had sensitized them, made them vulnerable to a group or a movement that claimed it had the ultimate scripture, the Ur-text behind all religion. It was no coincidence that he was hearing about Dagon, a god so mysterious that archaeologists and scholars of religion had very little hard information about it and what they have is contradictory. It was obviously an important deity, a creator god in some ancient cultures, who was half-man, half-fish: a hybrid being that controlled the weather, the crops, and victory in battle. The Kurds also have a hybrid deity that is part human, part snake, known as Shahmaran or the Queen of Snakes. Like Oannes, the being that came out of the sea to instruct the Sumerians on the arts and sciences of civilization, Dagon is a reference to some ancient event that was forgotten by most of the world's population. It was an underworld god, a chthonic creature that rose from the mud and slime of the first Matter to challenge all that was holy, pure, and good. And its high priest, according to the cult around Dagon, was called Cthulhu. *Kutulu.* The Lord of the Underworld. *Al-Qhadhulu*: the god who had abandoned the planet. If these associations were correct, then Angell expected to see them repeated everywhere in the old books, the dead languages, the lore of the dying gods.

The Yezidis claim a Sumerian origin. Yezidi legends and Zoroastrian legends share many tales and even deities in common. Where they were going now—to Nuristan—was a land whose gods were equally ancient and derive from north India as well as from Persia. The Seven Towers of Satan was the fanciful name given to a network that spans the globe, linking all these groups together. It is a continuum of belief and practice stretching from Mesopotamia to India that points to a subterranean channel of ritual specialists whose task it is to keep that particular door to the past firmly closed. You can only keep it closed if you know where it is.

And here was another cult deliberately and even gleefully trying to pry it open.

They bumped down in Kabul, and before they had even come to

a complete stop a truck running alongside was waiting for them to deplane. They looked like Special Forces, but they had no insignia and no nametags.

"Could be JSOC," said Adnan. "Or SOAR."

Angell looked out at the surroundings, and knew no matter who it was he was very far from home. Or even from any place that looked like home. For the first time he realized that he could die here.

The airport was filled with helicopters and military transport aircraft. This was the new normal for Afghanistan. Had been for decades. The Afghans were world-renowned as fierce fighters with swords and rifles; give them rocket launchers and field artillery and you had yourself a force to contend with. Unfortunately, they were mostly contending with each other.

More color coordination. A man called Brown and another called Magenta. They were driven to a hangar on the north side of the airport and transferred to a beat-up looking van.

"Don't worry about the transport," said Brown, in a voice intended to be reassuring. "It's got a lot of armor plate, bulletproof tires, bulletproof glass, and gun ports. Plus an engine that could tear a Ferrari a new asshole."

"We're not JSOC or SOAR, just in case you're wondering," added Magenta. "We're CTPT. Just another acronym, okay? Our team has been here, on and off, since 2005. Our job is to search and destroy, basically. Now, we are gonna be hugging the Afghan-Pakistan border all the way up to Nuristan. This is a fucking nightmare of an area, because you've got everything from Al-Qaeda to the Taliban to Chechen rebels—yeah, you heard that right—and every other godforsaken martyr-wannabe coming in from Pakistan, all looking to waste themselves a coupla gringos like you and me."

"We understand you guys are going to Kamdesh," said Brown. "It's none of our business why you want to go there, of course, but you couldn't pick a more remote location on God's green earth. You are going to the Hindu Kush, my man. We're going to do our best to get you in and out safely, but all I ask is that you get your shit done as soon as fucking possible. ASAFP, you know what I mean?"

"No worries. We don't plan on hanging around long enough to change shirts. We have a guy we have to see, and then we're out of here. We'll cut you guys loose as soon as we can."

"That's all I wanna hear. Okay. Need anything? Coke? Pizza? Dramamine? No? Okay, great. Mount up!"

The door of the van slid open and Adnan and Angell jumped inside.

It was a dirty and scratched up van of indeterminate color, mostly gray but that could have been the primer. It started up with a steady purr, however, which made Adnan feel a little better. Brown and Magenta sat up front; Adnan and Angell were in the rear of the vehicle where an inflatable mattress was set down in case either of them wanted to take a nap on the ride up.

"Normally we would take a helo up there, but that only works if you don't care about being visible. I know you guys wanna go in dark, so that's what we're gonna do," informed Brown.

"We're going up the Kabul/J-bad Highway. The drive is about six, ten hours, give or take, until we reach the point where we have to walk. Dirt roads, washed-out roads, roads hugging the side of a cliff for miles. No way a Humvee can make it. A Chinook would get us there much faster, but it attracts a lot of attention. We lost one in there a few years ago, you might have heard, along with a SEAL team. It's about 350 klicks to Kamdesh on a good day, so just sit back and let us worry about the drive," added Magenta.

Adnan knew what wasn't being said. This had reached a whole new level of lethal. They had a TACSAT phone, a lot of ammunition, MREs, and what looked like CLS bags: Combat Life Saver. Basically, field dressings for mortal wounds. He exchanged a look with Brown and Magenta, but didn't say what he was thinking. He didn't have to. He pointedly glanced over at Angell, and Brown and Magenta nodded. They would keep it light as far as they could. Until they started taking fire from the tree line.

Angell couldn't believe he was sitting in the back of another vehicle for another massively-long drive to the middle of nowhere. The military had an expression: hurry up and wait. This felt like it, but that expression left out the most important part: when you wait this long, you start to imagine the worst.

He wondered if Lovecraft ever thought of the events he set in motion more than eighty years ago. Lovecraft even wrote about the Yezidi, about theosophical cults, about "crazed Levantines" rioting in the streets. He had predicted, in his own way, the Arab Spring. He wrote about these things in a relatively small output of mostly short stories that were published in pulp magazines with monsters on the covers. Letters in a bottle. If someone were to go back and decode those stories, what would they find?

CHAPTER TWENTY

THE BIG UNEASY

A man may also become a shaman following an accident or
a highly unusual event …

— Mircea Eliade, *Rites and Symbols of Initiation*

Ti Frère returned with a dusty paper file from the archives. The
police records going back a hundred years had not been damaged
by the flood waters of Hurricane Katrina, but they hadn't been digitized, either.

Sneezing, he handed the file over to Detective Cuneo.

"I think this is what you were looking for," he told him, and
stood next to his desk, expectantly.

Cuneo looked up at him. "Am I supposed to tip you, or
something?"

"Oh, no," said Ti Frère.

"Then?"

"Oh. Right. Okay." He walked back to his own desk, the one
next to the coffee machine, to sulk.

Cuneo opened the file gingerly. The typeface on the cover was
itself an antique, like maybe the props department at Universal had
come up with it. He noted the signature of the investigating officer,
one Inspector John Raymond Legrasse. *Hmm*, thought Cuneo. *They
had "Inspectors" back then. "Inspector" Legrasse. It had a nice ring to it.
Inspector Cuneo sounded like the guy who checked your restaurant kitchen
for violations.* He sighed and went back to looking at the very old
police report.

Inexplicably, one of Cuneo's favorite films was *Angel Heart*,
which took place almost entirely in New Orleans and other parts of
Louisiana, and for a moment he felt like a character in that movie.
Just waiting for Lisa Bonet to show up, he thought.

The pages were loose in the folder. There were some faded photographs of what appeared to be a crime scene involving what looked like more than a dozen bodies hanging from scaffolds around a central figure on a pedestal, plus a record of the interrogation of a witness named Castro, which Cuneo thought was funny. *Castro*.

He glanced at the photos, which seemed to be of someplace in the bayou. A lot of tropical foliage and that weird statue.

He flipped past it, and then stopped and looked at it again.

That statue. It looked a lot like one of the drawings from his own crime scene.

The photos were monochrome and starting to turn yellow with age. He picked up a magnifying glass—feeling a little silly, like Sherlock Holmes—and peered intently at the statue. Damn, it was identical.

He walked the file over to the Captain.

"You see this?" he said, pointing to the old photo of the statue.

"What about it?"

"Now look at this," he said, showing him the digital photo of the diagram from the concrete temple.

"They're the same, alright," he affirmed, after studying both images for a few seconds. "What's your point?"

"These were taken 107 years apart. Is there some kind of, I dunno, voodoo cult around here that would be using this stuff all this time?"

The Captain shook his head thoughtfully. He looked at the pictures again, then set them down on the desk and regarded Cuneo with a pitying eye. "This has nothing to do with *voudon*, *cher*. And it isn't Santeria, *Palo Mayombe*, *Candomble*, or any of that other stuff, either. What you have here is maybe a resurgence, maybe a revival, of a group that used to operate in these parts around the time of Pierre Lafitte and the War of 1812. The Cajun people out in the bayous? They used to talk about this group. It wasn't your usual Haitian crowd, either. It had members from Cuba, Haiti, the DR, even Chinese sailors who belonged to it over on the other side."

"The other side?"

"Of the world, cher. Of the world. They were Chinese from Hong Kong, Taiwan, Singapore ... some damned place. Mongolia. That was it. Or maybe Manchuria? Anyway the records are all in there, if they haven't been lost by now."

"Captain, you're talking about a global ... what, cult ... that was operating here a hundred years ago?"

"Sure. Yes. Why?"

"Before the Internet. Before mass media, television, hell even telephones?"

"I see your point."

"And they're operating again, now? Killing people in the Lower Ninth?"

"Well, we don't know that just yet. The post-mortems haven't come in yet."

"Captain, they were shackled to that pole. With chains."

"Some kinda sex game gone wrong?"

Cuneo was silent a moment. He had seen that sort of thing before. It *could* be a sex game, he supposed. It would account for there being two corpses.

"But the symbol. Who would have known about that?"

The Captain nodded. "You have a point there."

Cuneo returned to his desk and read through the file. It was clear to him that the police had broken up some kind of murderous orgy out there in the bayou, mass murder or mass sacrifice however you wanted to call it, but what was weird was the involvement of so many people from so many different ethnic and cultural backgrounds. Usually, groups like this were homogenous: they were all from the same place with a shared cultural context. An Afro-Caribbean cult would not have Chinese members, for instance. But this one did. It was unusual, but hard to believe it would have lasted for any length of time with such a diverse membership. Yet it had. Or someone was trying to revive it.

It was the Faraday cage aspect of the whole thing that added a different wrinkle. Obviously the underground temple had been abandoned due to Katrina. You'd think the owner of that building would have returned in the months that followed in order to clean up the evidence, but maybe not. Maybe whoever it was had just taken off, gone as far away as possible from the scene.

That was when Ti Frère stopped by and dropped off another file.

"This is the real estate record for the site that was bulldozed. It went through a coupla hands before the Chinese guy bought it."

"Vietnamese."

"What?"

"Never mind. Thanks." Cuneo looked at the paper on the lot and its dilapidated building. There were no utility bills, of course; no electric or phone, but it had indeed gone through three different owners since Katrina probably as investments that never panned out because the value of the property kept falling with each sale. It was the owner who had it at the time of the hurricane that interested him.

Ah, there it was. A name, something to work with finally.

Legrasse.

Angell felt himself slipping away with each kilometer they traveled. They were in a mountainous region that might have been beautiful under other circumstances but which now was only sinister and foreboding. They were hugging a winding river, and were within a stone's throw from Pakistan. He overheard the two agents discuss how raiders from Pakistani towns would come over the border and engage with Afghan troops from time to time. He also heard how everyone in the area considered the Nuristanis to be pagans and devil-worshippers, not real converts to Islam, and how they were driving into a part of the country that even the Afghan security forces avoided. Even the Russians had avoided during the Soviet occupation. No one wants to go to Nuristan. They go because, for one reason or another, they have to. And they leave as quickly as they can.

The road itself was a narrow, single lane dirt track that hugged the side of the mountain and threatened to pitch them into the river at every turn. Adnan's head was sticking out the window on the left-hand side, watching the wheels to make sure that they didn't stray over the edge. It was nerve-wracking and slow.

They had passed the town of Naray on the way up, and suffered the stares of villagers as they passed. Although they were dressed like local Afghans, the villagers did not recognize the van so they knew they were strangers. Angell felt like he was living in a scene from *Dracula*, and it was Walpurgisnacht.

The last ten kilometers would take at least an hour of very slow driving. The two agents in the front seats debated walking instead of driving into the town, but came to the conclusion they would rather stay with the vehicle. They saw a pickup truck precede them into the town, driving as slowly as they were, but apparently unconcerned. A local farmer, probably, judging from the pile of corn in the bed of the truck.

And ahead of them, finally, after a very long day of driving, was Kamdesh.

It was a town built on the side of a mountain, from what Angell could see. Mud colored houses, made of something like adobe, crawled up the mountain like a peculiar form of organic life. Suddenly, for reasons he could not explain even to himself, Angell began trembling uncontrollably. This was something other than fear. Fear had a "fight or flight" component, and this reaction had neither. This was surrender in the face of an overwhelming force. Angell felt himself giving up, and he didn't know why.

He tried to keep his condition hidden from the other men in the van, and ignored the shaking of his legs and arms and the weird sensation of trembling in his chest. It felt as if his mind were leaving his body, as if he had already been killed, and briefly wondered if that was so: if they had been blown up or shot at or been the target of an RPG. He actually wondered if he was already dead.

"Sir, we're here. Welcome to beautiful downtown Kamdesh.

Now let's get the living fuck out of here, shall we?" It was Magenta, and Angell watched him check to be sure a sidearm was locked and loaded. Brown was doing the same, and had passed a nine millimeter automatic to Adnan who checked the magazine and then tucked the weapon somewhere within the folds of his Afghan costume.

Brown and Magenta knew that Adnan spoke Farsi and Arabic, and that Angell had a working knowledge of Pashto as well. But there were a lot of dialects in this part of the world, including Dari and Urdu, so they would have to be careful. Brown and Magenta knew Dari and Pashto and spoke the languages like natives, which was the whole point. They had the thick beards and thicker attitudes they would need to pass as Afghans. They knew they couldn't pass as Nuristanis and wouldn't even try. They would say they had come from Jalalabad, but that their relatives were from Kabul. That should explain any perceived strangeness in their accents.

The two agents already knew who they were looking for. They had been briefed by Peachy by phone and again by Adnan and Angell themselves. They were going to find the headman of the village and make their request known to him first, as was customary. Adnan and Angell were told to keep quiet and be respectful.

And no sudden moves.

They exited the vehicle and began walking slowly in the direction of the center of the town. People came out from their houses to watch them, but said nothing. There was an Afghan National Police building—a small adobe hut by the side of the road—but no one was there. Brown and Magenta walked point, with Angell walking slack and Adnan at the rear. Finally, a young man with blonde hair and the bluest eyes Angell had ever seen walked up to them and started chatting with the two agents.

After a minute, Brown turned to Angell and Adnan and spoke to them in Pashto, saying they were going to see the headman.

They followed the young man down a dirt path as Angell noticed another man, older, talking on a cell phone. It was the weirdest thing Angell had seen in a long time. A cell phone in a region that seemed to have no indoor plumbing or even electricity. He was about to say something to Adnan who knew what Angell was thinking, and whispered to him, "The word is going out that we are here. Someone, somewhere, is being notified. Let's just hope it isn't the Taliban. Stay alert."

There was another structure in front of them, looking pretty much like every other one in the village. They were asked to enter and as they did they saw several village elders already sitting in a half-circle on an old carpet. They looked up as the strangers walked in, and made some greetings first in Dari and then in Pashto. Brown answered for all of them. They were invited to sit down and join them for some chai.

The thick milky tea was poured and everyone settled down and tried to get comfortable. The two agents, Brown and Magenta, introduced themselves with Afghan names and talked pleasantries, as did their hosts. No one seemed to be in a hurry to discuss why there were there.

Angell for his part calmed himself down. He could not afford to look nervous in front of these men, and he had the mission objective firmly in mind. Well, maybe not firmly. What was firm was his determination to get out of all this alive. He sipped his chai, and looked around at the bare walls, the reddish carpet, and the long beards of the elders all around him as he listened to the conversation and tried to understand as much of it as possible.

The Nuristanis did not like Pashtun people, whom they viewed as invaders and interlopers. They didn't like the Pakistanis, the Taliban, or Al-Qaeda. They just wanted to be left alone. So Angell and his team were taking a chance by coming into Kamdesh in the first place. But the stakes were too high and, anyway, they had what seemed like the perfect excuse: the name of the man they were coming to see and a recommendation to see him from the Zoroastrian priest in Yazd. This was an acknowledgment that there was a network of brothers and that Angell and his crew were part of that network. That made Angell feel somewhat more secure.

Slowly, Brown and Magenta began to introduce this information into the conversation. Questions came in Dari, Pashtu and Urdu. Sometimes a mix of all three. Angell had a hard time following the dialogue between Brown and a man who seemed to be the village headman, but he heard references to the Katra more than once. The first time, there was silence among the elders as Angell could feel them appraising him and his colleagues in a new way.

Finally, the headman stood up and the others followed, including the four foreigners. He pointed up, straight up, and said something in Dari that Angell did not understand.

Then he pointed straight up again. This time his meaning was clear. The man they were seeking lived on top of one of the mountains outside the town.

Something about this didn't seem right to Angell. This was all happening too fast. But before he could say anything to any of the others he felt woozy. His vision blurred and he started to lose his balance.

He was blacking out. His last thought before he lost consciousness was *I've been drugged.*

All was darkness.

Angell could feel nothing, see nothing, hear nothing. *Is this death?* he asked himself. *Has it finally happened?*

Then, a sound. Distant. Terrifying. A plaintive chant, a base note thrum of anti-matter that threatened to overwhelm the material world. Sounds, ideas, memories all clashing in Angell's mind, crashing on the individual, sharpened rocks of his identity like waves of dystopian visions through the untranslated scriptures of the Original People.

Who the hell are the Original People? he asked, mentally. *Where does that come from?*

And why do none of my thoughts make any sense?

He vaguely remembered a room full of Nuristanis. A carpet. Chai. The sense of being drugged.

That sound again. A chant. An incantation. Male voices, he realized for some reason. All the voices were male. Or almost male. Almost human. As if humans were deliberately trying to sound non-human. To make sounds that humans could not make. Was that it? It sounded vaguely Tibetan, had none of the lilting quality of Gregorian chant. Could be Middle Eastern. *Can't make out the words.*

A smell now. Sharp. Pungent. He knew it. *Juniper.* Someone was burning juniper. Maybe he wasn't dead yet. Maybe he was being prepared for burial, though. An incense to cover the smell of decaying flesh. His flesh. His burial. Maybe he was dead, and his soul was lingering over his body. He tried to tell himself it wasn't necessary. He didn't have to stick around. What if they cut off his head? What if they cut it off and put it on a stake by the side of the road, a warning to Americans and foreigners *and professors of religion that they had no fucking clue what they were doing and what they were talking about.*

If you don't understand violence, he realized with a shudder that went through him like ague, *then you have no business talking about religion.*

The juniper smoke was rising all around him, but he still couldn't see. It was seeping into him somehow. His nostrils must be working. Either that, or the smoke was penetrating his body through its pores.

A phrase came to him in his smoked-out stupor. Funny words. Lyrics to a song, maybe. Or the punch line to a dirty joke.

Kutuluhu akhbar.

Toodle-do akhbar. Oodles of akhbar. No.

Kutuluhu akhbar.

Oh, God, no. He heard his voice as if it was booming from a boombox based in the Bronx. In the Baghdad section of the Bronx. In the Bronx neighborhood of Baghdad. Jalalabad. Asadabad. Islamabad. My bad.

Kutuluhu akhbar.

Someone was screaming. Screaming this insane phrase! Someone was …

Oh, crap.

It was him.
He vomited, and passed out.

A little while later, he came to. Someone had poured water over his head and clothes. Cold water. Ice cold river water from the Kunar River. How did he know that? But it was still dark, pitch dark. He shivered from the cold and tried to warm himself with his hands, but they wouldn't move. He tried again. He heard a sound. Steel. Steel on steel.

He was shackled to something. To something metallic and cold behind him.

He heard voices. He passed out again.

They undid his shackles. They lifted him up by the arms. They half-dragged him to another room.

They pulled the black woolen hood off his head so he could see. He blinked in the light of the room, which was dimly lit by candles and a kerosene lamp.

He looked around and saw an old wooden bookcase against a white-washed wall. In the bookcase were a number of gold-embossed Qur'ans, bound in leather, a few volumes on shari'a, and some computer and technical manuals.

The unreality of all of it made Angell believe he was still stoned, still high on something, tripping on some Kafiri kif, some Nuristani narcotic. Some Afghan horse, not the polo kind, extracted from the only crop that made Afghanistan any money at all: opium. Was that it? Was he on the nod? A Nuristani nod, courtesy of the Katra of Kamdesh?

He couldn't keep the alliterations out of his head. They were like song lyrics he couldn't shake to a tune he couldn't hear.

He just wanted to sleep.

There was a commotion outside, and three or four men wandered into the room and took up positions in the corners. They were all Afghans, wearing the baggy white trousers, the white tunic that went to their knees, the dark vests, and the strange, flattened beret or turban that was their signature hat. They all had long, black beards and carried AK-47s. The smell of their gun oil was heavy on the air. A fly buzzed into the room, making the only sound, and then it abruptly stopped. There was silence.

Into the room walked another man, rather tall and ascetic-looking beneath his turban and behind his full, black beard. His cheeks were sunken and hollow, but his eyes burned with intelligence and conviction. He sat down on the floor across from Angell and the room, if possible, became even quieter.

He spoke in English that had traces of an Oxford accent.

"You will be pleased to learn that your comrades are still alive and well. Their disposition will depend entirely on the outcome of this meeting. That is, on your cooperation."

"Where are they?" Angell managed to croak.

"They are safe."

"Who are you? Are you Taliban? Al-Qaeda?"

"My name is Omar Mansour. And that is the last question you will ask me. Your job is to answer them. First, what do you seek? Why are you here?"

"My name is …"

"We know who you are, Doctor Angell. We have been tracking you for some time. We know about your famous uncle, as well. We know how he died. Murdered, wasn't he?"

Baffled, Angell could only nod.

"Close to the ocean … in New England, I believe."

"It was a long time ago."

"Yes. Almost eighty years. But you have not answered my question. What are you doing here?"

"I am looking for a book."

Angell noticed the sound of shuffling behind him. Hushed voices. But only for a moment. His interlocutor watched him briefly, as if assessing him, and then replied: "A book? All this for a book? What book?" He gestured behind him at the bookcase before Angell could answer. "*We* have books. Many books. But the only book that really matters is *al-Qur'an*. Is that what you are looking for?" He smiled. "There are many Qur'ans in New York, where you live. You can buy them in Barnes and Noble, even order them on Amazon. There is no need to come to this place to find a Qur'an."

He leaned towards him.

"But perhaps the book you are looking for is something *haram*? Something unclean? Forbidden? Like that filthy text of the Yezid?"

Angell swallowed.

"It is not the Black Book of the Yezidi that I seek."

"Then why were you seen visiting their village? Asking questions of its elders? Observing that obscenity at Kutha?"

He didn't know how much they knew, or how much he could safely divulge. Angell was surrounded by armed men of what was probably an Al-Qaeda or Taliban cell deep in Nuristan. How had they known about his visit to the Yezidi in the refugee camp on the Turkish border, or the ritual at Tell Ibrahim in Iraq? Had he told them about all of that when he was stoned and chained to a pillar? Or was it an Al-Qaeda leader he was speaking with, someone with a network of informants throughout the East and especially here in Afghanistan?

If he was still in Afghanistan.

Hanging on the wall above the bookcase were swords. Two of them. Crossed. Curved scimitars. A familiar image from propaganda videos and decapitations.

Angell suddenly had a desperate urge to use the toilet. But he calmed myself, and placed a hand over his roiling bowels, to settle them. He knew he could not afford to show too much weakness now, even though he was their prisoner.

"I am looking for another book. I had information that perhaps the Yezidi knew of it, knew where it was."

"What is this book? What is the title? Perhaps we have it in our library?" The last was said with a sneer, and it elicited some amused sounds from the armed men around me.

"It is called *Kitab al-Azif.*"

The silence that greeted that statement was absolute. Even outdoor sounds were suddenly absent, as if every jeep, every crying child, every braying goat, had been shushed by some cosmic power. It was a silence that had a life of its own. Angell couldn't even hear his own breath.

His questioner spoke the next words slowly, even softly.

"That is a strange name for a book. Do you know what it means?"

He nodded.

"Something to do with the sound insects make."

"The howling of insects, you might say, although insects do not howl. Not normally, at any rate. Why do you seek this book? What value does it have for you?"

This could be his last day on earth. His last hour. If he answered falsely, and they knew it, he would die. Perhaps slowly, his head severed from his shoulders by inexperienced executioners with rusty blades. All those horrific video images ran through his mind of hostages beheaded by fanatics. He had no doubt that the man in front of him was just such a murderer.

If he answered truthfully he might still die at the hands of these fanatics. He had the same to lose no matter which way he answered, but he thought his chances were marginally better if he was truthful. And, by staying alive, that meant he still had a chance to find the book and stop the imminent bloodbath from happening.

In less than a second, Angell had made up my mind.

"The book is important. To a lot of people. To Sunnis. To Shi'a. To the Kurds. To the Iranians. To the Saudis. Yes, even to the Americans. And to you. The book is about evil, and how to stop evil. A worse evil than any of us can imagine. I know I can imagine a great many evil deeds. This surpasses any of them. It is a book written by a man who had seen this evil and who knew how to stop it."

The interrogator named Omar stroked his beard as Angell spoke to him, never once dropping his gaze from his eyes.

"Do you have this book?"

"No. Of course not. I have been searching for it the past week, from Turkey to Iraq, to Iran, and now to Kamdesh."

The interrogator nodded.

"We also want this book."

Angell returned his gaze as steadily as he could.

"What would you do with it?"

"This book is *haram*. It is forbidden for any Muslim to read it. But there are many Islamic scholars who have permission to read these books, if only to determine the contents in order to condemn them more … credibly."

"And to use the information contained, in order to become more powerful?"

It was a drastic statement, very bold under the circumstances, but Angell couldn't stop himself.

Omar Mansour smiled.

"As I said, it is *haram*. However, it is also powerful. The *idea* of it is powerful. True power comes only from Allah. I believe we must keep it out of the hands of our enemies. That is also your belief, is it not?"

"Of course."

"But why should I trust you? Why should I trust the American government?"

"I believe the feeling is mutual."

He gestured to a man standing behind his prisoner. Angell cringed, awaiting the blade, or worse.

"Some tea," he said.

And everyone in the room relaxed. Except the professor of religious studies.

As a well-armed waiter brought them a brass tray containing a teapot and some cracked cups, he thought over his options. The situation was obviously very fluid. There was no reason why they should let him go. He had seen them, seen their faces. Angell didn't know exactly where he was: the hood over his head had taken care of that.

He could not give up their location, or the identities of the mujahedeen who had snatched him. Did they need him alive? He hoped so.

"I hope you were not too inconvenienced by the drug we administered to you and to your colleagues. It was necessary that you be incapacitated for awhile."

"What was it?"

"It grows locally here. The shamans use it in their profane rituals. But it is valuable as an interrogation device. Like a ... a truth serum."

"I see. Did you get what you wanted?"

Instead, the terrorist leader changed the subject.

"Do you know how these Nuristani devils perform their rituals? No? I will tell you. They have shamans who contact the spirits of the dead and the spirits of their gods. Yes, it is all very *shirk*. The shaman will sit in a special room that has pillars carved in the shapes of their gods, who are not really gods of course but jinn. You know jinn?"

Angell nodded.

"And then they burn juniper branches."

"Juniper?"

"Yes, in order to disorient the senses so they may see through this world and to the next. They make communication with their jinn that way, and they learn many fabulous things."

So that was what had happened to Angell. They had treated him like some kind of Kafiri shaman. Why? What was the point of that?

"Their gods communicate with them in dreams, they say. Many Afghans believe this, but nowhere as much as in Nuristan. We should destroy all of them, of course. All the Nuristanis. They are not true Muslims. We should burn their villages to the ground and kill every one. We should sell their women and children into slavery in Pakistan. Have you seen their women? No? They have blonde hair and blue eyes. They are a very strange people, Doctor Angell. But we keep them alive and allow them to live in their arsehole of a country because they are useful to us. They sit between Pakistan and Afghanistan, and their loyalties shift with the wind. Today, Taliban. Tomorrow, Al-Qaeda. The next day, the Afghan National Army. But everyday we move across the border in Nuristan and back, with no problems. We could move an army across the river, and the kafirs would say nothing about it as long as we paid them more than they were getting from the Afghans. They know they are vulnerable, you see. They are surrounded by Muslims, and they are kafirs. They can lose everything in an instant."

"Yet they were the first to fight the Russians. And they are still fighting you."

Omar smiled. "You know your Afghan history, Doctor Angell. Yes, they are good fighters and fiercely loyal to their own people. They believe they are descended from soldiers of Alexander the Great. If they lived in any other part of Afghanistan they would have been wiped out completely by now. Their terrain protects them, but not for long."

"Why don't you just leave them alone? They are no threat to you."

"Have you seen their shrines? Their idols? We have tolerated their existence for far too long. As well as your precious Yezidis. The time has come to eliminate these kafirs from the face of the Earth." He said this calmly, with a half smile on his face, as if discussing a recalcitrant child or a troublesome tax collector. This was in May, 2014.

In December of that same year Omar Mansour, leader of a Taliban subgroup known as Tariq Gidar, would attack a school in Peshawar, killing 148 people, among them 132 children. He himself would be killed in a drone strike in July, 2016.

"Doctor Angell, we would like very much to see this book. Unfortunately, we do not have many people on our ... staff ... with the kind of expertise needed to locate it and then to verify that it is truly *Al Azif.* Only someone with your background ... I mean, with access to your grand-uncle's work, his files, his journals ... would be able to tell if any book was truly the one we seek."

Angell considered a moment before breaking the bad news.

"His file, the one on this book, is missing. It was stolen many years ago. I believe it no longer exists."

"Then … I don't understand. How do you even know to look for the book if you have not seen the file?"

"You should know the answer to that. It is no secret that this book is being discussed all over the world right now, and especially among dissident Islamic sects from the Middle East to China. There have been revolts, rebellions, massacres, even cultic activity involving human sacrifice, all over North Africa, the Levant, Iran, and elsewhere. Sunni, Shi'a, Sufis, Alawis, Druze … the whole Muslim world is excited over the prospect of this … scripture … being revealed in the next days or weeks. And not only the Muslim world, but sects as far away as Mongolia, Haiti, Nigeria … and even in the United States. You want this book because everyone else wants it—either to use it, to keep their enemies from using it, or to destroy it—which is how we heard of it in the first place. Which is why I was recruited to help find it."

"Then you understand that all these factions you mention, and many more besides, are united in their desire to find this 'scripture' as you call it. None of us can afford to wait until the other has it. We cannot accept that anyone other than ourselves own this book. We certainly cannot accept American ownership. They already have nuclear weapons. They cannot be permitted to have *Kitab Al Azif* as well."

"Then … what do you propose?"

The interrogator took a sip of his tea.

"We could kill you and your friends, of course. That would ensure the Americans would not find the book. It would take them too long to find another expert to help them, and by now the book is probably out of reach of their best efforts."

"If you kill me, then you won't find the book either."

"Yes, I have thought of that. Which is why I propose to release you and send you on your way."

At this, Angell almost dropped his tea cup. He looked at the terrorist and wondered if he had heard him correctly.

Mansour continued, "The book had been with the Kalasha people—the same as the Nuristanis—until they were converted in 1895. Even the Kalasha do not know the true origins of the book, however, only that it refers to the hideous practices of the Nabataeans of Kutha who used it to contact alien forces.

"Two days before your arrival, another group of men passed through here on their way to Kashmir. Foreigners. They also asked to see the Katra. They were more successful. When we heard that they were here, we naturally left our base in Pakistan to intercept them. But we were too late. Too late to capture them, but just in time to capture you. And the Katra himself: an old shaman, a trafficker in spirits and dreams. He is revered among the people here, just as they revere all superstitious practices and those who perpetuate them."

"Where … where is the Katra now?"

"I will take you to him. Perhaps you will have more success with him. He was not so forthcoming with me."

"What do you want from me?"

"To do just what you were told to do. Find the book. Find it quickly, for we are running out of time. There is a schedule involved, and each day that passes brings us closer to annihilation."

"And when I find it?"

"You will hand it over to me. Or to my people."

"Then you must release *my* people. I need them to accompany me. I am a scholar, an academic. I am not a commando or a guerrilla fighter."

"You're really in no position to be making demands, Doctor Angell. No. Your friends will remain with me until I have possession of the book."

"How do I know you will keep your word?"

"You don't. So let's stop bargaining like women and proceed to the next step." He took a map from a shelf in his bookcase and spread it out on the floor between them.

"You will be accompanied by some of my men. They will be with you day and night. They will get you to Kashmir and if you

leave at once you should be able to make good time. We know where
the other men are headed and we can get you there ahead of them
since we own the territory between here and Kashmir." He pointed
at their location—Angell noticing with some relief that they were
still in Kamdesh—and then drawing a line from Nuristan across
northern Pakistan into the disputed territory of Kashmir. "We will
slow them down, but just enough to enable you to get into position.
Then you will follow them to the book, and my men will seize it."

"Do we know where in Kashmir they are going?"

"There are seven unholy sites across the world from Iraq to
Mongolia. Seven towers, they are called, but they are not towers
the way we understand the word. These seven towers are nodes in
a network. Each of them is to be 'switched on' in turn. We do not
know how this is done, and we do not know where these towers
may be, except in very general terms. That is for you to discover. The
book is an essential part of this blasphemous ritual; without it, the
devil-worshippers cannot accomplish anything.

"And as I have said, there is a schedule. It depends on some kind
of astronomical observation. When the stars are right, the contact
between the dead gods and their followers will be at its peak. Keep
that in mind. Now, let us see the Katra of Kamdesh."

Omar rose and the others followed him, Angell in the center of
the group even though there was no chance of him escaping on his
own.

They went outside and passed a building and then another one.
Finally they came to a large hall of some sort. It was dark inside, but
the smell was almost overpowering.

There, tied to a wooden pillar in the middle of the hall was a
man, naked, and covered in blood. It was the Katra of Kamdesh.

His head was placed neatly in his lap.

CHAPTER TWENTY-ONE

THE RV

Their mode of speech was transmitted thought. ... When,
after infinities of chaos, the first men came, the Great Old
Ones spoke to the sensitive among them by moulding their
dreams; for only thus could Their language reach the fleshly
minds of mammals.

—H.P. Lovecraft, "The Call of Cthulhu"

A sheep herder walked slowly along the road outside Mandagal, a
town north of Kamdesh. He carried a long stick, and wore the typical flat-brimmed turban of the Pashtuns. Mandagal was a dangerous
town, filled with Taliban operatives as well as a handful of ISI agents:
members of Pakistan's own security services who were not supposed
to be in Afghanistan but who frequently crossed the border just outside Mandagal to keep their hand in.

The sheep herder was a little crazy, so people left him alone. He
was a herder without sheep, a man without a home. He had walked
to Mandagal from somewhere else, no one really knew. And he was
walking out of Mandagal the same way.

He stepped aside to let a military vehicle pass him on the narrow
single lane dirt road. He didn't bother looking up. The vehicle was
on its way from Kamdesh, and that is all he really needed to know.

He stepped off the road completely now, and found a quiet place
in the trees to sit and think. Jason Miller wiped the sweat off his
forehead with the end of his turban.

This was getting too dangerous, he thought. There were
Americans in that town, in Taliban custody, and they were on the
same mission he was. If he stopped to help them, the others might
make it to the book before him. But if he left them there, he would
have to carry that guilt with him for the rest of his life. They would

317

be killed, there was no doubt in his mind about that. They would
be killed, probably beheaded, and even tortured first. Just for sport.
He knew there was a bounty on dead Americans, something like a
thousand dollars each. All you had to produce was a digital photo
of yourself standing over the body. Easy money in that part of the
world. Throw in a video of the beheadings and whoever did this
would be a hero to the permanent underclass.

Miller knew there was no getting around it. He would have to
see to it that the Americans were rescued. There were four of them,
according to his informant at Naray (a town the four had passed on
their way to Kamdesh). They had stopped to relieve themselves by
the side of the road and that is when his informant snapped their
picture with a smartphone from his vantage point behind a cliff
overlooking the river.

Miller took out his own phone and looked at them again. They
were good, he had to give them that. They looked like Afghans. All
except one of them, who looked dirty and disheveled and scared
shitless. That would be the academic type they brought along.

He figured they would behead him first.

He didn't have the juice to call in an air strike. A drone would have a
hard time getting in here, too, and anyway Kamdesh was a target full
of civilians. They couldn't risk a Tomahawk coming in and blasting
a crater in the center of the town. If he was going to get anyone
out, he would have to do it himself without backup or reinforcements. The three men with the academic looked like hard types,
professional soldiers probably, so they would know how to handle
themselves once they were free. They could look after the teacher
or whatever the hell he was. He just hoped he wouldn't waste too
much time rescuing them. He was on a pretty tight schedule.

He checked the astronomy app on his smartphone.

Only a few more days to go before all Hell would break loose.

Literally.

In Baghdad, Aubrey was fuming. He had not heard from his people in two days. He knew their location due to the GPS positioning chips and that is what worried him. Angell and his Kurdish contact were in Kamdesh. He didn't have GPS on the other two; they worked for CIA and their group—CTPT, or Counter Terrorism Pursuit Team—was deep undercover in Afghanistan. The problem was: the GPS for Angell and the one for Adnan were now in different places.

Adnan's was still in Kamdesh, but Angell's had started to move. Something went wrong in Nuristan and he couldn't find out what. He tasked a drone to take a look, and got back the image of a truck going north out of Kamdesh, probably heading for Mandagal. It matched Angell's GPS. This was not good. Mandagal was enemy territory. If they were taking Angell there, he was a prisoner and they were going to take him to Pakistan.

He dreaded the phone call he had to make. Monroe would want to know immediately if Angell was off the grid. If he was, the whole mission had failed and all they could do now was hunker down and prepare for the worst world war in the planet's history.

New Orleans

Detective Cuneo sat in front of a sweet old lady in her living room in the comfortable Belle Chasse suburb of New Orleans, a long way from the Lower Ninth Ward in all senses of the term.

"Ma'am, I'm here inquiring about some property you owned in the city."

"That would have been my husband."

"Ma'am?"

"My husband owned property. He passed away some years ago. About the time of Katrina. Poor man. Worked all his life, fingers to the bone. Would you care for some coffee? Tea?"

"No, Ma'am. Thank you."

The living room was suffocatingly floral and bright. It was a cheerful room, or might have been had it not been for the heavy, well-stocked bookcase standing in a corner. It reminded him of a brooding raven on a bust of Pallas. Or something.

"Oh, you've noticed my library," the old lady gushed. She was dressed to the nines for early in the day. Tight, white hair that had been perm'ed to within an inch of its life. Floral print dress. Pumps. A little too much makeup. Jewelry that looked real, not costume. Pearl earrings and a giant diamond brooch that caught the light from the sun and held it captive, demanding ransom.

He looked closely at some of the spines and was startled by the subject matter. Authors he had never heard of—Regardie, Crowley, Montague Summers, Grillot de Givry, Waite, Randolph, Mathers, Levi—and titles that made the blood run cold.

The Book of Black Magic and of Pacts.

The Secret Lore of Magic.

Magick in Theory and Practice.

Goetia.

Books on Freemasonry and witchcraft; alchemy and ritual; secret societies and pagan cults. And there: on the lower shelf, books on voodoo and Santeria.

Cuneo stood up and looked down at the sweet old lady on the upholstered love seat. "These your books, ma'am?"

"Oh, indeed they are, Detective."

"Interesting hobby."

"Oh, it's not a hobby."

Cuneo really did not want to get into that discussion at this time. Instead he went back to the case at hand.

"I'm here to ask you some questions about the property in the Lower Ninth Ward, the one that presumably was abandoned after Katrina. What can you tell me about that?"

"Oh, dear. I was afraid of that."

"Sorry?"

"That property has been nothing but trouble since the day

Frank—that's my late husband, Frank was his name—since the day Frank got it from the Chinaman."

"The … Chinaman? You mean someone of Asian descent?"

"I mean Chinaman! A person of Chinese origin. Not descent. He was a real Chinaman! From China!" She was clearly put out that Cuneo had tried to be politically sensitive. She was clearly too old to care about the social niceties.

"Okay. When did Frank buy it from the, uh, Chinaman?"

"Young man, I never said that Frank bought it from the Chinaman. I said he *got* it from the Chinaman."

"It was a gift?"

"Not exactly. Frank was to take care of it for the man. Hold onto it. See to it."

"Like a … a caretaker? Something like that?"

"Well … no, not really. It was Frank's turn, you see."

"Mrs. Galvez, I am really quite confused."

The lady sat back on the couch and regarded the detective from New York—he obviously wasn't from New Orleans—with some irritation.

"Detective, the property in question has been in our tradition for generations. It's not so difficult to understand."

"Your tradition? And what tradition might that be, ma'am?"

She sighed, and fanned herself with an embroidered handkerchief.

"It was Frank, and before that it was the Chinaman, and before that it was that man from the islands, and so on, back to that unfortunate episode before the war."

"Before the war? World War Two?" he said, venturing a guess.

"No, young man. Before World War One. The real war. World War Two was just the sequel."

"So you're saying the property has been in your … in the possession of your … *tradition* going back to 1907? The year the police raided the ritual in the bayou?"

"Of course. Now you're starting to understand. You sure you don't want some tea? It's lapsang soochong. Imported directly."

"Uh, no, thanks, ma'am. So you know all about that incident in 1907? The ritual, the idol, the, uh, dead bodies?"

"Detective …?"

"Cuneo, ma'am."

"Detective Cuneo. Let's start at the beginning. You know about the Freemasons? The Rosicrucians?"

"Some. Secret societies that have been around for centuries. Like that."

"Well, they're Johnny-come-latelies when compared to the oldest secret society of them all. Our tradition has been on the Earth for thousands of years, with knowledge passed down from generation to generation, millennium to millennium. We were old when Sumer was young. What the police discovered in the bayou in 1907 was just a preliminary invocation of the Ancient Ones. And, yes, there were bodies. Dead bodies. But they weren't dead when they were brought there, I can assure you. That came later."

"Ma'am … Mrs. Galvez … what you're telling me …"

"Yes, yes, dear. I know. It's quite surprising, I suppose."

"Surprising? You're talking about mass murder. Human sacrifice."

She sighed and looked away.

"I suppose."

"And you're saying that the ritual in 1907 and the property we found this week are related in some way?"

At that point Mrs. Galvez dropped any pretence at good breeding and etiquette. She looked straight into Cuneo's eyes.

"Detective, how dense can you be? The proof is right in front of you. You found the 'box', the one buried under the house. You saw what was in it. You saw the crime scene photos of 1907, at least I assume you did or you wouldn't be here. You know the two things are connected, and now you know that I am living proof of that.

"I am a high priestess of our Order. I have been since I was a child. I was born into it, and raised within it. My mother was a high priestess, and her mother before her. My grandmother was present at that ritual in the bayou. She was only sixteen. She was possessed by six men before she was possessed by the High Priest. I am descended from that union, for she gave birth nine months later to my mother.

"The High Priest was my grandfather. He was also my father, for he possessed my mother, the high priestess, nine months before I was born. I have the blood of the Ancient Ones in my veins, Detective.

"We called on the High Priest in 1907, but that wasn't the first time nor was it the last. The High Priest has been with us since the very beginning, since before humans walked on the face of the Earth. When Christians talk about the Alpha and the Omega, they don't have a clue as to what that means. We do. Our High Priest represents the Alpha, the beginning of all life and all time, before humans were created in order to serve him and his gods, the Ancient Ones. He is also the Omega: he will wipe this planet clean of the filth that have infested it, the humans who revolted against him and tried to create their own history.

"The fools."

Cuneo now knew that the old lady was insane. She had lost her mind somewhere along the line, and this inquiry was triggering all sorts of weird psychotic fantasies, or something. He knew the answer to what happened in the Lower Ninth and who killed those people in the underground chamber was here, somewhere, but he was sure he wouldn't get a straight answer out of this old broad. He had to find a way to extricate himself and leave without closing this particular door behind him forever.

He got up, and started putting away his notebook, when a question occurred to him.

"Ma'am, you've been very helpful. Thank you. I just have one more question. What does this ... tradition ... call itself? Does it have a name?"

"Of course it has a name. We're not sleepwalkers. We know what we're about."

"Of course. I didn't mean to imply ..."

"Dagon."

"Pardon?"

"Dagon. We're named after one of the incarnations of the Ancient Ones."

"Ah. Okay, thank ..."

"And the High Priest. Certainly you want to know *his* name as well?"

"Well, sure, if you don't ..."

"Cthulhu," she said, pronouncing it *Kutulu*. "He may be dead, but he sees *everything*." And she started to laugh, and kept laughing as Cuneo left the house, got in his car, and left the neighborhood. He kept hearing that laugh all the way back to the station. All the way back home. All the way into the deepest sleep he had had in years.

All the way into his dreams.

Monroe got off the secure channel with Aubrey in Baghdad. He had known this would be a long shot, but it was one he had to take. He had no alternative, no option, but to enlist Angell. There were reasons beyond Angell's own obvious intelligence, knowledge of the region, linguistic ability. There were even reasons beyond Angell's family connection to the material, although that was important. And now he had sent Angell into the most dangerous place in the world.

Sure, there were other dangerous places. The Sudan, for instance. Syria, now that the rebels were carving out chunks of real estate for themselves. Libya. Yemen. But Nuristan? The old Kafiristan? It was like walking into a viper's nest. The Nuristanis hated everyone who wasn't Nuristani, and even then they had their doubts.

Monroe stood up and looked at the map he had pinned to his wall. He traced Angell's route thus far. Where the hell were they taking him?

By drawing an imaginary line between Tell Ibrahim to Yazd and then to Kamdesh he was starting to see a pattern. He knew that others were looking for the Book as well. He was getting reports on electronic traces and physical activity that pointed to a core group of the Dagon cult making its way across Central Asia, a group that had been in Nuristan only days earlier. That meant Angell might be headed in the same direction.

But where?

Angell was tied up in the back of a truck heading north out of Kamdesh towards Mandagal, a town on the border with Pakistan. There were two men in the front seat and another two sitting on either side of him. His bonds were not too tight, more of a reminder than anything else. He knew he would not survive sixty minutes on his own in the Hindu Kush and, anyway, he still needed to find the Book. The only question was what he was going to do with it when he found it.

The sense of isolation was heavy on him. Not only was he in a strange and forbidding part of the world, replete with terrorists, pagan cults, and the ever-present threat of violence, but he had lost his comrades to Omar and his crew, and had no idea what was happening to them. Or even if they were still alive.

Outside, the view was of mountains, trees, a rapidly running river, and buildings that seemed carved out of the cliff face. They passed an Afghan on the road who didn't even look up as they passed. Another time, under other circumstances, Angell might have found some peace in these mountains and in a simple life far from the constant pressures and demands of modernity. But one look at the faces of his guards and he realized that was a dream that had no basis in any kind of reality. Life here was nasty, brutish and short.

They arrived in Mandagal without fanfare. They drove down a dirt street with a tremendous view of the mountains and parked outside a nondescript mud-colored building with a narrow doorway and no windows.

They hustled Angell out of the truck and into the building, removing the rope that tied his hands in the process. The interior was dark, with some sunlight coming in from the far end. He could smell rancid cooking oil and cordite.

They made him sit down on the carpet in the center of the room
while his guards stood outside the building and smoked cigarettes.

Fifteen minutes later, another man entered the room and sat
down next to Angell without introducing himself. He spoke an
Indian-accented English and got down to business immediately. He
unfolded a well-worn map that was printed in English and which
looked like an old gas station map, the kind one used to see in the
pre-Internet days.

"The route we use goes through Pakistan and then to Kashmir,"
he said, tracing the route in broad strokes. "It's used by everyone
in the region, including by Lashkar-e-Taiba, and is well-known to
ISI, the Pakistani security agency. I won't lie to you; this will be a
dangerous journey. We have to blend in with the local traffic and not
arouse any suspicion. There is no problem when we are in our own
territory, of course, but there are many who will want us to pay a
tax to go through their territory if we are carrying an American. So
you are not to speak in the presence of anyone except those in our
vehicle. Others will make you for an American no matter how fluent
your Urdu or Pashtu may be."

Angell looked around at the men who had come in and were
sitting around them, then looked back at his host and nodded.

"We are going as far as the Pakistan border, and then we will
be picked up by our people using a somewhat heavier vehicle. The
passage will be rough, but we expect no attacks from either side,
unless there are units of Lashkar-e-Taiba in the region at which
point there may be some difficulty. They are not always aligned
with us. Sometimes they make their bed with Al-Qaeda, and their
interests and ours do not always coincide."

The sheer number and complexity of all these movements and
armies and groups was making Angell's head spin. He knew things
were worse in Syria and Iraq, but that was cold comfort.

These were all basically independence movements, or at least
they were in the beginning. The Taliban fought the Soviet invaders

and then tried to take over Afghanistan. Al-Qaeda was set up to drive the "Crusaders" from Saudi Arabian soil, and then became a worldwide terror operation with an ill-defined strategy and an unrealizable goal. Then there were Hamas and Hezbollah: anti-Israel groups allegedly fighting for the liberation of Palestine and the Gaza Strip, but funded by Shiite Iran. Not to mention al-Nusra, fighting to remove President Bashar al-Assad from power in Syria. And now something called the Islamic State of Iraq and the Levant, ISIL, that was organizing all over the region.

Lashkar-e-Taiba was the radical Pakistani group that was responsible for the bombing of the hotel in Mumbai a few years ago, as well as an attack on an Orthodox Jewish building in the same city. They were believed to have adherents within ISI, which made everything more complicated and inaccessible to reason.

Throw in at least three separate Kurdish movements, plus the fringe religious sects, and you had an ever-shifting jigsaw puzzle of agendas, missions, and alliances. Angell knew it was this tremendous diversity of interests and goals which contributed to their failure as political movements and which naturally resulted in a resort to violence. Add to that the criminal gangs who were enabling these movements with smuggling operations involving drugs and guns, and you had a world—an entire reality—that was so alien to Western conceptions it might as well have landed here, rather than developed organically. Yet, they all seemed to be on the same page when it came to a virulent hatred of humanity, a hatred that permitted them to mercilessly and joyously slaughter innocent men, women, and children wherever they were found.

Maybe Monroe was right, really right, thought Angell. Maybe this is all evidence of something much darker behind the scenes. Muslim groups are destroying each other, and it makes no sense. They are advertising their hideous executions on YouTube. This is the culture that gave the world suicide bombers, after all; maybe they, themselves, just want to die. Maybe this mass media approach—the heavily-televised and video-taped beheadings—was a plea to the rest of the world to end it all for them. How could they believe their message would be taken any other way?

He was reminded of that line from the movie, *Apocalypse Now*: "Even the jungle wanted him dead." Maybe it was the same thing. Maybe even the desert wanted them dead.

They bundled Angell back inside another vehicle as they made their way to a rendezvous point on the Pakistani side of the border. He heard the word "Chitral" mentioned once or twice, and assumed that was where they were going. Chitral is in the heart of Kalasha country, the same people as the Nuristanis except they are allowed to practice their indigenous religion unmolested. More "People of the Book," but not of the Qur'an.

As they bumped and jostled their way along the dirt track into the Pakistani frontier, Angell was alone with his thoughts.

What if, he pondered, the Book is some kind of pre-Islamic or non-Islamic text that questions the validity of Islam in some way? Like it was believed the Dead Sea Scrolls were going to do where Christianity was concerned. Evidence that could not be denied, but which could threaten the very existence of the faith? And now its existence has come to light, and the Muslim faithful of every sect and denomination have a vested interest in making sure it never sees the light of day. If it did, it would take the wind out of the terrorist movements completely because they claim precedent in the Qur'an and the Hadith. They could lose their legitimacy, at least among some elements of the population.

It made sense, to a certain point. The Yezidis are not Muslim; they claim descent from Sumer and Babylon. The Nuristanis were pagan until a hundred years ago, and even now they are considered to be kafir, unbelievers. The Kalashas fled across the border when the Muslim armies came, and preserved their pagan traditions. These are the ones they've been going to for information, not to Muslim scholars or specialists in Islamic history and literature. They've been going to these antinomian groups the whole time. They've been isolated, surrounded by enemies. And now they're the center of attention … by Muslims. By terrorists professing an Islamic faith, or at least one with Islamic trappings.

Jesus, thought Angell. Lovecraft … that racist, anti-semitic bastard … had seen all of this coming. He wrote about the Yezidis, about the "Mad Arab," about rioting Levantines. *About a book written by a Mad Arab*. About gates opened to the other side, of alien forces coming down and destroying the world. And what has been the defining meme of the last thirteen years since 9/11? Mad Arabs.

If Lovecraft had been right about that, was he right about the book, too? If he was, if he was even half-right, then Monroe had a point: this book must never see the light of day. More importantly, it must never fall into the hands of terrorists. It was a weapon with enormous explosive potential. It was an IED planted in consciousness that could go off at any time.

And if the terror cells got hold of it they could distort its message, corrupt its meaning, use it to create God-knows-what chaos and tragedy on the world stage. *Al Azif*. The *Necronomicon*: a code book for terrorists? An *Anarchist's Cookbook* from space?

Angell knew he was a prisoner of the Taliban, for that was the one group no one mentioned. That the Taliban were looking for the Book came as no surprise anymore to Angell. He had seen what people would do in pursuit of it. Since the attack on the refugee camp in Turkey people had been dying. He would have to make sure that the Taliban never got it. He would have to make sure no one got it.

He would destroy it first.

CHAPTER TWENTY-TWO

CODEX IV

Before leaving Key West, Lovecraft spent another night talking to Tanzler. Shaken by his dream of his dead mother, Lovecraft allowed himself to be taken to see Tanzler's obsession: Maria Elena de Hoyos, who by now was quite ill. Her doctors did not expect her to get any better, and her family was completely distraught.

At first, Lovecraft recoiled from the Latin atmosphere of the home. He had to be dragged through the doorway to Elena's bedside. Looking down at her, he was reminded a little of Sonia Greene. His wife was Jewish, and had dark hair and made a Mediterranean impression; Tanzler's Elena shared some of these characteristics. Unaccountably, Lovecraft felt guilt rise up in him at the sight of this poor young woman suffering from an illness for which there was no cure and no hope. He had already spent a lot of time visiting women in hospitals, and his dream from the previous evening had unnerved him.

Thus, when Tanzler bade him stay another night so that they could discuss strategies for reviving a dead body, Lovecraft felt he could not refuse. Tanzler also knew about his relationship to George Angell, and the theft of the Cthulhu File. To be honest, Lovecraft thought, he may also know more about that cult than he lets on. He may hold the key to understanding the relationship between madness and the paranormal, even if he is not aware of it, and Lovecraft needed that information. His own sanity may depend on it.

So he agreed to another night of long talks in the dim light of the shack, accompanied by copious amounts of iced tea and an array of Cuban pastries, filled with guava paste and *queso blanco*. They discussed death, the chemical and biological requirements to maintain life and to postpone the decomposition of the flesh and the organs. They talked about the stories of Edgar Allan Poe and Arthur Machen, and Tanzler insisted that there were truths buried in the religions and myths of ancient cultures, myths that could be decoded if you had the benefit of initiation into the mysteries. He introduced his guest to the works of L. A. Waddell, who had been to Tibet and who had written books demonstrating the Sumerian origin of the Chinese language, as well as proof of the existence of the Aryan race.

Kabbalah, theosophy and other practices were only fragments of the wide-ranging conversation that went on for hours. It was like late night talk radio, only a few years ahead of its time and with a very exclusive audience. Again Lovecraft saw the sun come up after a long night of endless talk and speculation, but Tanzler had what he needed. He had been taking notes during the talk, writing down odd bits of data in a small book he kept with him in the hospital's radiology lab where he worked. With his experience in the world's arcana and his knowledge of medicine, he thought, and Lovecraft's knowledge of the Cthulhu Cult—the cult of a dead priest who nevertheless communicated through dreams—he had the rudiments of a process that would keep Elena viable long after death and maybe even revive her once he removed the TB from her body.

Even better, he now had more information to send to Himmler. That would keep *him* viable a little longer, too.

1932. October 25. Death of Maria Elena de Hoyos, of tuberculosis, in Key West, Florida. Tanzler arranges for an elaborate, above-ground mausoleum to house her remains, but has it fitted out with custom equipment to enable him to maintain her body for as long as possible. That same year, Reverend Henry St. Clair Whitehead—expert on Afro-Caribbean religion and friend of Lovecraft—dies of an extended illness. At the same time, Lovecraft makes the acquaintance of Robert H. Barlow, a teenager who is a fan of fantastic fiction and who also lives in Florida. Lovecraft makes several trips to that state over the next few years, to visit Barlow and to keep current on the situation with Tanzler and his decomposing bride. Barlow will become the executor of Lovecraft's estate, and will collaborate with the older man on a story involving the Yezidi and Malik Taus the Peacock Angel, "The Battle That Ended the Century": a tale set in *New York City* on New Year's Eve *2001*. Imagination as Prediction.

1933. Hitler comes to power in Germany. Tanzler removes Elena's corpse from the mausoleum and brings it to his house, where he can perform more elaborate experiments on her body with the additional funds now available to him from Himmler. He later reports in an American pulp magazine that she opened her eyes, and held his hand. He reports further that he remained in telepathic communication with her on a constant basis after her death. He writes a letter to Lovecraft in great excitement with this news, showing that the claims of the Cthulhu Cult—that their High Priest communicates with his followers in dreams— are entirely possible. Tanzler believes that Lovecraft has exposed an important truth in "The Call of Cthulhu," and that readers missed the point of the story. It was not about Cthulhu, writes Tanzler, but about the Call. This letter is later removed from the archive by an increasingly nervous Robert Barlow.

1936. Robert E. Howard, author of the *Conan* stories and friend of Lovecraft's, commits suicide at the age of 30. His mother had been ill with tuberculosis for years. When she entered a coma and was not expected to awake, Howard shot himself. Lovecraft's letters to Tanzler concerning the illness of Howard's mother and efforts to find a cure have not survived. Lovecraft evidently believed that the four years since Elena's death and Tanzler's ministrations over her body should have resulted in some new procedures.

1937. Howard Phillips Lovecraft dies. He succumbs in the same hospital where his mother passed away. His efforts to notify Tanzler in advance were not successful. Barlow, as executor of Lovecraft's estate, takes charge of his manuscripts and brings most of them to Brown University in Providence. Neither the

Cthulhu File nor the Black Book—the *Kitab Al-Azif*—is part of the collection.

1938. Himmler's team has made progress in deciphering the Book. Based on sections of the *Necronomicon* and on coded information discovered in Lovecraft's "At the Mountains of Madness" Himmler funds an expedition to Antarctica and another to Tibet during this year.

1939. The invasion of Poland. World War II and the extermination of the Jews and other races begins: human sacrifice on a massive scale, accompanied by the theft of the world's cultural artifacts from museums and private collections throughout Europe, North Africa, and the Middle East. Hitler has his agenda; Himmler has his.

1940. The disinterred body of Elena de Hoyos is found in Tanzler's home by a family member acting on a tip. This threatens to expose Tanzler's network of Nazi agents, and when word gets back to Himmler he is furious. This happens at the same time as the Hess flight to England, which has tremendous repercussions for the occult groups in Germany once it is revealed that Hess was acting according to an astrological calendar. "When the stars are right." Himmler, fearing blowback from the Tanzler revelations, stops sending him money and changes the communication protocols and codes, effectively cutting him off. Tanzler is on his own. He is briefly jailed, then released. The statute of limitations has expired on the sole count of grave desecration.

1944. Tanzler leaves Key West, and moves near Zephyrhills, Florida, outside Tampa, where he has family from Germany.

1945. As the war comes to an end, vitally important occult texts— among them the Black Book as well as the famous Egyptian Scorpion Papyrus (arguably the oldest esoteric text in existence, a set of incantations to the Egyptian god of chaos, Set)—go missing.

1946. American occultist and rocket scientist Jack Parsons begins the Babalon Working: a series of magical ceremonies in the Mojave Desert designed to open the Gate between this world and the next. His partner is L. Ron Hubbard, who will become the founder of Scientology.

1947. The Dead Sea Scrolls are discovered. The modern UFO phenomenon begins, with Kenneth Arnold, Maury Island, and Roswell. Modern day magician Aleister Crowley dies. Tanzler publishes his story of Elena de Hoyos in the same pulp magazine, *Fantastic Adventures*, that publishes the new "flying saucer" stories of that year. His editor is the famous Ray Palmer. The same magazine will publish a story by L. Ron Hubbard in 1950, "The Masters of Sleep."

1948. Robert Barlow goes to Europe, seeking the missing documents, especially the Black Book now referred to with the name by which it would become famous: the Book of Dead Names. The *Necronomicon*.

CHAPTER TWENTY-THREE

BLACK BOOK, BLACK SITES

A book is not an isolated being: it is a relationship, an axis of innumerable relationships.

—Jorge Luis Borges, *Other Inquisitions*

Jason Miller had made his way to Jalalabad after a brief visit to Kamdesh and was in a small café near the medical center, drinking thick, sweet coffee and planning his next move. Wondering about his motivations, he had spent a few gold coins and whatever good will he had stored up in this country to convince the elders to release the Americans unharmed and get them to Jalalabad, and the Nuristanis had gratefully complied. His only requirement was that they do not tell the Americans who he was or why they were released.

The Jalalabad Airfield was an obvious choice for them, but he couldn't use it. He was a wanted man. He had been traveling for the past two weeks on forged papers but didn't know how long his luck would hold out. Monroe was looking for him, and protocol dictated that Interpol was, too. Therefore, hitching a ride on a military transport was probably out of the question.

It would have been nice to work with Monroe and his people on this. If he had, the whole thing would have been over by now. But he knew what Monroe wanted with the Book. He wanted to keep it, and maybe use it one day in some weird-ass remote-viewing experiment with demons or aliens or dead gods or some shit. Miller was not about to let that happen. Once he got hold of the Book, he would destroy it. At once. Not a second thought.

In fact, Miller had known what was going on with the Book even before Monroe had a clue. It was due to those remote viewing sessions and the hunt— first for Bin Laden and then—for every other Al-Qaeda asshole on the scorecard, which led to looking in Afghanistan that Miller gradually became aware of the whole scenario. His visit with Eco in Turin had tied it all together for him nicely.

It was funny, thought Miller. Eco insisting that the *Necronomicon* didn't exist, that it was a hoax. As if that would make any difference at all to the people he had sworn to fight: the enemies of reason and the foes of civilization. *Sure, the* Necronomicon *was a hoax. So was the friggin' Bible,* he thought. *Look at how that turned out.*

He got up from his table and walked to the street. Tucked inside his tunic was a map of Asia from Turkey to Mongolia. He liked to have paper in case his phone ran out of batteries or was otherwise compromised. Miller didn't get to where he was in life by taking shortcuts. Anyway, he needed a big map—something his smartphone could not accommodate—in order to get the big picture. And he needed somewhere to sit down in peace and privacy for a few minutes to look at it.

Hence his choice of a café next to the medical center.

It was a modern building, several stories tall, all steel and glass. He went inside and found the restrooms. There were no seats, as in the West, but porcelain trenches in the floor where one had to squat to relieve oneself. And, of course, no paper. There was water all over the floors and a suspicious odor, but there was a stall with a door and that was all he needed.

He went inside and shut the door, listening. There did not seem to be anyone around, not even the ubiquitous cleaners. Standing, he quietly unfolded his map and began retracing his steps.

There, marked clearly on the map in his own personal code, were the Seven Towers. Another code showed those sites around the world that were connected with the underground cult that was "plugged in" to them: a spider-web of connections criss-crossing the Earth. In some cases, these sites were identical to locations where interrogation and torture centers had been established, the so-called "black sites." They existed in foreign countries, outside US legal jurisdiction, but there were analogous sites in the US as well. There was a famous prison at Moundsville, West Virginia, which is where the Manson Family member and would-be presidential assassin Squeaky Fromme was held; it is also an ancient Native American burial mound site. Then there was the State Prison at Chillicothe, Ohio, built on the site of another famous mound complex. And so on.

Other sites are the locations of temples sacred to the most arcane or violent sects. Still others are sites notorious as the locales of famous slaughters, massacres, and mass killings of all kinds. And there are a few sites that do not have any associations at all, being in the middle of featureless desert or in the depths of the world's oceans.

It was a map copied from the Lovecraft Codex before Miller went AWOL and augmented with his own remote viewing ability, plus intel that came in from a variety of unorthodox sources in the occult underground. Miller had been the only one to know of the existence of the Codex, and the only one who knew where it was and how to access it. Unfortunately, he didn't have time to read the whole file or copy it. It was the map that grabbed his attention, and he found it was easy to memorize the seven core locations he needed because they formed a pattern that was easy to remember. They formed a constellation.

Ursa Major. The Great Bear.

The Big Dipper.

Mosul and Yazd comprised the first two stars in the handle of the Dipper. That was easy enough. There were five more stars that were assigned to five more sites on the map of Asia. China's White Pyramid near Xi'an was one. Urumqi in Xinjiang Province was another. But Miller intended to grab the Book long before anyone made it that far. He knew where Monroe's team had to be headed next, for he knew where the Keepers of the Book were headed. The Keepers had been in Kamdesh a few days before Monroe's people. They had been in Yazd. They had left Kutha only hours before Monroe's team had arrived. And they would be in Srinagar next.

Alone in the restroom, the only sound that of dripping water from somewhere and the smell of untreated sewage in his nostrils, Miller closed his eyes and moved his consciousness out of his body and down, down into the contours of the map.

For a remote viewer, sometimes the map *is* the territory.

The Keepers of the Book were moving fast. Miller saw enormous mountains covered in snow. The sun was rising ahead of them, so they seemed to be moving southeast with the mountains on their left. The Himalayas, most likely. But he couldn't "see" the next Tower. They would have to cover all seven towers, in order. And they had to do it so that they were at the last tower when the stars were right.

There were seven Keepers, according to tradition. Yet Miller saw only six. It was possible that one died along the way. If that was the case, the Keepers would keep moving anyway because of the schedule. There was no time to bring up another Keeper through the complicated initiation process. That meant they would be somewhat weaker when the time came, but with the Seven Towers, the Book, and the Stars they would have enough of the ingredients to facilitate their goal. They would awaken the Sleeper, and the world would know Reality with a capital "R."

He viewed the likely outcome. He saw that all the crackpot theories of conspiracy nuts, ancient astronaut cranks, and occult archaeology addicts would seem to be coming true, but in reverse. A Gate would be opened—that was the terminology the cult used—and the separation between this world and another would dissolve. Forces had been gathering outside the Gate since the end of World War Two; even earlier according to some prophets of the cult. There had been a gradual awakening of the Sleeper going back centuries, thought Miller in his self-induced hypnogogic state. But the real pressure had started to build in 1945. And then, in 1946, the rituals in the Mojave had accelerated the program, so that by 1947 the first of the Ancient Ones had begun to materialize on the planet, in full view of human beings.

He came to, the session ending of its own accord. He was leaning against the wall of the bathroom stall, the map in his hand. He noticed that his finger was pointing at a specific spot on the map. It was in Nepal. High up in the mountains east of Kathmandu.

How perfect, he thought. *The hidden valley. The Keepers must be on their way there now.* He just might be able to beat them to it.

Angell's vehicle had driven for hours into the Swat Valley. They were on their way to a Kalasha village where they had a contact: a man who was compromised because of his love for a Muslim girl from another village. The Taliban were holding that information over him, to force him to cooperate.

The Taliban hated to go anywhere near the Kalasha, unless it was to burn their villages to the ground. The Kalasha of Pakistan are non-Muslims who still openly practice their ancient religion, ancient even when Alexander was a baby. They were a thorn in the side of the Taliban but Pakistan was not Taliban country and there was little they could do about it. They were just passing through, and any attempt to throw their weight around in the Swat Valley would be reason enough for ISI to turn on them and have them all arrested. Or worse.

They did not get the information they wanted from the Katra of Kamdesh, not even after torture and interrogation. The village elders were too frightened of the Taliban to offer more than token resistance, and even then it was more in terms of persuasion than threats of violence. However, Omar Mansour knew that the villagers would eventually rise up against them and that the longer he and his men stayed in Nuristan the more likely a firefight would be. Mansour's own position within the Taliban was precarious as it was. Should he lose fighters to the kafirs he would become the laughing stock of the movement, if he wasn't executed himself as an example. His only defense was the fact that he was aggressively seeking the Book; if he didn't acquire it, however, he would be the next to lose his head.

The Kalasha of Pakistan were, in a sense, the "Vatican" of the Kalasha clans. As they had not converted and as they had kept the old ways they knew the rituals, the legends, and the ancient lore concerning the Book. At least, that is what Mansour was depending on. His people had been overzealous in their interrogation of the Katra—a shaman who aroused nothing but disgust in them—and they had allowed their feelings to overwhelm their common sense.

He had also received intelligence that a group known as the Keepers of the Book had passed through the region only days before. There was only one place they could be going, and that was to the Kalasha homeland. He knew they must have talked to the Katra, the one person in all of Nuristan who knew the old ways and was a person they could trust, but his interrogators had been foolish and had allowed the man to die before he could reveal any secrets.

So they cut off his head and arranged it neatly in his lap, as a warning to the Americans.

As for the prisoners, Omar Mansour would deal with them himself. There was no reason to keep them alive. He could string Doctor Angell along for quite some time by telling him everyone was in good health, but Angell was really in no position to bargain. Briefly, he considered keeping one or more of them alive as something to trade in the event he needed something else, or safe passage out of Nuristan without losing any men. He would see how he felt. After all, it was known that Omar Mansour was a man of many moods.

As he stepped outside of his temporary command post at the outskirts of Kamdesh he saw figures in the shadows all around him. Villagers, elders, even children. Everyone was afraid of him. Everyone hated him. But that was no matter. It was better to be feared than to be loved. He read that somewhere.

There was a cry as if from a dog howling at the moon. Dogs were disgusting creatures. Coprophagic. Islam says that dogs are unclean, the eaters of filth and dead bodies. The mere sight of a dog was sometimes enough to make him ill.

He started walking down the dirt road between the buildings

on his street. His men were walking behind him, looking in every direction, armed to the teeth. It was then he noticed that there was only a waxing moon, a sliver of light in the heavens. The rest of the sky was filled with stars. For some reason, the sight of all those stars filled him with a kind of dread, as if they were faces of a jury and the sliver moon was the prosecutor assigned to his case.

The howl came again. He heard a shuffling sound as more and more villagers came out of their homes to stand in the dirt road and watch him pass.

Mansour was the head of the Taliban in Pakistan, and as such was a wanted man by the Pakistani authorities. He was tall and thin, with a long black beard that came to the middle of his chest. In his thirties, and the father of three children, he was a charismatic leader who loved to play volleyball. He only had a high school education, plus some time spent in a madrassa: a religious boarding school. Other than that, he was self-taught, having learned English by listening to the BBC. He joined the Taliban in 2007 and rose to prominence within its ranks. His men loved him and called him Emir, "prince," and even Khalifa, or "caliph"; he was considered an uncompromising supporter of jihad and an opponent of everything that was decadent and western.

He loved the tribal regions and tribal people. He loved their simplicity and honesty, and their pure faith untainted by materialism and slavish devotion to western culture. The only exception to this rule was Nuristan. They were tribal people, too, but they represented a time before Islam, before even Christianity or Judaism. They were from before Abraham, worshippers of jinn. They were people of darkness, and if he could get away with it he would slaughter them all.

More people left their homes and simply stood on the streets, watching him and his entourage pass. They had no expression on their faces. It was as if they were all dead, spirits of the dead, come to accuse him of murder.

He strode among them, through them, without a word. He was

heading to the place where they kept the prisoners and he had a
decision to make. If he slaughtered them now, he and his men could
leave and make for the border. If he didn't, he could either take them
with him or stay there another day or so until he heard back from
his men in Kalasha territory.

He kept walking.

Another howl in the night, another dog or some other animal.
It meant the jinn were out in force. Dogs could see them and alert
their masters.

Then he passed the building where the dead shaman was still
chained to the pillar with its obscene carvings, and the howl became
stronger: a rolling, deep-throated sound that vibrated the stones
underneath their feet.

Omar exchanged glances with his men, then gestured for them
to enter the building. They nodded, locked and loaded, and carefully
went through the door.

They froze when they got a few feet inside. Omar followed and
walked through the midst of them to face the source of the howling.

It was the head of the shaman in the corpse's lap, eyes wide open,
mouth distended in an unending, animalistic bellow.

They opened fire on the shaman's head and corpse in a deafening
roar in that enclosed space, splintering the body as well as the pillar
to which it was chained. Omar shouted at them to cease firing. They
were only wasting ammunition, and were firing out of absolute
terror at something that was already dead.

"Stop! Stop firing! It is dead! Stop!" He slapped his hand down
on the arm of the man closest to him, then moved to the next. Soon,
the ringing in their ears from the automatic fire subsided and the
smoke from the barrels of half a dozen AK-47s drifted away. What
was left of the shaman was now nothing more than an indentation
on the dirt floor of the temple.

That is when Omar realized that they had been had.

"*Where are the prisoners?*" he shouted at his men. "*Where are they?*"

Adnan and the two CIA anti-terrorism agents were running on the road south of Kamdesh, armed and free. The two Taliban who were guarding them had their throats slit by a group of villagers who had appeared out of nowhere, distracted them, then overpowered them. They untied the prisoners and handed them the weapons. They were told there would be a pickup truck going south on the road out of town that would take them as far as Jalalabad. Then the villagers melted back into the town just as the firing began at the shaman's temple.

The terrorists began searching the town, looking for the escaped prisoners. Omar was furious, both with his men and with the villagers. If he tried to exact revenge, however, the wrath of Nuristan would fall on him. The Afghan National Army would probably take that opportunity to finish them off. He consoled himself with the thought that Angell was on his way to find the Book, and that no matter that he lost his prisoners there was nothing they could do to interfere with his plans.

Adnan heard the engine first. They scattered to the side of the road to make sure that the truck coming down the road was their contact. When the vehicle came slowly around a bend in the dirt track Adnan spotted the driver and recognized him as one of the men who had freed them. He waved him down, and the truck stopped. The three men jumped on the bed in the rear of the pickup and covered themselves with a tarp that had been spread there for the purpose. The truck then set off for Jalalabad.

Near Chitral
Afghan-Pakistan Border

Angell was jostled awake by the sudden stop of the vehicle and the attendant shouts of the men. They seemed to have reached their destination.

He was pulled roughly onto the road and was able to get some idea of where they were. The mountains were in the distance, and in his immediate surroundings he saw a young man dressed in black clothing. He was handsome, with very pale skin for a Pakistani, and with shocking blonde hair and blue eyes. He was their Kalasha contact, and stepped over to the side of the road to talk to the Afghans.

Angell couldn't hear their conversation. He wasn't meant to. Instead a guard was posted to keep an eye on him while he relieved himself on the other side of the road. He thought briefly of making a run for it, but realized at once it was a plan doomed to failure. He had no real idea of where he was, and was surrounded by armed men. If he made it to a Kalasha village there was no guarantee that they wouldn't hand him over to the Taliban anyway. He needed a scorecard to keep track of all the players in this game, and knew that the rules of that game changed by the hour. If you weren't immersed in it, you would become the one being played.

The men broke up and started walking back to their truck. Angell could tell that there was something disappointing in the news they received from the young Kalash.

One of the men helped him back into the truck, and said, "We have a long drive ahead of us. The Book has had a head start. We have to cross to Kashmir."

Kashmir? That was in a disputed no-man's land between India and Pakistan.

"Not to worry," said the Afghan. "We will not make it in this vehicle. We will have some help." His smile, missing a few teeth and an eye that had been shattered during a rocket attack in Chitral, was not reassuring.

The Taliban raise most of their funding through taxes imposed on criminal gangs in the region—basically protection money—and funds derived from kidnapping and ransom, as well as through the extremely lucrative drug trade. For them, Nuristan is a good place to hold kidnapped victims due to its isolation and the difficulty of get-ting armed troops into the region. The local villagers will be forced into either supporting them, or tolerating their presence.

Once inside Pakistan, however, a different set of parameters is encountered. To a certain extent there is cooperation with ISI, Pakistan's security services, who can use the Taliban as pawns in their byzantine machinations concerning Afghanistan. They also derive some income from the drug trade that flourishes, virtually unopposed, in the border regions from Waziristan to Nuristan. The fact that Osama bin Laden lived quite freely in Abbottabad—not far from Nuristan—in an area dominated by the Pakistan military, is evidence of this *realpolitik*. America and the West may be fighting a global war on terror, but in Central Asia the dimensions of this conflict are quite different, and involve the sentiments and cultures of local people who see what the West calls terrorism through a local lens. Angell has fallen into the midst of this environment, and has no idea about the proliferation of terror groups and their relationships with criminal gangs in that part of the world. As a religious studies professor he has been blessedly unaware of this complex collection of competing groups, all of whom claim some identification with Islam but whose very idiosyncratic interpretation of that religion—combined with local tribal and pagan elements—has contributed to an environment that seems more like a bad LSD trip than the neat theological arguments of a Thomas Aquinas or an Abu al-Hasan al-Ash'ari.

The reality on the ground in Afghanistan and Pakistan has more to do with tribal conflicts, criminal activity, and political maneuvering than it does with religion. Religion provides the moral justification for activities that would take place anyway and which are based on centuries of historical context. People, however, are still people and are still motivated by the same needs and desires as everyone else on the planet. Angell was gradually coming to realize that this intense focus on a book that had a blasphemous reputation wherever it was discussed represented a desire for power that was basic to all human endeavors. This need was more powerful than theological differences or even ethnic or tribal differences, for it was a lens for understanding the world and gaining control over the invisible machinery that hummed beneath its surface. Some groups claimed they wanted to obtain the Book in order to destroy it, but Angell didn't believe that for a second. Others claimed they wanted it to use it, and Angell appreciated their honesty. No one, however, claimed they knew what was in it, or who wrote it, or what its message may be.

No one, of course, except the group he heard mentioned in whispers among the Afghans: the Keepers of the Book. Who they were, and how they were organized, remained a mystery to him.

And now they were headed for Kashmir, an area of the world that was as heavily contested as Israel and Palestine. Both India and Pakistan claimed the region, and there was intense conflict between Muslim and Hindu factions that often resulted in violence. In fact, there is a strong local tradition that Jesus Christ himself had traveled to Kashmir after the Crucifixion and was buried in Srinagar, its capital. That meant that two locations associated with the founder of Christianity—Jerusalem and Srinagar—are centers of religious violence and political struggles. The irony of this was not lost on Angell.

A heavy truck appeared about an hour later. They were proceeding east, across northern Pakistan, on another dirt road to nowhere when the truck's engine could be heard above their own. When it finally came into view, it was an incredible sight.

The so-called "jingle truck" was an enormous affair when compared to their own Toyota Hilux pickup truck. It was painted in elaborate colors and designs and had a bed that was reinforced to carry as many logs of firewood—or bags of opium—as possible. The walls of the bed rose up far above the cab and even extended over the roof of the cab to permit more freight to be carried. It was a vehicle whose appearance would have made Ken Kesey proud, as psychedelic as a Peter Max poster.

Both vehicles stopped, and Angell was dragged out and brought to the rear of the jingle truck. From the rear bumper hung dozens, if not hundreds, of chains which was the reason for these vehicles being called "jingle" trucks. The entire vehicle was covered in meticulously-executed and extremely colorful artwork. Many of the designs were familiar to Angell from his study of Sufism and other mystical schools. But there were others—not quite as conspicuous—that had a different pedigree.

There were symbols from the occult workbooks of the European Renaissance, so out of place here except for how they were drawn and painted which made them look like the rest of the art. He recognized seals from the *Keys* of Solomon and magic squares from the *Book of Abramelin*. There were demon sigils from the *Goetia* tucked in between geometric figures that would have been at home in Istanbul or the Alhambra. And, to top it all, at the top of the rear of the truck like an enormous tail light was a heavily ornamented Eye in a Triangle. If the Illuminati had a party bus, this was it. Angell marveled at the décor but was so wired he thought no more about it, except for odd moments here and there when he wondered at the artist and his source material.

There were bags of what appeared to be opium on the truck but it was a light load, more for appearance than for trade, and they formed a kind of surface on top of which Angell and his guards arranged themselves for the journey to Kashmir. No one would stop a truck carrying opium, since Afghan opium accounted for more than ninety percent of the world's supply. Even Army generals use military trucks to transport Afghan opium to augment their income, so one interferes with opium transport at one's peril.

The engines started up again, and the Taliban's modest pickup drove back in the direction of the border while Angell's jingle truck shifted gears and made its way to the other side of the country.

It would leave the dirt road in another few kilometers and join the highway going east. Angell and the guards became drowsy with the movement of the truck and the relative comfort of sitting on the bags. Angell watched them, and saw that he had an opportunity to grab a gun from the nearest man whose eyes had closed but knew if he did he would not get very far. He could shoot the guards and maybe force the driver to take him to a town or a city somewhere, but where? And how would he be received? His mission was to get the Book under any circumstances and, oddly enough, his captors provided the best chance he had to accomplish that goal, even as every instinct in his body told him to *run*, run into the forest, head for the mountains, and get as far away from these murderers as possible. Just run! But that would be suicidal. He knew that, even if the adrenalin coursing through his body didn't.

So, he decided to take advantage of the lull in activity and get some sleep himself. He didn't know when he would get such a chance again.

Adnan and the two CIA agents had made it as far as Jalalabad Airfield where they were welcomed by US Army personnel and offered hot showers and food. Their Nuristani driver did not hang around, but instead sped off as soon as his charges were at the airfield gate. He had fulfilled his duty and did not want to appear to be any friendlier with the American authorities than he had to be.

Adnan welcomed the comparative luxury of the facilities with relief, and when rumors began to spread as to where he had been and the fact that he had escaped there were many intelligence officers who wanted to talk to all three of them, but that had to wait. First, Adnan had to get on the blower and talk to Aubrey who by now was fairly frantic in Baghdad.

Once the preliminaries were over and the appropriate codes exchanged, Adnan got right into it.

"They're taking him to Kashmir. At least, that's what we've heard. He left Kamdesh with a contingent of Taliban about the same time we did. They must be halfway across Swat by now."

"Are they holding him for ransom, then?" That was a common practice among the Taliban when it came to foreign captives.

"That's a negative, sir. They know about the Book and they are doing everything they can to be the first to get hold of it. They need your man for that, so they won't harm him until they have the Book in their possession."

"So they know where the Book is?"

"They have a pretty good idea. Another group passed through Kamdesh several days earlier. They talked to the local shaman there. We don't know what was said, but we do know that the Taliban were very interested. And then they took off for Kashmir."

"Where's the shaman now? Can we talk to him?"

"Negative, sir. The shaman is down. They interrogated him. Harshly. They would have done the same to us, but some villagers released us and killed our guards. We don't really know why. They told the Taliban leader, guy name of Omar, that mountain vampires did it. They didn't buy it, of course, but they pretty much had no choice but to accept the explanation. For now. I have the feeling Omar will be back one day soon to execute some vengeance on the town."

"Omar? That would be Omar Mansour?"

"Not sure, sir. They called him Emir, though."

"Yes. That's him. He's the leader of the entire Pakistani Taliban. If he's in Kamdesh over this affair, then he's taking it very seriously indeed. He can field hundreds of fighters on an hour's notice."

"What are your orders, sir?"

Aubrey was in a bind. He needed eyes on Angell. He had GPS data and knew that the professor was nearing another dangerous locale. He also knew the man's days were numbered as long as he was in Taliban captivity.

But he also needed the Book. He needed the Book more than he needed Angell alive or anyone else, for that matter. Monroe had made him understand the disaster that would take place if a religious fanatic—any kind of religious fanatic, from Islamic jihadist to Christian fundamentalist to any other kind—got his or her hands on the text. It was a lit match to the gasoline soaked rags of religious fanaticism and once the conflagration started there would be no way to stop it.

Aubrey didn't believe that the legends told about the Book were true, despite Monroe's paranoia and his weird collection of old newspaper clippings and ancient star charts. He didn't believe using the incantations in the Book would open some kind of weird interstellar Gate that would allow space monsters unfettered access to the planet. *I mean, who came up with* that *arrangement?* he thought. *Who says we would have to let them in? If they existed, why couldn't they simply break open the door and have their way?* But that wasn't important. What was important was that these people believed in the Book and its power and they knew that the reputation of the Book was more than enough to guarantee at least some of their followers would believe in its power, too. And for most political and religious leaders a shared fantasy was enough. If it didn't seem logical, its proponents could always claim that elements of the argument remained a "mystery."

"How fast can you get to Srinagar?"

Adnan looked over at the base commander, who gave him a thumbs up.

"They'll get us helo to the site once we know where it is, but the base commander says it'll be hairy. We'll be pissing off both the Indians and the Pakistanis at the same time. Quite a diplomatic accomplishment."

"Based on your own take, what do you think the chances are of getting our man out alive?"

"There's no margin in their killing him. That would be their last option. But they would take him out if they thought we were getting to the package first. We'd need a SEAL team to do this right, and days of planning, like Neptune Spear. We don't have that luxury." Operation Neptune Spear was the one that killed Osama bin Laden.

Aubrey consulted a file in front of him. Adnan could hear the anachronistic rustle of paper.

"We've got JSOC standing by, in Karachi. I've already tasked UAV to monitor the border region, using his GPS as tracker."

UAV meant Unmanned Aerial Vehicle: a drone. JSOC—or Joint Special Operations Command—had a team embedded with the Pakistani military in Karachi. They reported directly to the White House, which meant the mission had approvals at the highest level.

Adnan thought furiously. They could do no better than have JSOC involved in a rescue attempt, but Adnan was worried about a leak that would jeopardize Angell's life. He knew JSOC was tight as a drum, but if they operated out of Karachi there was always a chance that—with a mission as high-profile as this one, with crazed cults all over the world scouring the countryside looking for the Book—someone would talk. Even a rumor at this point could get Angell killed.

"Sir, could we run the op out of here?"

There was silence a moment on the other end.

"We don't have a team in J-bad," he answered.

"You have me, sir. And the two CTPT assets. This would be right up their alley. And we both know the players by sight. A helo could get us into Srinagar before a team is brought up to speed in Karachi."

"That's just the three of you."

"And the helo crew, but they wouldn't have to leave the ship. Sir."

Aubrey checked his computer.

"They won't be in Kashmir for another four or five hours at least if they are on schedule. They are north of Abbottabad now. How much time do you need?" He was referring to the fact that none of those men had slept in days or had very much to eat. If they tried to undertake a mission as delicate and dangerous as this one in a state of fatigue they would make mistakes, and those mistakes could be fatal. Aubrey was also a political animal, and he didn't want to see a bunch of dead or captured American special ops people on the evening news.

"An hour or so, sir. We'll catnap in relays."

Aubrey did some math and looked at his computer screen. He watched the progress of the drone as it flew high over the Pakistan-India border. It was being controlled out of Creech AFB in Nevada by some twenty-something drone jockey with a can of Coke and bag of chips next to his console, probably. Aubrey could not get his head around that, but there you go. He just hoped the kid would wipe the grease from his fingers before hitting the button that would send a Hellfire missile up the ass of the Taliban leader holding Angell. You know, just to be respectful.

"Take two hours. You'll need every bit of it. Let me talk to the base commander."

Angell's jingle truck made a pit stop on the way to the Kashmiri border. It was in a line with other trucks and similar traffic on the road. The men got out and stretched their legs, including the driver who casually walked over to Angell.

"*Assalaamu aleikhoum,*" he said.

"*Wa'aleikhoum salaam,*" Angell responded.

"How's it goin'?" the man said, in perfect English, to the astonishment of the American.

"Uh ... okay?" he replied, a little confused.

"Don't worry, dude. I studied at UC Berkeley."

"That's ... weird."

"Yeah, right? Anyway, I'm not Taliban. I'm just a contract hire, you know? I'm not even really Muslim, but don't tell them that." He nodded in the direction of the others who were standing next to each other, urinating.

"I'm Kalasha. You know Kalasha?"

Angell nodded, wondering where this was going.

"When I was at UC Berkeley I got turned on to all this other stuff, you know? Since I'm Kalasha, I'm hip to the arcane shit they got goin' on around there. That whole Wicca scene, Golden Dawn, astrology, Reiki ... you name it, dude, I was into it."

"That explains the artwork on your truck."

"Oh, you noticed that shit? Cool. Yeah, I got heavy into ritual magic my senior year. Almost flunked out because of that ... well, that and the pot ... but whatever. Listen, these guys are probably gonna waste you once they're done with you. I thought maybe they would ransom you out to your peeps, but from what I hear of them talking, I don't think so."

Angell swallowed heavily, and could only croak a "Thanks."

"Hey, listen dude. Don't sweat it. I'll get you out of this. We gotta stick together, right?"

Angell looked at him quizzically. "What do you mean?"

"You're Professor Angell, right? From Columbia? I recognized you from the photo on the university website. I read all your work, man. You got a fan base at Berkeley."

"You're kidding me."

The Afghans began moving back to the truck, some of them smoking cigarettes and talking, reluctant to get back on the truck even though they were under a tight schedule.

"Later, dude. I gotta get back in the cab. Won't pay to let them see me talking to you. Peace."

Angell realized he didn't get the driver's name.

They finally set off again, and by his estimation they were about three hours from the border. He had no idea how they planned to get across, but he knew the Taliban ran smuggling operations through there all the time. He wondered if Aubrey was still monitoring his GPS chip or even if it was still working.

More than that, he worried about Adnan and the two CIA agents who had been taken prisoner by the Taliban. He had no idea if they were still alive. He would do his best to get proof of life from his captors before doing anything to translate or analyze the Book.

Not for the first time, he asked himself why he was so essential to this mission. They could have asked Schiffman or Tabor, someone else with a background in ancient Middle Eastern languages, maybe with a track record at archaeological digs and experience working with the government. He wondered again if his personal history was an important element, and he didn't understand how it could be. It was a problem without a solution, as far as he was concerned. But a problem that meant life or death to him.

There was a new guard sitting in the back with him. They had been taking turns sitting up in the cab with the driver, and this one had been hogging that seat until the others complained. Now he was in the back with them and not too happy about it. He glared at Angell, muttering words in Pashtu under his breath not realizing that Angell understood that language. He was calling Angell an unbeliever, a man who should be killed and not coddled. The other man argued with him, saying that their orders from the Emir were to make sure the *kafir* studied the Book when they got it and told them how to use it, otherwise getting the Book would be half of the mission only. The other half would be their heads.

The angry man said he didn't think this was God's mission. He said that the book was *haram*, and everyone knew it. Even to touch it would be *haram*. It was an unholy scripture, one that taught the ways of *shirk*, of idolatry. Why not simply burn it, and the foreigner, too?

CHAPTER TWENTY-FOUR

CODEX V

1948. Robert Barlow, Lovecraft's executor, has tracked the *Necronomicon* to Bolzano, a town in the Tyrol.

After Lovecraft's death in 1937, Barlow was involved in sorting all of Lovecraft's papers—including unpublished stories and notes—and giving the bulk of them to Brown University. He then went on to study anthropology and won a Fulbright scholarship to Mexico, where he eventually became the head of the Anthropology Department at Mexico City College. He was a renowned expert in Mexican languages, religion, and culture, inspired by the work of his mentor on ancient cults and by the work of Reverend Whitehead on Afro-Caribbean religions.

However, he also began a quiet search for the *Necronomicon*. He had learned of the Book's existence not only from the Lovecraft stories—a theme that was picked up by other writers in Lovecraft's circle and expanded to include all sorts of extraneous material—but also from his conversations with Lovecraft and with Count Karl Tanzler von Cosel who regaled the younger man with stories of the war and of his attempts to resuscitate his dearest Elena using Lovecraft's understanding of reanimation.

Finally, word came to him of an SS officer who had escaped to Mexico after the war and who had specific knowledge about an occult bureau within the SS known as the Ahnenerbe, or the "ancestral heritage research bureau." This sounded like a promising lead to Barlow, who followed it up with a meeting with the renegade SS man.

"The one you need to speak to," said the officer, "is Johann von Leers. He is an expert in Middle Eastern languages and is probably the one who knows the most of what was going on with occultism within the Reich."

Barlow eventually tracked Leers to the town of Bolzano, in the Italian Tyrol: a famous way-station for Nazis on the run. It was here that some of the members of the SS-Ahnenerbe escaped in the years after the war, living out their lives day by day as they awaited transport and false papers to South America. The trail was cold, but Barlow found a local priest who knew the Nazi he was seeking. The priest told him that the man disappeared some time ago, but that he left behind a suitcase in his rush to get away before the American CIC agents found him. He showed Barlow the suitcase and in it was a file of papers that had belonged to Leers and an envelope that had Julius Evola's name written on it.

Barlow eagerly opened Evola's envelope first. This, at least, was a name known to him: a crackpot philosopher who promoted a kind of fascist esotericism, a man who had been ordered by Himmler to investigate the horde of stolen occult books and manuscripts the Reich had seized from Masonic temples, secret society archives, and personal libraries throughout the occupied territories. These were priceless works that were never recovered by the Allies, most of which made their way to private collections around the world (those that did not remain within the core of Nazi supporters that formed ODESSA, the Nazi underground network). Inside the envelope was a sheaf of papers that were collections of strange symbols and even stranger verbiage. At the top of one page was the word—written in Greek letters—*Necronomicon*. Barlow stopped breathing for a moment. *Is this it?*

He riffled through the pages, noting almost immediately that they were too few in number to represent the manuscript. He put them down and went through Leers' file.

It was in English and marked "Cthulhu Cult." Barlow did not realize he was looking at the very file that was stolen from Lovecraft's Brooklyn apartment more than twenty years earlier, but he took it and the Evola paperwork with him anyway. He thanked the priest and left the Tyrol forever.

On his return to Mexico City he learned that the bloody sacrifices of the Aztecs have resonance with those of the Cthulhu cult he read about in the Leers file. He also realized with both horror and excitement that his idol, H. P. Lovecraft, had encoded much real information in his stories. He understood that he must now go back and re-read everything—stories, letters, foul matter—with a view towards decoding the texts. Lovecraft's use of specific dates and places are the clues he needs to calculate the cult's future plans. He continued his study of the rituals and lore of the indigenous peoples while at the same time conducting a greater search for Leers and the *Necronomicon*.

The following year, while still deep in the study of arcane religious practices, he doesn't notice a new student who enrolls in his class: William S. Burroughs.

CHAPTER TWENTY-FIVE

THE LURKER AT THE THRESHOLD

The strong emotions, the fear, the terror, so skillfully aroused by the scenarios just described, are to be regarded as so many initiatory tortures.

— Mircea Eliade, *Rites and Symbols of Initiation*

The jingle truck came to a complete stop, pulling off the road as it did so. In the distance was the town of Garhi Habibullah, essentially a suburb of Abbottabad. The idea was to go across from there to Muzaffarabad on the Kashmir side and from there across the mountains to Srinagar. There was no way a jingle truck was going to make it the rest of the way. From now on, they would have to switch to a smaller vehicle with a good engine, four-wheel drive and a low profile. Angell was afraid he would lose the driver at this point in the journey, as the driver was the only one who seemed to be on his side.

The Afghans sit down by the side of the road. One of them seems to be in telephone contact with someone in the town. Angell catches part of the conversation which seems to indicate a pickup truck will be leaving soon to meet them. Until it does, they tell the driver to wait, just in case there's a delay or a problem.

Once again, the Afghans pull out their cigarettes for a smoke. Angell walks around a little to stretch his legs, looking at the scenery—which, in spite of everything, is breathtaking—and trying to assess his chances if he starts to run.

It is a good time of year to be in this region. There is a profusion of greenery everywhere and majestic mountain peaks in the distance. A fast-running river divides Pakistan from the Kashmiri border, and one look at it—even from a distance—tells Angell he would never make it across by swimming.

He thinks back on what he knows of Srinagar as the town

rumored to be the final resting place of Jesus. According to the legend, famous in Kashmir, Jesus faked his own death and traveled with his mother from Palestine all the way to northern India where he was welcomed as a guru, eventually died and was buried in a shrine in the town. Somehow, this story is comforting to Angell. It's Christianity without the bloody crucifixion, the torture, the violence. Jesus as guru seemed more palatable than Jesus either as zealot or as victim. Briefly, Angell wishes it were all true; that using some magic of DNA and genetics scientists could prove that Jesus was buried in Srinagar. What a change that would inaugurate in the world's religions. Peace to replace war; love to replace fanaticism. And maybe there would be a different sort of cult: a Jesus cult of mantras, meditation and yoga instead of ceremonies that involve the devouring of the victim's flesh and blood. Even then, the Yezidi would still have been taken off a bus and massacred in Mosul. No way out.

For a moment, Angell admits that atheism is the one characteristic that he shares with his nemesis: H. P. Lovecraft.

Just as Angell is lost in these thoughts, a man is seen walking towards their party from somewhere in the woods on the Kashmiri side. The Afghans jump up and ready their weapons.

It's just an old man, alone, whimpering. He is old and disheveled, and seems to be blind. Angell is startled, thinking of the old Zoroastrian priest from Yazd. The man keeps walking towards them, his unseeing eyes a milky color, his arms outstretched before him. He ignores the shouts of the Taliban to stop, to turn back, to go away. They train their weapons on him, even knowing that he appears to be harmless, but knowing all about suicide bombers and how they can be anyone, any gender, any age.

The old man is making straight for Angell. The driver of the jingle truck jumps down from the cab and stands behind the American.

"Dude," he whispers. "This is weird."

Then the old man starts to speak. In English.

"Go away, Gregory. Go away! Turn back!" The voice is clear,

unaccented, an American voice, a voice with the tones of Rhode Island all along it like Christmas lights hanging on the tree. It is his father's voice, and he is terrified.

"Go back!"

The Afghans don't know what to do. They hear English, but the man is obviously local. The cognitive dissonance that takes place is unsettling. The Taliban look around them, in every direction, expecting a congregation of English-speaking jinn.

Then the man with the voice of his father, his long dead father, stops in the middle of the road and points at Angell with a bony finger creased with age and tanned with working in the sun. A mindless, wordless scream escapes from his mouth.

Qhadhulu!

A shot rings out from somewhere behind the old man, and he falls dead at their feet. Angell is horrified and frozen in place. The Afghans look at him as if he is some kind of evil spirit himself, for the dead man spoke in English, pointed at him, and spoke the word they hoped never to hear for they knew damned well what it meant. Everyone did. That was the joke, wasn't it? *They all knew.* They knew from Turkey to Syria, from Iraq to Iran, and now from Afghanistan to Pakistan. That one word. That curse for all humanity. That term of *shirk.* That detestable word. The one that sums up in a single sound all that is wrong with religion and with God and the gods and all the ritual and prayers and incantations. The word *Qhadhulu.* The *Abandoner.* It is not a word of the jinn, of the devil, of the evil spirits. No. *It is the name of God himself.* The one who abandoned his people, his creation, his planet. The one the blasphemers and the kafirs are trying to call back to life.

Those thoughts and worse coursed through Angell's brain like the icy, rushing, poisonous waters of the river Kunar, the boundary between Pakistan and India, between Muslim and Hindu, between Central Asia and South Asia. A frontier that is neither here nor there, but worth slaughtering each other over. In the distance, on the other side of the river, they could see a man stand up from a hiding place, from his "god spot," and look down at his kill. It is an Indian soldier. He looks down, looks at the men gathered by the side of the truck, and walks away.

Stunned, the Taliban fighters open up on the place where the shot came from. They are far out of range, their AK-47s no match for the reach or the precision of the sniper rifle across the river. They are panic firing, and their shots are going wild. Angell hits the ground and covers his ears with his hands.

This is never going to stop, he thinks. *Automatic weapons fire. The church bells of the twenty-first century.*

With all the ringing in their ears, no one notices a pickup truck coming their way down the road from town.

CHAPTER TWENTY-SIX

WHEN THE STARS ARE RIGHT

… that cult would never die till the stars came right again, and the secret priests would take Great Cthulhu from His Tomb to revive His subjects and resume His rule of earth.

    — H.P. Lovecraft, "The Call of Cthulhu"

Jason Miller is at the observatory on Mount Saraswati, near Leh in the province of Ladakh. The very names of Leh and Ladakh summon up Lovecraftian associations, but these are real places, on the map near the India-China border. Another border, another frontier. This constant crossing of borders—this aggressive liminalism—must mean *something*, thinks Miller, but only briefly. His attention is concentrated on the astronomers who are showing him their equipment. They think he is an official from the US government, and he lets them think that.

They are excited about some trans-Plutonian space objects they have sighted, traveling in the wrong direction around a distant star. They are losing Miller, who can't seem to focus on the math, but he takes advantage of a lull in the conversation to ask them a pointed question about the largest known supernova in history—one that exploded in the year 1006—and they become suspicious. They answer his questions politely, acknowledging that the supernova exploded in the constellation Therion—the Beast—and that it was synchronous with the explosion of a volcano on the island of Java that obliterated an entire kingdom and buried the largest outdoor Buddhist shrine in the world under a mountain of lava. Borobudur would not be discovered again for another eight hundred years or more.

He then asks more pointed questions concerning recent supernovae, such as the important SD 2011 Fe—which took place in the tail of the Great Bear a few months after the assassination of Osama bin Laden—on the night "when the Great Bear hangs from its tail in the sky" according to the *Necronomicon*. When supernovae from that area of the sky are listed in tabular form it becomes obvious that there is a pattern to them, a kind of cosmic pulse.

This is what Miller was afraid to learn, and it gives him greater impetus to finish his quest for the Book as quickly as possible. That cosmic pulse—he believes—is nothing less than the opening and the closing of the Gate that will allow tremendous sinister forces to penetrate the Earth's atmosphere when summoned by the followers of Cthulhu.

He stays with the astronomers for another thirty minutes or so, to be polite, and says goodbye. They want to invite him to share their lunch, but he begs off: playing the busy government official. His jeep is outside and he is eager to get back on the road. He was on the way to Nepal when he decided to get verification for what he had seen during a remote viewing session. So he hopped the forty-five minute flight between Srinagar and the small airport at Leh. He hired a jeep and drove the few hundred klicks to the village of Hanle and from there to the small observatory. The drive was long and Miller was getting tired of the constant traveling even though he was now in a relatively safer part of the world, replete with Tibetan Buddhist monasteries and temples against mountain backdrops and scattered among small villages and snow-choked streams.

But the detour was worth it. He was getting a better idea of what he was up against and confirmation of his worst fears about the intricate connections that exist between the uprising of the Cthulhu cult and the movement of astronomical objects. He was not a believer in astrology, but he had a healthy respect for astronomy and the effect of meteorites on the development of human civilization. The ancient Egyptians used meteorites as a source of metal for their mummification ceremonies, the rituals designed to resurrect the dead Pharaoh. And it was a meteorite that became the object of veneration in the Arabian city of Mecca. At the time of the Prophet

Muhammad, the Ka'aba in Mecca held 360 idols in proximity to a chunk of meteorite that was believed to have sacred characteristics. Today it is the cornerstone of that shrine, albeit without the idols, and every Muslim in the world turns to face that meteorite five times a day to pray. That the tribe responsible for maintaining the Ka'aba was the Prophet's own tribe, the Quraish who originated in Kutha, was a fact not lost on the American remote viewer.

Astronomical events have figured prominently in religious and political history everywhere on the planet. The supernova of 1006 was just one of these events, but astrologers were not charting these objects any longer. Not like in the old days. And the Book was composed at a time when astronomical observations were of utmost importance.

The constellation Therion is known today as Lupus, the Wolf. But Miller preferred the old name, for it summoned up associations with Aleister Crowley, the English magician who called himself *To Mega Therion*, or The Great Beast, after the same concept in the Biblical Book of Revelations. The Great Beast was ridden by the Whore of Babylon, yet another set of associations with tremendous symbolic potential, pointing to Iraq and Tell Ibrahim, the homeland of the Quraish and the gateway to the Underworld. He would have to discuss all of this with Professor Eco one day. For now, though, he had to make haste to a remote area of Nepal, high in the Himalayas and dangerously close to the border with Tibet, for it would be there that the showdown would take place with the Keepers of the Book.

Chapter Twenty-Seven

The Beyul

They all lay in stone houses in Their great city of R'lyeh, preserved by the spells of mighty Cthulhu for a glorious resurrection when the stars and the earth might once more be ready for Them. But at that time some force from outside must serve to liberate Their bodies. The spells that preserved Them intact likewise prevented Them from making an initial move …

— H. P. Lovecraft, "The Call of Cthulhu"

The Afghans are afraid to touch the body of the dead man, so Angell goes over and lifts the body by the arms. He sees the driver standing there, and waits to see if he will help him out. He finally gets the message and crosses the road, lifting up the old man's legs.

"Listen," says Angell. "I've had it with this shit. I'm going to make a break for it."

"You can't be serious, dude. There's nowhere to go from here. They'll cut you down in a heartbeat anyway."

As they're arguing there is a sound of the vehicle approaching them. That has to be the ride from Garhi Habibullah, the one that will take Angell to Srinagar. If he wants to live, it is now or never.

They place the old man gently on the grass. Still bent over, Angell looks over at the road and watches the Hilux pickup truck approach, waiting for the distraction to give him a few moments' head start.

That is when he notices something strange about the truck. Or, to be more precise, about its passengers.

The truck pulls up right in front of the Taliban fighters who casually walk over to the vehicle, guns at the ready but not aiming at the men in the truck.

But Adnan, the Kurdish-American spook, is aiming his AK-47

out the passenger window and right at Angell's driver. The other two men in the truck are similarly armed and have taken the Afghans by surprise. The Taliban attempt to raise their weapons to fire on the Americans, but it's too late. No one is brave enough to start a firefight they know they can't win. And the Afghans did not have time to reload after their panic firing across the river.

"Drop the weapons!" shout the CTPT agents in Pashtu. "Drop them! Now! Do it now!"

There is a slight hesitation in one of the Taliban and Adnan aims at his head.

"Go ahead, asshole," he says in English. The man drops his weapon.

The jingle truck driver raises his hands in surrender and confusion, looking over to Angell.

"Dude?"

"It's okay. They're with me."

The Taliban were caught with their guard down. They saw the truck approach with men inside dressed as Afghans and thought it was their ride. They did not know that their phone calls were intercepted by Aubrey's people once it was realized that they were being made from the same location as Angell's GPS. Since the Taliban in question were not observing operational security but using their cell phones along the route into Pakistan, it was a simple matter of isolating those cell phones that were making calls in the near proximity of the GPS signal over a period of time.

Aubrey intercepted the last call, made by one of the Taliban guards to the contact in Garhi Habibullah. Adnan and his two CIA colleagues were already in the air when the call was made. They were dropped off outside the town and waited by the dirt road that was used by the jingle truck: spotted long ago by Aubrey's drone. They commandeered the pickup truck and put its driver in the bed, tied up and covered with a tarp.

The element of surprise was necessary to keep Angell from being shot by one of the Taliban.

"How ya doin', guy?" asked Adnan. "Miss me?"

"That's what I call riding shotgun. How the hell did you know where I was?" Angell held the jingle truck driver by the arm and brought him over to Adnan who had left his vehicle and was standing over the three other Afghans who were kneeling on the ground with their hands on their heads. As one of the CIA agents held a gun on them, the other tied their wrists behind their backs with plastic cable ties.

Adnan pointed skyward. "A little birdie told me. By the way, the old man sends his regards."

"Which old man? There are so many."

Adnan only smiled. He pointed to the driver and spoke to him in Pashto. "You. Down there with the others."

"It's okay. He's not Taliban. He's Kalash."

"No shit? Well, it doesn't matter. He was one of them."

The driver took his place next to the others and his wrists were tied.

The two CIA men were going through the pockets and personal possessions of the Afghans, looking for identification papers and anything that might be of interest to the other intel guys. They started speaking to their prisoners, in Pashto, Urdu and Dari, asking questions and not getting any answers.

"These are high-value targets, if only because they work directly for the Emir. We should be able to get some useful intel out of them."

"Go for it," answered Adnan. "You want to take the pickup, or this friggin' monstrosity?" He pointed at the jingle truck. They would head back to the extraction site with their prisoners. Their orders were to take them back to Karachi for interrogation but they wanted first crack at them in case the Pakistanis gave them any trouble.

"The monstrosity is the right size. We've got four prisoners and the four of us. Unless we take both vehicles."

"Let's do that. It's better if we split up anyway. You guys take the big truck, and I'll ride with the professor here. We better move, though. I don't want to stand around here too long."

The driver was dry-mouthed and perspiring heavily. He figured he was going to be executed, and looked imploringly at Angell.

"Look," Angell said to Adnan. "This one's not a threat and he probably doesn't have much intel. Guy went to UC Berkeley for chrissakes. He's just the driver. This is his truck. How about we cut him loose?"

"You must be joking, man. We can't just let him go. He could sound the alarm back in town. He's probably an opium smuggler anyway. Nah, we take him with us. But once our ride shows up, maybe we can cut him loose then. He won't be able to do us any harm at that point."

"Thanks. I could use a silver lining. Anyway, I thought you guys were goners for sure."

"The villagers helped us escape. They said something about a foreigner giving the money. I have no idea what that means. They even killed two Taliban in the process which took guts. Listen, we can't wait around here. We gotta get back to base and you need to be debriefed by the Man. We got intel on the whereabouts of that thing you're looking for but we can't talk about it now."

"Understood. How do we get out of here?"

"There's a helo standing by. This whole mission has gone into overdrive."

Angell got into the pickup with Adnan driving. There was still the original driver of the pickup under the tarp in the bed of the truck. They pulled out and headed back the way they came. The jingle truck soon followed with its complement of two CIA agents and four prisoners. The agents left the Taliban's weapons in the dirt near the highway after smashing their firing mechanisms with rocks.

"Are we going back to Baghdad after this?"

Adnan kept his eyes on the road, alert to any sign of trouble. They were in Pakistan and nominally cooperating with the ISI and the Pakistani military, but the region was a hotbed of the new group that was forming up in Waziristan across the border. The Islamic State was attracting disaffected elements of the Taliban and Al Qaeda.

They were scary players in a region already replete with sociopaths and utter raving psychos with more guns than brains. After a minute, he answered Angell's question out of the side of his mouth.

"I understand that Nepal is beautiful this time of the year. You know, or not."

"Ah, fuck me."

They were silent the rest of the way to a clearing outside the town that has been designated their LZ. They dragged the prisoners out of the jingle truck and arranged them in a row on the ground. In a few moments, the sky was darkened by the approach of a Russian-made MI 17 helicopter that had been standing by. It settled gently on the ground and the prisoners—all four of them—were bundled into the helo along with the other men.

"I thought we were gonna cut him loose," said Angell above the noise of the rotors.

"In Karachi. We have to make sure he isn't one of them."

"Who's gonna look after his truck?"

"Not our problem."

Angell just nodded, resigned to fate—his and everyone else's—and remembered to be grateful that he had been rescued and now was in relatively safe hands. If Adnan was right about Nepal, that should be a piece of cake compared to what he had already been through. Nepal wasn't at war with anyone, and even though they had some problems with Maoist guerrillas it was still a predominantly Buddhist country with a primitive infrastructure that was known more for hashish and mountain climbing than terrorism.

Piece of cake.

Instead of heading for the base at Karachi they made straight for PAF Shahbaz, a Pakistani Air Force base located at Jacobabad, about halfway to Karachi. Shahbaz also held a drone site run by the US Air Force, and was the location from which the drone was launched that kept an eye on Angell's itinerary through Pakistan. CIA would take custody of the prisoners from there, and Adnan and Angell would get on the SAT phone and contact Aubrey who was still in Baghdad.

Angell watched as the prisoners were removed and led away with black hoods over their heads so they could not identify where they were or who their captors were. Angell felt bad about the jingle driver, but kept his thoughts to himself. When this was all over, he would try to find out what had happened to him.

He and Adnan went into the comm center and raised Aubrey.

"I am very glad to hear your voice, professor," said Aubrey when contact had been made. "I'm sorry this has taken you so far from your original mission and subjected you to such harsh treatment. You must be terrified."

"There is no need to play me, *sir*." He had been warned not to use Aubrey's name over the secure line because nothing was *that* secure. "I survived. And now I understand my itinerary has been modified."

There was a pained silence at the other end. Aubrey knew he deserved whatever animus Angell had for him and for the whole mission but he was willing to take that on in order for the mission goals to be fulfilled. If Angell wanted to kick him in the balls, that would be okay, too. As long as they got the Book.

"Yes, professor. The intermediate location is no longer viable," he said, meaning Srinagar in Kashmir. "We have intel that the package is headed for Nepal. Information is being forwarded to you by secure link now. We estimate another twenty-four hours total and this will all be over. You'll then be put in a first-class seat on the first available flight home." What he didn't tell Angell was that there probably would be another two or three days' worth of debriefing in a safe house in the States somewhere. No need to bring that up now. He also didn't mention that Angell's basement apartment had been broken into by NYPD; his people had gone in and cleaned it up, bringing it back to the way it was before the break-in, so perhaps he wouldn't notice anything amiss. Except for the broken spirit pot.

"Is your colleague there next to you? Let me speak with him, please."

Angell handed the receiver to Adnan, and walked out of the comm center, looking for a place to sit down.

When Adnan came out of the center a few minutes later he found Angell sitting on a folding chair in the canteen, head on a table, fast asleep.

Thirty minutes later, Adnan and Angell are having coffee in the empty mess hall. Although they are alone in a secure facility, they are keeping their voices low so as not to be overheard. There is no SCIF at the base, and they need to discuss the upcoming mission to Nepal.

Angell is still exhausted, but is getting a second wind. There will be time enough to sleep once this is all over. He sips the bitter coffee, black, then decides he needs as much lactose and sucrose as possible and starts pouring in the cream and sugar.

"There's this guy, name of Jason Miller. He used to work for us. Now he's freelance. He's after the same thing we are. They say he was behind that rocket attack in Syria. He may have been the one to arrange our escape in Kamdesh."

"Jesus. So he's been onto us from the start. Who is he working for?"

"Aubrey says they don't know, only that we have to make sure he doesn't succeed. Not knowing is worse than knowing in this business."

"Okay. So what's the plan?"

"We know Miller has been as far as Ladakh. We intercepted some email messages sent by one of his contacts and that got us on the right trail. Miller's pretty cautious when it comes to leaving a trail—he has an operational background—but some of his network is composed of contract hires and they're not always professional. Anyway, there's an observatory on a mountaintop that's run by the Indian government, and we have reason to believe he was there.

Some astronomers reported that someone who said they were from our government visited the site about eight hours ago. No one from our side went there, and the visitor matches the physical description of Miller."

"How does an observatory have anything to do with us?"

"I'll get to that in a minute. I don't know much, only what they tell me. And they told me he is heading to Khembalung. It's in the Himalayas, some distance from Kathmandu."

"What's that all about?"

"Beats the shit outta me. All I know is that Miller is headed there as well as some other people Aubrey has been keeping an eye on. A real convention of book lovers, I guess."

"Okay. Let me get this straight. An observatory in India, and Khembalung in Nepal. This is all a far cry from some Arab cultists in Iraq." Angell sipped some of his coffee, made a face, and added more sugar. "We are all way out of our depth here."

"What do you mean?"

"You know I'm a scholar of religion, right?"

"Yeah."

"I mean, that's one of the reasons I'm here, right?"

"Okay." Adnan didn't know where this was going.

"You tell me Khembalung, and to most people that's just a bunch of sounds strung together. But it has some significance. And what you're telling me is making me nervous, as if I wasn't freaked out to begin with."

Angell swallowed a long draught of the coffee, and put his cup down. They were still all alone in the mess hall.

Adnan was silent, just watching him.

Finally, Angell started to explain the reason why he thought they were going to Khembalung, a place Adnan had never heard of before that day.

"Khembalung is one of seven *beyul*. A *beyul* is a 'hidden country.' You've heard of Shangri-la, right?"

"Sure. A mysterious kingdom in the Himalayas. No one knows where it is."

"Right. They made a movie about it. *Lost Horizon*. Anyway, there are seven of those places, according to Tibetan tradition. Except we know where Khembalung is. It's not invisible. You can get there. But it's tricky. It's a cave complex beneath the Himalayas. And it's sacred to the Tibetan Buddhists."

"So, then, that's cool, right? It's all Dalai Lama stuff. No guns. No terror plots."

"Yes, and no. There are different kinds of Tibetan Buddhists. Some, like the Dalai Lama and his crowd, are pretty much how we think of them. All sweetness and light. Except for some really strange rituals associated with Tantra, it's Buddhism. But there are two other main groups, the Red Hats and the Black Hats."

"Uh oh."

"Well, the Red Hats are more esoteric than the Dalai Lama's Yellow Hat sect. And the Black Hats are closer to the indigenous religion of Tibet, the one from before Buddhism came to the region. More shamanistic, you might say. And then there is the real Bön tradition, which is whatever the Tibetans were before Buddhism. Now all of these groups have some practices that would be considered a little weird by many people, such as using skeletal remains as sacred instruments. Cups made of human skulls, drums made of human skulls, leg bones used for trumpets, and the like."

"You're shitting me."

"I shit you not. This is pretty much SOP among the Tibetan Buddhists. And they also have a strong shamanic tradition. The State Oracle of Tibet is a guy who becomes possessed by a god and who utters prophecies in a strange language. It's an official position, to this day. *And* he works for the Dalai Lama. Imagine the shamans who work with some of the other sects."

Adnan sat back in his chair and just shook his head.

"I thought my people, the Ahl-e-Haqq, were strange. But this takes the cake."

"What worries me is the fact that with Khembalung, there is even a more apocalyptic tone to this whole mission; putting a *beyul* into the mix only emphasizes that."

"What do you mean?"

"Shangri-la, right? It's called Shambhala in the Tibetan texts and according to Tibetan tradition the Kalki Avatar—a kind of warrior god—will come riding out of Shambhala at the Last Battle, destroying the unbelievers with fire and sword. It's the Tibetan version of the Apocalypse. Shambhala is a 'hidden country,' a *beyul*. I think these guys—maybe this Miller, or the other ones we've been following all over the place—are going to Khembalung to awaken this force, by whatever name you want to call it."

"You don't really believe all this stuff, do you?"

"No. I don't believe a word of it. But they do. I don't believe in this secret Book or anything connected with it. But they do. So not believing in it is a luxury we can't afford right now. A consolidation of the worst elements of all the world's religions in one spot could have disastrous consequences. The kind of thing our Aubrey is most worried about. This sacred site, Khembalung, conjoined with the secret Book, along with a few dozen psychotic cult leaders … there's only one thing missing."

"What's that?"

"A schedule. This stuff usually needs a sacred calendar of some sort. The Muslims have their own calendar, the Buddhists theirs, the other cults all have different systems for measuring time. What schedule would they all agree upon?"

Adnan swallowed heavily and took a deep breath before responding.

"Well, see, I just might have the answer to that one."

"According to the astronomers at Ladakh, Miller—or the guy we think is Miller—was asking them about supernovas. In particular, one that exploded in the year 1006 and then another that exploded in 2011. He seemed very interested in them and kept mumbling something about the word Therion and Lupus and the Bear. He thought there was some kind of connection between the supernovas and other events or effects on Earth.

"This might be your schedule, right?"

"You said Therion, Lupus …?"

"Yeah, because the astronomers told him that the first one he asked about, the one in 1006, took place in the constellation that used to be known as Therion but which is known today as Lupus. I have it right here." He took a tablet from his backpack and turned it so that Angell could see the screen. It was the data transmission from Aubrey.

Angell studied the contents quickly but carefully. It was as if the file was written specifically for him.

"It came in while you were … resting," Adnan added. "Aubrey mentioned it to you, I think."

"Right, I remember. This is … interesting. If your guy Miller has any kind of background in this stuff at all he would have been bouncing off walls when he saw this."

"Can you explain? Because, man, I am totally at sea here …"

"It's like this. It's all symbol systems and icons and mysteries within mysteries. It's a kind of language all its own. Therion is the Greek word for 'Beast.' Any kind of animal, really, but it has resonance for some modern cultists because one of their heroes, a man called Aleister Crowley, called himself 'The Great Beast' or in Greek *To Mega Therion*. It's from the Bible, the Apocalypse: the Book of Revelation. Now the Beast in the Apocalypse is depicted being ridden by a woman, the Whore of Babylon. Now, I was just in Babylon—or what's left of it—a few days ago, back in Iraq. Babylon was the center of a religious system that was based on the earlier, Sumerian, one."

"You're making me dizzy."

"It's like this. What Miller saw at the observatory was

confirmation of a number of things that he probably suspected all along. The connection between that supernova—when did it take place?"

"Uh ... in 1006."

"That's CE, right?"

"Pardon?"

"AD. Same thing."

"Right. 1006 AD."

Angell thought for a moment.

"Yeah. That fits. It's the same year that one of the greatest Indian civilizations was wiped out. In fact, look at this," he pointed to a field on the tablet. "You see that date? It's incredible, really. But there it is. April 30, 1006. That was the date the supernova was seen. It's also the date Mount Merapi exploded on the island of Java. The two explosions happened simultaneously. One in the heavens, and one on Earth. The one on Earth destroyed an Indian, Tantric civilization and buried Borobudur beneath a mountain of volcanic ash. It stayed that way for almost another thousand years."

"Okay, that's pretty interesting, but ..."

"April 30 is a day that is sacred to European paganism. It's called Beltane. But in some parts of Europe it's known as Walpurgisnacht. It's the day the witches gather for a major sabbat on top of Mount Brocken. It's like Halloween for us. Oh, Christ ..." Angell's voice trailed off, as it often did when he was on a mental journey, connecting dots in a puzzle that was practically invisible to form an image that most sane people would reject.

"The other constellation ..."

"Lupus?"

"No, that's just another name for Therion. The last one, the Great Bear?"

"Right."

"The Great Bear has tremendous significance throughout the world. It was often referred to as The Chariot. The Arabs referred to it as a Bier or a Coffin. To the ancient Egyptians, it was the Thigh of Set. In any case, it's a symbol of immortality, of journeying to the stars to achieve eternal life. It's also a symbol of rebirth, resuscitation, the reanimation of dead matter. As in mummifying the Pharaoh."

"Okay, but where does that take us?"

"The Great Bear points to the Pole Star. The stars of the Big Dipper, part of the Bear constellation, can be used to find True North. Sailors and navigators used it in ancient times and still use it that way. But it has another purpose, too.

"It's also a clock. A cosmic clock. It can be used to tell time. In other words, *it can be used to create a schedule*."

"When was the next supernova Miller asked about?"

"Uh … here. SN 2011 Fe. That was in August of 2011. Why?"

"What constellation did it appear in?"

"Oh. Uh … ha. It appeared in the Big Dipper. The Great Bear. That one."

"What happened in August of 2011?"

Adnan shook his head and flipped through the tablet's pages, looking for data.

"There would have to be a connection somehow. Something Miller was looking for."

"Oh, shit. Here it is. You're not gonna believe this."

"What?"

"It's when they shot down our helicopter in Nuristan. Same place we were just … That was with SEAL Team Six aboard. It was the heaviest day of casualties for American servicemen in Afghanistan to that point."

"SEAL Team Six? Wasn't that …"

"Yeah. It was. It was the same unit that got bin Laden."

"What was the official name of the operation?"

"Neptune Spear."

"That's spooky just by itself. Neptune's Spear caused hurricanes and earthquakes, according to Roman mythology." Angell was thinking of Neptune, God of the Sea, and the strange drawings he had seen, in Mosul and then at the Towers of Silence. Sea monsters. *Dagon.*

"And the raid took place earlier that same year."

"Bin Laden was killed on May 2."

"Close enough to April 30."

"Close enough for government work."

Both men were silent, afraid to give voice to their thoughts. Were they seeing things? Ghosts in the data? A Ghost in the Machine?

It was Adnan who broke the silence.

"Wasn't April 30 the day Hitler committed suicide?"

Angell nodded.

"And *sixty-six* years later SEAL Team *Six* kills bin Laden. On almost the same day."

"Sixty-six and six. The number of the Great Beast. Therion."

"Both bin Laden and Hitler were anti-Semites."

"And no one's seen the corpse of either one."

"April 30, 1975 was the day Saigon fell to the Communists."

"But April 30 has already passed. We're in May now."

"And Bin Laden was killed in May. The calendar has shifted. They're using the Big Dipper as a kind of clock or pointer for their rituals. Maybe something to do with the precession of equinoxes or something."

"What?"

"I don't know. I'm not an astronomer. But I bet Miller heard something that made him realize the right time is approaching. And along with the right time you need the right place."

"And the right Book."

"We've got to get to Khembalung, and we've got to go *now.*"

CHAPTER TWENTY-EIGHT

THE TULKU

The shaman stands out by the fact that he has succeeded in integrating into consciousness a considerable number of experiences that, for the profane world, are reserved for dreams, madness, or post-mortem states.

—Mircea Eliade, *Rites and Symbols of Initiation*

Permission was granted by the Nepalese government to have a US helicopter fly into their airspace. The excuse given had something to do with a meteorological survey in the mountains.

Adnan, Angell and six of their new best friends were onboard and would be inserted as close to the cave entrance of Khembalung as possible using a helo in the Himalayas. They had pretty good coordinates based on an expedition that took place there a decade earlier, and a set of photos of the entrance to make it easier to locate. Everyone was heavily armed and wearing Kevlar body armor. They would do a flyover first in order to see if there was a welcoming committee. If there was, orders were to drop Angell and two men off at a suitable LZ while the others would go on ahead to neutralize any opposition.

They got as close as they could get in the MI 17, which was a very versatile craft in that part of the world. Made by the Russians, it seemed everyone had one. The Pakistanis, the Afghans, the Indians all had MI 17s and had more on order. Although the Americans favored their own Black Hawks and Chinooks, the sheer prevalence of the MI 17 in the region made it imperative that US helo pilots were checked out on them as well.

It also enabled this particular team to travel relatively incognito. A fully-armed Black Hawk with all the trimmings would have been much more conspicuous.

They found a relatively flat space that was not crowded out by tree branches or low hanging rock. It was still at least two miles to the Khembalung entrance as the crow flies, probably twice as long considering the route they would have to take. The helo crew reported no sign of human life in the immediate vicinity; infra-red and thermal all came up negative as well. At least, outside the mountain. Inside, they were on their own.

Angell was getting tired of commuting in helicopters. But he was tired of commuting in jingle trucks and Japanese pickups, too. He got a change of clothes at Shahbaz before they left, and a shower and shave for the first time in days for which he was eternally grateful. There was no longer any need to have him pass for a local. He was in the company of well-trained, well-armed men of his own country's military. They were JSOC, and this fact alone made Angell relax. Had he thought about it, though, he would have realized that the White House didn't send JSOC teams on routine missions.

He was dressed warmly, in a fur-lined parka and hat with ear flaps. This was over body armor that covered him from the neck to the groin. He was already too warm, but was grateful for the added protection. It would get cold soon enough, once the sun went down which was in about an hour.

The team trudged up the mountain and along a small stream. The sound of the running water was like bells tinkling. It was a peaceful scene, but the JSOC men were on their guard. Adnan was up front with the team leader, and Angell was in the middle of the file. The countryside was shrouded in a fine grey mist that seemed to come from nowhere, and which reminded Angell of the weird fog that appeared suddenly at Tell Ibrahim during the ritual to Kutulu. They were walking along the west side of a river called Chhoyang. It was a popular trail for trekkers and tourists from abroad; it was also used extensively by local villagers, none of whom had become visible as yet.

Their intel had told them to avoid the main cave entrance as it was a destination for tourists and pilgrims and did not lead to the deepest part of the interior where, it was believed, Miller and a group of unknown individuals called the Keepers of the Book were headed. Angell and his team had the benefit of military transport and official approval for their mission; it was entirely possible, even likely, that they had beat Miller to the site and could set up and wait for him to appear. As for the mysterious Keepers of the Book, no one knew when they arrived or if they would arrive at all.

A digital map on a small tablet attached with Velcro to the team leader's arm revealed another point of access that was downriver from the more popular one, and hidden by a stand of trees. Above them at twenty thousand feet was another UAV, a drone, that was tracking their every move as well as transmitting valuable data on weather, physical obstacles, movements of people and vehicles, etc. In addition, video was being uploaded from cameras attached to the body armor of the JSOC men. The whole thing made Angell feel as if he was a character in a video game.

As they walked, he thought back to the man shot to death by a single bullet fired from the rifle of an Indian sniper. He was a local Pakistani villager, a man who probably never went further than a few miles from his home in his life. Yet, he spoke to Angell in his father's voice. In English. And told him to go back. He couldn't get his head around that. His father had been dead for years. Cirrhosis of the liver was the official cause, but it was really a slow suicide. Angell didn't like to think about any of that. There was no point, really. He never knew his father, not in any kind of normal father-son relationship. He didn't feel he had missed anything when his father died. Yet, here he was, hearing his father's voice warning him out of the mouth of a man on the other side of the world. One day he would have to figure out what that meant. Obviously, it hadn't really happened that way. He must have imagined it.

Shit, he thought. *This whole mission is about imagination. At some point we have to decide that at least some imaginary data or experience is real data or experience.*

The team leader raised his hand and held it. That meant for the group to stop in their tracks. Adnan could be seen talking to him, and looking around at the mountain face.

Then he pointed.

Angell couldn't see it, but it was there. An outcropping of rock that looked natural enough, because it was natural. The alternate cave entrance was behind it. The column of men moved up, off the path next to the river, and along a straight line to the rocks. It was already growing dark, and for security the JSOC team turned on their night vision goggles rather than use flashlights which would have announced their existence for miles in any direction.

Angell didn't have night vision goggles, but was able to follow the man in front of him up the steep incline. One by one the men disappeared into the mountain. One of the team reached down for Angell's arm and led him up and around the rocks to an even darker patch of night. Once inside, they turned off their night vision and turned on their flashlights.

They seemed to be quite alone in the cave entrance. Further down they could just about make out a narrow tunnel that was wide enough for a single person to wedge through. Past that point there seemed to be something flickering. A lantern, possibly, or a butter lamp. That was the best-case scenario anyway.

The JSOC team leader held a confab with his men. He would lead a group into the tunnel to see who or what was there. They didn't want any surprises. He would leave Angell there with Adnan, and gave the latter a fully-loaded pistol.

"You could hold off an army from here with that nine mil. The entrance is designed to let only a single person at a time get past the rock and into the cave. We're going inside. If I hear shots from here, I'll send reinforcements your way, don't you worry."

"No problem, sir. Got it covered."

"Outstanding. See you in five," and with that he squeezed into the tunnel after his men, leaving Adnan and Angell to guard the entrance.

Adnan had kept his beard, but otherwise looked like a different person. His reason for keeping the beard was that he was due to go back online in Kurdistan once this mission was over and he couldn't afford to wait a few months to grow another full bush. But seeing him now as more American than Kurd was an interesting sight to Angell. He marveled at how people had multiple forms to suit different occasions. Yesterday, an Iranian Kurd; today, an American intelligence officer. Same person in each case. He was about to say something about it, to draw Adnan's attention to the observation, when they both heard a sound at the cave entrance.

Adnan drew his automatic and leveled it at the entrance. There was a shuffling sound, and Angell shone his flashlight directly at the place the sound was coming from.

It was a Nepalese villager, it seemed. Short, in his forties probably, weathered skin. Unarmed.

"What are you doing here? What do you want?" said Adnan, uncomfortably aware that *he* was the interloper, not the villager.

"Shouldn't you ask who I am first?" said the man, in Indian-accented English.

"Okay."

"I am the priest of this place. You would call me a shaman, probably. Although we don't use that term. A little too colonial for our taste, like you gentlemen have priests but we poor beggars only have shamans. Or medicine men, or something. My name is of no consequence. You couldn't pronounce it anyway. May I sit down? It's a long walk for an old man."

Another old man, thought Angell. *An old woman would be nice for a change.*

"Nicer for me than for you, I imagine," said the shaman, reading his thoughts.

Angell turned to Adnan. "Put that thing away. This may be the one we are here to see."

The shaman sat down on the ground as if it was an easy chair, old and comfortable, and he began to speak.

"I know why you are here. I will have to speak quickly, so please do not interrupt. You are in a *beyul*, a hidden country. But it's not what you think. I am a Tibetan, but I am not a Buddhist and this is not a Buddhist *beyul* no matter what the guidebooks tell you. This place once concealed a great *terma*. You know *terma*? Many of Buddhism's most important texts were originally *termas*. A *terma* is a hidden text, a spiritual document that was buried and appears only when times demand it. The great sages of Buddhism have discovered buried termas, which basically makes their reputation as great sages. The *Bardo Thodol* was one such terma. You know it as the *Tibetan Book of the Dead*, an unfortunate and wholly inaccurate characterization, but there you have it. These 'hidden treasures'— for that is what the word terma means—are well-known in Bön religion, too. The sacred books of the Yezidi are termas. Those of the Kalasha are still lost, buried when the armies of the Prophet swept through their country.

"Unfortunately, not every terma is benign. Some are very dark indeed. They were buried not to be rediscovered at some later time but to remain hidden and buried forever ... or at least until human beings were capable of reading them without losing their minds. The Book you seek is one such terma. It is a terma of darkness and death. It is a true 'Book of the Dead,' unlike the *Bardo Thodol*. It was buried here, in this place, centuries ago. But then some Chinese explorers found it, long ago, and its influence began to be felt around the world.

"Your Book concerns a being known as a *kusu-lu*. In our language, that means a shaman who has come back from the dead. I believe your people pronounce it as Kutulu or Cthulhu? No matter. It is the same being. A *tulku*. A tulku is a being sufficiently spiritually advanced that it can choose its own time and place of rebirth.

"The Dalai Lama is a tulku; he is reincarnated constantly, out of love for humanity. The kusu-lu, though, is a tulku who returns out of hatred for humanity. They are both spiritually advanced, just not in the same way. I believe it was the English author Arthur Machen who wrote that there are sacraments of evil as well as of good. He understood the concept. Many do not.

"Your Book, your *Necronomicon*, is a terma that was buried by the kusu-lu, the high priest of the Old Ones, until the time came for the destruction of the world. You see, the kusu-lu sees the world as a prison from which he desires to be liberated. The *Necronomicon* is the Tantra of his particular Liberation, his *kusulu-pa*: a word that can mean mysticism as well as exorcism, for the *Necronomicon* contains not only the mechanisms to open the Gates and free kusu-lu from his slumber of death; it also contains the formulas to imprison him forever.

"Kusu-lu, or Kutulu, resides in one of the beyul, in Aghartta. This is a kind of anti-Shambhala, a domain of dark powers. Khembalung leads to the Gate of Aghartta, but it is only one of many. Even now, at this very moment, devotees of Kusu-lu are making their way to the Tomb from different spots on the Earth. This is only one entrance. There are many more, all over the planet."

Angell had heard enough. He stood up from where he had been squatting on the ground and addressed the shaman.

"What you are telling us are legends, old wives' tales. Buried books, a high priest, Aghartta, Shambhala, and now you expect us to believe that there are multiple entrances to this spot from places around the planet. A physical impossibility! All we want to know is the location of the Book so we can get it out of the hands of terrorists and murderers who would use it for propaganda purposes. Instead we get fairy tales! What you have told us is impossible and irrational …"

"When the stars are right, such considerations will mean nothing."

But before the shaman can explain what he means, a flash-bang grenade is tossed into the cave from outside. Adnan hits the ground but he is too close to the device. Angell dives for cover in a corner of the entrance. The shaman simply sits where he is. There is a blinding light and an explosion, and when the smoke clears no one is moving.

CHAPTER TWENTY-NINE

THE CODEX VI

The Nazi that Robert Barlow has been seeking—Johann von Leers—has left South America for a permanent position in Egypt. A linguist fluent in Arabic and Hebrew, Leers has used what leverage he has with the Nazi underground to buy his way into Nasser's government. In Egypt, Leers converts to Islam and takes a Muslim name, Omar Amin, but his real agenda is the destruction of Israel and the rebirth of the Nazi Party.

He begins to form alliances with Nazi occult groups around the world, including the National Renaissance Party in New York City, which is run by the crazed theosophist James Madole. Word begins to spread in occult circles that Leers has access to the *Necronomicon*, taken out of Europe with him when he fled to Argentina. Rumors of Leers and the *Necronomicon* reach Barlow in Mexico City.

When Barlow realizes that the Black Book is out of his grasp and in the hands of Nazi maniacs, he falls into a deep depression. He begins contacting American and Israeli intelligence to urge them to seize the book from Leers in Cairo. Word of his campaign reaches the ears of ODESSA operatives in Mexico City, who approach him and threaten to reveal his homosexuality to the university authorities. It is 1950, and such a revelation would destroy him both professionally and socially.

On New Year's Day, 1951, Robert H. Barlow commits suicide in his room at the college. His body is witnessed by William S. Burroughs, one of his students, who would become famous as a Beat writer and author of *Naked Lunch*.

He is also famous for having accidentally shot and killed his wife later that same year in Mexico City.

(In 1977, he would write a letter praising the publication of one recension of the *Necronomicon*, calling it a "landmark in the history of spiritual liberation.")

The last of the Lovecraft circle is now dead: Barlow, Robert E. Howard, both suicides, the Protestant minister and expert in Afro-Caribbean religions Henry St. Clair Whitehead, and Lovecraft himself. By this time Carl Tanzler is also dead—an effigy of Elena de Hoyos in his arms, unsuccessfully reanimated without the benefit of the *Necronomicon*—and the circle is now closed. The only ones who knew anything of the *Necronomicon* are Nazis, a scattering of cult leaders around the world, and a handful of impoverished academics. The Yezidi in Iraq and Turkey and the Nabataeans—as well as some Shiite and Sufi sects—are aware of the Book and its links to their own Sumerian origins, but do not possess the text.

After the death of Leers in 1965, the Yezidi in Lalish hear rumors that the Book has wound up with a neo-Nazi enclave in the United States from which it was stolen by two Eastern Orthodox monks, who then allow portions of it to be translated … but the original disappears again, only to resurface at the Baghdad Museum after it has been purchased on the black market by agents of Saddam Hussein. The invasion of Iraq and the attacks on the Baghdad Museum give a clan within the Yezidi an opportunity to seize the Book and conceal it at a secret shrine in Lalish, but word spread to agents of Al Qaeda, Hezbollah, Hamas, Lashkar-e-Taiba, the Druze in Lebanon, and the Alawis in Syria, as well as Jemaah Islamiyyah in Southeast Asia and the Iranian Revolutionary Guard—as well as new players such as Boko Haram in Nigeria and the Islamic State in Iraq and the Levant—that the Book is in play, and that it is both a threat to their ideologies and a potential source of great destructive power to vanquish their enemies.

But there is another group for which the Book has always been a core scripture, a terma, a buried treasure that has been discovered and which will be used to resurrect the tulku, the First Priest. This group is older than all the others, and is the root religion of all religions— for it is the religion of the founders of all life on the planet Earth, the source of its genetic code, the breath and blood from beyond the stars that gave life to the human race before trying to take it away again. And the followers of this cult, this Cult of Cthulhu, this priesthood of Dagon, has been waiting for this moment, this post-atomic age moment, this wholly integrated internet-enshrouded, spider-webbed world of data and instant messaging, to reappear. The message of their Gods, of the Ancient Ones, is perfectly structured for this moment in human history when a thought, a word, an image travels from one end of the globe to the other in microseconds. This, they know, is consciousness: a simulacrum of the electrical signals of the brain's neurons, firing in meaningful patterns, providing a material basis for the incarnation of their Gods.

The Book is both a guide for the worshippers of Kutulu / Kusulu / Cthulhu—the High Priest of the Ancient Ones, the Lord of the Underworld, the Shaman risen from the Dead, the Promised One, the Hidden Imam, the Mahdi, the Christ, the Anti-Christ, the Kalki Avatar who will return from his secret place of death below the earth and the oceans, to restore ownership of the planet to its original colonizers from beyond the stars—but it also contains the methods for stopping them. It is a Book about the opening of a Gate, but also the means of closing it. It is a Gospel that cannot be allowed to see the light of day: not by its adherents and devotees, and not by its fiercest opponents. This is a Secret that must remain a Secret. At least, until the stars are right.

And the global electronic-neuronal firing, the planetary cerebellum, begins to form new patterns as the Cult becomes emboldened, knowing that the day for which they have waited millennia is about to dawn. The cable television channels begin saturating the airwaves and high speed fiber optic networks with specials on Ancient Astronauts, Jonestown, Satanic cult murders, Aztec sacrifice, alien abductions, serial killers, the video-taped beheadings by members of terrorist groups, the murder of Muslim Rohingya by Burmese Buddhists, the crackdown on Tibetan Buddhists and Muslim separatists by Chinese Communists ... internet podcasts and blogs reporting the presence of aliens and illuminati everywhere ... insane speculation about lizard-like amphibians inhabiting the bodies of political and cultural icons ... and everywhere else—the slaughter of women and children, their forced labor and sexual servitude, the gradual genocides in Africa and the elimination of religious and ethnic minorities—gradual so you don't notice it and don't do anything about it—are ignored, lumped in with the aliens and the illuminati and satanic cults so that the entire message is devalued, marginalized, stripped of any shred of journalistic integrity ... a world where fiction becomes fact, and fact fiction ... into all of this, into this Poesian maelstrom, the *Necronomicon*.

The ancient plea of the Sumerian high priests—Spirit of the Earth, Remember! Spirit of the Sky, Remember!—is about to be answered.

BOOK THREE

THE BLACK BOOK

CHAPTER THIRTY

THE TERTON

The real hero is always a hero by mistake; he dreams of being an honest coward like everybody else.

— Umberto Eco, *Travels in Hyperreality*

Adnan was the first to recover, pointing his pistol at the cave entrance and getting ready to fire at anyone or anything coming through. Angell still had ringing in his ears and a halo of light where his vision should be, due to the effects of the flash-bang grenade. The shaman was nowhere to be seen, but then no one was seeing much of anything at the moment.

Adnan yelled out to Angell, "You okay?"

Angell couldn't hear him, so Adnan asked again, even louder.

It was then that Adnan realized that maybe Angell was answering him and he couldn't hear.

He crawled along the floor of the cave, keeping his eyes on the entrance, towards where Angell had been when the grenade went off. He finally saw the professor leaning up against the cave wall, rubbing his eyes and trying to get his vision back.

He grabbed him by the leg and shook him, so that Angell had to look down and listen.

"Don't rub your eyes. It will only make it worse. Wait a few minutes. Your vision will come back."

Angell just nodded, numb with the effects of the blast.

"When they come in I will hold them off as long as possible," he shouted into Angell's ear. "You go through the tunnel after the other guys. Tell them what's happening."

Angell nodded again, and started crawling over to the tunnel entrance. Adnan noticed he was trembling like a leaf, but said nothing. Once he made contact with the JSOC guys he would be okay.

Instead, he turned his attention towards the cave entrance. The blast had only been seconds ago but it seemed like an hour. At any moment whoever lobbed that grenade would come through, blasting away at anything that moved.

Angell got to the tunnel entrance. His vision was coming back. He could see the tunnel. He turned to look at Adnan, who had stationed himself off-center from the cave entrance, still sitting on the ground, and holding his automatic straight out in front of him with both hands.

Angell took a last look and squeezed himself through the tunnel aperture.

It was almost tall enough for him to stand upright, and wide enough—once past the aperture—that he was able to walk freely for some time. The tunnel permitted only one route for the first few hundred feet, but after that point it branched off. Ahead of him was the route the JSOC team took, because that is where they spotted the distant light. He was about to go that way when someone grabbed his left arm.

"Wait!" said a voice in the darkness.

Angell twisted his arm away and peered into the gloom.

"Who's that?" he whispered, thinking it was one of the team.

"*Namaste,*" came the sarcastic reply.

It was the shaman.

"You had better follow me," he told Angell. "The other way is a death trap."

"Who are they? Who tossed the grenade at us? Al Qaeda? Taliban?"

The shaman pulled at Angell's sleeve, leading him down a separate tunnel running roughly perpendicular to the main tunnel system.

"You might as well ask 'Christians? Muslims? Buddhists? Maybe even the Jews?' What difference does the uniform make? They are all fighting for the same side."

"What side? God, or the Devil?"

The shaman turned on him, nearly screaming in his face:

"There is no God! Don't you understand? There is *no God*! There is *no Devil*! There is only *us* and *them*!"

From the cave entrance they could hear shots being fired. Angell froze, thinking of his friend standing there all alone with a limited supply of ammunition and no one coming to help him.

"We've got to go back. We've got to find help!"

"There is no help the other way. You have to trust me."

He dragged the confused professor down the tunnel. They seemed to be descending. There was dampness on the walls and floor, water seeping into the cave structure.

"If there is no God or Devil, then who are you? *What* are you? What is a shaman or a priest without Gods and Devils?"

The shaman considered how to answer the college professor in a way he would understand, but eventually gave that up as hopeless. Training, even academic training, creates a kind of worldview that is difficult to dislodge, even with the challenge of living experience of the world.

They descended a few more feet, the angle of descent becoming uncomfortably steep, requiring them to hold onto the wall for support to keep from tipping over. The sound of their footsteps echoed ahead of them.

"It is not about the gods and devils that populate the storybooks we give children. And when it comes to God, we are *all* children. There is no mature way of understanding the concept of God, except maybe total disbelief. The problem is that disbelief does not proceed from knowledge but from suspicion."

The distant sound of another round fired made Angell sick to his stomach, and this pontificating old shaman was not helping.

"I have read all your atheists. Dawkins, Hitchins, even the French. What do they have in common, all these atheists? They complain about religion because of religious wars. As if you could separate violence from men by removing religion. They do not write as scientists, but as jilted lovers. Dawkins, Hitchins … they are schoolgirls whose boyfriends have dumped them. They have seen only one aspect of God, the fact that he has abandoned them. So they say he does not exist, because he does not exist where they are. Just like schoolgirls who cover their ears, or who cross out their boyfriend's name from their notebooks. Abandonment does not mean non–existence."

That word again. Abandonment. *Al-Qhadhulu*: the Abandoner.

"So what do you believe?"

"Believe? Nothing. There are things that I know, and things that I suspect. As what you call a shaman my job is to keep looking."

"And who are you looking for?"

"The King of the World," he replied, as they turned a corner in the tunnel they were in and came upon a large area in which they could stand upright. The shaman took a match from a pocket in his padded tunic and lit a lantern, casting a soft glow of light around the tunnel walls.

"And the King of the World is here."

At the cave entrance, Adnan has made every shot count.

Two men are on the ground at the entrance, either dead or dying. The leaders of the assault know that they cannot afford an all-out attack without blowing up the entire cave entrance, an option they don't really have because they need to get into the cave. They discussed simply blowing up the huge rock that stands in front of the entrance, thus allowing them to rush the shooter. They know they would lose a few men in the process but they would eventually gain access.

As for Adnan, he cannot afford to get too close to the entrance in case they have a sniper good enough to pick him off. He is much safer staying where he is, but he can't help wondering what has happened to Angell and the reinforcements he desperately needs.

He checks his ammunition. He still has seven bullets. In a

moment, he will carefully approach the two bodies in the entrance and see if he can relieve them of their weapons. He can use every gun, every round of ammunition.

He tries to slow down his breathing and calm himself, knowing he needs a steady hand now more than ever before in his entire life.

"The King of the World?" asks Angell in disbelief. The situation is dire, and the fate of everyone is in the hands of this maniac.

"He is everywhere."

"And still you can't find him?"

"You don't find him. He finds you."

Angell shrugged his shoulders in impatience. "That sounds like a fortune cookie."

"The King of the World is everywhere, you understand? The surface of the Earth is quite big," he moved his hands out from his body, indicating the girth of the world. Then he drew his hands together in a single fist. "The center of the Earth is quite small. Every point on the surface of the Earth can be connected to the center, to Aghartta. Aghartta is the hidden country, the *beyul*, of the other world—just as Shambhala is the center of this world."

What the hell does that mean? thought Angell.

For the first time, as his eyes grew accustomed to the dim light in the shaman's cavern, he saw words written in gold letters at the top of one wall:

མཛོད་ཕུག

"What does that mean?" he asked the shaman.

The man looked up, and back to Angell.

"It means 'the Cavern of Treasures.'"

"Is that what this place is?"

"Not exactly. It's where a terma was found. *The Cavern of Treasures* is a Bön text, a terma, and a critical one for it is written in both the Tibetan language and the language of Zhang-Zhung: the land of origin of our ancestors and their ancestral tongue. Another 'hidden country.' It was discovered in the eleventh century."

"Is that why we're here?"

"Oh, no. This is just one of many entrances to the sleeping place of the High Priest, the one you call Kutulu."

"So ... Kutulu is the King of the World?" Angell was by now thoroughly confused. It seemed no one was defining his terms, and if you didn't agree on definitions then what sounded profound was most likely nonsense, and vice versa.

"From the point of view of certain European mystics of the nineteenth and twentieth centuries, yes. He is."

"What about from your point of view?"

"We have a history, as human beings, of having kings who routinely destroy their kingdoms. In that sense then, yes, Kutulu is the King of the World. He is certainly its Destroyer."

"Then ... then why do these others call him? Why summon a King if the King can destroy them?"

"From fear, perhaps. They fear his power and rush to appease him, swear to him their allegiance, hoping to escape his wrath. From love, also. Some of his devotees truly love him and the destruction he represents. They want to see an end ... and end ... to all this." He gestured to the cavern, the tunnels, the entire world.

"And they have a point. We are a failed experiment, a genetic mistake. The Neanderthals should have conquered us, not the other way around. The human race would have stayed stupid and naïve. Instead, we ate the forbidden fruit, started to think for ourselves, and here we are."

It was silent outside the cavern. No longer any sound of gunfire. Angell was hoping this was a good sign, but he wondered where the others had gone to. Had they not heard the firefight?

"The place of Kusu-lu is the palace of Death. The Underworld. In the language of the old people, the people from before Babylon, he was called the Man of the Underworld. Kutulu.

"In our language he is a tulku. A tulku of darkness and hatred, to be sure, but a tulku nonetheless. He has had many names, was known to many tribes, all over the world. Some called him a god. Others, a devil. You know about the asuras and the devas?"

Angell nodded, wearily. "Of course. In India, a deva is a god and the asuras are demons. In Persia, asuras were gods and the devas were demons. That is where the English word devil comes from. From the Persian word for demon, from the Sanskrit word for god. Devil, and divinity. Same root, opposite meanings."

"So you see. It is all a matter of a point of view. Which side you are on, which side you oppose. In the end it matters little.

"The book you seek is what we call a terma, as I said. A buried treasure, a sacred writing that has been hidden for centuries. For millennia. Until the right time comes for it to be revealed. Many of Buddhism's most important texts began as termas. But there are termas of evil as well as of good, just as there are evil tulkus. There are treasures whose burial place is a well of serpents rather than the gems and flowers of the Pure Land. They have been hidden by the tulkus so they will not be destroyed. As evil as they are, they are still sacred because they reveal spiritual truths, and in a world with so many lies even an evil truth is something to treasure.

"This text, this evil terma, what you call the *Necronomicon*, calls upon the High Priest of the Great Old Ones. It can be discovered by high initiates, it is true, but only by those who have been summoned by the High Priest himself."

"How does he summon followers if he is dead and buried?"

The old Asian pointed to his own skull with a boney forefinger.

"With dreams. With visions. He calls upon them with his mind. He is a master of dreams. When the stars are right and when the number of his followers is great enough, they can raise the High Priest from his underworld sarcophagus."

"With the Book."

"Yes, with the Book. It contains formulas human beings require in order to communicate with the High Priest. With Kutulu. While the High Priest can forge the dreams of the unconscious or sleeping mortal, the mortal needs the formulas in the Book to open the Gates and awaken the Priest. He who does this, he who discovers not only the Book but understands its formulas, is what we call a *terton*: a discoverer of a terma. In other words, a kind of guru or teacher but more than that. Prophet, maybe. " He looks pointedly at Angell.

"But you said 'when the stars are right.' Is this some kind of astrological ..."

"This calculation of the stars is not astrology. It is pure astronomy. But it is not *our* astronomy, not a science of the Earth from the perspective of the Earth. The astronomy of the Great Old Ones is an arcane method that betrays its origins ... how do you say this? ... Out of space, out of time."

Angell felt his heart sinking. The old guy was insane. This whole thing was insane. And now a decent human being, a brave man who is risking his life for him and for his mission, was in danger of dying a horrible death in an empty cave in the middle of nowhere. And what was he doing? Standing there, trying to reason with a madman.

The time was up. He had to go. He had to do something to salvage the mission and save his friends. He had no weapons, didn't speak the local language, had no contacts in this part of the world, and didn't believe a blessed thing this guy was telling him. But he had to do something.

He turned to leave.

Chapter Thirty-One

Extraordinary Rendition

The shaman is the man who knows *and* remembers ...
—Mircea Eliade, *Rites and Symbols of Initiation*

Jason Miller was on his way to the same location, but from a different approach.

He was running a penetration of the caverns below Khembalung from the Sino-Tibetan border side. The Chinese had been constructing a clandestine tunnel complex from the Tibetan side of the Himalayas, using a pre-existing tunnel system that had been known to only a few Bön priests in the past. Using a map that had been drawn long ago by the Chinese adventurers who had first come upon it in the days before the Boxer Rebellion, and amplified by details picked up during more recent interrogation sessions of Bön initiates, the Chinese had found the tunnel and had proceeded to enlarge the opening as well as dig deeper into the complex than even the Bön priests had before. So, while the JSOC team was penetrating deeply below the mountain on foot and by flashlight, Miller's group was riding a rail car supplied with electric lighting. They were making good time. Their intelligence had shown them that the Keepers of the Book—whoever and whatever they were supposed to be—had preceded them into the caverns but they were sure there was no easy way for them to escape except through Miller's tunnel.

The men accompanying Miller were members of a Tibetan underground movement with whom he had made contact years before when he was still working for the US military. If they were caught by Chinese security forces they would all be executed on the spot. Miller knew they were taking a terrible risk, but they knew the risk would be much greater should they fail. The Tibetan calendar

was showing some of the same details as those he had obtained
from his own research and that of the astronomers at the Indian
observatory at Mount Saraswati at Ladakh. His calculations showed
that he—and the Keepers of the Book—had only a few hours before
the alignment of stars and supernovae in the Great Bear signaled the
time of the opening of the Gate. Miller's intention is to make certain
the Gate remains closed, and in order to do that he must seize the
Book before Monroe's people get hold of it. He believeed Monroe's
intentions were sinister, and that if his people have the Book or get
it in time, they could—deliberately or accidentally—open the Gate
themselves.

He recalled a moment shortly before he went AWOL. It was
during the time of the Arab Spring. North Africa was being overrun
by "mad Arabs." Miller was getting messages through his remote
viewing sessions that he was keeping from Monroe, Aubrey, and the
rest. Messages he thought were for him, personally. When Monroe
got wind of this, he went ballistic.

"Do you think you're immune because you're psychic? Or a remote
viewer? Your talents can be used against you. If you don't realize
that, you're not an asset to us anymore. You're a liability. It used to
be, remote viewers could watch and observe from a distance. They
could see what was going on, on the other side of the world, without being seen themselves. But this is a different story, my friend.
When you started viewing on your own time you opened yourself
up to them."

He had never seen Monroe so agitated before. Hell, he had
rarely ever seen Monroe at all. It was usually Aubrey, his errand-boy,
who visited, chatted, debriefed him. But here was Monroe because
somehow he got wind of what was happening to him.

"They use your sensitivity to control you. Not only you. Other
viewers as well. Plus artists, writers, musicians, preachers. Exorcists!
Christ, even tea-leaf readers! Gypsy fortune tellers! Whoever has a
real gift, a genuine sensitivity to what we used to call 'vibes' back in

the Sixties. You thought you guys were like sneak thieves, reading people's minds without their being aware of it. And you were right. But these are not people. I don't know what to call them, but they are not *people*. They are here, and they are among us, but they are not even remotely human. They control through the same medium you use to view remotely. They are in telepathic touch with thousands of you, perhaps more, all over the globe. The deterioration of the planet is causing their resting places to be disturbed. The melting of glacial ice is loosening their bonds below the Antarctic ice shelf. They are in a state of excitement, but they are still asleep. Do you understand? They are in that twilight state between sleeping and wakefulness, and they are using you—and others like you—to help them through that last bit of sleep to full, conscious awareness.

"Your gift, your ability to view remotely … *it can be reversed*. Like a transmitter and receiver. Someone is on your channel and using it to issue commands. Their transmitter is a lot stronger and more ancient than yours. The technology they use—the biochemical apparatus that is their nervous system, something we never understood because we never really believed they existed—is overpowering your ability to resist. Instead of *you* spying on *them*, they are using *you* to spy on *us*. You have become a double agent, and you don't even know it."

Miller recalled those words in detail, for each one was like a nail driven into his flesh. And Monroe, God bless him, was almost right. Almost. Because it wasn't a *them*. It wasn't a group or a collection of beings.

There was only One.

As they proceeded deeper beneath the mountain the air got thinner and the atmosphere danker. He thought back to everything he had been through the past few months as he raced to find the Book before Monroe and his merry men. And as he began his search, the whole world started going to Hell.

It really began ten years earlier, only no one noticed. Not even him. In 2004 a starquake—a *star*quake!—took place whose radiation reached the Earth on December 26, 2004. It was the single largest stellar explosion witnessed by human beings for four hundred years, making the magnetar (a kind of neutron star) that caused it—SGR 1806-20—the single most highly magnetized object in history. The gamma rays and X-rays produced by the blast were enough to fry the circuits of satellites in Earth orbit and partially ionize the Earth's atmosphere.

At the same time, same month and day and year, on planet Earth a tsunami—the largest to hit the region since 1300 AD—struck the east coast of India and the west coast of Indonesia and Thailand and took almost two million lives. However, it also revealed the existence of temples buried beneath the sea. The Seven Temples of Mahabalipuram in India were revealed to the world as the waters rushed back from the shore during the tsunami and then rushed back in, removing centuries of sediment. Huge buildings made of stone, constructed in the eighth century AD, rose above the waters including foundations that dated more than two thousands years in the past.

A starquake, a tsunami, satellites blinded, and ancient temples rising from the sea. The astronomers had told him that one, not realizing what they were saying. Not realizing they were validating the prophecy encoded in the Lovecraft story about a sunken city called R'lyeh and the sleeping Priest in his Tomb.

Then, as he made his way to the Middle East, in mid-January of 2014 came the revelation of a supernova in the Big Dipper, the Great Bear asterism, the one so important to the Cult. This was SN 2014J, an exceedingly close supernova that was so bright it could be seen by amateur astronomers all over the northern hemisphere. Another signal that Cthulhu, great Cthulhu, was awakening.

This recalled the oceanic turbulence of 2001 and the discovery of an ancient city below the waves of the Gulf of Khambat, south of Mumbai on the western coast of India: a city older than Sumer, older than Mohenjo-Daro.

The Earth and the seas began giving up their secrets and the Cult of Cthulhu was becoming more excited by the hour. He could feel them, feel their agitation and their communications like tiny needles pricking the flesh all around his skull. The Ukraine was in flames, instigated by a neo-Nazi militia, and its president escaped to Moscow ... a cult in Nigeria slaughtered all the students in a school by locking its doors and burning the building down ... a few days ago they seized nearly three hundred schoolgirls and are holding them in captivity, swearing allegiance to Al Qaeda ... This much blood, this much violence will provide the energy necessary to raise dead but dreaming Cthulhu from his sarcophagus beneath the Earth, from his coffin in Aghartta.

From his Tomb beneath his very feet in the *beyul* of Khembalung.

Like a terrorist or spy, dragged unconscious and drugged, tossed onto a helicopter or a plane going to an undisclosed location, Cthulhu—the High Priest of the Ancient Ones: dreaded alien entities who were even now crowding around the soon-to-be-opened Gate—disappeared into a black site. Extraordinary rendition. A place far from the haunts of men, far from the civilized world that lived and dreamed a fantasy of right and wrong, of good and evil. And there he should stay.

Even as the cries of the Cult and the booming voice of Cthulhu, Kutulu, the Man of the Underworld, were making themselves known in his head, echoing from one side to the other of his cranium, cerebellum, cerebrum, commanding him to open the Book and say the words, Miller resisted. Resisted mightily. For the terma must be destroyed, and the terton along with it.

It was almost time.

CHAPTER THIRTY-TWO

DEATH AND RESURRECTION

For, as we must not forget, initiatory death is always followed by a resurrection...

  — Mircea Eliade, *Rites and Symbols of Initiation*

Adnan's back was against the wall, both literally and figuratively. He heard voices outside in the Nepalese night, muttering voices, the occasional cough, and curses spit in five languages. It was completely dark, but Adnan did not dare turn on his flashlight because it would give away his position.

What are they waiting for? he wondered.

He had managed to sneak over to the two dead bodies in his doorway and remove their weapons and what he could find of their extra ammunition. That was a plus. What was bothering him a little was the fact that he could not identify who the bodies were: not their unit, their ethnicity, nothing. They didn't carry any ID that he could find. They looked vaguely Asian but that was all. They could have been from anywhere.

He had two AK-47s with extra magazines. As long as they didn't lob any grenades or blow the rock standing in front of the entrance he could hold out for quite some time. But he hadn't heard back from Angell or the JSOC team. There was a very good chance that they were all dead and he was the only one left. That thought gave him no comfort at all for it meant that he would die, and die alone, in that antechamber to Hell.

He was not aware that the timing of this night was of the essence. He didn't know that the forces outside the cave were planning a major offensive that would get them inside the cave and down the tunnels to the Tomb of the High Priest in time for the Opening of the Stellar Gate.

He was not aware that he had, at most, fifteen more minutes before the antechamber to Hell became Hell's studio apartment.

Angell had lost consciousness.

He had turned to leave the "Cave of Treasures" and the crazy old shaman when something hit him in the head. He blacked out for what must have been only a few minutes for the light from the lantern and everything else in the cavern looked unchanged.

"What the *fuck*?"

"Sorry, professor. But I couldn't have you going off like a mad man." He was holding what looked like an antique knife with a very heavy handle. That was evidently the weapon he used to knock Angell down.

"Me? *Me*, the mad man? Are you ... you're insane!" Angell struggled to get up from the floor but he suddenly felt nauseous from the blow and stayed on his hands and knees while trying to collect himself.

"You are not in any position to save anyone right now. You will do more harm than good. Give me five minutes to explain, and then I will help you out of here so you can save your friends."

"I don't think they have five minutes," Angell said in an anguished voice.

"Oh, they do. You see, the forces arranging themselves outside the cave can't do anything until they hear from me."

"Who the hell are you?"

"I am the one they are all looking for, out there," he said, pointing in the general direction of the cave entrance. "I am one of the Keepers of the Book."

"Jesus. I'm surrounded by megalomaniacs with god complexes ..."

"Yes, probably. But in my case, I am just a kind of Listener. It's a hereditary title, passed down in initiation from generation to generation. My title is ambiguous, actually. The word means both

'Listener' and 'He who is heard.' Even in Hebrew. Depends on the circumstances."

"Like asura and deva," Angell replied, his pain subsiding and his strength gradually returning. He looked around for a weapon to dispatch this crazy old man once and for all.

"Exactly. You're getting the hang of this, I see."

"So? Now what?"

"So now, let us raise famous men."

"You mean, 'praise.' Let us praise famous men."

"No. I mean 'raise.' As from the dead. That is what this is all about, isn't it? Raising the dead but dreaming Cthulhu from his ancient slumber beneath the Earth (a phrase with more than one meaning, by the way). Raising the dead, reanimating the dead. The ancient Egyptians were famous for it, weren't they? They believed their Pharaoh would ascend to the Pole Star by means of the Big Dipper. What they called the Thigh of Set. Your Carl Tanzler tried to do the same."

"Who the hell was that?"

"They must have told you. German agent? Sent by Himmler to contact your great-grand-uncle George Angell? He was also the man in Florida who tried to bring his lady love back from the dead, and consulted with Lovecraft on the case. Well, that's what they said, anyway. In reality he built a modern sarcophagus and mummified her so she could fly to the heavens, just like a Pharaoh. Did you know he made love to her corpse? For *years*? Imagine the Tantric implications. I mean, talk about a great rite."

"What the living *fuck* are you talking about?"

"Forgive me. I so rarely have an audience. This is all about raising the dead. Your Book, *Necronomicon*: Dead Names. The *Bardo Thodol*, called the *Tibetan Book of the Dead*. The Book of Coming Forth by Day, which most know as the *Egyptian Book of the Dead*. Death, Professor Gregory Angell ... yes, I know who you are ... Death is all the rage around here."

And soon to be the rage outside if I don't get to Adnan in time, thought Angell.

"The sooner you understand this, the sooner you can help your friends out there. If you don't understand it, you're all doomed and your whole planet with you. Pay attention, and stop looking for a weapon. I'm not an idiot.

"Raising the dead is not a technology restricted to humans and animals. It can also be used to raise ... things ... that are not human and not of this Earth. Easier, actually. What Tanzler was doing in Key West ... what Lovecraft wrote about in his stories ... what the Nazis tried to do during the war (remember Operation Barbarossa? Why do you think they called it that?) ... and what the Cult intends to do here, are all part of the same process. Once the method is perfected it can be applied to anything. Jesus raised Lazarus from the dead, then he rose himself after he had practiced on Lazarus. This is why he was buried twice: first in Jerusalem and then in Srinagar. This is all about raising the dead, Doctor Angell. But not only dead people. Not those poor souls you watched being butchered in Mosul. Or at Kutha. What they intend is to raise the First Priest, the High Priest of the Old Ones, and with him to instigate the rebirth of the planet ..."

"And the destruction of humanity."

"Certainly. Isn't it about time? The planet is exhausted. People are tired. All we know how to do is slaughter each other and we have gotten progressively better and better at it. First it was hundreds, then thousands, then millions at a time. Now it's tens and hundreds of millions. We can't begin to speak of saving a million people from *anything*. But we *can* kill them in huge, unthinkable numbers! We've run our race, and now it's over. All those people you weep over will be reborn, Doctor Angell, but in new bodies, bodies better suited to interstellar travel. They will be reborn as what you call aliens, yes. So what? They were aliens to begin with. Our origins are in the stars. It's time for all of us to go home. And the Book you seek will help open the Gate to allow those forces—our ancestors—to come back and reclaim what was rightfully theirs. And you, Doctor Gregory Angell, by your very flesh and blood, by your genetic code, you are the missing piece of the puzzle! That is why you are here. That is why that wizened old sorcerer back in Washington recruited you and sent you here. The Place, the Time, the Book, and the Priest."

"Morphic resonance," Angell whispered to himself.

"What?"

"Morphic resonance. That's why I'm here. When one member of a species learns something new, the other members of the same species learn it at the same time, across space and across time. It's a theory that was proposed by Rupert Sheldrake decades ago."

"Your point?"

"You and your followers are in some kind of telepathic contact with this Kusu-lu, Kutulu, or Cthulhu, right? Psychics are also in contact, if we believe Lovecraft. Artists, musicians, sensitives. That was the whole point of the Lovecraft story. If true, it proves the existence of the morphic field. It means that Sheldrake is right, and that once they have raised their High Priest the same effect will take place across the universe. The dead will rise. Everywhere. They will have learned how. Not just your Old Ones, but beings of which you have no knowledge or understanding, beings that share the same morphic field.

"*That's why I'm here*. I'm the descendant of the man who discovered the Cthulhu Cult. The man they say was murdered by a German agent. The man who knew Lovecraft personally. The man who gave him the idea for the stories about Cthulhu. The man who knew about the existence of the *Necronomicon*. I'm the key to accessing Lovecraft's morphic field. He had no children! He has no descendants. I'm all there is!"

The shaman sat back on his heels, squatting unceremoniously in the Cave of Treasures, apparently speechless.

"Since Cthulhu is in contact with human beings he shares the same morphic field as the rest of us. He is similar enough ... what did you say? Genetic material from the stars? ... that what happens to him happens to all of us. This planet could well become the battleground for forces unimaginable, for monstrous beings that cannot die, or stay dead. Dead but dreaming, isn't that what the Book says? And when that Dreamer wakes up … when he becomes a Dreamer of the Day … so will all the others," he ended in a whisper, as if talking to himself.

"They have the Book," said the shaman, whispering like Angell.

"Who does?"

"The other Keepers. They have the Book, and they will open the Gate on time."

"When? What time?"

"When the Great Bear hangs from its tail in the sky. When the stars are right. It could be at any time now."

"I need to get to where they are. Now!"

"That's the Tomb of the High Priest. Kutulu. I can take you there. It's not far. Another mile or so in the tunnels. But you won't like it."

"Let's go!"

"I warned you."

They made to leave the cavern.

"Why won't I like it?"

"Because giving up disbelief is much harder than giving up belief."

At the moment they exited the cavern, the stuttering of automatic weapons reverberated off the walls. Angell's heart sank, and he turned on the shaman with murder in his eyes.

The battle for the cave had just begun.

CHAPTER THIRTY-THREE

WALPURGISNACHT

SN 1006, the largest supernova in human history, exploded on April 30, 1006 CE in the constellation of Therion. Mount Merapi on the island of Java exploded on the same day, burying Borobudur beneath volcanic ash.

April 30, 1492: the day Christopher Columbus received his commission to set sail for the Indies.

April 30, 1776: the eve of the day the Illuminaten Orden was founded.

April 30, 1789: the day George Washington took the Oath of Office as first President of the United States. The Washington Monument is exactly 555 feet high; the number of the word *Necronomicon* in Greek numerology.

April 30, 1919: the day seven Thulists—members of the Thule Gesellschaft, the secret society that practiced occult rituals in the Four Seasons Hotel in Munich, alongside the nascent German Workers Party—were murdered by Communists. It was the instigation for the Freikorps Revolt against the Communists that introduced Adolf Hitler to the Thule Society and the German Workers Party, which became the Nazi Party.

April 30, 1945: the day Adolf Hitler is said to have committed suicide in the Berlin bunker.

April 30, 1966: the day the Church of Satan was founded in San Francisco by Anton Szandor LaVey.

April 30, 1975: the day Saigon fell.

April 30, 1978: the day the Democratic Republic of Afghanistan was proclaimed, with disastrous consequences.

May 1, 2003: Operation Iraqi Freedom officially ends. Iraq war begins.

May 2, 2011: Osama bin Laden executed in Abbottabad, Pakistan.

Chapter Thirty-Four

The Beast in the Cave

Life and death have been lacking in my life.
— Jorge Luis Borges, *Discussion*

Adnan had rapid-fired one of the AK-47s as three men tried to force their way into the entrance around the rock. He dropped all of them but regretted the expenditure of ammunition. He did not dare approach the bodies for more since it seemed they were now tired of waiting and would pour more troops into the opening in a desperation move.

They had fired on their way in but their shots went all over the place. They were not wearing night-vision goggles and, like him, were afraid to use their flashlights in case they telegraphed their intentions.

But now all bets were off. He knew they were fixing lights to their automatic weapons and would simply start barreling in the entrance regardless of the risk to themselves. He slid across the floor to the other side of the cave, figuring they had a fix on his earlier position. His eyes had gotten accustomed to the dark and could make out silhouettes positioned around both sides of the rock. He wouldn't waste ammunition on warning shots but would wait until he had a good target.

Just please, God. No grenades.

He heard a sound behind him. He swung in its direction, holding the AK out in front of him, when he heard Angell's voice.

"Adnan. You all right?"

"Yeah. I'm right here."

"Are you hit?"

"Not yet. What kept you?"

"Never turn your back on a shaman."

"What's that supposed to mean? Never mind. Where are the others?"

"I haven't heard or seen anything from those guys. I have no idea where they are."

"Is that someone with you?"

"Yeah. The old guy from before. The Tibetan."

"I thought he disappeared when the flash-bang went off."

"He's still here. Listen, we better go back down the tunnel. Time is running out."

"What about these guys? As soon as we leave they'll come flowing into the tunnels."

"I'll take care of that," said the shaman, pushing past them and walking straight to the cave entrance.

"What the fuck! Get him back here! They'll kill him for sure!"

"He says they'll listen to him."

"Really? Seriously?"

"He's like their leader, or something. Look, while he's doing that let's get the hell out of here and down the tunnels."

The shaman walked up to the rock and said something in Tibetan. There was sudden silence from the other side. Then he said something in a different language. It might have been Zhang-Zhung. There came a low growl from the assembled forces outside. The growl rose in volume to become a chant. It was one Angell had heard too many times already.

Ku Tu Lu! Ku Tu Lu!

The shaman came back to Angell and Adnan.

"That will hold them for awhile. They know I am a Keeper, and they will await my orders. Let's go. We're running out of time."

He led the way through the tunnel aperture and began moving quickly in the darkness like a blind man. Angell and Adnan could do nothing else but follow suit.

"Where are we going?" whispered Adnan.

"To the Tomb of the High Priest," answered Angell. "It's where everybody who's anybody is gonna be tonight. My mission is to grab the Book and then get out of here. Problem is, I don't know where JSOC is. They were our ride."

"Let's cross that bridge when we come to it."

They descend deeper and deeper, the air getting thin, the darkness absolute. The walls of the tunnels are covered in dampness and ichor, a thick slime that they cannot see but which they can feel and it disgusts them. Adnan has given one of the AK-47s to Angell with a brief instruction as to how to use it. The shaman is armed with his ornate knife.

At the same time, Jason Miller is approaching the same area but from his own direction. The Tibetans are filing along behind him, growing increasingly nervous. They have heard about these strange tunnels from the Bön-po, the old monks, and remembering those tales does not fill them with peace and joy. They also sense something talking to them, just below the level of their hearing. A kind of muttering. And it is unnerving.

Miller, on the other hand, hears it clearly. It is the dead High Priest in his ancient Tomb. Calling to him.

He reaches a large, nearly empty cavern. There is the sound of dripping water, and a smell of camphor mixed with something bitter and fetid. He shines his flashlight around the walls, as do the men with him. The height of the cavern must be more than thirty feet. It is enormous, almost overwhelming after the long trek through narrow tunnels.

The architecture of the cavern is an insult to the senses. Walls seem to end and fold in on themselves; there are columns that seem to support nothing. The ceiling is high above their heads but at the same time seems to be dipping close to the floor. There are more corners than there are walls, more space than the walls and floor would allow.

And covering the walls: paintings. Icons. Creatures painted ten, fifteen feet high. They seem to be wearing vestments of some kind but there is something off about them. The colors are vibrant, a lot of red and gold and green, but somehow in the wrong places. It is as if the Twelve Apostles were depicted as animals, or as human beings but with indescribable defects. The paintings were ancient; older than Sumer, older than Mohenjo-Daro, older even than the cave paintings of Lascaux; but with incredible precision of detail. And the water, dripping down the sides of the cavern over the paintings, only serves to make them seem somehow alive.

That is when Miller notices a strange bas-relief on the floor of the cavern, a half-man, half-fish, part octopus-looking thing that fills him with dread, but before he can study it there is a noise from the other side of the cavern.

Angell appears from the other direction. He has his weapon out with the safety off. The shaman has made himself small, sidling over to a wall on a far corner. Whatever happens now is what was written.

Adnan follows Angell into the cavern and they both notice Miller and his entourage at the same time.

Guns are raised, but no one is firing. No one really knows who the others are. They may be fellow devotees, come for the reading of the Book and the Opening of the Gate. Angell didn't really know what to expect, but it wasn't another American and what appear to be half-a-dozen Asians with automatic weapons.

One of the Tibetans spots a torch covered in what looks like asphalt. He lights it with a cigarette lighter, and the cavern begins to glow with a sickly yellow light. More torches are found, and the cavern grows brighter, the eerie and unsettling icons on the walls growing even more disturbing. Still, Miller and Angell are at a standoff, staring at each other, with Adnan covering Angell and wondering what the next move could be.

"Do you have the Book?" It is Miller's voice, coming from a curved space, half in shadow, on the far side of the cavern.

Adnan raises his weapon to face Miller.

Angell replies, "No."

"Well, that sucks. Where do you think it is?"

"You're an American," says Angell.

"You got that right. You?"

"Yes."

"You one of Monroe's boys? One of his problem children?"

"He sent me here. Yes. You?"

"Oh, I used to be. I put in my papers some time ago."

"So I guess we're both here for the same thing."

"Yeah. Hey, let me make you a deal. I get the Book, but I run off a copy for you. You know, on Kindle."

"Nice try. But I kinda need the original."

The Tibetans don't know what to make of this exchange. Two Americans talking to each other, but neither one puts down his weapons. The Tibetans keep theirs trained on the hard-looking guy with Angell. This could all go sideways very soon.

Then there is another sound, something droning above the dripping water and the heavy breathing of anxious, worried, armed men. It is a chant, but like nothing Angell has ever heard before in all his fieldwork in the Middle East and Central Asia. It is in a kind of minor key, but in a scale that no human composer would have created. The words are impossible to make out, in a language unknown to Angell. And there is something else, an instrument vibrating below the chant, a sound not unlike those of the long Tibetan trumpets, the *dungchen*. It gets louder and louder, like a jet engine about to take off.

The chant grows louder, coming from another section of the cavern entirely. And this one reveals a mass of devotees approaching them, their leader holding the Book in his raised hands above the heads of his followers.

These, then, are the Keepers of the Book.

CHAPTER THIRTY-FIVE

THE BABYLONIAN PROTOCOL

So rituals have a kind of deliberate and conscious evocation of memory, right back to the first act. ... this conservatism of ritual would create exactly the right conditions for morphic resonance to occur between those performing the ritual now and all those who performed it previously. The ritualized commemorations and participatory re-linking with the ancestors of all cultures might involve just that; it might, in fact, be literally true that these rituals enable the current participants to reconnect with their ancestors ... through morphic resonance.

— Rupert Sheldrake

Ancient Sumer. Night. A ziggurat: the seven-stepped pyramid that is both temple and communication center between the Earth and the Sky. A pattern of stars can be seen above the horizon to the north. It is the Great Bear constellation, hanging from its tail. A high priest ascends the pyramid carrying a pot of burning incense and muttering an incantation in a language that was old when Sumer was just a Mesopotamian swamp.

He reaches the top of the pyramid where there is a small chamber and a cauldron in front of it with a fire of burning cedar wood. He enters the Holy of Holies, beseeching the Old Ones: "Spirit of the Earth, remember! Spirit of the Sky, remember!" In the distance, visible only from the top of the pyramid, can be seen other ziggurats with fires burning on top of them, making a pattern in the land like a modern landing strip.

In the chamber is a statue of a strange Creature, half-cephalopod, half-humanoid, the image from the Cthulhu File. Before it is a young woman, drugged, dressed like the Sumerian goddess Inanna or the

Babylonian Ishtar. She reclines on a low couch. As her face turns in
the light of the fire we see a marked resemblance to Jamila, the Yezidi
seeress. The high priest reveals a curved blade.

From the other side of the chamber a Being enters. A human
in a mask, perhaps. Or perhaps not. It is a man, but with the face
of a bird and large wings like a peacock. He has come to take the
sacrifice away, to entice the Old Ones to return. To rescue their
weak and vulnerable creation from the horrors that will come. Wars,
famines, pestilence. Holocaust. The sacrifice is the elixir that revives
and restores. It is the blood of the priestess, the earthly representative
of Inanna, of Ishtar, the Goddess who descended to the Underworld
and then let loose the demons and the dead who dwell below.

Below the ziggurat there is a large pool of water. The Absu, the
abyss. It is the entrance to the Underworld. To Kutu. Gudua. Cutha.
The sacrifice will be thrown from the mountain of the ziggurat into
the ocean of the Absu, to entreat the First Priest, the Kutu-lu, to
awaken from his timeless chamber of death to return to the World
and call forth the Old Ones again.

Miller shakes his head, coming to consciousness. That last viewing
was intense, and dangerous because he lost contact momentarily
with what was happening around him. It was an involuntary viewing, and it frightened him. His eyes focus and he sees that the devotees—the followers of Cthulhu, the Keepers of the Book—have
arrayed themselves around the walls of the cavern, facing towards
the center.

A woman is being brought out. Angell, on the other side of the
cavern from Miller, recognizes with a jolt young Jamila from the
Yezidi camp. As his eyes grow accustomed to the torchlight he can
make out many nationalities, many races among the cultists. There
are even a few faces he recognizes: from the news, from celebrity
sightings, and even from the journals of religion and spirituality he
subscribes to as a professor. This is not real, he tells himself. This is
a kind of nightmare experience. A hallucination, probably brought

on by whatever herb it is they are burning as incense. Juniper? He noticed it grows in profusion on the mountainside. Maybe the sense memory of it, the association with the scene in Kamdesh …

Jamila—it *is* Jamila, from the refugee camp—is speaking in tongues. A kind of satanic glossolalia. Her eyes are turned upwards in her head and she appears to be in a trance. Miller is responding to it, fighting the urge to join her in this unholy communion with the Other. His men, the Tibetans, have totally lost their concentration on Angell and Adnan, and are transfixed by this young woman in the center of the cavernous temple, the templous cavern, this Tomb of the High Priest. They have heard of such things before. They have seen their shamans and their monks perform miracles; have watched as the State Oracle of Tibet went into a similar trance, speaking in tongues. But this … no, not this. This is not right. This is … wrong.

Jamila is dressed in a costume of some kind, chaste but somehow degenerate at the same time, as if the material that covers her from neck to toes is swimming on her or around her, a gauze like silver smoke. The leader of the cult is bald, a head like a torpedo, and large. He is arrayed in a black and gold vestment with symbols embroidered on it that were derived from the Black Book in his hand, the one he still holds over the heads of the congregation. He is speaking, inaudibly, an incantation and his devotees are responding in kind in a sub-vocal chant that nevertheless stands Angell's hair on end.

Adnan wants to shoot something. Almost anything at this point. This is truly out of hand. And the JSOC team is nowhere to be found. He eyes the Book in the leader's hands and calculates the distance and the time needed to get to it and grab Angell and get the hell out of the caves.

Then abruptly Jamila's voice changes and what comes out of her mouth is a sound unlike any Angell has ever heard. It has more in common with the ululation he heard at Tell Ibrahim, but it is coming out of a single throat and not dozens. He doesn't know how she is doing that. It is not a human voice, but something halfway between animal and machine.

Miller and Angell come to the same realization at the same time: Jamila is channeling the creature in the Tomb. She is channeling Cthulhu and giving orders to his devotees. The floor—the wide, geometrically-impossible stone floor with the weird bas-relief in Riemann-like dimensions—begins to tremble, and it is at that moment that Angell realizes that the enormous stone floor beneath his feet *is* the Tomb. They have all been standing on it the entire time.

The cult leader opens the Book to begin to read from it aloud.

CHAPTER THIRTY-SIX

LOSING MY RELIGION

In war magic, anger, the fury of attack, the emotions of combative passion, are frequently expressed in a more or less direct manner. In the magic of terror, in the exorcism directed against the powers of darkness and evil, the magician behaves as if himself overcome by the emotion of fear, or at least violently struggling against it. Shouts, brandishing of weapons, the use of lighted torches, form often the substance of this rite.

—Bronislaw Malinowski, *Myth in Primitive Psychology*

As the Keeper of the Book begins to intone the incantation that will raise Cthulhu from his Tomb, Chinese troops begin to mass on the Tibetan-Nepali border in anticipation of a massive terrorist campaign being run out of Khembalung, or at least that's the cover story. The Indian and Pakistani armies respond in kind, and a major military confrontation between three countries over the territory of a fourth appears to be inevitable.

Half a world away, Russian troops pour into Ukraine at the same time as Boko Haram accelerates their process of slaughter in Nigeria, especially of women and girls. Child soldiers run amok in Cambodia while Burmese Buddhists begin a campaign of eradication against the Muslim Rohingya. Crack-addled former soldiers of Charles Taylor's Liberian militia come out of hiding; dressed in odds and ends of women's clothing and sporting Halloween masks they go on a rampage of rape and murder. Women as the enemy; women as objects of desire. Desire as enemy.

In Afghanistan, former leaders of the Northern Alliance gather for a celebration. They know something is in the air. A change is coming. The world will never be the same. So they are hosting a dance competition among their boys. The infamous practice of *bacha bazi* is all the rage among these grizzled elders, who steal or buy boys as young as six or seven and groom them to be exotic dancers who wear women's clothing and make-up and who service the adult males sexually until they age-out at seventeen or eighteen at which time they are discarded. An underground nationalist network as an underground pedophile network. The Taliban put a stop to *that* in their territory, thank Dagon; instead they buy or steal women and girls as slaves for their friends and colleagues in Al-Qaeda, or as commodities to be sold on the open market for easy money. And when the Taliban frees one of the boys used as a sex slave by the Northern Alliance, they turn him into a child soldier and send him to kill Afghan policemen. Jesus may have wept, but Cthulhu laughs. "Suffer the little children," he gurgles in his putrescent palisade. "Indeed."

A US Los Angeles class submarine detects strong seismic activity at or near Point Nemo in the Pacific Ocean and what appears to be frantic escape maneuvers by a school of giant cephalopods. The seismic activity seems to stop abruptly … then just as abruptly turns into an undersea earthquake as volcanoes around the Ring of Fire begin shooting jets of rock and lava into the sky and the submarine is tossed like a paper boat on shockwaves emanating from a deep fissure in the sub-oceanic soil.

Of course, none of this is known to the inhabitants of the cavern. The Tomb of the First Priest is trembling with what might be more seismic activity, following a fault line that runs from somewhere below the Indian Ocean and into the sub-continent itself. Is this what the shaman meant when he said the Tomb of the First Priest could be reached from various places around the world?

Adnan notices Angell starting to move towards the cult leader. The professor is slowly raising the muzzle of his weapon and Adnan knows he is about to fire. He reaches over and whispers, "Just what do you think you're doing?"

"I have to stop him. Whatever he's doing, whatever he's saying, he's making it worse."

Angell doesn't have to explain what 'it' means. There is a growing tremor from beneath the floor where they stand. The chanting from the crowd is building in intensity. Even Miller is swaying a little, eyes closed, lost in his own reverie. And Jamila … the Yezidi woman seems to be an extension of the Tomb itself, moving in its oddly-syncopated rhythms, lowering herself closer and closer to the floor. What histories are in her head! What a collection of arcane lore, spirit possession, violence, assault, and finally the kidnapping by the Cthulhu Cult to bring her to this place: first from Iraq, then Syria, then a refugee camp in Turkey, and finally across half of the world and all of Central Asia to reach this cavern in this tunnel below this Himalayan mountain in the company of men who do not speak her language, far from her beloved neighbor Fahim, far from her homeland in Lalish. She knows, but cannot say, that another cult of death and depravity—ISIL— is now moving on her people at Sinjar with the intention of killing every last one. Like the Cathars from a land she never knew, like the Jews of Masada, they will climb to the mountain top and resist, and hide their books and their sacred implements while they await the call of Melek Taus, the Peacock Angel.

But Jamila knows this is *now*. Jamila knows this is *here*. If anyone is going to defend her people, her Yezidi family, the thousands of men, women and children who have been reviled and oppressed and slaughtered throughout all of human history since the days of ancient Sumer, it will have to be now, and here, and with this god they call Kutulu.

Because no one else will.

The leader, the one she was told to call the priest of Dagon, has the Book in his hands, the Book she had rescued herself from the Mukhabarat so many years ago. He defiles it even as it defiles him. He has begun to intone a chant over the droning of his followers, in a rising and falling tempo that seems simultaneously desperate and angry.

Before he knows what he has done—a question he will ask himself for the rest of his life—a shot rings out and it dawns on Angell that he has fired it, fired the weapon and put a bullet through the heart of the chanting priest.

Miller's eyes slam open at the sound which has sent an echo running in ovoid spheres around the cavern, cutting off the priest's voice in mid-oration. Angell doesn't know what he is doing, but he knows that if he doesn't put a stop to the ritual, somehow, that terrible things—sick, hideous, loathsome things—will take place, and these diseased human beings will be sent to run wild in the streets of the world's cities and towns, causing more chaos and bloodshed than the world has ever known ... and that's saying something. Maybe he has been infected with the same bloodlust as the people who now surround him, hatred in their eyes, as they raise ceremonial daggers and scimitar swords to flay and slice the flesh from his body.

All he knows is that, for the first time, he has taken a human life. The sensation of the weapon bucking in his hands. The smell of the cordite. The sickening sense that he has somehow been changed, been ruined, soiled—that is replaced by a deeper disgust that he has come to this. He has killed. A man is dead or dying, leaving the world forever, because of him and a book. A book ... a book has become the reason that human beings die. He can't stand the thought. A book! But he has no time to grieve.

Angell fingers the trigger on his weapon, heart pounding, ready to take a few with him but knowing that his life is over no matter what happens next.

More shots ring out. Adnan opens fire on the advancing cultists as Miller and his men begin shooting in the same direction. Miller is shooting and running, heading for the body of the slain priest just as it starts to fall. Angell knows Miller is going for the Book. He fires into the crowd himself, suddenly a commando—telling himself *it's okay, it's alright, they're trying to kill me, too*—trying to shoot his way through to the Book before Miller can reach it. Others have the same idea and Angell knows he will never make it in time ... when the Book seems to rise into the air of its own accord.

It is Jamila, who seems to have come out of her trance at the sound of the gunfire—unwelcome reminders of an entire life lived at the mercy of armed men—and who has seized the Book and is now moving with it towards Angell. There is something about her at that moment that nags at something in Angell's own memory but he can't place it. With no time to wonder about it he races towards Jamila, stumbling over falling bodies as he goes, hearing Miller's frantic shouts at his men to cut him off and seize the Book.

Then, in a replay of what transpired in the basement in Mosul in 2003 with Fahim, the Mukhabarat, and Jamila, there is a shudder that runs through the entire cavern and the sound as of a beast growling either in pain or in hatred or both, and a feeling of almost unbearable warmth runs through Angell's body as if an ocean of heat was pouring through his veins and running from the soles of his feet to the crown of his head, nearly blinding him on the way. The warmth, the heat, the vertical ascent ... Angell knows enough to realize it is the Serpent, the one depicted on the side of the Yezidi shrines, the rising Serpent, the Goddess herself, call her Shahmaram or Kundalini, the real source of life and energy, not that ... that Thing in the Tomb. But it is happening *to* him, not from him. It is coming from *Outside*. This is no yoga meditation happening here. It is violence and death and ... and initiation.

There is a sudden, almost deafening silence, as all action stops and all eyes turn towards Jamila and the Book.

Her mouth opens, and a low but sensuous voice speaks a phrase in Kurmanji, the Kurdish dialect of the Yezidi tribe to which Jamila belongs. It is her language, and it is a language known to Angell, of course. And he does not believe his ears.

"In his house at *Ur Il At*, dead *Kutulu* waits ... dreaming ..."

Ur Il At, a Sumerian phrase that Angell roughly translates as "The Supreme City," but which just as easily could be the fictional *R'lyeh* of the damned interloper who started all of this, Howard Phillips Lovecraft. His mind racing, he is struck by the way she pronounced the word *Kutulu*. It was not exactly the Arabic *al-Qhadhulu*, for "the Abandoner', but more like the Akkadian *qatalu*: a word meaning "to kill."

He tries to make sense of what she is saying because it seems to be central to the solution of all of this. The sense of inner heat is almost overpowering; the silence is as heavy as an anvil all around him in that wretched cavern. He looks up, finger on the trigger.

And Jamila hands him the Book.

"Terton," she says. Naming him. Anointing him.

Identifying him.

CHAPTER THIRTY-SEVEN

"Is R'lyeh Burning?"

As I think of the many myths, there is one that is very
harmful, and that is the myth of countries.

—Jorge Luis Borges, *Artful Dodge* (April 1980)

Monroe has been out of contact with his people for almost two days
and is growing frantic. GPS chips in the uniforms and radios of the
insertion team reveal that they are in the region of Nepal close to
the border with Tibet, as planned, but that they have not been moving for almost twelve hours. That can only mean they are all dead.

Angell's chip, however, showed movement until the signal
became faint. It is possible that he is still alive, which means the
Book still may be in play. The signal was lost in Khembalung and
Monroe knows only too well that Angell could easily be wandering
anywhere in the series of underground caves and caverns that
comprise the "hidden country."

Reports coming in from the US Seventh Fleet in the Pacific
are alarming to a great degree. Even more worrying is the chatter
coming in from all over the world. Expert at seeing patterns in
seemingly unrelated phenomena Monroe sees that the seismic
activity in the Pacific is linked to the political unrest in Asia and
to a series of smaller earthquakes in Pakistan and Afghanistan. The
potential for armed conflict between China and India—with Nepal
as the battleground—is very real. Central Asia is in an uproar, with
government leaders in Turkmenistan, Uzbekistan and Kazakhstan
fleeing for their lives and holing up in safe houses in Iran and
Armenia. The government in Iraq is no longer functioning even with
a Shi'a majority and a Shi'a leadership. In Lebanon, Druze militia
have been engaged in a life-or-death battle with Hezbollah. The
Sunni population of the Middle East and the Maghreb, previously

so splintered and factional, are now dangerously united. There can only be one reason for that: a perceived threat that is greater than their differences.

Chatter about the "First Priest" is mixed with references to the Twelfth Imam, which is itself confused with mention of the Kalki Avatar: a purely Indo-Tibetan idea of a warrior king who will come out of the "hidden country" to wreak death and destruction on the world. Apocalyptic cults of Islam, Buddhism, Hinduism, and Christianity all claim that their Apocalypse is at hand, and all centered around the same figure of the First Priest. This is further conflated with rumors concerning the Old Ones returning to the Earth, and no one but Monroe understands what that means. How such a concept became common currency among the terror cells and popular movements throughout the developing world frightens him. It means a paradigm shift in religious thinking, the kind of thing that concerned the Vatican years ago when talk of UFOs and life on other planets forced the cardinals to come up with some policy positions on aliens so that their hegemony over their followers would not be threatened. Islam—apparently alone of the major faiths—never had a problem accepting the possibility of life on other planets. But this?

A middle-aged man is arrested in the Ninth Ward of New Orleans, covered in blood, a scimitar in his hands, standing in the middle of the street. Detective Cuneo is the first on the scene. He walks up to the man carefully, slowly, and hears him chanting an incantation to Cthulhu. Cuneo has left his file on the Ninth Ward homicide case in his car, sitting on the passenger seat. He tries to approach the man, to get him to put down the sword, when he turns and rushes Cuneo, screaming "Kutulu!." Cuneo has no choice but to fire, and the man is down.

Standing over him, he recognizes the face. It is on a photograph in his file, the one from 1907. A man called Castro.

Cuneo knows it's impossible. The coroner's van arrives at the scene and they remove the body. He asks if the man had any ID on him. They pull out the wallet from the man's left back pocket.

Sure enough, the man's name was Castro. Same name, same face as the guy who answered all the inspector's questions more than one hundred years ago. It's just a coincidence of course, but as he is looking down at the driver's license and realizes that the address on the license is the same as the house with the double homicide there is an explosion that rips through the Ward from a few blocks away.

His crime scene has just exploded. Gas main leak, they will tell him later.

Sure.

In Beijing, in Tiananmen Square, a beautiful spring evening. A local woman from one of the *hutongs* off Wangfujing is standing in the center of the square. She is holding a string shopping bag and wearing sensible shoes. She looks very frightened when two men of the Public Security Bureau approach her because she has not moved from that spot in more than an hour. She is terrified, both at the fact that she cannot move and at the fact that the police are questioning her. She tries to answer their questions, but her responses come out funny.

She is speaking Sumerian.

In Chile, in the commune known as Villa Baviera—formerly a torture and interrogation center known as Colonia Dignidad, whose former Nazi leader was a convicted child molester—incense is being burned and the old flags, the swastika flags, the Blood Flag, are being raised as torches are lit in anticipation of the return of the Dark Lord.

In Uganda, the ritual killings of children as human sacrifice are on the rise.

In Bangkok, more than two thousand fetuses are found in plastic bags at a Buddhist temple. The smell alerted the authorities.

The United States now boasts the world's largest prison population, of which the majority of inmates are African-American.

In Beijing again, a 350-year-old temple to a dragon deity is unearthed near the Olympic Village complex. Close by, another temple—this time to a fertility goddess— is also discovered.

In Houston, local law enforcement reveals that their city is now the world capital of sex trafficking.

In the United States, the number of suicides of returning veterans from the Iraq and Afghanistan campaigns is larger than the number of those killed in action.

In Jerusalem, Mecca, and Rome the faithful gather by thousands and then millions to pray for help from … they know not what. But it is not working. The old banishings and exorcisms do not seem to work. If this is not about God and the Devil, then what is it?

Monroe's hands are tied. Due to the super-secret nature of his investigations and the off-the-books mission of Angell and the JSOC insertion team there is no one he can go to for help, not without jeopardizing the mission even further while he wastes time explaining things to someone over at DHS. The JSOC cowboys are on a need-to-know basis and believed they were taking orders from the White House. He was desperate then, so he took the chance of pulling a string and sending in JSOC to ensure success. That decision will come back to haunt him, he knows. He will face terrible legal repercussions from his actions, even criminal charges. But that did not matter to him now. What was important was the success of the mission. If it failed, prison time or even execution for treason would be the least of his problems.

While figuring out what to do next he sees a television report that shakes him to the core. He grabs the remote and un-mutes the sound only to learn that the latest earthquake in the South Pacific has revealed the existence of a city that was buried long ago, possibly an island that sank to the bottom of the ocean. Grain film footage taken by the crew of the US submarine shows some kind of architecture rising from the sea bed as the waves rush outward in a tsunami that threatens New Zealand and Australia. It is larger than the submerged temple complex at Mahabalipuram, uncovered by a tsunami on December 26, 2004; larger and older than the city complex at the Gulf of Khambat, discovered off the coast of India in 2002 and judged to be more than nine thousand years old.

It was as he feared all along, and as his accumulated evidence suggested. The stories of H. P. Lovecraft were not fantasies but *predictions*. The tales of ancient aliens and their rule on this planet were not inventions.

They were *memories*.

Monroe knows what he has to do. He closes his eyes and takes a deep breath. His entire life, from the Korean War to this day, flashes before his eyes in a sad parade of battles won and lost and the sacrifices he made to keep his country—and now his planet—secure and safe from all its enemies, domestic and foreign. All of that is now in jeopardy. All of that may soon count for nothing.

He picks up the phone.

CHAPTER THIRTY-EIGHT

THE PANDORA EFFECT

May Heaven exist, even if my place is Hell.

—Jorge Luis Borges, "The Library of Babel"

Jamila holds out the Book to Angell. Everyone else is frozen in place, except for Miller who is inching his way towards the couple, immune to the power emanating from Jamila, or the Book or both, but insistent on getting the Book away from them.

Angell reaches out and takes the Book, his eyes never leaving Jamila's, feeling with unease the strange leather that covers the ancient pages. He later will learn that the Book was rebound by Leers in Berlin during the war, using leather made from human flesh from the death camps. At this time, though, all Angell knows is that the mission entrusted to him by Monroe is nearly accomplished. He has the Book in his hands.

Jamila drops her arms to her sides and lifts up her head to stare at the impossible curvatures of the ceiling, as if listening.

At the observatory in Leh, at that same moment, the astronomers sight what they have expected, and in precisely the same spot in the sky that was predicted: another supernova, emanating from the tail of the Great Bear. It is sighted simultaneously around the world, visible in daylight and at night, the brightest ever recorded since SN 1006. It is the signal the Cult has been awaiting: the sign that the Gate is opening.

In the cavern, Miller seems to sense it as well. Desperate to stop it from happening, he leaps over several supine bodies and races towards Angell who is staring down at the Book in his hands. Miller shouts at him: "You must close the Gate! Close the Gate!" But Angell is oblivious to everything but the force boiling up from the pages of the *Necronomicon*.

He reaches Angell and grabs the Book just as Jamila returns her attention to the scene around her. She sees Miller open the Book and lets out a long, terrifying scream.

Meanwhile Adnan has been trying to make sense of everything he is seeing. He doesn't know who are the bad guys and who are the good guys. He sees Miller has taken the Book away from Angell, and he knows that Angell's mission is to seize the Book and bring it back Stateside. So, he makes a decision.

Miller runs through the pages, half by sight and half by touch, until he comes to a page he has seen so many times over the past six months or more. In his dreams, in his visions. He places his hand over it as if reading Braille and begins to intone a prayer that will close the Gate and stop the alien/demonic hordes from swarming into the Earth's biosphere. Angell hesitates between shooting Miller or allowing him to finish, because the rest of the demented assembly in the cavern has come out of their collective trance at the sound of Jamila's scream and are steadily advancing on the trio.

Adnan moves slowly towards them from the other side, angling for a clear shot at Miller. The woman is in the way, and then Angell himself. On top of that, the freaks in the cavern have started moving again.

Jamila raises her arms to the heavens and begins her own insane chanting, an antiphon to which the cultists respond. The image that was plaguing Angell since he first saw Jamila has now coalesced into something he recognizes. Jamila is reciting an ancient hymn, the *Descent of Inanna to the Underworld.* Jamila has identified herself— or been identified—as the Sumerian goddess whose three-day sojourn in the realm of the dead and the demons has resulted in her resurrection but at a cost to humanity. For, as the hymn tells us, "her demons preceded her." Angell realizes that these psychotic, deluded fools around him are performing a ritual that has not been celebrated in more than five thousand years. They want the demons released. They want the First Priest, the High Priest of the Old Ones, Cthulhu, to resurrect from its dead stupor.

Tanzler and his reanimation experiments. The Nazi cult that employed Leers, Evola and all the other occultist cranks at the SS-

Ahnenerbe. The Twelve Shi'a and their belief in the imminent
return of the Hidden Imam. Hitler and his Operation Barbarossa,
an invasion of Russia named after a Teutonic king who is "dead but
dreaming." All those pop novels and movies about zombies, vampires,
and the other "undead," preparing the world psychologically for
what their creators secretly believed would happen in reality. All of
this, and Angell's mission too, predicated on the insane belief that
the dead could be revived, even after thousands or millions of years.
Jurassic Park. With demons.

He didn't know if Miller believed in any of this or not, but
he understood that Miller knew that *they* did and, no matter what,
he had to use that belief against them. He had to prove that they
had closed the Gate. But Angell could not deny the evidence of his
own senses: the eerie underground cavern that served as a Tomb for
a being of impossible size and unearthly contours that even now
was vibrating wildly under his feet like a tea table at a Victorian
séance; the Pythoness that was Jamila, an otherwise sweet daughter
of the Yezidi who suffered so greatly under Saddam, channeling
the Creature in the Tomb; the spiritual sickness that he was feeling
even now, so much worse than he experienced at Mosul all those
years ago when the Yezidi—Jamila's people—were taken out and
slaughtered. This was religion?

"*There is no religion here,*" he heard the voice shout in his head,
reminding him of what he had been told only an hour earlier. The
voice of the shaman. How was that possible? Angell stared madly
around him at the sound. Where was he?

"*This has nothing to do with religion! This is not ideology, or theology.
Not some battle between the forces of Good and Evil. There are* no angels,
no demons. *There is only* Us *and* Them*!*"

Adnan sees his opening, and takes it. He fires a short burst at
Miller that plows into his chest, sending him crashing to the floor.

Miller is stunned, more at the fact that he has been shot at all and
less at the fact that he is dying and has at most only a few seconds

to live. His life telescopes in front of his eyes. Events from his child-hood are squeezed together with things he experienced only days, or weeks, ago.

You thought everything was a joke, something to entertain adolescent boys. Monsters from space. Haunted houses. Depraved cults. Forbidden books.

And then it happened. Lovecraft died before World War Two began. He died before we learned of the Holocaust. He died before the atomic bomb was dropped. Before Cambodia. Vietnam. Before UFOs and The Exorcist *and* Ancient Aliens. *Before the Manson Family and serial killers and Jonestown. Before the Arab Spring. Before Erich von D niken and Zecharia Sitchin. Before the* Anarchist Cookbook. The Sayings of Chairman Mao. The Story of O. ...*

Before television.

Before 9/11 made terror cults common knowledge and household words. Haunted *household words.*

Before the modern world made Lovecraft's world a reality.

Not so funny anymore, is it? Lovecraft as seer, as prophet of the New Age? An atheist as visionary?

Isn't it ironic?

Don't you think?

The crowd begins to converge on Angell as Miller drops to the ground. He grabs the Book with one hand and begins firing at the crowd with the other. Panic firing. He is not even sure how he is able to fire an AK-47 with one hand. Miller's Tibetans rush into the crowd, firing their own weapons, and the din is horrendous in the enclosed space. Adnan ... where was Adnan?

Jamila's screams can be heard over the gunfire and the moans of the wounded. Something is happening and it is not certain that even Miller or the accursed Book was ever able to stop it.

Something ... someone ... is rising from the stones and tiles of the cavern's floor. Rising from the floor and from the walls and from the ceiling, all at once, an effect that is contrary to every law of the third dimension. As the blood of the maniacs spills and pools on the ground, spattering the walls, raising a stench of copper that competes with the awful incense and makes Angell wonder, crazily, if copper is sacred to Venus because it smells like spilled blood, the crowd pulls back with a collective sigh—an "Ahhhh ..." that seems to go on forever.

Jamila is now silent. Her face has become almost beatific. The only sound in the world is the strange buzzing of a horde of invisible insects, like a delegation from the East. The buzzing rises higher and higher. *Al-Azif,* he thinks. *This is why. When Kutulu rises from R'lyeh* ...

Jamila points at Angell, her smile becoming flirtatious and seductive. She glides over to him, ignoring Miller's corpse and the Book in Angell's hand, and puts her fingertips tenderly on his shoulder as the shadows around the cavern gather and become more concrete, more sinister, more lethal.

Above her head, Angell can see what appears to be a face coalescing out of angles and tricks of light and darkness and the clouds of incense and cordite. It is something that partakes of the sea and the land, of the swamps and marshes of Mesopotamia as well as the sunken temples of Mahabalipuram and the Gulf of Khambat; of the forgotten cities of the Hadrahmut buried under aeons of sand and fear. There are tendrils—of smoke, or of flesh?—what appears to be an eye, a nightmare of mismatched organs and limbs, yet at the same time incredibly ancient. A nagging memory of DNA and wrong turns on the evolutionary path.

Jamila puts her other hand on Angell's gun arm. He looks down at her, afraid to glance into her eyes, and he sees not only Jamila and Inanna—but this scholar of religions and religious studies sees Ishtar, Sekhmet, Kali, Tanzler's Elena, and Dante's Beatrice, Poe's Lenore, the Kurdish lizard goddess Shahmaran, and the Whore of Babylon.

Babylon. Of course.

And Jamila's tender and flirtatious finger pulls the trigger of the AK-47.

CHAPTER THIRTY-NINE

CLIMATE CHANGE

The future is inevitable and precise, but it may not occur. God lurks in the gaps.

—Jorge Luis Borges, *Other Inquisitions*

Monroe is getting data directly from the drone flying over the Khembalung area. He has been on the phone with Aubrey almost constantly. Aubrey is understandably freaked out by the whole affair. There has been no word from the JSOC team and that is especially worrisome. The military buildup along the border with China is proceeding unabated.

The Raptor drone is equipped with the latest in infra-red cameras and they have not picked up any life forms near any of the entrances to the cave complex. The entire mountain shows up black on the screens as if there isn't even any vegetation there.

The drone is also equipped with two Hellfire missiles, should it come to that.

Aubrey is a physical and emotional mess. He has been with Monroe for decades and he knows what is at stake. They are at the finish line, but that's when everything can go wrong. He knows that from bitter experience.

He has been in Baghdad now for too long. He wants to get back to the States. He thought it would be good to get back in action again, an old man like him, but realized too late that this was a young man's game. He had the experience and the wisdom, but he couldn't transfer any of that to the people for whom he was responsible. They knew what they had to do, and they made choices in the field, in the heat of the moment, that were not always the right choices, and that's when he had to have backup plans.

Right now, he didn't have any. He had to get Angell and the Book out. Barring that, then just the Book.

He had come to like Angell; well, a little anyway. He was serious, depressed, cynical about life more than other people his age. And he had a right to be. But Aubrey had seen much more, been through much more, and had been responsible for a hell of a lot more, and still managed to retain his sense of humor. As he thought back to the last few days since leaving Brooklyn he realized he had never seen Angell actually smile.

He hoped there were still some smiles in Angell's future.

His screen came to life again. More telemetry from the UAV. And his phone was ringing. It was Monroe.

Monroe hung up from the call to Aubrey. Still no word. He looked down at his desk, where the long-lost Cthulhu File sat there like a witch's toad, fat and threatening. The Cthulhu file was the backbone of the Lovecraft Codex. It was retrieved from poor Barlow's room at the university after the professor's suicide. William Burroughs had handed it over to an official from the US Embassy in Mexico City in return for the US government looking the other way concerning the writer's accidental shooting of his wife. That official—whose real job was hunting Communists for the CIA—later became part of Monroe's team.

All he needs is the Book, and his life-long quest will be complete. With the Book and the Codex the answers to thousands of years of human history would be revealed, putting everything into a new context and permitting an enormous realignment of powers, capabilities, and government focus. It could save the world, he thinks. Especially now, as the new cult that called itself the Islamic State was blatantly advertising its links to these ancient ideas and to the Cthulhu Cult. The black flags, the ninja costumes, the videotaped beheadings, the mass executions, the rape of women and young girls … didn't anyone get the joke? It was the Manson Family again, except with Toyota Land Cruisers instead of dune buggies. That was ironic, thought Monroe. They're in the desert, like the Manson Family. They should have dune buggies.

The news coming in from all parts of the world is more than alarming. He knows the White House is running scared, in complete disarray because it has become impossible to focus on any one—or any dozen—crises as more and more keep appearing. He is using that distraction to his own purpose and maneuvering to divert the resources he needs to Nepal, but he feels for the administration. They were used to dealing with existential threats in a more twentieth century fashion: find the bad guys, root 'em out, done. But the bad guys were just the witless tools of some *really* bad guys, and these *really* bad guys were taking orders from some lifeless but dreaming *corpse* buried beneath the mountains and the seas. The source of radicalization—Islamic, Christian, Jewish, Buddhist, whatever—was not the Internet, which was just the medium. The source was not economics alone, or history, or religion. These provided what the magicians call the "material basis" for the manifestation of the Evil Spirit: a Force and an Entity that is not so easily defined, identified, and neutralized. For that you needed an exorcist, and the last exorcists with that kind of juice died sometime in the sixteenth century.

As the reports coming in show the outlines of an ugly and sinister Force coalescing out of the pain, bloodshed, and horrors of ancient antagonisms, natural disasters, and technology gone amok, Monroe can almost look into the face of Cthulhu itself, like that demon face that some people claimed they saw in the fires of the Twin Towers on September 11, 2001.

Even the increasing warmth of the world's oceans is contributing to Cthulhu's resurrection as his undersea abode rises to the surface. Schools of giant squid, jellyfish, and all manner of bizarre sea creatures are swarming in incredible numbers. The Antarctic ice sheet is melting, revealing structures and terrain impossible to imagine only decades ago. The dimensions of Cthulhu are staggering and defy any rational, Euclidean sense of geometric proportion. It is simultaneously in the deep Pacific, under the Himalayas, channeled in Louisiana, Mexico,

Kiev, Lagos, Beijing, Yogyakarta, a farm outside Perth, a crack house in Brooklyn, among child prostitutes in Cambodia, drug-crazed militia in Peru, a mosque in Somalia ... It is rising from all points on the Earth, all at once, as if shrugging off the dimensions of space and time, one by one.

In a town in Missouri that night an unarmed black man is gunned down in the street by two heavily-armed police officers. As the man is dying on the asphalt in a pool of his own blood, the people begin to come out from their homes, their shops, their churches and word-lessly they start to surround the two officers...

Why didn't we pay attention, asks Monroe of himself and the world. *Our artists, our writers, our musicians see farther than we do. The rest of us just play catch-up. And now it may be too late.*

Chapter Forty

Raptor/Rapture

> ... I will merely say that caves played a role in prehistoric initiations ...
>
> —Mircea Eliade, *Rites and Symbols of Initiation*

The shot that Jamila has fired from Angell's weapon has hit the old shaman, center mass. Angell twists around at the sound of the blast and sees the man against the wall, a flower of his own blood blooming across his chest. In his right hand, he was holding his antique knife and was about to plunge it into Angell's back.

No time to lose, Angell returns to the Book and the closing of the Gate. The Book is open to where Miller had left it, and Angell feels he has no choice but to continue Miller's work.

He stares at the page in front of him, the one Miller had been reading, and realizes that he can make it out as a Sumerian chant written in Greek letters.

He believes none of this, he tells himself. None of it. But he sees the growing fog around him like the one at Tell Ibrahim, and he smells the stench, the foetor of that fog like the offal of a badly buried dinosaur. He cannot deny the tremendous vibration of the entire chamber as the floor itself begins to disappear, replaced by a thin transparency like a caul over the newly-forming cranium of a thing about to be born from the corpse of its own body. *There is no God!* Screams the shaman in his brain. *There is no Devil! There is only Us and Them!*

He is standing between the *Us* and the *Them*; he is standing at the juncture of two worlds. He is enough of a scholar to understand liminality and knows he is standing at the Mother of All Liminal Boundaries. And so, he chants. Between two worlds.

What the hell else was he going to do?

And Jamila still stands before him. Hearing the words of the Closing of the Gate, eyes closed in a kind of existential ecstasy, she grabs the weapon from Angell's hand. He releases it, thinking that she is relieving him of it so he can better hold the Book.

But she *is* the Gate. She had been channeling Cthulhu in Cthulhu's own Tomb. She cannot trust herself not to be used again. Like Miller and his involuntary viewing, she does not want to become possessed by the Thing in the Tomb once again.

Angell is chanting, his voice becoming more confident with each line.

The Tibetans have crowded around Miller, and have dropped their weapons. They want to pray Miller into the Bardo, so that his soul will have a safe journey to his next life, but they do not want to interfere with the Closing of the Gate, so they wait patiently.

The body of the cult leader—unnamed and unknown to Angell—has been dragged away to feed the vultures. The other devotees—seemingly hundreds of them—are standing, attentive, knowing that whatever happens in the next few moments it will be something to remember, to record for posterity, and to tell their diseased and vicious offspring that they were there when the Gate *almost* opened.

Angell chants on. Between two worlds.

Jamila takes the muzzle of the AK-47 and presses it against her chest. She tries to reach for the trigger but her arms are not long enough. She adjusts herself and tries again.

Angell looks up and sees what she is doing.

If she kills herself, she may open the Gate. A chain reaction of all the dead who have been sacrificed over the millennia to the Old Ones. Morphic resonance! Giving it the power it needs to break free. *I know why she is doing this. She thinks she will close the Gate by killing herself. But I can't let her do it.*

Without missing a beat in the incantation, Angell swings and slams his fist into her head. She drops the weapon and falls to the ground, dazed.

He continues the chant.

On the other side of the world, the instruction that passed down the chain of command that began in a small office in a Washington, DC suburb—Monroe's office—is executed. The submarine that was nearly sunk by the rising of a submerged city in the middle of the Pacific Ocean has fired a nuclear missile into the sunken city's center mass. The effect is two-fold: it re-submerges the city (what's left of it) but it also creates a tsunami that effectively covers other risen architecture from the South Pacific to the Indian Ocean. The ancient "hidden countries" of Cthulhu and its followers are being submerged again.

As bodies of giant squid and other cephalopods rise to the surface of the oceans, Angell completes his chant. The expected supernova in the Great Bear constellation dims. The Gate is closing and Cthulhu is once again in its Tomb: a coffin built of eldritch dreams, stale blood, and conflicting dimensions. Miller is dead, but Angell can hear his voice in his head begging him to destroy the Book.

Monroe sees that the global conflagration is stalling. The first sign was the unexpected dimming of the supernova. The second was the destruction of the sunken city. The Gate must have been closed, he thinks. Somehow, something went right.

Now he has a decision to make and it must be made immediately.

If Angell is still alive and has the Book, there is no guarantee he will get out of Nepal safely. If someone else manages to get the Book, they could all be back where they started. Does he take a chance that Angell will emerge in one piece and safely hand over the *Necronomicon*?

Or does he make the hard choice?

Aubrey has just hung up with Monroe. The decision has been made. He sits down with his head in his hands. There is nothing else to do. They have won, but the cost is high.

The cultists are milling around, all dressed up and nowhere to go. Jamila is regaining consciousness. Angell looks around for Adnan. Finds him on the floor near the rear wall. He has been shot through the abdomen.

"Don't know who did it. There were bullets flying ... I thought for sure you were dad ... I mean, dead ..."

"Hold on. I'll get help."

Adnan grabs the professor's arm.

"Yeah? Where? I've got a sucking chest wound, son. There are no medics for miles around here. I'd die before I could make it out of here, much less to a doctor. And no one is coming in here after us."

"No! This is not going to end this way!"

"Hey, I'm Ahl-e-Haqq, remember? We believe in reincarnation. I'll be back," he said in his best Schwarzenegger impression.

"You got the Book, right?"

Angell could only nod.

"Hey, then. Mission accomplished, right?"

"We did good, Adnan."

And then Adnan answered him, but in his own Kurdish dialect. He was losing consciousness. Hallucinating. And there was not a damned thing he could do for him.

One of the Tibetans who came with Miller walked up to him, and looked down at Adnan.

"Bad," he said.

"Yes," replied Angell. "Bad."

"And her?" he asked, pointing to Jamila. "Nepali? Lepcha?"

"No. Yezidi."

"Ah, Yezidi. Yezidi no good." He waved dismissively.

Angell, in a fit of fury, jumped up and knocked the man down with his fists, the second time he had to strike another human being.

"We are *all* Yezidi," he told him.

Adnan has died. Miller is dead. The nameless cult leader is dead. Others are also dead, he doesn't know their names. The Tomb of Cthulhu has become the tomb of so many others. He wants to bring Adnan's body at least out of the tunnels but he has no idea how to do that on his own when he doesn't even know how to get out himself. He goes through Adnan's pockets and finds a letter he has written to his parents, sealed and ready to be mailed. The sight of it causes Angell to lose it. He just sits there, soaking in his friend's—yes, he thinks, his friend's—blood and weeps.

Jamila finally stands up, and looks around in a daze. The smell of the firefight has mixed with the noxious incense and the atmosphere is stifling. She reaches down and touches Angell on the shoulder. After a minute he looks up at her. She nods, and points back to the way she entered with the cultists. *That way*, she seems to say. *That way is out.*

Angell walks out of the hidden country into the crisp night air. He is alone. Jamila has stayed behind to care for the wounded, something she has learned how to do. Angell, however, has to go. He cannot afford to be captured and the Book must not fall into the wrong hands.

He walks off into the Nepalese mountains as the Raptor drone fires one of its Hellfire missiles at the cave entrance.

And Angell disappears.

EPILOGUE

From all this, one common characteristic emerges—access to
the sacred and to the spirit is always figured as an embryonic
gestation and a new birth.

—Mircea Eliade, *Rites and Symbols of Initiation*

Monroe gets reports from his extraction team. Angell is nowhere to
be found. Neither is the Book. Miller's body is discovered and he
appears to have been shot by a round fired from Angell's weapon.
That's the story, anyway. He will replace the ballistics report with
one that matches Angell's nine millimeter, the one in Aubrey's possession. It gives Monroe the option of labeling Angell a murderer
and a traitor, which would give him the authority to track him
down anywhere in the world. It's an option he will remember.

Aubrey believed Angell to be dead, his body to be discovered
eventually somewhere in the tunnel complex. Then Adnan's body
is recovered. Oddly, his parents receive a letter from him that was
mailed after his body was discovered. It was mailed from Hong
Kong. Everyone is confused, except Aubrey. He makes inquiries in
Hong Kong, but Angell is long gone by then. He hopes Angell is
smiling somewhere.

The missing JSOC team is eventually recovered. They were
drugged by some noxious herb in a burning censer carried by an
old Tibetan man in the tunnels. There was no ventilation, and they
succumbed immediately and were out for twelve hours. No one
thought to bring gas masks.

The Cthulhu Cult continued to organize and attempt to
resurrect their High Priest, their connection to the alien forces they
believe will save them. But without the Book, they are handicapped.
They will try again, however. They always do.

Angell never returns to his apartment in the Red Hook section of
Brooklyn. He is alone in a remote area of the world—Mongolia—

following a hunch that one of the Seven Towers is located there, near the Singing Sands of the southern Gobi Desert. He has found a rock with an inscription. Something about strange aeons and the death of … death. But he really is pondering his next move. He has the Book safely hidden. His atheism has been shaken to its core by the things he has seen and done. He has witnessed what can only be described as the paranormal. But that doesn't mean he has to believe in God and the Devil. After all, the old shaman didn't. And he saw no evidence of God in the cavern.

He thinks the spirituality of the world is not based on God and the Devil, but on a struggle between what it means to be human and those alien forces that care nothing for humans except as beasts of burden or food, if they even care at all. They say that the Devil's deepest wile is to persuade us that he does not exist. Angell thinks that Cthulhu's deepest wile is to persuade us that the Gods we worship are really on our side; he knows that those Gods are used as masks by a deeper, darker Evil than we can ever imagine for it demands our destruction even as it demands our obedience and our love.

He hopes—ironically, he *prays*—that he is wrong. That he's got it *all* wrong, and that his new belief system is the product of the diseased mind of that Thing in the Tomb, calling out to him, seducing him with its thoughts. The Call of Cthulhu.

There is only one tool to stop this force from gaining power the next time a Gate is about to open. And Angell has it. And is never letting it go.

The Book. The Black Book.

The *Necronomicon*.

Gregory Angell and the Book will return in *Dunwich*.

ACKNOWLEDGMENTS

First, I would like to thank Bill Corsa, my long-suffering agent who tried for more than a decade to sell this property because he believed in it (or, rather, did *not* believe that anyone would *not* want to publish it). So this is a culmination of all those book proposals—so many book proposals to so many publishers—over all those years. The book has changed considerably in that amount of time, not least because the political situation in the world changed so fundamentally and so quickly, requiring extensive rewrites and re-imaginings. Thanks for all the yeoman's work you've put into this project, Bill. You can relax now. It's done!

Next, many thanks and genuflections go to Yvonne Paglia. Although I have published considerable amounts of non-fiction with Ibis Press and Nicolas Hays, Inc. in the last few years, this is my first published work of book-length fiction. She is taking a chance, and for that I will be forever grateful.

Stuart Weinberg of Seven Stars Bookstore in Boston. His voice forcefully was raised in support of this project as well. Like Bill Corsa, he didn't understand why someone would not want to publish a book about Lovecraft and the *Necronomicon*, international terrorism, devil worshipping cults, intelligence agencies, necromancy, necrophilia and all the other necros, as well as the breakdown of human civilization generally. I mean, come on. What's not to like?

Donald Weiser. For his good humor and patience, with my projects and with me especially.

James Wasserman. (Sigh.) I tried to keep the Crowley material to a minimum, man, but you know … well … it's not easy. Jim also was a major supporter of this project and urged Yvonne to publish it. He has been a designer of my books for a long time, and a friend for even longer. I am grateful to him, Stuart, and Bill for their unwavering moral support.

(Also, having a book contract meant I actually had to finish writing the damned thing.)

To Whitley Strieber and Christopher Farnsworth, both busy and successful writers who very generously took time out of their schedules to read an early version of the novel and comment on it. Many thanks!

To good friends (if they're still speaking to me) Maya Gabrieli, Sophie Kaye, Adrian Anderson, Nina Rojas, and Captain Bates, to name a few: all people I have been avoiding the past year because writing is a solitary practice that does not permit of much socializing. There are others, mostly family, who are not mentioned here by name for their security in case everything I've written about in this book turns out to be true!

And thanks to all of you, dear readers. You have supported my efforts through the years to investigate and reveal the hidden structures of our world through my non-fiction works. This book is an attempt to do the same, only using fiction as a medium instead of the heavily-footnoted, bibliographed books I normally write. Consider this as me, after a particularly hairy overseas trip, hanging out with you, thinking aloud in an unedited way about the cosmic implications of things I've read and seen: the kind of conversations I have in my own head all the time.

And for those of you who don't understand how I can write about Nazis one day and about Tantra or Alchemy or Religion the next, I hope this book ties it all together for you.

A wise man (probably a lawyer) once wrote that some truths can only be expressed in fiction. This is my attempt to do just that.

Enjoy!

ABOUT THE AUTHOR

Peter Levenda is a well-known author of many published works on esoteric subjects. *His Unholy Alliance: A History of Nazi Involvement with the Occult* bears a foreword by Norman Mailer and has been translated into six foreign languages. *Ratline: Soviet Spies, Nazi Priests, and the Disappearance of Adolf Hitler* broke new ground when it revealed the Far East segment of the Nazi escape routes after the fall of Germany. *His Hitler Legacy: The Nazi Cult in Diaspora: How it was Organized, How it was Funded, and Why it Remains a Threat to Global Security in the Age of Terrorism* explores the pernicious Nazi influence on the modern interpretation of Jihad. Levenda is also the author of the three-volume study of the influence of esoterica on American politics, *Sinister Forces: A Grimoire of American Political Witchcraf.* His Ibis Press book *Dark Lord: H.P. Lovecraft, Kenneth Grant, and the Typhonian Tradition in Magic* explores many of the esoteric themes exposed in this novel.

ALSO FROM PETER LEVENDA

THE DARK LORD

H.P. Lovecraft, Kenneth Grant,
and the Typhonian Tradition in Magic

PETER LEVENDA

One of the most famous—yet least understood—manifestations of Thelemic thought has been the works of Kenneth Grant, the British occultist and one-time intimate of Aleister Crowley, who discovered a hidden world within the primary source materials of Crowley's Aeon of Horus. Using complementary texts from such disparate authors as H.P. Lovecraft, Jack Parsons, Austin Osman Spare, and Charles Stansfeld Jones ("Frater Achad"), Grant formulated a system of magic that expanded upon that delineated in the rituals of the OTO: a system that included elements of Tantra, of Voudon, and in particular that of the Schlangekraft recension of the *Necronomicon,* all woven together in a dark tapestry of power and illumination.

The Dark Lord follows the themes in the writings of Kenneth Grant, H.P. Lovecraft, and the Necronomicon, uncovering further meanings of the concepts of the famous writers of the Left Hand Path. It is for Thelemites, as well as lovers of the Lovecraft Mythos in all its forms, and for those who find the rituals of classical ceremonial magic inadequate for the New Aeon. Traveling through the worlds of religion, literature, and the occult, Peter Levenda takes his readers on a deeply fascinating exploration on magic, evil, and *The Dark Lord* as he investigates one of the most neglected theses in the history of modern occultism: the nature of the Typhonian Current and its relationship to Aleister Crowley's Thelema and H.P. Lovecraft's *Necronomicon.*

AND FROM IBIS PRESS

THE NECRONOMICON

31st Anniversary Edition of the Schlangekraft Recension

EDITED AND INTRODUCED BY SIMON

In the past decades, much ink—actual and virtual—has been spilled on the subject of the *Necronomicon* (also called the "Simonomicon"). Some have derided it as a hoax; others have praised it as a powerful grimoire. Despite the controversy, it has never been out of print for one day since 1977.

The *Necronomicon* has been found to contain formulae for spiritual transformation that are consistent with some of the most ancient mystical processes in the world—processes that involve communion with the stars.

In 2008, the original designer of the 1977 edition and the original editor joined forces to present a new, deluxe hardcover edition of the most feared, most reviled, and most desired book on the planet. With a new preface by Simon, this 31st Anniversary edition from Ibis Press is available in two versions. The first is a high quality hardcover bound in fine cloth with a ribbon marker. The second is a strictly limited, leatherbound edition, personally signed and numbered by Simon. A small number of leatherbound copies are still available.

POPULAR HARDCOVER, BOUND IN HIGH QUALITY CLOTH

$125.00 • ISBN: 978-0-89254-146-1 • 288 pages • Printed on acid-free art paper • 7¼ x 10¼ • Ribbon marker • Sold everywhere

NUMBERED & SIGNED, DELUXE LEATHERBOUND EDITION

Strictly limited to 220 numbered books, signed by Simon.

$275.00 • ISBN: 978-0-89254-147-8 • Three sided silver-gilding • Special binding boards • Deluxe endpapers

Signed edition available exclusively from www.studio31.com